TURIT'S
RISE

THE *SAGA OF THE SINGING SWORD BRIGADE* SERIES:

AND COMING SOON:

SAGA OF THE SINGING SWORD BRIGADE
BOOK FIVE

TURIT'S RISE

J.M. MACLEOD

AMBASSADOR INTERNATIONAL
GREENVILLE, SOUTH CAROLINA & BELFAST, NORTHERN IRELAND
www.ambassador-international.com

Turit's Rise

Saga of the Singing Sword Brigade, Book Five
© 2024 by J.M. MacLeod
All rights reserved

ISBN: 978-1-64960-420-0
eISBN: 978-1-64960-697-6

Cover Design by Hannah Linder Designs
Interior Typesetting by Dentelle Design
Ebook Conversion by Anna Riebe Raats
Edited by Kate Marlett

AMBASSADOR INTERNATIONAL
Emerald House Group, Incorporated
411 University Ridge, Suite B14
Greenville, SC 29601, USA
www.ambassador-international.com

AMBASSADOR BOOKS
The Mount
2 Woodstock Link
Belfast, BT6 8DD, Northern Ireland, UK
www.ambassadormedia.co.uk

The colophon is a trademark of Ambassador, a Christian publishing company.

To Rex & Kayleen
And their kids:
Jackson
Rachel
Brooke
Luke
For allowing me the pleasure of working on my manuscript in their
Pennsylvania farmhouse

THE SINGING SWORD

The sword gleaming ancient runes,
Pulsing out heroic tunes,
Hummed a strain one cold, fey night,
Ere the battle joined full might,
To keep safe from hurtful woe,
And guard from death's sorrow.
Hear a tale that will inspire,
Told by every rune afire.
Of caves and snows, hills and dells,
Grand oaths tell, deceivers fell,
This tale though new, is old as stars,
And blest are all that bear the scars.
Wise they are that live and learn,
Truth their cause, the false they spurn.
"Lives for the King," their battle cry.
And for their Prince, they dare to die.

CHAPTER ONE

A CLAP OF THUNDER RUMBLED down the cobbled street as if storm daemons were playing at ninepins. Jorna lowered her head, tugged her shawl tight, and pushed on into the gusty winds splattering the first drops of what promised to be a gulley-gusher. In her mind's eye, Hod-ya's cold, calculating eyes still stared at her. It chilled Jorna's blood more than the storm's dropping temperature. Encountering the Majestic Madam face to face revealed how woefully understated were the tales about the mistress of Lurcan's castle. Hod-ya was, indeed, a very real menace, especially to clandestine kingsmen meeting secretly throughout the Cosmopolisian region.

Jorna's steps quickened; she snuggled close to the brick-and-mortar buildings lining the street. Most edifices in this sector of the city had been converted into shops or taverns, but a few of the ramshackle buildings still served as home and hearth to a few impoverished or elderly folk who'd been unable to flee as the neighborhood decayed into an urban slum replete with thieves, drunkards, and ne'er-do-wells.

A suspended sign held by two slim chains dangling from a corner of the building identifying Ward Street swung wildly in the gusts; Jorna turned left to escape the windy blast. She hoped to get home before the ominous, gathering thunderheads released their burden. But would home even be safe? Nowhere seemed safe since her confrontation with Hod-ya at the tavern where Jorna worked as serving girl. Jorna's pace slowed as she pondered the consequences. A rogue wind whipped the fringe of her shawl, forcing her to instinctively clutch at it.

Her thoughts immediately returned to the more pressing issue. After she had left The Boar's Tusk, might Hod-ya have badgered the tavern owner to reveal where she lived? The underside of Jorna's chin, which Hod-ya's fingernail had pierced during the brief interrogation, smarted. Lurcan's henchwoman sounded so confident when she accused Jorna of being an Ecclessite . . . but then curiously let her go. Why would she do that?

Jorna leaned into the wind that had switched direction and now blew directly into her face. Home was just a little way down the street. Hopefully, her husband, Flan, would be there and have a fire going; so she could seek his comforting embrace and ward off her chill by the fireside. She couldn't wait to relate her chilling encounter to him.

Flan, the trusted leader of their furtive coterie of a kingsmen brigade meeting secretly in the very heart of the empire's capital, Cosmopolis, would know what to do. Logon had established this underground brigade behind enemy lines many years prior, despite the extreme risk. Though recruits were not required to stay, for the most part, the kingsmen chose to remain in peril rather than seek Ecclessite brigades in safer regions where chances of imminent capture, torture, and/or death were minimized. Thus, the stalwart brigade, constantly in jeopardy, remained in Cosmopolis simply because King Elyon and the king's son, Logon Xychirion, asked it of them.

The intrepid little band had burrowed beneath the surface of the empire's capital city to invite Carnalians to their secretive meetings where they could hear and respond to the king's amnesty. Carnalians came and listened, at first unaware how they had offended Ecclessa's king. If they accepted his amnesty, he would freely pardon them—although they certainly weren't expecting to be thrust through the heart with an Ecclessite sword as part of that amnesty.

The rain descended in torrents, flooding gutters and runoff ditches within minutes. Jorna splashed ankle-deep through puddles, soaking her skirt's hem. If Hod-ya followed up on her suspicions that Jorna was Ecclessite, the brigade's mission of rescuing Carnalians from the coming destruction of the empire would come jolting to a halt; kingsmen would be rounded up and tortured to disclose the whereabouts of other kingsmen; and Logon's offer of amnesty would be silenced throughout Cosmopolis.

A brilliant flash of lightning accompanying another thunderclap struck a lamppost not twenty feet away. Jorna, temporarily blinded, reeled, her ears ringing and her body tingling from foot to scalp. Had she not clutched at the wall, she would've tottered into the gutter. She steadied herself against a wooden door frame.

"Logon," she uttered, "is this . . . Am I . . . " Then her vision cleared; and looking around, she realized it had been nothing more than a lightning strike. Another lightning bolt some distance behind displayed her shadow on the wall. She braced for the ear-splitting crack and wasn't disappointed as her innards vibrated with another sonic concussion seconds later. Regaining her balance, she flew down the street, gratefully sighting the doorway of her frame house at the far end of the street where she and her husband dwelt.

She took but a moment to glance behind to see where that last lightning bolt had struck and saw three dark-clad men sprawled face-down on the road, steam rising off their inert forms. Hod-ya's spies? Had they been secretly following her? Jorna, serving girl and chambermaid at the Boar's Tusk Inn, was, indeed, under suspicion of being Ecclessite. If caught and subjected to inquisition, would she break under the severe methods of questioning and denounce other kingsmen in and around Cosmopolis?

Jorna's fingers tripped the door latch; she leaned into the heavy, oaken door, forcing it open. The room was dark; no welcoming fire greeted her from the hearth. She entered and leaned against the door's backside, closing it with a thump, then stood still, collecting her wits. Droplets cascaded off her garments and formed little puddles on the wood plank floor. She shivered as she stepped into the room.

"Fire; I need to get a fire going. And where is Flan?"

Crossing to the hearth, she seized an iron poker and stirred the ash pit. Orange-red coals gleamed from under a thin layer of gray ash. Jorna dumped a handful of kindling directly onto the embers. Spirals of smoke curled up the flue, followed by sparks, then crackling flames timidly spreading to larger sticks she added. Satisfied the fire would take, Jorna retreated to her bedchamber to change into dry clothing.

Minutes later, she emerged in a dry, homespun blouse and surcoat; floor-length skirt; and shawl, all overtop her Logon-dress. Jorna added medium-sized logs to the greedy flames. The fire's warmth was already seeping into the room. Jorna half-filled a water kettle, hung it on the swing-arm, and nudged it over the flames. A cup of tea would soothe her frazzled nerves just now. She took a firebrand from the hearth and touched it to the wick of an oil lamp on the table and lowered the glass chimney. The flaring wick sent a cheerful glow into the room. Jorna leaned back in her chair, shoulders slumped. The warmth of the fire and cheery lamp-glow, however, did little to assuage the icy chill gripping her nerves.

A brief memory of Dancel's friend flitted across her mind—Jima, was it? No, Jana? No—wait, Jeda! Jeda of the house of Kway, carried off to Pitland . . . Whatever had become of her? She'd been pierced with a

Child of the Stars at her first and only meeting and sent back to Hod-ya with no other encouragement than "Trust Logon" ringing in the poor girl's ears. Weeks after that, there were rumors of an Ecclessite maiden slated to duel to the death in Pitland's barbaric Scrarth and Avangar tournament. The brigade that met in their house felt responsible for the girl because they had coaxed her into allowing them to pierce her heart with one of the king's swords.

At first, they had often mentioned her to Logon, hoping that the Ecclessite girl rumored to fight in Pitland's ghastly duel wasn't Jeda. They'd received no comforting word to the contrary, nor had they heard how the contest ended. It had been a few weeks since the contest was held; news from southern lands traveled slowly. After a while, their petitions to Logon on Jeda's behalf faded.

Had Jeda fallen under the power of the emperor? Would she report Flan, the kingsman who had pierced her with an Ecclessite sword? Was that why Jorna felt such a chill during the tavern encounter? Did Hod-ya already know? Was she playing some cat-and-mouse game? Was their clandestine brigade even now under surveillance?

Steam billowed from the kettle. Jorna slowly rose; took a mug off the hutch; sprinkled some dried clover blossoms, mint, and alfalfa onto the bottom; and with a dipper, added hot water. A soothing aroma wafted to her nostrils; she stirred in a dollop of honey, took a sip, and sat at the table again.

"Oh, Logon." She raised her eyes to the overhead rafters. "What are we to do?"

It was then her eyes detected a faint bluish glow in the corner where she and Flan stashed their swords in baskets under overcoats and stormy-weather gear. There should be no glow from that corner of the room! Had someone searched their home, rummaged through their belongings, and discovered their swords? Were Hod-ya's dronnets bearing down, perhaps at this very moment, through rain-glutted alleys toward her home, ready to break through the door and catch her in possession of illegal weapons? Jorna's gaze returned to the doorway. Was it about to be shattered asunder by the crushing blow of a sharif's battering ram? She closed her eyes to shut out the dizzying thoughts.

Unbidden, a runesong crossed her mind:

> *Fear not the kyllorn, man or beast,*
> *Though breathing threats of doom.*
> *Logon's heel their pate hath creased*
> *Cause their hearts gave him no room.*

Her pulse slowed. She hurried to the corner and saw the basket's lid askew amid several garments carelessly tossed aside. Only one sword remained, the one with a diminished shine—hers. Beads of perspiration broke out on her brow as she exhaled. "Flan must have taken his sword when he went out and didn't remember to cover the basket. I've told him betimes . . . "

She lifted her blade from the basket and took it over to the table, withdrew a toller from its secret niche beneath the tabletop, and was about to touch it to the sword when she realized that a rune was already aglow, one she'd not sharpened.

"Logon, is this a message for the brigade?" She then traced the rune with her finger and read aloud from the runes of *Atel's Ecclessite Manifesto*:

In hardship abundant,
In stripes above measure,
In prisons more frequent,
In death encompassing,
In enemy custody, denied life's treasures.
In beatings with rods,
In this trail not soft,
In suffering ransack,
In left then, to die,
In deep lamentation,
In Logon's debt am I.

In peril of waters,
In peril of thieves,
In peril by my countrymen,
In peril by villains,
In peril in cities,
In peril in wild fens,
In peril at sea,
In peril among Ecclessites false.
In weariness and pain,
In hunger and thirst,
In night-watching, oft,
In cold and heat,
In quandary, but . . .
In all glad celebration,
In Logon's great name!

Jorna sat back, her lips pursed and brow scrunched in reflection, toller loosely hovering in hand.

The door suddenly lurched open. A windy blast of rain swept in as a dull thump of thunder followed a large, cloaked, shadowy figure invading from outside.

Jorna nearly knocked the lamp over in surprise.

The door slammed to, and the form turned around. "Sorry, love, I didn't mean to startle you. Why, you look pale as a cusp!"

Jorna ran to Flan in relief. "Oh, Flan!"

"Who'd you expect, the captain of Lurcan's guard?" Flan shucked off his oilskin and hung it on a nail. "Nasty as tophet's breath out there tonight." He shook his head, sending droplets in all directions from his hair and beard. "Say, something really has you spooked. Tell me."

Jorna enfolded herself into his arms. "Oh, Flan, I might have betrayed our brigade."

Flan gave a slight nod and led her to the table, where he seated her and settled into his own catty-cornered chair. He took and rubbed one of her hands. "It can't be as serious as all that." Furrows on his brow belied the confidence his voice tried to convey.

Jorna sighed. "I'm afraid it is. Hod-ya and Captain—"

"Hod-ya?" Flan repeated, making sure he'd heard right.

"Yes, the witchy woman herself, and her toady Captain—er, now *General*—Mileer, unexpectedly showed up at The Boar's Tusk Inn late this afternoon returning from some wilderness campaign."

Flan released Jorna's hand and edged his chair closer to the table, then laid his hand on her shoulder. "Go on."

"Unenra and I were clearing tables—you know, setting up for the girls that tend the late shift's after-dark crowd—when I overheard Hod-ya and Mileer talking at a nearby table in low tones. Flan, I clearly heard Hod-ya say something about preparations for a coronation feast, and these were her very words: *'It isn't every day a condemned man assumes leadership over an empire. His name will be tattooed on every person.'*"

Flan whistled low. His eyes shifted to Jorna's sword on the table. "And that?"

"This," she said, tapping the newest glowing rune, "was reflecting off the ceiling, because *somebody* forgot to properly cover—" A chagrined expression crossed her features. "I'm sorry it's just that when she interrogated me, I—"

"Interrogated? You were interrogated?" Anger flushed Flan's neck up to his face. "Did she hurt you?"

Jorna's gaze dropped to her sword, then she tilted her chin and pointed at the inflamed slit. "Her fingernail scratched me, that's all. It still smarts some."

Flan's white-knuckled fist thumped the table, making the lamp jump and the wick flicker.

"I'm all right, really. But do you make of what they said—about this coronation and tattooing—the same omen I make of it?"

Flan again eyed the sword on the table. "And why did you pick that particular rune that warns Ecclessites about suffering?"

"I didn't. It was glowing of its own accord." The pair sat for some moments in silence. "It's happening, isn't it? The prophecies, the days of extreme danger, the Tremendum?"

Flan sat back, rubbed his eyes, then leaned forward. "It must be. It all adds up—sending the Kway girl to the castle and possibly Pitland."

"I was thinking about her today, too."

"And Dancel coming less and less to meetings because she thinks she's under suspicion . . . and then that ominous trumpet blare resounding from the skies throughout the empire, putting the entire city on alert."

"I still think that was the beginning of the prophesied Trumpets of Doom that precede the Tremendum."

Flan nodded and tenderly beheld his wife. "You may be right. Add to that the constant movement of empire troops toward the front, crowding the streets, as well as daily rumors of outlying kingsmen brigades being overrun . . . "

"And the propaganda that Logon's Bridge has been crossed and Ecclessa is in flames."

Flan stood and stretched. "Yes, well, we know that hasn't happened yet; or else, there'd be nothing left of Cosmopolis but raze and ruin. But if they're planning a coronation, destroying Logon's Bridge must be in their plans—"

The door burst open; and several armed men rushed inside, surrounding the Ecclessite brigade leader and his wife.

CHAPTER TWO

"FLAN, JORNA, HAVE YOU HEARD the news?" blurted a heavy-set man even before the last of the kingsman patrol entered and closed the door.

"Shremp," Flan addressed the burly man leaning over Flan's shoulder and dripping water on the table, "you've been told time and again that it's necessary to knock and use the password."

"Uh, oh yeah. Sorry, Flan, didn't mean ter barge in like thet. But . . . but it be's important news usn's gots."

Flan crossed the room to the front window, lifted a corner of the curtain, and peered out into the misty street. "If you were followed . . ." he almost growled.

"We weren't, Captain," said another. "The few people and sharifs brave enough to venture outside in this storm are down by the tailor's shop on the main road, gawking at three dronnets struck dead by lightning."

"Dronnets?" Jorna rose and joined Flan at the window. "I just came from there not twenty minutes ago." Then under her breath, she said to Flan, "They might have been following me."

Shremp continued, "Done kilt 'em dead as stone, it did."

"So, that's your earth-shattering news?" Flan returned to his seat, with Jorna following. The six men gathered around, making the floor slick as their garments shed raindrops. A dull thump of thunder again resounded through the rafters as a fresh downburst of rain beat against the window.

"News? Oh, no, no, no, it be's more important than that, although ain't that be's something 'bout them dronnets bein' kilt? High an' mighty officer—short little guy—like Mileer hisself, commandin' lotsa respect . . . Oh, what be's his name? Spletched! That be's it? Second in command o' the castle's defenses was hoppin' around, cussin' and shoutin' an' slappin' inferiors like he be's the one what got hit with lightnin'. Seems them blackguards was on some kinda secret mission. Whatever they knew died with 'em, upsettin' the little guy."

"So, what news is there other than some dead dronnets in the street?" Flan demanded, nostrils flaring in exasperation.

"It's about Pitland, sir—er, that is, it's no more," Feckle answered for the chagrinned Shremp, who finally realized that he was annoying Flan and thought it wise to hold his tongue.

"What nonsense are you babbling on about? You six burst in here, claiming important news, telling us a lightning strike killed a couple of dronnets down the street, then nonchalantly say that Pitland doesn't exist anymore?"

Another of the intruders stepped forward. "Perhaps I can make sense of their babble."

"I wish you would, Cleese." Flan gave full attention to the tall, dark-haired corporal. "Pull up a chair."

Cleese handed his slicker to one of the others as they retreated to hang their raingear on hooks beside the doorway. He sat and faced husband and wife. "Only a couple of hours ago, bedraggled troops wandered in from the wilds of Ra-Amawl, telling about the Scrarth and

Avangar contest. It's only hearsay at this point, official word is mum."
He glanced around the room at the men who'd entered with him. "But
I get this from a reliable source, a man in Mileer's regiment who saw
the whole thing from start until—well, until they had to flee for their
lives. I think I can piece the events together well enough to explain."

"Does this have anything to do with Jeda of Kway?" Jorna lifted
her head.

Cleese's eyes widened. "How did you know?"

"I was afraid of this, Flan, dear. We shouldn't have sent that poor
girl to her death. We should have taken whatever necessary risks to
hide her—"

"But wait! You haven't heard? It turned out for good. Logon used
that girl, Jeda, to equip the king's prisoners, who were slated for
execution, with the swords of Vadiv—the same as Children of the
Stars before the generals inscribed them. They rose up and gained their
freedom; hundreds upon hundreds of tophets and cusps were banished
to the swamps from which they spawned. Then Pitland itself erupted
in a huge volcano, a caldera! From what we heard, Pitland, the entire
country, is now nothing but a seething bowl of lava."

"Are you sure?" Flan sat back. "'Cause in that case, I have some news,
too. But it may not seem as fortuitous as yours."

Jorna lay her hand on Flan's arm. "Perhaps all these reports should
wait until we can call a brigade meeting. That way, we'll not keep
repeating ourselves every time someone comes in."

"Good idea. But there's no time to waste; we must call a meeting
for tonight! Cleese, take your squad back out. Split up and spread the
word that there's to be a special gathering tonight. No one should miss

it, not even because of the storm. In fact, it may be that Logon sent this storm to cover our comings and goings tonight; neither Mileer's nor Spletched's troops will be eager to venture out and hunt down our gathering this stormy night, I'm sure."

~

Squall after squall rolled through Cosmopolis and nearby hamlets all that night, threatening to overflow creeks and storm sewers as well as inundate low-lying roads, not to mention the rampaging winds that tore tree limbs loose and sent debris skittering down streets. No Cosmopolisians, civilian or official, ventured into the violent evening storms, other than furtive kingsman covering up against the pelting rain and braving the windy blasts as they made their way toward the nondescript house on Ward Street. An urgent meeting had been called; attendance was of utmost importance.

Only one candle lit a second-story, un-shuttered window shining outward on Ward Street as a beacon penetrating through the raging tempests, guiding those who dared face the downpours to the meeting. Jorna kept busily admitting brigaders into her home as soon as they appeared, seating them at a table with refreshments as a ruse before ushering them through a doorway hidden behind a tapestry and into the warehouse-meeting hall behind. If sharifs or dronnets were to suddenly barge into their home, even the ruse of entertaining guests on a night like this would be implausible.

Flan leaned against the wall in the large back room that got fuller by the moment as Ecclessites entered and seated themselves in concentric rings around him. Kingsmen brigaders softly sang runesongs and sat cross-legged, swords on laps, tollers in hand, ready for rune study as they awaited the rest of their brigade to assemble.

"Deep flows the river, crimson red.
Those bathed in love's purest flow,
Fear not the tophet, cusp or dread,
No matter where they chance to go.

Shades of dark, their powers fail.
Threats subside, short their reign.
For rescue comes midst assail.
The salvage work; the king will gain."

There were some seventy persons—adults and older youths repeating the chorus, meditating on the words, letting the message of hope soak in, especially considering rumors that portended imminent danger on a grand scale. Still more Ecclessites filtered into the hall until it seemed Jorna had no sooner sent one couple through the secret doorway behind the tapestry than another couple appeared at the door. Upward of a hundred souls soon crowded to the walls, soberly taking the various canticles upon their lips.

After several minutes passed with no one else entering, one final person lifted the tapestry and joined the assemblage. It was Dancel, followed by Jorna, who, having shut the front door, now meandered through the seated brigaders to her husband's side. She whispered in Flan's ear, "I think everyone is here; the entire roll of adults are present. Even elderly Dimchas and his wife, Eunille, braved the storm. And as you see, Dancel caught the secret sign Cleese left outside the castle gate; she's taking an exceptional risk to be here. She told me this may be the last time she'll risk coming for a while." Jorna then took her seat on the floor near Flan.

Flan raised a hand, drawing the attention of all in the room. He waited as they finished the last verse:

"Fulfill the call; rise to your part.
Cleansing comes at his command.
Waste not the day, but guard your heart.
Great power supports the king's demand."

The room quieted.

"Logon"—Flan fixed his eyes overhead as if seeing beyond the rafters—"we especially need your wisdom, guidance, and comfort this night."

Everyone in the room closed their eyes; attentive to Flan's petitioning the one they all loved and served.

Flan continued, "Speak to us now through Child of the Stars or the Advisor's gifts, so we can hear and know your bidding m'liege, for it seems that the long-anticipated Tremendum has arrived."

A collective gasp coursed through the assembly, and not a few eyes popped open. Had Flan lost his mind? Sure, things appeared bleak, but they'd survived other hazardous times that seemed as dark. Did Flan truly believe the end of Carnalia was at hand?

"Look up here," Flan addressed the assembly. "I see many startled faces among you; believe me, you're no more alarmed to hear what's on my heart than I am to share it tonight. But before I do, Cleese has some news. Though it's only rumor at this point, it coincides with the runes I'm compelled to share tonight. Take note how swiftly things are happening in regard to the mystery runes. Cleese?"

Cleese picked his way through the crowd toward Flan. All eyes were on him; they trusted him because of his care and helpfulness, encouragement, or wise counsel. Additionally, Cleese's grasp of rune-warfare was almost as highly regarded as Flan's. He was a great help to Flan in the administration of mundane brigade duties, especially since, as of yet, their small contingent had no other senior staff officers, nor even a sergeant-at-arms.

"Well, I, uh . . . " Cleese shyly faced the brigade. "Heard by way of rumor—I want to emphasize, it's just hearsay at this point—but we got wind that Pitland has become a lake of fire and bubbling lava, just like the mystery runes predict will literally occur prior to Logon's returning in power."

An excited murmur ran through the crowd. One man arose, pointed at Cleese, and said, "Hear now, if it's only rumor, why get everybody all shook up until you know for sure? The brigade where I was originally trained expected Logon to gather all Ecclessites safely out of Carnalia before Pitland became a 'bubbling lake of pitch,' as the rune says. So, if what's happened is what you think it is, wouldn't Logon already have summoned us?"

Several voices rose in agreement; but others disputed, each individual espousing his or her own understanding that allowed Pitland might turn into lava before Logon gathered Ecclessites safely to Splendora. Here and there, men angrily rose to their feet, pointing fingers, their voices tense and loud, as if volume added weight to their argument.

Flan clapped his hands for quiet, pleading, "Hush, hush, they'll hear you out in the streets . . . " No one paid any mind until he put fingers in the corners of his mouth and blew a shrill whistle, bringing immediate silence. "What is this, a free-for-all? Any loud argument will do? Let us thank Logon that the night is filled with storm and fury, or the racket you've made would surely draw a *passel* of sharifs down on us. Now settle down, all of you, settle down; hold your peace. There's more. And you're not likely to find much comfort in this information either."

Everyone settled to the floor, except the elderly Dimchas who remained standing. "I have aught to say, Flan." He started picking his way across the crowded floor, carefully placing his cane as he wended his way between brigaders sitting cross-legged on the floor.

"Brother, stay, stay where you are. We can hear you from there. I know how difficult it is for you to get around and am grateful you even came out on such a night. I—*we*—respect your age and the wisdom Logon has given you, so speak your mind."

"Well, I don't mean to remonstrate with you, Flan. You're a capable and worthy captain. But if you'll recall, there was a time, upward of three years ago, when I advised—due to mutually exclusive viewpoints on this very subject and because settling on the erroneous view or treating all views as equally valid could prove hazardous—this brigade to come to an agreement on the precise meaning of the mystery runes before those days overtook us and found us unprepared. Now, if Cleese is correct about Pitland, it's almost too late. If we fail to unite now, we'll squander our strength by bickering with each other and possibly fall out altogether; dividing us, making us even more vulnerable, not to mention ineffective in rescuing lives. The greater our unity, the greater our victory. But if we are disunited—"

"As it is now," Dancel interrupted, rising to her feet. "I'm sorry to interrupt, but most of you know me—that I work in the palace, though secretly am an Ecclessite. That's why I risked coming tonight, though it probably seals my doom; for the castle bustles with activity morning, noon, and night. Hod-ya will surely call for my services tonight and find me missing; but I came to warn you: it's no rumor. What remains of Pitland is in flames. I heard it from Hod-ya's own lips. Bablo-ya, Hod-ya's sister, for so long sated with the blood of Ecclessites, is fallen to rise no more. Pitland has become a place of torment for those who reject Elyon as their king. I've pieced the story together from conversations I overheard while running errands between highly placed officials."

A hush gripped the crowded room.

Dancel continued, "Even more significant is the fact that right this very moment, preparations are underway to appoint a supreme leader, a Feuhr, over all of Carnalia, Craniantium, Eroton, what's left of Pitland, and other far-flung duchies on the outer borders."

Blank stares greeted her words.

Dancel looked to Flan. "Don't they get what that means? Don't they know what total empire rule under one utterly evil person portends?"

Cleese stood to his feet and moved beside her. "Dancel, there have been other human potentates from time to time who tried to dominate the empire; but after a short reign, their dominions fell apart. Why should this particular coronation be any different?"

"Because"—Dancel waved her hands in exasperation—"this time, all manner of evil entities have been summoned to attend and will be unleashed into the empire immediately following the ceremonies to inflame the citizenry against Ecclessites with all manner of lies and calumny. I heard Hod-ya proclaim that Lurcan himself will take up residence in this human emperor, investing powers in him, summoning tophets, firedrakes, cusps, and even releasing the *apyonis* to assist this

Feuhr, the *emperor-kyllorn* in the flesh, as he induces all mankind to do obeisance to him."

"Bosh!" several voices rang out around the room.

"It's true." Flan raised his voice above the hubbub. "It's true. Jorna and I came to the same conclusion ourselves late this afternoon, though we didn't associate the release of the *apyonis* with the coronation."

"The what?" several voices cried out.

"May I answer that?" asked Dimchas, still on his feet but leaning heavily on his cane.

Bowing to the elderly, gray-mustachioed gentleman, Flan nodded. "Please do. I'm sure your understanding exceeds my own."

Dimchas surveyed the crowd around him. "This is what comes of not tolling your swords when you had the time. If you'd taken the pains to toll those difficult runes on your swords and gain some understanding for yourselves, you'd know who the *apyonis* are and what they're capable of. Bear with me . . ."

"Long ago, Brida broke away from King Elyon and led a violent rebellion against the king and his son. Those roamers not seduced by Brida's lies were outraged when Brida turned his Elyon-given magnificence inward to adore himself instead of gratefully acknowledging the one who created and adorned him. Thus, Brida devolved into Lurcan—a howling, jealous dog—who slandered Elyon and Logon throughout Splendora and Psychanan."

"Aye, aye, we kens all o' that," Shremp called from the middle of the room. "But what 'bout them *ayopniks?*"

"*Apyonis,*" Dimchas corrected. "Well, Lurcan was nearly captured and condemned to a well-deserved punishment when suddenly from among the ranks of Elyon's *prectores,* several powerful, key warriors joined Brida's revolt, surging to his aid. Though Elyon and Logon weren't caught off guard, many of their faithful roamers were. It's difficult for humans like us to comprehend the kind of injuries *kyllorn* can inflict on each other, for they don't have mortal bodies like ours. Nevertheless, vicious, brutal warfare ensued."

A crashing boom of thunder directly overhead resounded as if to emphasize Dimchas' tale. Many eyes were drawn overhead; some girls squealed, and not a few men ducked, fearful that the roof was caving in.

"Yes, I'm sure that battle sounded much like that." Dimchas paused and surveyed his listeners. "At any rate, those fallen *prectores* who were seduced by Lurcan became much more malignant than other fallen roamers; they were especially cruel against defenseless humanity. Therefore, Elyon put a binding curse upon them and isolated them to a vile, noisome place to await the moment he'd allow them to play out their destructive role in the final days of mankind's rebellion. Duje, half-brother to Logon, inscribed a short rune on our blades concerning those foul creatures:

> *And fallen prectores taking hark,*
> *Cast from Elyon's habitat,*
> *Waiting under moist and dark,*
> *'Til near the day of judgment sat.*

In other words, they're so dangerous and cruel—in some ways, worse than cusps and tophets and the like—that to spare mankind from their spite, the *apyonis* had to be locked away in some pit and kept under guard until the beginning of the fall of Carnalia. They were stripped of their glories but not their malice; and although their destructive power was reduced, it wasn't entirely removed. Mortal men will be tormented by them at the sounding of the Fifth Trumpet of Doom, though at first, Carnalians might consider them as allies. But they'll not be allowed to harm anyone belonging to Logon and so will turn and vent their outrage against Carnalians."

"And that," said Flan, "brings us to what I need to share and why I called this meeting tonight. Thank you, Dimchas, for that explanation."

Dimchas nodded and lowered himself beside his wife. Dancel returned to the floor. Cleese picked his way through the crowd and sat beside her. All eyes turned to Flan.

Sounds of rushing water suddenly swept through from the outer room into the meeting hall, accompanied by a gust of wind that lifted the outer doorway's concealing tapestry. The secret meeting was exposed to the street, where the storm raged.

Against the backdrop of the doorway stood several warriors silhouetted by a lightning flash.

CHAPTER THREE

THOSE NEAR THE TAPESTRY SCRAMBLED away from the invading military squad in panic. Around the room, swordsmen jumped to their feet brandishing weapons in response to the challengers disrupting their clandestine meeting.

"Fear not!" boomed the strangers' leader holding forth a glowing Child of the Stars. "We come in peace; we're kingsmen."

A collective sigh was heard throughout the room. Swords were lowered but not put away.

Flan waded through the crowd toward the strangers. "Hail, and well met. We were unaware of other brigades near Cosmopolis. How is it that we've never encountered you?"

"Because we've come a far piece. We hail from the depths of Ra-Amawl, where we've been extremely careful to conceal our existence in the jungle, revealing ourselves only if and when the Advisor gives us clearance," the spokesman said. "Forgive me; I'm Knarsh, squad leader, sent by Captain Varter to locate the kingsman brigade in Cosmopolis."

"We, too, have taken pains to conceal our existence in Cosmopolis. How did you know we existed, much less find us?" Flan replied.

"We're blessed to have a seer in our brigade," said Knarsh. "Her name is Kyleah. Three weeks ago, the Advisor gave her word to send a delegation here"—with a sweep of his arm, Knarsh indicated the four men and two women standing behind him—"to rendezvous with a kingsmen brigade in Cosmopolis, trade information, and plan a coordinated assault on Lurcan's castle in order to rescue as many empire citizens as possible while there is still time."

"You have a seer in your brigade? And how do you know she speaks truly?" challenged Feckle. "Many brigades hold that that gifting has long since passed. After all, Lurcan uses soothsayers and prognosticators and has even covertly sent some to infiltrate brigades with false messages, bringing ruin. And now you, arriving from deep inside Ra-Amawl . . ."

Knarsh nodded. "You be the judge. We were told to enter Cosmopolis during a night of storm, when most of the citizenry would be shut inside their homes. Kyleah told us that a light would guide us. Not quite sure what she meant, we waited atop a hill overlooking this quadrant of Cosmopolis; we beheld the gleam in your window, the only light visible in the entire city. That's how we located you; trusting Kyleah's instructions, we followed your light. As for whether we validate the gift of seer . . . if there still are generals, recruiters, and captains, wouldn't it make sense there are still seers?" Knarsh held his sword out for Flan's inspection, tapping a glowing rune as he read:

"At Logon's descent, in time of moment,
Freed from confines in Logon's ascent,
Releasing the trapped, his own he unbound,
Bestowing great gifts, with power renowned.
Generals to plan and lead the attack,
Captains to guide to make up the lack,
Sergeants and corporals to build up and bind,
Seers who hear show paths yet to find.

All officers give to strengthen his corps,
Love's force striving to bring to his door,
Carnalia's lost souls, stolen to die,
But amnesty clutch forever and aye.

"These runes are just as valid as when they were first inscribed," Knarsh insisted. "We know Kyleah's messages are true—and from Logon—because she has been tested and proven. Several months ago, she received word to dispatch a patrol to the main road cutting through Ra-Amawl to waylay the coach of the witch-woman, Hod-ya kar Psa, take the occupant captive and bring her to our hidden campsite." Knarsh paused and surveyed the hall. "We were, of course, quite skeptical. But our captain insisted that Kyleah's previous oracles had an unblemished record; therefore, we should trust her counsel. I, myself, was on that patrol. To our surprise, we found not Hod-ya but two girls who'd gotten in over their heads and were on their way to the Scrarth and Avangar duel. Not only that, but we also found one of those girls was a newly recruited Ecclessite—"

"Jeda! You rescued Jeda?" Jorna scrambled to her feet.

Knarsh's mouth opened and closed. "That's right. So, you did know her?"

Flan explained, "Jeda met with us but once; but on that night, of her own choice, her heart was pierced by a Child of the Stars. She was whisked away immediately to Logon's Rock. Afterward, we sent her off with heavy hearts, knowing she was slated to go to Pitland, but the Advisor gave reassurances that she wasn't alone."

"Ah, I see. So, this is the brigade that she mentioned to us." Knarsh rubbed his beard thoughtfully. "Unfortunately, she was with us only a short while; we began teaching her Logon's ways, but she soon got lost in the forest. We've heard nothing more since. But her traveling companion, Glend, who was also delivered from Hod-ya's coach into our keeping, was also eventually pierced by a kingsman sword—though it took some doing, eh, Glend?"

A petite, pretty, young blonde stepped forward, pushing the hood back off her forehead, saying bashfully, "I'm Glend. When I heard a patrol was going to Cosmopolis, I hoped to meet the people who guided Jeda to Logon; for without Jeda's influence, I would never have surrendered to him."

"She insisted we allow her to come, pestering us until Captain Varter relented, despite the peril."

"Well, we have good news for you on that account," said Flan. "Just today, we've learned that Jeda was indeed a contestant in the Scrarth and Avangar duel. Somehow, with Logon's help, she was used to turn the tide, resulting in the utter destruction of that foul contest forever—and, apparently, most of Pitland as well. Please, come seat yourselves among us. Our meeting has just begun. I have a rather urgent word to report that may well indicate why Logon timed your arrival among us for this very night."

Dancel moved alongside Glend and whispered in her ear. Glend turned, smiled, and embraced her friend; then, the two sat side by side.

Around the hall, people resumed their seats, while Flan returned to his place along the back wall. Jorna briefly disappeared behind the tapestry to secure the outer room, shut the door, and quickly returned, letting the tapestries fall back into place. She signaled Flan that all was in order.

Flan nodded and resumed. "Earlier today, my wife overheard Hod-ya and Captain Mileer—"

"*General* Mileer," Dancel called out. "He's promoted himself."

Chuckles at Mileer's well-known hubris greeted this interruption.

"Yes, well, as I was saying," Flan continued, "that nefarious duo of Mileer and Hod-ya kar Psa came out of the wilderness to stop for refreshment at The Boar's Tusk Inn, where my wife overheard brief snatches of their conversation; they were talking about coronating a new leader over all the empire, a *Feuhr*. From my studies of the mystery runes, I can only conclude that that leader will be indwelt by Lurcan himself by dark and mystical ceremonies. After that, an even greater hatred against Elyon and Logon will be unleashed throughout the empire. Lurcan's man will be obsessed with wiping out every kingsman brigade and coercing every captured Ecclessite to renounce fealty to Logon on pain of execution."

"But"—Cleese stood to his feet—"doesn't Logon come first to gather us to a place of safety before all that occurs?"

"In response, I can only say the mystery runes depict certain events that Logon said must happen immediately prior to the 'end of this age,' which events do indeed, seem to be happening even as we speak. Yet Logon hasn't appeared. Instead, he's apparently uniting us as allies and revealing specific tactical instructions." He turned from Cleese to Knarsh. "Your arrival from Ra-Amawl, fellow kingsmen, is confirmation."

Shremp rose to his knees, challenging, "But I was always taught ter 'spect Logon ter come and rescue usn's afore the Tremendum; but if'n that hain't happenin', mebbe none of what usn's been told be's true!"

Flan pointed a forefinger at Shremp, "That's exactly why Lurcan's agents, seen and unseen, have infiltrated kingsman brigades in an effort to confuse our understanding of the mystery runes, hoping kingsmen will either get fearful, or else frustrated, trying to discern truth from error so that they'd doubt the runes Logon had inscribed on the sword! But we must not trade the plain meaning of the runes for specious theories; rather, we should evaluate current events in light of the runes. I admit the mystery runes tend to be vague on many points—and with good reason. Nevertheless, too many have become dogmatic in their interpretation, insisting that the runes can only mean such and such, when quite clearly those same runes could be understood another way. Rather, we must hold to the meaning of those runes as compatible with other runes and then interpret recent events in that light: Pitland is burning; a supreme emperor is about to be crowned; and kingsman brigades are mercilessly assaulted with unprecedented fervor.

"In addition, we hear of increasingly frequent and intense storms on land and sea, floods, earthquakes, landslides, wildfires—not to mention unrest along the bordering states. But the culminating issue, as far as I'm concerned, is what Jorna overheard Hod-ya and Mileer say: Every person is to be branded with this supreme emperor's name as proof of fealty to the empire." He tapped a rune in the middle of his blade. "As one of Atel's runes says:

> As I wrote you before, so I say again now,
> That day cannot come, till the mark and the vow
> On all mankind is forced and is taken.
> An evil one rises when truth is forsaken.
> But undone will he be, by the breath of a word
> And rescued are all that embrace the truth heard."

A collective gasp arose from the assembly. Husbands drew their wives closer; wives looked fearfully to their husbands, then back to

Flan; youths looked nervously to their parents, shaking their heads, not wanting to believe that this ancient prophecy was about to be fulfilled in their lifetime. What of their hopes for the future, their plans for family and livelihood?

Flan stared at Knarsh, "If you feel confident enough to speak for him, would your captain concur that we are on the threshold of the end?"

Soft weeping broke out here and there; otherwise, a somber silence brooded upon all.

Knarsh cleared his throat and said, "We, uh, haven't quite gotten that far in our deliberations of the mystery runes. I guess we didn't want to consider that possibility. But I will say this: before we were sent to you, our brigade was rousted from an insecure campsite and led to an amazing, new, utterly impregnable base camp. You might say it is a fortress of high cliffs replete with a labyrinth of caves and flowing with fresh water, all in the midst of a lush, fruitful forest and bountiful hunting ground.

"And what's more, one of our lieutenants, Bonu, went out on a private mission and encountered group after group of Ecclessites fleeing errant kingsmen brigades that no longer trust, teach, or obey the swordrunes. Truly, we hear that some brigades have outright abandoned the Children of the Stars, following false leaders who encourage counterfeit weaponry. Those refugees still holding to the swordrunes were directed by Bonu to our hideout. Because of that, our numbers have swelled to regimental strength and probably have increased even more since we embarked on our journey here. Logon is surely preparing for something tremendous."

"There is our evidence, if we dare accept it," Flan proclaimed. "How many events have to dovetail before we accept this as more than coincidence? Our responsibility, as I see it, is to prepare ourselves to receive Logon's battle plan and not fearfully draw back in the hopes of some sudden rescue that might not come. If that sudden rescue comes, well and good; but if not, we'd best be ready to resist whatever Lurcan plans. For too long, we've tolerated a divided motive: Yes, we sought to bring Carnalians to Logon, but was not our striving also to preserve our relatively comfortable lifestyles?"

Flan gazed at the sea of faces around him. "Did Logon die to keep us warm, clothed, and well-fed? Or did he yield his life and rise again to deliver us from Lurcan's power? These brothers and sisters from the depths of Ra-Amawl know about a sparse lifestyle that honors Logon's sacrifice; but in the final analysis, we all owe Logon our very lives, regardless of cost. After all, we enlisted voluntarily as soldiers in his cause, did we not? What loyal soldier demands a right to determine the limits of the mission he's assigned?"

Silence hung like a shroud in the room. Many eyes were fixed on the floor. Few dared look directly at Flan.

Cleese spoke up. "Flan is right. I believed what I wanted to believe; I chose comfortable concepts instead of what's plainly engraved."

Several agreeing murmurs echoed Cleese's sentiments.

Cleese lifted his eyes to the rafters. "Logon, forgive my fear; I'm at your service. Whatever you bid, I'll do; wherever you send, I'll go . . . "

Soft whispers ascended from every corner as kingsmen remembered Logon's love and sacrifice on their behalf, recalling how grateful they'd been when they were first rescued from Carnalian ways and desires and solemnly took an oath to live and die for the king and his son.

A crack of thunder rattled the building; everyone's eyes popped open.

A figure shining bright as lightning and girt for war stood in their midst. It was Logon himself, wreathed, as it were, in a fiery whirlwind, his eyes blazing like lamps and his skin glowing like molten metal. For several moments, his eyes swept the gathering, all of them feeling as if the prince looked into their hearts.

"Fear not, beloved. The day to vent my wrath against all rebellion approaches. Lurcan's crimes have reached full harvest; I will thresh his empire thoroughly, separating wheat from chaff. This is why I send you into battle—to offer amnesty to as many as will listen to you. Yet in that fray, many of you will face difficult choices. You will suffer indignities, rejection, insult, and harm; Lurcan will cunningly offer false amnesty and relief from your torments. I warn you now that anyone who defers suffering for my name's sake to get a moment's peace with Carnalia is not worthy of me. I am with you to embolden, strengthen, and enable you to endure the insufferable, even as I endured for your sake; but you will need to deliberately choose to reject the false and cling to me.

"You are commissioned to use my weapon to resist hatred and death. My ways of love and life defeat terror and death. You will best their hatred by your love for me and refusing to deny loyalty to me, even though your life be forfeit."

A mournful look crossed Logon's face. "Not all of you will overcome; but those who do will receive great honors from my father and me. Those who follow me, placing their lives in jeopardy for my name, will never die but will be granted the privilege of reigning with me over my vast, ever-expanding kingdom. Those who forsake me remove themselves from my protection; so, remain steadfast!"

There was another crack of thunder, accompanied by a blinding flash of light. Logon was gone.

Everyone was awestruck; each searching his own heart. Few noticed, but one of the mystery runes glowed yellow on everyone's sword.

CHAPTER FOUR

INDIVIDUAL COMBAT WITH SERGEANT LOVE'S Carnalians came to a halt, the combatants from both sides intrigued by the deadly struggle between the two former best friends grappling with each other. Bilrood momentarily maneuvered himself atop Artka in a sitting position. Pinning him to the ground, he launched himself upward and then down on Artka's torso, thrusting a dirk at Artka's throat.

At that moment, an intense flash of light burst forth from the kingsmen's swords. Carnalians howled, instantly stepping back in pain and surprise, dropping their swords, knives, axes, spears, halberds, and bows from blistered palms to the ground.

Bilrood's dirk bounced harmlessly off Artka's jerkin and lay sizzling in the mud. Bilrood, still sitting atop Artka, leaned back, mouth agape, clumps of sweaty hair hanging over his eyebrows, staring wide-eyed at his blistered palm. "What sorcery is this?" he demanded of Artka.

A quiet hum filled the air which gradually intensified, swelling in volume until the Carnalians clamped hands over their ears, crying out, "Stop it, stop it; make it stop!"

Artka shoved Bilrood off his chest and regained his footing. The kingsmen found the wavering tone delightful, stirring their hearts. In unison, they shouted, "Logon Xychirion!" at the top of their lungs.

Gulundur danced in a circle as he triumphantly waved his sword overhead and quoted:

"A great mountain burning, cast into the sea,
Bubbling and boiling a third of its beasts,
Roamer the second blows, unhindered, free,
As ships and crews become death's feasts."

After several minutes, the tone faded away. Dumbfounded, the Carnalians stood rooted to the ground, unable to do anything but stare at their blistered hands. Some whimpered while others cursed. Suddenly, upon seeing the Ecclessites still brandished swords, they realized how vulnerable they appeared.

"Retreat!" Sergeant Love shouted, limping uphill as fast as he could go on his injured foot. Smag, Poppitt, Rilf, and the others churned uphill, struggling for traction in the rain-slick mud.

One of them cried out, "The Magician did this!" which spurred them all to greater effort.

Bilrood scrambled away from Artka on all fours.

Artka lunged and seized his friend by the boot, staying his escape. "Bilrood, you may not get another chance. Let me pierce your heart; you'll see I tell the truth."

Bilrood twisted around and flipped onto his back, gazing helplessly after his fleeing comrades, his face reddened, his eyes wide. Turning back, he glared at Artka. "Don't you come near me with that accursed blade," he threatened.

"It won't hurt you." Artka touched his sword point to Bilrood's chest. "You'll see, life comes from this blade despite the lies you've heard; Logon Xychirion will forgive you of all the wrong you've ever done and he'll heal your wound."

Bluskie, pointing after the other fleeing Carnalians, tugged Gulundur's sleeve, asking, "Shouldn't we give chase?"

"Eh? What's that, young man?" Gulundur looked away from Artka and Bilrood. "Give chase? Oh, uh, yes, I guess . . . "

Scang laid a hand on Gulundur's shoulder. "T'aint nobbut use, Cap'n; them's too far gone by now. An' usn's jest a standin' here starstruck like ninnies watchin' 'em high-tail it over the hill. But at least we gots that 'un." He pointed at Bilrood. "Go ahead an' stick 'em good, Artka."

"No, no, no!" Bilrood flailed his arms trying to break free of his once-best friend. Getting to his feet, he spun around and churned uphill, kicking mud chunks into the air, pausing only a moment to look back and sneer at Artka. "We'll meet again—when your Magician isn't nearby giving you an unfair advantage. Then you'll know the taste of my steel." He turned and immediately found himself encircled in the brawny arms of Scang.

"Gotcha!" Scang flipped Bilrood around to face Artka. "I be's holdin' him fer yer ter skewer."

Artka lowered his sword. "It's no good that way, Scang, and you know it. He himself must realize how much he needs Logon's forgiveness and then must want it. Until he's ready, piercing him would only be cruelty, not to mention more dangerous for him."

"But yer tol' me yer warn't ready when Tren stuck yer. Mebbe he be's ready but don't know it?"

"Release him, Scang. Lurcan has him so full of fear and lies that he'd bolt the first chance he got. The Advisor must first prepare him." Artka stepped close to face Bilrood, who dangled in Scang's grip. "And

I'm going to petition Logon for that every day. You're right; we will meet again, and then you'll see I'm telling the truth. Let him go."

Scang opened his arms, and Bilrood hit the ground, churning through the mud. Within a minute, he was gone over the top of the hill, even bypassing Sergeant Love, who gimped along leaning on a tree branch for a crutch.

The kingsmen, ankle deep in mud and all safe and sound except for a few bruises and scratches, gathered around.

Gulundur remarked, "Well, that's that, I guess. Time to return to the castle. Hopefully, Metid's column has safely returned." So saying, Gulundur led downhill to the road leading back to the castle. The others followed single file; Artka and Scang brought up the column's rear. Artka turned to watch Bilrood and Sergeant Love vanish over the brow of the hill following the other Carnalians.

"Thet be's a rough go, eh, Artka? Havin' ter let yer best friend go free an' hope Logon be's able to draw him in."

Artka quick-stepped to keep abreast of Scang's longer strides. "He *was* my best friend, Scang. Now I have others—comrades with much more in common than just having lawless fun and getting in trouble. Now my companions and I share Ecclessite values."

Scang smiled. "Right yer be's, laddie. Me, too."

The patrol diagonally traversed the lower slopes where the brushfire hadn't scorched the grass. Though the ground was damp, there were neither ashes nor barren ground, hence no slick mud was churned up by their passing, expediting their descent to the road and their march to the King's Gate Fortress West.

Bluskie and Skujj were intensely curious about the trumpet blast that had filled the air and the blinding-white flash erupting from the glowing runes on their swords. Bluskie spoke up for both. "Why did the Carnalians drop their weapons? And why didn't we?"

"Mystery runes, lads," Gulundur replied, lowering his head and forcing his weary legs forward. "Answers are in the mystery runes, and I'm no expert, I'm afraid."

"But you're a captain, aren't you?" Corporal Albesht intruded, double-timing alongside. "I thought captains were supposed to know all the runes."

Gulundur sighed. "Yes, I suppose there are a great many things I should know about the runes but don't. Some things I just took another captain's word for; other times, I was just too busy with the details of running the fortress. All those excuses seem so feeble now. I mean, there were times I could have set aside to further examine those runes. At any rate, Saygus would be the one for you to ask; for his brigade, sequestered away over the winter in the mountains as they were, made a serious effort to light up the entire sword."

"Well, I admit I'm ashamed that I never put the effort into finishing my first shine of the entire sword, let alone a second," joined Lieutenant Syramna. "But to the best of my knowledge, what we experienced back there, I believe was an event predicted in the Trumpets of Doom."

"The second trump, I think," Gulundur added. "The first sounded some months ago."

"Second? How many are there? What do they mean?" Bluskie probed.

"Seven, in all," said Gulundur. "They signal events which Logon warned would herald the Tremendum, the severe and final judgment on Carnalia. The trumpet blasts are a warning for Ecclessite brigades to expect and be prepared for a time of great chaos and distress, culminating in Logon sweeping from the skies over all nations, gathering his faithful and taking them to Splendora. Perhaps when we arrive back at the fortress, Captain Metid—providing he's arrived—can fill you in as to what he knows about the Trumpets of Doom. He probably knows more than I do.

"This much I surmise—if that was the second trumpet, five more have yet to sound, each one announcing a judgment more severe than the preceding. But not to worry, as far as I can tell, kingsmen are immune, providing they haven't soiled their tunics." He glanced at Bluskie and Skujj.

The flush on their cheeks indicated that the duo were painfully aware of the stains on their tunics.

"Now enough of this chatter. This old man's legs and lungs aren't used to all this traipsing about the countryside uphill and down, through mud and rain. I'm worn out from slogging through mud, not to mention getting soaked to the skin." Gulundur lowered his head again and picked up the pace.

Clouds scudded in from the east, covering the sky as the rag-tag kingsmen patrol drew within sight of the King's Gate Fortress West. The lowering sun lit the underside of the clouded-ceiling, casting a reddish-purple hue over the glacis before the castle, causing it to appear like a field of blood. The castle itself stood in silent shadow before the beleaguered warriors who skirted the inside tree line along the field's edge.

"T'ain't no sign o' life, Cap'n," Scang huffed. "Seems ter me if'n Metid got back safe, troops oughta be wavin' a welcome ter usn's off'n them parapets."

Gulundur paused to scan the hill's dusky crest, then grunted and lowered his head, continuing his upward hike.

"Mebbe usn's oughta send a scout?"

"Won't change anything, Scang. If the enemy has taken the fort . . . well, you know the consequences of that. Either way, we'll have to convince them to yield to Logon's amnesty."

"Ewert!" Bluskie muttered, remembering his wounded friend left alone in the castle. He dipped his hand into his rucksack and extracted his friend's muddied tunic. "If Carnalians control the castle, then Ewert didn't get his tunic back afore they—"

"Belay thet thought, laddie." Scang laid a hand on Bluskie's arm.

"That's right," Artka said, "Logon wouldn't let anything happen as long as his intentions were to get his tunic back."

Skujj looked hopefully from the giant Eroton to Artka.

"Look on the wall above the portcullis." Gulundur pointed. "Someone's waving a glowing sword! They do see us. Kingsmen still hold the fort and the bridge." He chuckled and vigorously waved his sword overhead in reply.

Clanking chains echoed across the meadow as the portcullis was raised. Soon, several men and women holding torches aloft scurried through the knee-high grass of the glacis toward the returning war party.

Despite their weariness, Gulundur's squad quickened their pace. Evebryl, Sejisca, and Cocee were in the forefront of several women bearing waterskins and food to refresh the exhausted fighters.

"Sejisca." Artka opened his arms and embraced Saygus' eldest daughter. The other women greeted sweethearts, husbands, fathers, and brothers with fond embraces and kisses. Within minutes, the merged companies plodded uphill amid much excited chatter about the most recent glowing rune and the musical tone that rang out over all the land.

"Evebryl," Gulundur asked, "any word from Metid?"

"Afraid not. A couple of hours ago"—Evebryl indicated—"we saw a sudden flume of smoke rising over that way, as if a forest was ablaze, despite a sudden downpour. We thought it might be Metid under attack."

"Rest easy on that account. We started the fire. And a brilliant scheme it was, too, eh, Scang? Routed the rascals in front of us, made them scatter like chickens from a fox just so we could get the tunics back to these men. Had a bit of a row with some Carnalians, too, but the trumpet blast put an end to their resistance. Hard-hearted lot they were. Couldn't penetrate a one of them! Not even Artka's friend from his pre-Logon days."

Sejisca took Artka's chin in hand, turning his face toward her. "Was it that Buldoor friend you grew up with?"

"Bilrood—and yes, it was him. And others that I trained alongside of in the Roaring Lion's Brigade. I have a hunch we'll meet again."

The war party passed beneath the portcullis and entered the keep's inner doors to find a roaring fire in the hearth. Women and older children attended to various chores around the keep, especially helping the wounded. Even elderly men, too infirm for strenuous duty, found ways to be useful. This was the camp following—the weak, halt, and infirm that had been left in Sajon's care now held the fort and protected the bridge.

Bluskie and Skujj spotted Ewert in a corner and rushed to his side, producing the lost tunic, to Ewert's great relief. They assisted their friend, slipping the garment over his head and smoothing it out.

The rest of Gulundur's patrol settled in, stowing their gear along the walls before going to the dining hall to receive a meal prepared under Evebryl's oversight. The recently arrived soldiers were given seating preference; those who had already eaten took turns serving.

There was little talk as the evening came on. Most ate in silence, pondering the increasingly intense events of the past few days, especially the latest rune and the tone that reverberated from the skies and disheartened their enemy.

"Movement out on the glacis!" a voice echoed down through the keep from one of the tower guards.

Sajon and Gulundur, seated across the table from each other, glanced at one another.

"You go, Captain." Sajon nodded. "I only had temporary charge of the fort in the absence of a senior officer, but you have rank. Besides, I'm still somewhat incapacitated." He rubbed his thigh. "Running up and down the stairwells isn't something I can do easily at the moment."

"Yes, well, it's not something I can do with ease either, what with slogging through swamps and thickets the live-long day; but I suppose I might be able to ascend the stairs better than you." Gulundur smiled and headed for the staircase.

Artka abandoned his seat and bounded to the bottom of the stairway, arriving just ahead of the captain. "I'll be glad to go in your place, sir. Just let me know what you want done."

"Kind of you, lad, but I'd better have a looksee for myself. You stay down here and get refreshed."

"I'd rather know what's going on."

Gulundur nodded, suppressing a smile. "Of course, you would," he intoned under his breath.

The pair climbed the spiral staircase, Artka impatiently following Gulundur's labored steps. Upon reaching the top, however, Artka zipped around the captain and trotted down the walkway and through the upper guardroom mess hall where he'd first met Scang. Dismissing the fond reminiscence from his mind, he exited the portal to the catwalk behind the crenellations that ran the length of the wall to the next block house. He silently drew alongside Hudge, who had grabbed a fistful of muffins off a platter on the way to his self-appointed lookout.

"Where away?" Artka whispered, staring into the misty gloom rolling upward into the lower field from the valley.

Hudge indicated the tree-lined fringe along the left side of the field. "Either a large company of men in very tight formation is keeping to the shadows just inside the fringe of the forest; or a very large, slithering creature is stealthily stalking up toward the fortress, taking advantage of the cover provided by the woods in this misty darkness. I've seen no light, neither torch nor sword."

Gulundur, breathing heavily, joined them, peering where Hudge indicated.

"I know it's a lot to suggest, and I'm as exhausted as anyone from our excursion," Hudge urged. "But I believe the fort ought to be put on alert."

Gulundur leaned with both hands atop a crenellation and sighed. "You're right, of course. I'd hoped we'd have had a respite from our last fray. Hudge, go below and quietly put the post on alert. Assign some men to join us on these ramparts; secure all entry points and display the banner along the riverbank with a bonfire requesting assistance from Ecclessa's shore—just in case any more kingsmen have arrived at the eastern shores in the last few hours. Artka, stay with me; I'll need you to relay messages."

"Shouldn't we hail whatever or whoever is creeping up along the edge of the field?" Artka asked. "It may be kingsmen forces cautiously approaching, not knowing if the fort is in enemy hands."

"Hmm, I think not; if it's Metid and his forces, it won't make any difference. If it's an enemy, be it human or *kyllorn*, surprise is our ally. In fact, we should wrap our blades, lest our presence be inadvertently revealed, ruining the slim advantage we have."

Both men wrapped their Child of the Stars in their capes and held them down below the wall, leaving only their heads poking above.

The shadow, darker than the surrounding murkiness of the woods, was barely discernable, gliding silently just inside the edge of the trees, undulating ever nearer. Artka longed to raise *Sky Saber* to eye level and examine the mysterious intruder, but the tiniest glimmer of light at this point would only alert the enemy that the fort was occupied, forewarning the approaching menace.

Gulundur held his breath as if he was listening for sounds that might reveal the nature of the approaching menace. But there was no noise except the breeze whistling softly through the crenellations. Nevertheless, the barely visible, undulating line of darkness progressed steadily uphill, keeping just inside the fringe of trees, purposely obscuring its presence along the forest's edge.

Artka estimated its length being some two hundred paces. Either it was a file of a few hundred men—more if in double or treble files—or one very long, snake-like creature. The hairs on his neck stood erect.

"Captain, it might be a disembodied dread, like the one that assaulted my troops in the Daggerman Castle."

Gulundur turned toward Artka, considering the implications. Finally, he turned back to the field again, whispering, "Elyon forbid! But if it is, well, we'll do what we can. Spread the word: let no light shine until I give the word."

Urgency overriding formal protocols, Artka left without saluting or even giving a verbal response, dashing away to accomplish his mission.

Artka jumped halfway down the spiral stairway to the center of the keep, catching everyone's attention. In hushed tones, he rehearsed Captain Gulundur's directives to not let any light shine or noise carry to the outside.

Hudge already had assigned the ablest warriors to defensive posts. Women, children, the elderly, and wounded huddled close to interior walls, swords in hand, prepared to present Logon's offer of amnesty to their assailants, no matter the cost.

"Just so you know," Artka announced, "we may be facing a powerful *kyllorn* instead of mere men."

Reddy, Harnet, Scang, Brendle, Clepy, and Braxmore rose from their seats in the circle and approached Artka. Reddy spoke for them. "Since the seven of us, uh, seem to have been together longer than any of us were assigned to anyone else, we'd like to tag along with you."

Artka bit the inside of his cheek, hoping his glistening tears didn't show. "I wouldn't have it any other way."

"Any firedrakes out there?" Scang said. "I'm kinda gittin' the hang o' thumpin' 'em."

Artka laughed. "I'll see if we can drum some up for you, Scang." So saying, he remounted the stairs two at a time, his companions close behind.

Once on the walkway, the seven gathered around Gulundur, who had a steady watch on field and forest.

"Any change?" Artka asked.

In the quietest of whispers, Gulundur replied, "They—or it— arrived at the top left corner of the fortress moments ago. It seemed to shrink in size like it's either a band of soldiers bunching into a tight-knit assault force, or it's your serpent-like thing coiling as if ready to strike. If it's the latter, we need to spread out a bit, lads, lest it take us all at one bite."

Sajon arrived at the top of the spiral staircase and limped over to Gulundur.

"Glad you made it up to see this," Gulundur said. "Look, over there in the upper corner of the field just outside the fort's corner—whatever it is, it seems like it's gathering itself to pounce but seems hesitant so far, unsure."

"I'm glad your patrol made it back in time to bolster our meager defenses." Sajon sighed. "If it was only women, children, elderly, and wounded with me to defend Logon's Bridge . . ."

The others nodded, grimly envisioning the scene.

Hudge returned to the walkway and stood alongside his brother as he reported to Gulundur, "All's ready, sir."

Gulundur nodded. "Now, we wait."

CHAPTER FIVE

BONU AWOKE ABRUPTLY. SOMETHING HAD disturbed his sleep, but what? Everything around him was still dark; nearby, the others slept soundly. He sat up; brushed off his leafy camouflage; stood upright to inspect his sword; adjusted his belt; and, with a leftover limp from his tussle with the waterdragon, headed silently into the undergrowth to check the pickets. Ever since the previous day when Roton had alerted him that he'd discovered traces of a large military force maneuvering on the shores opposite their cabin on the island, fatigue weighed heavier on him than ever. The thrashing the waterdragon had given him and resultant injuries, though not too serious, were taking a toll. That, combined with needing to be alert to sounds and smells as they trekked through Ra-Amawl, Bonu's energy was near depletion. And they were still a couple days' journey, at least, from Captain Varter and the safety of the cliffs. And, with an empire task force hot on their heels, Bonu dared not head directly to the encampment until they'd shaken all pursuers.

Bonu turned away from the others slumbering in the campsite and step by cautious step stalked along a deer trail, listening, watching . . .

A pinprick of blue light flashed upward from beneath a bush and headed straight at his chest, stopping harmlessly as it touched him. "A life for the king," a nervous voice challenged.

Bonu smiled, grasped the sword behind the glowing tip, and lowered it toward the ground. "Nicely done, Roton, only . . . oh, never mind. Nicely done. Had I been Carnalian, you certainly would have sent me to an audience with Logon." Bonu squatted beside the recruit. "Anything pass this way?"

Roton shook his head, then realizing Bonu couldn't see him, dark as it was, replied, "Nary a thing. Maybe . . . too quiet."

Bonu tapped his forehead. "Of course, that's what awakened me; it's too quiet for Ra-Amawl. That means only one thing."

"Something ominous is nearby and on the prowl." Roton swiveled his head. "Small, nocturnal animals usually snuffling about this time of day are still in their dens, sensing danger."

"Precisely! We must move out immediately. Go find the other picket—Grennace, isn't it? I'll wake the others and meet you back here in five minutes."

"Are we heading to the cliffs?"

"Too risky. Besides, I need somewhere to lay up for a day or two to recuperate. I'm functioning on half strength and less than that mentally; if I don't get some deep sleep soon, I'll make a disastrous blunder. We need a discreet place to lay low until the empire troops hunting us give up or wander off." The thought of jumping off a high cliff into a shallow pool crossed his mind. "I know just the place."

"Right, I'll fetch Grennace." Roton disappeared with barely a rustle in the bushes. If nothing else, Bonu mused, Carnalia trained their dronnets well.

Bonu returned to the sleeping forms scattered beneath a large cedar and, going to each, lightly touched their shoulder and whispered, "Check for irks," before moving on to the next. Lastly, he roused Jeda. "How are you at climbing?"

Jeda sat up, peered at her betrothed through the dawn's fading fog, blinked twice, and asked, "Climbing what? Stairs? Ladders? Ropes?"

"Sheer rockface cliffs."

"The difficult isn't enough, must you require the impossible?"

Bonu rightly interpreted the gleam of her smile through the misty dawn as a tease.

The others, yawning and stretching, gathered around, ready to resume the trek.

"There's an enemy in the vicinity," Bonu bluntly stated. "We need to hole up where they can't find us. I know the perfect place, providing you girls can climb."

Artil stepped forward. "You doubt Scrarth and Avangar contestants are up to a challenge? After Logon used us to pull down Bablo-ya and her corrupt principality, you ask if we're up to little cliff-scaling?"

Bonu tussled the girl's head. "My friend Scung would love your attitude, little one. You have the same unconquerable heart as he. I apologize. I should've known better than to doubt your abilities."

"Yeah, thanks, Artil," Spoena wryly muttered as she adjusted her cape and sword for travel.

"Well, we can, right?" Artil shot back.

"Not so loud," Bonu cautioned. "We'll find a way; and if not, Logon will reveal how. Now, fall in behind me . . . and maintain silence."

"Another impossibility." Jeda sighed as she fell in behind Bonu.

The others came single file with three of the ex-dronnets bringing up the rear to erase all sign of their passing. Grennace and Roton were waiting at the rendezvous; then as a group, they proceeded deeper into the jungle.

Two hours later, the ten stopped long enough to refresh themselves at a trickling rivulet. Renn, Olpuc, and Gravic stood watch, while the girls and Bonu, Grennace, and Roton resorted to a mossy bed. Bonu sat leaning forward and, with a stick, scraped a patch of ground clear of detritus to draw a crude map of the territory. "In case anything happens to me, this way is Captain Varter's cliff fortress; the cliff I jumped from into a pool of fresh water is over that way"—he tapped the etching on the ground—"which is where I'm taking us now. There's a small cave on top of the cliff, where an owl often dens up to consume his prey; you'll be safe hiding there."

Jeda knelt beside him to wash and redress his leg wound as he discussed topographical details. She shook her head and interrupted his discourse. "I don't like the look of that puncture, Bonu. It's angry-looking and smells unhealthy. Does it hurt?"

"Now that you ask, it's the only wound from the waterdragon that still bothers me."

"Let me have a look." Grennace leaned over Jeda's shoulder and lifted the bandage. A sharp intake of breath revealed his concern. "Bonu, that'll cripple you if it's not soon taken care of. The flesh will rot, and you'll lose your leg." His hand touched Bonu's forehead. "Why, you're burning up. Why didn't you say something?"

"Can't waste the time. We must attain the rocky cliff hideout; after that, we can tend to this. I think we can make it there before it gets worse."

"It's already worse. You shouldn't have been walking on it. This needs immediate attention." Grennace called to one of his men, "Renn, go find a *bhurga* tree, strip some of its bark—keep it moist, mind you, and bring it here."

Renn wordlessly disappeared into the shrubbery.

Grennace turned back to Bonu. "The more you use this leg, the worse it'll get. We need to stabilize it and make a litter to carry you."

"Out of the question. I need to lead the way; besides, constructing a litter will consume valuable time, not to mention announcing we were here by leaving a mess."

"Can't be helped. I know what I'm talking about; I was trained in battlefield medicine and herbal remedy. I believe King Elyon invested his creation with helpful things; just because the empire also has such knowledge doesn't necessarily disqualify kingsmen from using such things, unless they're intertwined with mysticism of the *kyllorn*. You're too valuable for us to lose. I'm sure Jeda would agree."

"Indeed, I do. But what if we apply the tip of a sword to the wound?" Jeda searched Bonu's eyes.

"Did that suggestion come from the Advisor, or is that your own idea?" Bonu stared steadily at her.

"What difference does it make?" Dalicusi posed, looking on with concern.

Artil knelt beside Bonu and examined the wound. "Laying a sword on a wound isn't a normal method to induce healing; what you're suggesting requires a suspension of natural laws, which would be a miracle. Miracles in Logon's name only happen if the Advisor prompts them. I, too, had thought of that and sought Logon about the possibility but can't say that I was encouraged to try."

"You're pretty uppity, little sister. I don't care if you did 'toot' a trumpet of doom; you're still my little sister and should stay out of things beyond your years."

"Careful, Spoena." Bonu wagged his finger. "You tread on thin ice when you rebuke one of Logon's choice servants. Artil has been entrusted with unique abilities. To disparage her position could be considered as an affront to Logon. And I agree with her. I've been asking Logon since last night to heal this wound but get no release in my heart to apply my sword. For whatever reason, Logon seems to have shown Grennace what to do."

"Well, can't we at least try?" Jeda posed.

"You still haven't answered my question. Is it you or the Advisor who prompts this action?"

"Well, doesn't Logon's having been beaten severely before his impaling guarantee healing of his followers' wounds and diseases?"

"Ouch!" Bonu winced as Grennace's finger probed deeper. "Careful there, Lieutenant; that hurt." Then, turning back to Jeda, he said, "Yes, Jeda, but there are differing thoughts on how to understand that rune." He shifted his sword around to the fore and ran his finger down the blade searching for the rune in question. Tapping it with his fingernail, he read aloud:

"Logon bore calamity,
His striped back our sorrowing.
Grieving paid our amity,
Impaling day, most harrowing.
Wounded for our wayward life
Bruised was he as our shield,
Victim of our hate and strife,
Yet by those stripes, we're healed."

Bonu grimaced again as Grennace finished his examination. "There are those who hold that kingsmen have a right to claim perfect health all the time based on this rune, that Ecclessites have a right to expect Logon to heal all hurts and sickness. However, that can't be true. Atel's runes reveal he had chronic eye trouble that Logon never totally removed, not to mention other ancient generals and brigade leaders who suffered health problems and resorted to natural remedies for relief.

"At the same time, the runes also declare that miraculous healings happened to various ones—even bringing them back to life. But many who asked in full faith, like Atel—perhaps the most full-of-faith general who ever lived—were denied. Logon's provision was to give us the Advisor, who, in accordance with Logon's will, dispenses special, supernatural abilities when needed. These are to be used with discretion and only at the Advisor's urging. Think about it: the main difference between Ecclessites and Carnalians is our willingness to submit our own wills in a given matter to Elyon's will, as Logon did. Thus, supernatural healing is dependent on the Advisor's prompting. Look at it this way: one special ability the Advisor gives is supernatural healing, right?"

Those gathered around nodded.

"So why is 'special healing' among the abilities the Advisor distributes to certain kingsmen if all Ecclessites have a right to claim healing anytime? It would be superfluous if physical healing was already guaranteed in the amnesty! We don't need to have a special unction of the Advisor to administer forgiveness for disobedience, for that's included in the amnesty."

Jeda turned her eyes away, tears glistened on her cheeks. "It's just that I hate seeing you suffer so."

A rustling in nearby bushes announced Renn's return with a handful of white bark.

"Ah." Grennace stood. "Splendid. Here, help me scrape and make a pulp from the inside of the bark." The two men scraped the fibrous, moist inside of the bark, then pounded it into a mash. "Now, Bonu, this may sting, but the juice will draw the inflammation out. We'll bind it tight, immobilizing your leg, which also demands we carry you."

Bonu started to protest.

Grennace interrupted, "This is absolutely necessary if the poultice is to work."

Olpuc and Gravic approached carrying a crudely constructed litter of two stout poles with webbed seating made of vines stretched between. Strong hands hoisted Bonu to an upright position, so he'd be able to direct the way.

"Renn, Roton, and I will clean up any evidence of our work here," Grennace said, "while you lead. The women will go between. Tut, tut, the matter is settled." He forestalled Bonu's objections. "Your job right now is just to be our guide—which you can do from that sedan-chair rig." Grennace smiled, adding, "After all, I know how to assume leadership, too."

The entourage slogged across spongy moss beds and waded through fern beds growing amid stands of saplings and clumps of underbrush, around thick bole trees replete with vines dangling from limbs of great height that allowed rare splotches of daylight to illuminate the ground through sparse spots in the canopy.

Bonu scowled as he directed Olpuc and Gravic, pointing his sword this way and that, uttering a terse word whenever a change of direction was necessary. Their progress through Ra-Amawl was slow; extra care for silence had to be exercised in case pursuers were close.

By mid-afternoon, they had reached an overgrown trail that Jeda, Spoena, and Artil recognized as the trail along which they'd lugged sacks of scavenged goods from Psa's Burn. Twenty minutes later, Bonu's patrol arrived at a charred clearing and paused to catch their breath, observing the severely blackened earth at the lower end of the field. Charred banks lined the pool that shimmered in the fading rays of sunlight, giving grim testimony that many had died as Psa met his demise.

Renn, Roton, and Grennace caught up to the group as they were halfway down the burned area between forest and clearing. "We've left spare trace of our passing," Grennace assured Bonu. "Is yonder cliff where your hideout is?"

Bonu nodded. "We'd best make haste while it's still light; there's no vegetation to cover us now until we're safe in my owl's den up top."

"How's your leg?" Jeda asked.

"Smarts but does feel less fiery. My headache feels somewhat better, too."

"And your complexion is returning to normal, I think." Grennace rested his hand on Bonu's forehead. "The fever has diminished—not gone yet but better."

"Let's move on," Bonu urged.

Olpuc and Gravic gratefully changed places with Renn and Roton before setting forth. The patrol slowly jogged down over the remainder of the burn, mindful of their patient. Green shoots had not yet sprouted near the pool during the intervening months, despite open sky and direct sunlight; it was as if some toxin from the desecrated Psa polluted the grounds around the waterfall's basin. The ex-dronnets bringing up the rear did their best to erase any sign of their passing over the hillside littered with charred trees.

The patrol slowed their pace as they neared the cliff's base. Scattered along the base were several sizable rocks that had some time or other tumbled from higher ledges, all but forming an irregular wall. The patrol members searched about and, with some difficulty, finally spied the overhanging shelf of the owl's den some eight or nine feet shy of the cliff's top. "This"—Bonu gestured like a lord inviting guests to his castle—"is the gateway to my cave."

"And you leaped from way up there into that small pool?" Spoena's tone was incredulous as she assayed the ledge above the pool and imagined his heroic leap into the pool of unknown depth to challenge a company of Erotons, several dronnets, and a dread.

Even Bonu didn't remember it as being quite that high.

Roton broke the spell. "Well, hadn't we best get about scaling the rock?"

All eyes turned from the ledge above the pool to the rockface before them, examining it for chinks that could serve as footholds. Some vines dangled down the cliff face but didn't appear strong enough for weight-bearing like the ones Scung had used to carry Bonu safely aloft out of the enemy's clutches.

Renn and Olpuc took an upward leap and, with grasping hands, caught crevices on the rock face some ten feet off the ground. They then nimbly scaled hand over hand, helping each other by pointing out footholds, guiding each other to higher perches.

Grennace, standing alongside Bonu on the ground, watched their ascent. "They were in the empire's mountain troops before joining the dronnet corps. If anyone can ascend a sheer rockface, they can. Once they attain the top, they'll scrounge around for vines to fasten to anchors, then drop them down and haul up the rest of us."

Spoena had already launched herself upward, catching one of the handholds the ex-dronnets had used. "We know how to climb, too, don't we Artil? You can do it, like we were taught, remember?" Spoena clambered up the sheer rock almost as nimbly as the dronnets, matching pace with them.

"We learned cliff-climbing from our father," Artil explained to the others gazing in amazement at Spoena, "but we never climbed cliffs this high or steep." Calling up to Spoena, Artil exclaimed, "I can't reach the first hold, Spoena."

"I'll give you a boost, Artil, if you think you can make it the rest of the way," Grennace offered. "Anyone else willing to give it a try?" he turned to Jeda and Dalicusi.

Artil called, "Spoena, do you think I can reach the other chinks and nooks once I get started?"

"Sure, they're not so far apart. Come on."

"Artil, are you sure? I mean, one slip is all you get." Bonu sat on a boulder, watching.

Artil nodded, looked up, and called, "Heave away, Grennace."

Grennace fairly tossed the girl up to the first handhold, which she caught and clung tentatively to for a moment; then securing both hands, she swung and hooked her foot over a slim nook and pulled herself up, following her sister's route.

Renn and Olpuc had attained the upper shelf by that time and quickly disappeared from Bonu's view. Seconds later, their faces reappeared, looking down over the cliff face. "Found your cave, Bonu. Looks like your owl or something has been living in it."

Bonu smiled for the first time in hours, remembering how he'd frightened the owl away and then ate its meal. "Check for vines up above on the plateau."

Bonu watched the sisters reach the halfway mark; the two men who had gone up and over the cliff passed out of view again. Spoena reached the ledge by the cave and slipped down into the opening, calling back, "I'm in the alcove."

Artil attained a spot just below the ledge and stopped, stretching her hand as high as she could but without success. "Ugh! Spoena, give me a hand. I can't quite reach . . ."

Spoena bobbed back into sight, smiling as she reached down. Their hands gripped, and Spoena hoisted Artil just enough to be able to swing her leg over and scramble to safety. Bonu watched anxiously from below, as did Jeda and Dalicusi. Suddenly, Spoena grabbed Artil's cape, hauling her rapidly out of sight behind the ledge. Her face again peeked over the edge as she hissed at those on the ground and pointed uphill to the burn.

Bonu immediately understood. "Down," he commanded.

Grennace, Dalicusi, Jeda, Gravic, and Roton instantly flopped to their bellies behind the line of fallen rocks. A second later, Bonu rolled off his seat and hit the ground with a thump and a groan. "Seems our pursuers found our trail after all, or else they're very good at guessing our intentions. They're spread out all over the hillside, inspecting every little gouge in the dirt for our spoor."

"How many are they?" Grennace whispered.

"Hard to tell in the failing light. Couple of hundred, maybe more."

Jeda drew close to Bonu. "Why would Hod-ya detail so many to chase after us? Is her revenge that important that she'd send such a large contingent?"

"Pitland has no fury like a witch-woman scorned, eh," Grennace quoted a Carnalian proverb. "And no witch-woman has fury like a Majestic Madam cheated of her prey," he added.

"What are we going to do now?" Dalicusi whispered, her eyes wide, even in the fading light her face appeared drained of color.

In the next instant, the end of a thick vine thudded to the ground.

Bonu looked up and saw faces peering down from atop the overhang; it was Olpuc and Renn dropping a suitable climbing vine to those on the ground. Spoena's harsh whispers at the two explorers carried to the group below. "Enemies, on the rise of the hill; don't you two ever look to see if all is clear?"

Olpuc and Renn instantly ducked out of sight. A hoarse whisper floated down from above. "Sorry! We didn't expect—"

Bonu faced uphill, peeking over the top of the rock to observe the troops sweeping the hillside in a grid search pattern. He estimated the remaining time as to whether the Carnalians could finish their search before twilight faded away altogether.

He whispered to the men on top, "I don't think they see us. They're too far away to hear us as long as we keep our voices low. They're so focused on searching for our trail that they've probably not even taken a brief look downhill. Don't make any sudden movements that might draw attention. Move slowly and deliberately and you'll be able to secure the other end of that vine around a rock or tree up there."

Olpuc answered in a heavy whisper, "Aye, then what? Haul you up slowly?"

"No, no, quick as a wasp on a fly, they'll swarm to any movement they see rising up the rock face. No, wait until it's completely dark and they've made camp for the night. In the meantime, stay out of sight; we'll dig in down here under this fringe of rocks along the cliff base. I'll *scree* like a nighthawk when I think it's safe to proceed. Hopefully, they won't extend their investigation down here till morning. They won't likely risk trampling on any tracks by trudging around in the dark."

Olpuc ducked out of sight.

Those on the ground scraped out shallow ditches behind the rocks, providing a hollow behind the rocks to hide in. It was an adequate hideout if none of the search parties broke away to explore down by the pool before dark.

Bonu lay back and listened to the small trickle of water tumbling off the cliff into the pool, providing a calm gurgle. Over such a short time, the persistent flow of water had cleansed the pool's immediate environs of the filth left over from Psa's demise, though desolation still marred the hillside around and the entire slope above the pool.

Several campfires sprang up across the ridge as night came on. Weary of vainly searching, the troops settled around the fires, unrolling bedrolls, and talking quietly—unusual for rowdy empire troops who'd normally be guffawing at bawdy stories, quarrelling, and singing pub songs—but then Ra-Amawl had a tendency to dampen even the most rambunctious of rowdies, Bonu mused.

Deep darkness gradually stole over the cliff, contrasting with the widespread campsite fires spewing sparks into the night sky.

Jeda snuggled into the crook of Bonu's arm, looking hopefully into her fiancé's face. Dalicusi nestled in beside her, glancing up at the sky, her lips moving in silent commune with her newfound liege. Grennace, Roton, and Gravic lay belly down near the dangling vine, ready to pull it taut and provide tension on the line when it was time for them to ascend.

Another two hours passed. The moon, well into its second monthly phase, skimmed the treetops lining the edge of the charred field. Bonu stayed alert, hoping to grab a momentary glimpse at their pursuers through the light of his sword, *Quickblaze*, to ascertain if it was safe to begin the ascent of the cliff face. Surely, he thought, they'd watch the forest, expecting anything that might be dangerous to come from the jungle beyond, not the sheer cliff at their back. When the pickets became drowsy, Bonu and company would ascend one by one up the cliff unnoticed as the enemy slumbered the night away.

Finally deciding a quick glimpse through the shine of his sword was worth the risk, Bonu withdrew *Quickblaze* and laid it atop a flat rock.

Jeda held her breath.

Bonu panned the blade from right to left until he spotted the nearest sentry. The man faced uphill as Bonu expected. He was watching the campfires along the high ridge and the jungle growth beyond. Bonu swiveled his blade left and found another picket, also facing uphill. Upon spotting two more sentries likewise looking away from the cliff, it was decided. Bonu pursed his lips and *screed* like a nighthawk.

The signal was immediately answered by a shake from the upper end of the vine.

Gravic grasped the vine in both hands and braced his feet against the cliff base. Roton did the same; the two of them provided a firm anchor to prevent the vine from swinging wildly about as each one ascended.

"Jeda, Dalicusi, grasp the vine in both hands and place your feet on the wall, then walk up the cliff face hand over hand, bracing yourself in whatever chinks your feet find," Bonu instructed.

"I know. I've done this sort of thing before," Jeda said, "in the short time I was with Captain Varter's brigade."

"Me, too," Dalicusi added. "It was part of the training Deparis insisted Stullo and I master in preparation for Scrarth and Avangar."

"Only," Jeda whispered lowly, "I didn't fare too well . . ."

"Well, my test was nearly as high. I'll go first." Dalicusi gripped the vine and planted her feet against the rock wall. Roton and Gravic pulled against the vine as Dalicusi ascended hand over hand and step by step.

"How will you get up, Bonu?" Jeda asked.

"One leg will do the work of two," Bonu replied, watching Dalicusi's shadowy form ascend in the moonlight. "My arms are strong enough to carry me up, despite the wounds from . . ." Bonu froze, staring upward.

The others looked up to see why Bonu stopped mid-sentence and instantly realized their jeopardy.

The glowing point of Dalicusi's sword hung below her hemline, swinging back and forth with each step, sending a tiny, albeit bright, beacon of blue light out into the night.

Bonu swiftly turned toward the field. Had they seen? He bit his lip and looked up again at Dalicusi slowly ascending the cliff, then back at the pickets on the slope. If one of their pursuers became restless and turned, they'd notice the tiny blue dot swinging back and forth against the dark cliff face.

Dalicusi finally attained the summit, slipped her leg over the ledge, and dropped out of sight behind the natural parapet.

Bonu breathed freely. He studied the slope several more minutes before taking Jeda's elbow in hand. "Jeda, make sure you secure your sword from sight."

"I will." She checked her sword's rigging and, when satisfied, gave Bonu a quick kiss on the cheek, stood on tiptoe, seized the rope, and firmly planted her feet against the cliff. Instead of watching her ascend, Bonu focused on the troops bivouacked in the charred field uphill. Her ascent seemed unnoticed.

"You needn't anchor the vine for me when I go," Bonu whispered hoarsely to the ex-dronnets beside him. "I'll go hand over hand. You both go on ahead."

Roton started to protest, but Bonu's finger touched his lips. "No, if anyone gets caught, it's better that it be me. You both need more training in Logon's ways. Grennace has a rough idea of how to find Captain Varter's cliff, if it comes to that. Now go."

Reluctantly, Roton and Gravic, each in turn, seized the vine and, hand over hand, hauled themselves aloft. When they were well underway, Grennace gave a final nod to Bonu and ascended the vine so vigorously, he almost overtook the other two.

Taking one final, sweeping look at the slumbering field of Carnalians, Bonu secured his sword, gripped the vine, and hoisted himself off the ground. He no sooner reached one hand over the other when his wounded leg snagged on something; he tried to kick free. Whatever snagged his foot wouldn't release it; in fact, it felt like an animal playfully tugging on his legging. Suddenly, it yanked painfully hard! Bonu lost his grip and fell to the ground with a grunt.

Brawny arms encircled Bonu's chest, and a gravelly voice chortled. "Ere now, yer'll nobbut be gittin' away as easy as thet! Not arter I be's a trailin' yer through thicket an' briar, field an' fen, an' jest losin' yer spoor every time I be's ready ter pounce."

"Scung? Scung, is that you?" Bonu could hardly believe his ears.

"Aye, Lieutenant, it be's me! I wondered if'n mebbe yer warn't headin' fer our little hideout in this here cliff. Then, when I espied a wee, twinklin' light a swingin' ter an' fro on the cliff face, I kenned it hadda be yers."

"How? You mean . . . it's been you dogging our trail, nearly boxing us in on the island, trailing us through the jungle?" Even in the dim moonlight, Bonu recognized the tangled beard and toothy grin of his friend.

"Aye, me bucko, aye. Yer be's a might hard ter catch, even wi' a sore leg." He eyed Bonu's wrappings and the poultice bound securely to Bonu's thigh for the first time. "What happent?"

"Eh, this? Encountered a waterdragon before we reached the island cabin."

"A waterdragon? Did yer now? Bored wi' duelin' dreads, eh?"

"Who's with you? What task force is trailing us?" Bonu took out his sword and openly viewed the quiet campsite through his sword's shimmering glow.

"Them be's yer genr'l friends, Tren, an' Ollo, Leton. In fact, it be's most o' the kingsmen Jeda liberated from Pitland, joined up together. Usn's climbed out o' Pitland on another stairway what was carved inter the cliffs at the lower end o' the White Castle afore the lava flow sealed the land shut. Usn's swept up through the southern marches o' a savannah an' eventually had ter duck inter Ra-Amawl. There, we fought a brigade o' empire troops an' rescued summat o' Mileer's men who told usn's thet seven dronnets done captured yers an' was takin' yers ter Cosmopolis. Thet's why usn's didn't jest reveal ourselves; we thunk yers was captive o' them dronnets an' thet they might slit yer throats if'n we tried ter rescue ya afore we could surprise 'em."

Bonu balanced on his good leg and arched his back, laughing heartily. "We wore ourselves out dodging you, crawling through undergrowth where a warthog wouldn't go, taking the most difficult paths, trying to shake an enemy off our trail and avoid capture; and all the time, it was just you, our own brothers-at-arms!"

"Bonu?" Jeda's whisper floated down from above. "What's going on?"

Several shadowy heads peered down over the ledge.

"Jeda, Dalicusi, Grennace, come back down. We've been fleeing kingsmen."

"What?"

"It's safe. Logon apparently provided an army to escort us to Varter's cliffs. They aren't Carnalians after all, but the kingsmen you armed and released, Jeda, during the Scrarth and Avangar, now banded together into one tactical group. Come down, we'll get warmed at their fires and enjoy good companionship and some hot food." Bonu waved his sword high overhead.

Bonu and Scung's conversation carrying uphill and the unexpected appearance of a brightly-lit sword at the cliff's base caused a growing stir throughout the Ecclessite camp. Men stood to their feet at their campfires, waving swords in reply; excitement buzzed through the camp, and a few jogged downhill toward the cliff.

The girls were the first to descend, making use of the vine as Scung held it taut. Jeda descended first, followed by Dalicusi, then the sisters. Grennace came last, following his men until they all stood at the bottom and met the welcoming war party scurrying downhill to greet them. Introductions were made as Tren, Leton, and Ollo stood near, flanked by several of their men.

Tren stepped forward, placed his hands on Bonu's shoulders, looked him full in the face. "Well done, Lieutenant! You've led us a merry enough chase, eluding us time after time in the worst jungle— something few can lay claim to accomplishing. And now Scung tells me you singlehandedly bested a waterdragon? And not only that, but rescued five dronnets?"

"There were seven; two were taken by the waterdragon. And I, as you can see, suffered somewhat from the encounter. Besides, I take no credit for the fact that these men are now following Logon. Artil here"—he reached over and drew the girl to his side—"initiated the primary sortie of their rescue."

"Is that so?" Tren gazed into the girl's face illumined by the light of his sword. "Ah yes, I remember, the trumpeter-lass. You've changed, even in the short time since then. You may be young, but you're no longer a child; there's an aspect of sagacity in your eyes. Logon has set his mark upon you. Tell me, has anyone in your family ever been used . . . uh, shall we say, to deliver specific words from Logon?"

Spoena stepped alongside her sister. "Our mother is a seer in Captain Varter's brigade, if that's what you mean."

Tren smiled. "Valiant daughters, both." Tren turned to Bonu. "Come to my campsite. We'll catch up on events and set a course for Varter's camp. I presume you realize that the second trumpet of doom has sounded, reportedly creating havoc on Carnalia's oceans and seaports?"

CHAPTER SIX

DANCEL PASSED THROUGH THE BENIGHTED, rain-swept streets, darting between inset doorways and second story overhangs, twixt wooden frame and brick-and-mortar dwellings, occasionally pausing just long enough to make sure no one had seen her before lighting out for the next sheltered alcove. The most recent squall that had roared through the streets kept the Cosmopolisian citizenry sheltering behind shuttered windows and latched doors. Only furtive Ecclessites slipped inconspicuously into the streets from Flan's home by twos and threes under cover of the raging weather.

Dancel was the first to leave the meeting, anxious to get back to her castle duties before her absence was noted. A sudden windy blast buffeted Dancel so hard, she swayed off balance and had to lean into the gust to maintain her footing while shielding her eyes from horizontal rain. Dancel leaned against a brick wall for several moments, composing her wits as the squall's fury intensified. She was compelled to keep her eyes downcast as she felt her way along the wall to the next inset entry, where she pressed close to the doorframe to await the subsidence of the stormy blast. A gust caused her to inadvertently bump the door behind her, causing it to *clunk* against its frame.

"Wh—who's there?" challenged a high-pitched voice from inside.

Dancel froze. No excuse for being out on a night like this would be acceptable. Perhaps if she remained quiet, the resident would think it was just the wind . . .

"I know somebody's out there; give answer, or I'll sic my dogs on you." It was no bluff; low growls and scratching claws emitted from the other side of the door.

Dancel pondered only a moment. If she took flight, she couldn't outrun dogs. Even if she could, she'd not escape their ability to sniff her down.

A bolt clicked, but the heavy, oaken door remained closed.

Dancel tried to swallow the lump in her throat.

A third bolt clicked open, followed by a latch clink.

"I'm . . . I'm only seeking a moment's shelter in your alcove until the weather passes. Then I'll be on my way." Dancel chided herself for letting her voice sound so shaky.

The door yanked open; a splash of yellow lamplight flooded into the street, casting Dancel's shadow across cobblestones. Silhouetted in the doorway was an old woman bent with age; leaning on a cane; cloaked in an elegant, floor-length, velvet, red garment. At her feet clamored two small lap dogs, growling through bared teeth but staying safely under the fringe of their mistress' garment.

"Why, you're just a girl! Hush, Cinnamon! Quiet, Clovis!" The old woman swatted at a dog with her staff. "Don't you worry, dearie; they're harmless. What in Splendora's name are you doing out on a night like this? Come in, come in, child, take off that wet wrap and warm yourself at my hearth."

"I . . . I really shouldn't. I'm late, and my mistr—er, family will be wondering after me."

"*Tush*, child, you're white as a banshee." Then lifting her cane again and pointing outside the doorway at the storm, she said, "It's not likely to abate for quite some time. Come in, come in." The old woman took Dancel by the elbow and tugged her inside toward the fireplace.

Securing the door behind, she announced, "My name is Tillie, short for Tiladith. My parents were apparently fascinated with ancient Ecclessite tales, hence my name. They were such romantics." She sighed. "But everyone knows me as Tillie—'Old Mother Tillie Ba-tel,' they call me." She lifted a hand to her lips, and her eyes widened. "Oh, my! I never tell anyone my real name for fear they'll make some association with kingsmen legends." She eyed Dancel, tilting her head to one side. "Please don't repeat what I just said to anyone!"

Dancel asked, "Are you . . . an Ecclessite?"

"Am I—I might be old, child, but I've not lost my senses. What would a kingsman be doing in Cosmopolis?"

"I'm sorry. I didn't mean to imply—"

"No, of course you didn't, child. I foolishly blurted out my secret like an old woman; but I'm no Ecclessite, I tell you."

"I'm Dancel." She lowered herself to a three-legged stool near the hearth and loosened her wrap.

Tillie's eyes narrowed. "Dancel? Dancel . . . Pretty name, that." She seated herself in a rocking chair opposite Dancel and picked up her knitting. "Oh well, gone like water through a sieve. I can't seem to remember anything these days. What did you say you were doing out on a night like this?" The old woman gestured subtly with her hand toward Dancel's feet.

Cinnamon and Clovis rose from the rug before the fire and sniffed Dancel's shoes, making little grunts and lapping up droplets falling from Dancel's outer garment. Dancel tentatively reached down to pet the dogs, letting them lick her fingertips while she pondered optional answers to the old woman's question. Finally, she looked up at her hostess but instead of answering, said, "Did I hear you mention 'Splendora' when I first came in? It's not a term Carnalians often use. Did your parents mention Splendora or legendary kingsmen heroes as you grew up?"

"Oh, I suppose I heard those words from someone. Why? What do you know of such things?"

With the portentous events that had just happened during the night's gathering at Flan's house, compounded by her need to return to her duties and the unexpected stormy blast that had brought her to this old woman's dwelling, Dancel was confused as to whether she should mention Logon's amnesty to this dear old woman who sheltered her or just play ignorant. After all, the lives of everyone in the brigade were at stake. Since this innocuous, old woman's fate now seemed to lie in Dancel's hands, ought she not do all she could to rescue her to Logon's kingdom, despite the risks?

Dancel lifted her head. "Did you ever want to know about Splendora and Ecclessite things?" There was no going back now; just asking that question marked her.

Tillie put her knitting down, rose to her feet, and stood over Dancel as she lifted a poker from the fireside. She stood a full minute, motionless as a statue regarding Dancel.

"Well?"

Turning to the fireplace, Tillie shoved two logs together with the iron implement, sending a fresh spurt of sparks up the chimney. Flames leaped up between the andirons, spreading a wave of warmth into the room. "Of course, I'd like to know more. Like . . . is it true"—Tillie replaced the poker, resumed her seat, and gathered up her knitting again—"as some say, that the prince of Splendora, Logon Xychirion, is alive?"

Dancel smiled. Reaching around behind, she released the leather ties in her skirts that secured her Child of the Stars. "Suppose I let *Bluefire* answer that."

Tillie gasped, and her knitting fell to the floor as she beheld the sudden introduction of a glowing Ecclessite sword. "Is that—is that what I think it is?"

"Have no fear, old mother; this blade cannot bring harm. It holds the answer to your question about whether Logon lives, if you really want to know." Dancel pointed the sword tip at Tillie's breastbone. "Do you?"

"Oh, my dear child, you may put that weapon away. I already know the answer." Tillie rocked forward, picked her knitting off the rug, tilted her head toward a tapestry that veiled off a secluded portion of her home and called, "Heard enough?"

The curtain parted, and out of the dim recesses emerged a tall, slender form. "Well done, Mother!" cackled the woman. She then stepped fully into the light. "As good as a signed confession."

"Hod-ya!" Dancel paled, and her lips parted as her sword slipped from her grasp and landed on the floor with a thump.

"Have they taken the scent?" Hod-ya stared at the dogs. "Can they retrace her trail, despite the rain?"

"Oh, I'm certain they'll do as bid, dearie." The old woman stood, now tall and straight—no longer frail and bent over. "Glad I could be of service, especially after what her kind did to your sister." Tiladith turned and glared with steely eyes at Dancel. "And you had the audacity to point that accursed piece of iron at me, thinking to dupe me into

becoming Elyon's mindless slave. Ha! Fool! Now, you'll see what comes
of betraying the empire. What should I do with her until you return,
Hod-ya?" Her bony fingers probed Dancel's shoulder. "She'll make a
dandy snack for your pets. Just don't forget Cinnamon and Clovis
when you divvy up morsels."

The two canines licked their lips at the mention of their names.

Hod-ya didn't answer. Instead, she strode to the outer door, undid
the bolts, then flung it wide open, and shouted, "Farber, get in here!"
Hod-ya turned back inside, leaving the portal open to the diminished
rainstorm. "Never you mind about her; my guards will see to her.
Unfortunately, Mother, you and your little fiends have work to do—
out there. And by the way, you'll not get meaty shares from this one,
at least not for a while. Oh yes, I've known for some time that you
yourself aren't averse to the taste of, shall we say, 'prime rib'? But I
know the mettle of this one; she had me fooled for quite some time.
She'll not easily divulge what I want to know; it'll take time and effort
to extract the information I need. Abject terror and continual pain will
eventually accomplish their work. And when we're finished, I doubt
there will be much left over."

Dancel's benumbed mind slowly regained function as she realized
they were discussing what to do with her. Her eyes alighted on the
sword at her feet. Sucking in a deep breath, she lunged.

The old crone's vicelike grip on the nape of her neck held Dancel
suspended in mid-air, her splayed fingers mere inches short of her
trusty Child of the Stars, clutching naught but air. "Now, that's not a
nice way to return my hospitality, dearie." Tillie's foot clumped down
heavily on the sword at mid-blade, extinguishing the light. "Is that
what you were reaching for? Yes, you'd love to slice us all to the heart,

wouldn't you?" She reached down and with one hand and hoisted Dancel up so that her feet dangled. "I'm sure you understand why I can't let that happen."

Hod-ya sarcastically chided, "Mother, like you used to scold me, 'Quit playing with your food.' Ah, here come my guards."

Lieutenant Farber entered the room, wiping rain from his brow. Three guards and one dronnet entered and stood at attention. "So, it *was* her all along. Sure had me fooled." Farber shook his head, spraying water droplets.

"Doesn't take much to fool a dolt," Hod-ya replied.

"Now, see here, I'm only on loan to you from Mileer. I don't have to take your abuse."

"You'll take whatever I care to dish out, even if I decide to pluck out your eyes. Say, aren't you the oaf-in-charge who lost that little girl, my third contestant, when we stopped at Willow House Inn?"

"Your own dronnet lost the girl, not me or my men. I can't be expected to play nanny to your dronnets."

Hod-ya momentarily seemed taller, as if towering over the lieutenant. Farber backed away, averting his eyes to the men waiting behind.

"Humph!" Hod-ya said.

"Are you going to take such insubordination from the likes of him?" asked Tillie. "When I was a Majestic—"

"You're retired, Mother. Besides, other matters take priority here. You have a small, but necessary, detail to perform. So, turn that wench over to Flymag and Scrimmit and get on with it. Take this fool, Farber, and this worthless tracker with you. Grashunk lost the trail of not only my Scrarth and Avangar but also several dronnets-in-training. I don't suspect the kingsmen you seek will give you any more trouble than this girl did. But go along in case these fools bungle another mission."

Tillie nodded and wrapped a shawl around her shoulders as she and her lap dogs prepared to follow Grashunk and Farber. Tillie turned around in the doorway, pointed at Dancel, and asked, "And just what exactly are you going to do with her?"

"Well, if you must know, she has an appointment with the Inquisitioner. Satisfied?" Hod-ya took Dancel's arm and shoved her toward Scrimmit, the sole dronnet in the room. "You and Flymag take her down to the lowest dungeon level, down where Caldon's kitchen serves the vilest of inmates. Tell Caldon she's to be locked in the deepest hole, chained both feet and one hand to the wall. She's only to be fed B'n'B broth, understand? No bread, meat, fruit, or sweetmeats. Just enough to keep her alive."

Scrimmit rasped, "Isn't you-know-who chained there?"

A smile crept across Hod-ya's lips. "Not anymore—his time has come. Now, off with you. I must attend to another detail in preparation for the coronation. Mother, as soon as you know anything, let me know."

Tillie held a handkerchief under her dogs' noses, which she'd cleverly and discreetly taken from Dancel, commanding, "Seek."

Farber backed out the doorway, and the two mutts scurried outside into the drizzle, followed by Tillie, Grashunk, and Lieutenant Farber.

Dancel raised her head as she was dragged past Hod-ya. "How did you know I'd be here?"

Hod-ya stretched her arm across the open portal, momentarily blocking the procession. "Take a look outside," she taunted. "It's just drizzling now. The real storms have long passed. Did you forget that I can manipulate very small, localized weather inversions? As I watched the streets from an upstairs window, I cast a stormy blast at you when you drew near this doorway. I conjured a minimal squall to drive you into my mother's doorway, though I wasn't sure if it was you or someone else. When I spied your brightly gleaming sword reflecting from under your skirts off wet cobblestones, I knew I'd found my traitor. You were one of my suspects, of course. Who else had such complete access to the castle and its secrets? But you were always so clever.

"After you dodged into this alcove, I came down the back stair and into my mother's house, telling her to draw you in. Just think, if, instead of seeking shelter, you had forced your way through the storm to the next street over, you'd have been out of range of my powers and would now be freely going about your duties in the castle. I'd have had to concoct another scheme to discover and catch you. I was never quite sure if you were the one I sought. You were quite valuable to me with your knowledge of the passages, and it takes so long to train another . . . Ah well, all that will soon be unnecessary."

Hod-ya turned aside to Scrimmit, "If she gives you trouble, there's no need to treat her gently. Just keep her alive and securely bound down in the hole."

~

Hod-ya watched from the inset doorway as her mother and the two waddling dogs headed up one street and Farber led his prisoner the other direction. She pulled the door to behind her and turned down a side street toward the massive house dominating the far end of the block.

The last of the storm clouds drifted away; windy gusts had ceased, and now stars peeked through lingering mists. A crescent moon hanging low on the horizon created a hazy glow. Hod-ya bared her teeth in a wicked grin like a predatory feline sniffing a blood scent; a nasty inner thought occupied her mind as she strode toward her destination. Psa's demise and Bablo-ya's overthrow excepted, things were still turning out—more or less—according to schedule. It was time to initiate the ultimate gambit that would crystallize Turit's rise as supreme emperor over the mindless masses.

She drew up outside and silently observed the edifice: the corner spires, flying buttresses bracing the sides; darkened high-arched windows; decorative false portals replete with pillars and various intertwined engravings all along the multi-tiered stairway that comprised the outer façade of this mammoth, ornate structure. It had been established centuries, perhaps millennia, prior, and now housed a peculiar fraternity of isolated monks, who placated the masses with rites and pseudo-Ecclessite myths.

In earlier years, Hod-ya had wondered why the emperor allowed this bastion of pseudo-Ecclessites to remain unmolested in Cosmopolis. After all, many of the monks researched Ecclessite swords and accidently discovered fragments of knowledge about King Elyon and Logon Xychirion. And some of those abandoned this sham institution of sanctimonious old men, who paraded about garbed in effeminate robes on high holy days. Hod-ya had argued that anything even slightly resembling Ecclessa should be considered dangerous; a true seeker could stumble across truth, despite this institution's prevarications, especially if they studied Ecclessite swords wanting answers, albeit unlighted as they were. But Hod-ya's years of studying mystical parchments, tomes of the soothsayers, and dark writings of the oracles eventually revealed the malevolent purpose Lurcan intended for the inhabitants of this globe-encompassing organization. Hod-ya smiled. The duped followers of these sham rituals would prove quite useful as a unifying factor, indeed.

Hod-ya paused. "Ah, poor, poor Bablo-ya, beauteous fool! You chose the quick and easy path, expecting your beauty to lay the world at your feet; instead, it led to your untimely demise, whereas I chose the slow, tedious, lonely paths of delving into the dark writings that slowly but surely yield power." Her smile broadened as she played her tongue over spiked teeth.

She ascended the seven courses of stairs—each level named for one of the seven major nations loosely allied that comprised the Carnalian Empire. She rapped on the door upon attaining the top tier steps. Her sharp ears heard the knock reverberate inside through the hollow hallway. After several minutes with no answer, her smile turned into a thin, grim line. She pounded the door with the heel of her fist, rattling the ancient, oaken door against its frame.

"Old buzzard-bait ought to hear that," she muttered.

Again, the echoes faded away with no apparent response. Just as she was about to assault the door again, she detected the sounds of slow, shuffling feet.

The door creaked open. A white-haired, shriveled old man with torch in hand grumbled, "Oh, it's you. Come to see 'His Eminence,' I suppose. I don't know if he'll see you, though. He's retired for the evening; it's late, very late."

Hod-ya's teeth gritted with a squeak. She brushed him aside and wordlessly strode down the torch-lit hallway.

"Here now, you need to be escorted. He won't see you—"

She called back over her shoulder, "Oh, he'll see me all right. Don't bother, I know the way. I'll rouse him, old man. You just go back to your pitiful dreams of bygone glories."

"This is very irregular. I must protest."

But Lurcan's house-governess was already halfway down the passage, muttering imprecations well beyond the range of the door-tender's hearing. He shrugged, locked the door, and shuffled back to his quarters.

Hod-ya passed several paintings, statues, and various obscure objects of veneration in the long hallway filled with a multitude of doors that led to various chambers—some large, some small—lining both sides of the concourse until she arrived at the box end, where a massive door dominated. Without announcing her presence, she heaved the door open and swung it wide, knocking over a stand and porcelain washbasin that had been tucked too closely behind the door. The basin shattered on the slate floor with a crash.

The occupant of a canopied bed bolted upright, his eyes wide, mouth agape. "Who's there?" his shaky voice croaked.

The occupant of this room was an important personage in the eyes of many Carnalians but not in Hod-ya's. To her, he was a foolish old man slavishly devoted to nonsensical customs. Though it was dark, Hod-ya's eyes easily discerned objects around the room. His Eminence, as he preferred to be addressed, quaked in fear under multi-layers of blankets. A display of opulence surrounded him: overstuffed chairs draped with bejeweled, floor-length garments of grandeur and chains of office, as well as gilded staves and scepters used for various ceremonial occasions. A cluttered table was surrounded by a dozen shelves piled high with scrolls, codices, files, official dictums, and reams of prepared homilies meant to console and delude the masses that attended his audiences.

"Get up, Your Eminence," Hod-ya snarled, "there's work to do that must be started this night."

"Ho-Hod-ya? Is that you? What are you doing here? What do you mean bursting into my chambers like this and disturbing my sleep— what o'clock is it, anyway? Where's my doorman? Did he allow you—"

Hod-ya was beside his canopied bed in a single stride. She seized a sable robe from the nearest chair and tossed it at him. "Get dressed and attend to matters at hand. There's much to do and no time to waste."

"Now see here, wouldn't business that important better wait till the light of day?"

"Do I have to personally—"

"No need to be hasty; I'm up. Pitland's chimes, what the rush?" He wrestled his pudgy form out of his nightshirt and into the fanon, stole, and chasuble denoting his office.

Hod-ya lit a lamp and busied herself rummaging through scroll after scroll, casting them aside until she found what she wanted. Sweeping the remainder of the papers off the tabletop to the floor, she muttered, "It's about the coronation; we must make changes. One of my trusted messengers, a keeper of the keys, has played me false; she's an Ecclessite and, judging from her sword, has been one for some time. If you and your adepts had been doing your job of keeping people satisfied with counterfeit platitudes—"

"How can you expect mystics to effectively do their job when you, Mileer, and Lord Kway do all you can to persuade people that there's no such thing as a *kyllorn* potentate? Of course, we know him, but not everyone caves in so easily to our propaganda about Elyon. Either way, your will is done. So how can you hold me accountable if we're not as successful as you'd like? There are always those who sense there's something more and go off seeking."

Hod-ya ignored his whining. "We must hasten the coronation before word of our scheme leaks out and you-know-who tries to thwart our plans."

"Hod-ya, I've had my spies persistently searching for Ecclessites; there are none within fifty miles of here, I assure you."

"Says you, Virac! I've just apprehended one coming fresh from a meeting this very night. Even now, trackers are sniffing out their meeting place. I expect when we're done planning, I'll have some suspects to interrogate back at the castle. I need your Inquisitor to lend official sanction to the proceedings. Now, as to our schedule of events—"

"Spand, the Inquisitor? Are you sure? It's been some time since we—ah, you've—called for his services. He may not be up to his usual skill level."

"Just the terror of his presence should be enough. Just make sure to send him to me in the morning. Now as to these changes . . ."

CHAPTER SEVEN

STALACTITES REFLECTED A FAINT, SURREAL, green glow as they dangled over a luminescent algae bloom. The two somewhat worse-for-wear rafts yawed back and forth in a current that was stronger than expected and of which the neophyte mariners struggled to maintain control. The algae bloom didn't help matters, slowing the rafts by clinging to the edges, undersides, and rudders like a makeshift sea anchor. It seemed as if the vessels attracted the floating slick of aquatic goo, for only the immediate area around the rafts was congested with algae; some fifty feet or so away, the waters were clear.

Jemele was the first to note this curiosity just after being startled out of daze by what appeared to be two huge orbs rising out of the water beyond the algae infestation. But the illumination was too dim to be sure, and the orbs didn't appear again.

When told, Saygus merely replied, "Staring off into darkness so long probably caused you to imagine it."

The nine raftsmen sat in a semi-circle on the foremost and largest of the rafts facing their leader. The soft glow of blue-hued swords combined with the ambient, greenish sheen of their surroundings blended to produce an ethereal, turquoise reflection on their faces. The topic at hand was what to do about the fact that day by day, their rafts floated a little lower in the jostling waves. That, and since the *spidercat* attack, a large portion of their supplies had to be jettisoned overboard lest the sailors be floating castaways in the midst of this vast, uncharted, underground sea. Even so, they'd occasionally landed fish that swam too close to the rafts; but every time, the algae bloom clustered around them, such serendipitous fish disappeared.

"It be's a quare algae what thrives wi'out sunlight," Flonkry noted, trailing his hand in the water, making little eddies. "Oncet in me life, afore I kenned Logon, me 'n' summat o' me mates was a-piratin' off'n the shores o' Craniantium. Usn's gots becalmed in a sea wi' algae 'thick as soup' a-clingin' ter our hull, slowin' usn's down to a stop. So usn's hadda launch longboats an' lay ter oars an' row our way out. Took near a week."

Saygus pointed at Flonkry. "If you want to keep that hand, I'd suggest getting it out of the water; we have no idea what creatures dwell beneath."

"Maybe he's using his hand as bait so we can catch another big 'un, eh?" Skitter taunted.

"An' mebbe I'll jest dangle yer off'n the aft fer bait, jest ter see if'n yer fit 'nuff fer anythin' ter eat."

"That's enough," Saygus sternly warned the two with a glance. "I know it's been . . . how many weeks now? I've lost count. We have almost no supplies to speak of and not much luck fishing. We're all hungry and sick of this unending green darkness." He looked around at the sea with its distant green sparkles stretching beyond the rafts. "But we must remember our mission."

"And exactly what is that mission, Saygus?" Fleb lifted his head in challenge. "Remind me; I forget. You goaded us to come on this merry mission of glory; but so far, there's no glory or even a mission! All we get is tasteless raw fish and dim green light everywhere all the time—and oh, yes, all the slimy water we can drink."

The eyes of the others focused on the bubbles foaming up between the gaps in the deck's logs. None joined Fleb in his complaint, but neither did any disagree.

Jemele pointed aloft. "Does that large, funny-shaped stalactite look familiar to anyone else? I could almost swear I've seen it before."

They all looked to the distant ceiling and the peculiar stalactite.

"Well," intoned Bismeta, "if it is the same one, that means we're caught in a circular current instead of advancing to our mission; we've been going round and round the same circuit for who knows how many days, wasting time."

A murmur arose among the men, but they avoided looking Saygus in the eye.

"Okay, time for a rune study." Saygus extracted his sword and laid it over his lap. His left hand poised his toller above a glowing rune as he waited for his men to comply.

But they didn't.

For the first time since launching from the beach, Saygus sensed impending mutiny. At the beginning of their voyage they'd balked, but their resistance was easily nudged aside when Saygus exposed the source of their fear was cusps assaulting them as they slept. Even the skirmish with the *spidercats* hadn't dinted their zeal like this. But day after day of monotonous drifting with little nourishment—even the food they got was bland and scarce, thanks to the loss of supplies—had taken a toll on them. There were no diversions from the relentless rocking of the waves, except rune study and sword drills. And seeing the same faces day after day in close quarters for more than a month— or was it two months?—was tediously irritating.

Mental fatigue, they discovered, was a new kind of battle; even Saygus wasn't immune. But he resisted the temptation to complain, disciplining himself to rehearse the mystery runes in regard to the details of the mission as far as he understood them.

Secluded away for years in his mountain lodge, he'd applied himself to unlocking the secrets of Dread Bane, trying to grasp the symbolic meaning of the mythological underground sea mentioned in those runes. When he accidentally stumbled upon Artka and his companions in that subterranean tunnel and learned the underground sea wasn't mythological but reality, it all became clear to him. Logon was calling him to spearhead a sneak attack into Carnalia via a subterranean water route.

The sounding of the First Trumpet of Doom that followed soon after confirmed that the Great Tremendum was about to begin. He had a hand-picked brigade consisting of his own family, Artka and his friends, and the contrite lion poachers, all delivered to his doorstep, as it were, for training. And train them he did, drilling into them the skills and lessons necessary for defeating the powerful enemy hosts they were likely to encounter upon breaching Lurcan's den. But then, Logon seemingly diverted his trainees to another battle front—after all the preparation he'd invested in them. Now instead, here he was, saddled with recruit-level, dull-sword, inexperienced, ill-equipped soldiers. Sure, at first when the swords all lit up the same rune, marking the men Logon selected for this underworld, seafaring expedition, he was optimistic that he could complete their training in time. But now, the longer the mission dragged on, the more it seemed hopeless—as it evidently appeared to his crew, too.

"What good's another rune study or practice drills if we ain't ever gonna put the metal of our swords against Carnalian ways and beliefs?" Fleb looked not at Saygus but the others for support.

Saygus' jaw muscles worked as if chewing tough jerky.

Osk finally gave in, sighed, and laid his sword across his knees. "It's difficult to recall," Osk confessed, "but I woke up in such a dark mood today, I seem to remember dreaming . . . " His eyes rested on his sword." Anyway, when I glanced at my Logon tunic, it looked gray. With nothing but this dull, green glow everywhere all the time, I can't really tell, but I think I detected some dark spots."

The others wordlessly examined their own tunics, finding, to their surprise, blotches that even the dim ambient light didn't conceal. The spots were small and individually insignificant; but taken together, they produced an overall dingy effect on each garment.

Saygus nodded. "This is a different form of warfare, men."

The nine lifted their eyes to Saygus.

"I've been foolish. I should have seen this coming."

"Seen what?" asked Bismeta and Skitter simultaneously.

"Remember the fear attack you all had after exiting the tunnels and just before we launched off the beach? That same cusp lord hasn't given up trying to discourage us. Even though he may not have discovered the purpose of our mission, it's his duty to discourage, distract, and delay us if he can't outright stop us. My dreams also have been disturbed, as I suspect most of yours have been."

Murmurs of agreement and nodding heads settled that question.

"Look at your Logon tunics, men. They're not vividly stained with shameful acts or intentions, but there's a graying so that the light of our swords no longer reflect as brightly. It's quite possible to stray from Logon in our thoughts and attitudes simply by not making the effort to stay sensitive to the Advisor as surely as if we'd committed some offense. Just because it's not evidenced externally doesn't mean it hasn't affected our inner relationship with Logon. In fact, it's sometimes easier to deal with the outer, ugly stains we get from wrongful words and actions because they're so noticeable and grievous to our hearts. But we tend to ignore this gradual graying, thinking it of little consequence. But it is of consequence because it creeps in and grows without our awareness until we become accustomed to the Advisor's silence, thinking and living like mere Carnalians rather than kingsmen."

"But my sword still glows, and new runes are uncovered," challenged Benio.

"That may be," said Saygus, "but examine your heart and your love for Logon at this moment."

Silence.

"You see," Saygus touched his toller to the blade on his lap, "we can become so habitual in outward performance of duties that we internally neglect intimate times of communication with our liege. I believe the enemy's subtlest attack has been launched upon us. Sure, our circumstances are boring with no end in sight; our patience has been stretched more than seems reasonable. Because of that, we've let the joy of Logon's presence fade, as indicated by our tunics. And I'm as guilty as anyone. Apply your tollers to the beginning lines of the mystery runes." He read:

> "Seven stars dispersing light,
> Seven lamps a-burning bright,

Warriors sent into the fight
Before day ends and comes the night.

I see your gains; I know your pains.
Through your strains, your pledge remains.

You've sifted those who were found false
And cast them out with quickened pulse.

Tho what you've done is not faulted,
Your first love is locked and vaulted.

Come back, beloved, be not in doubt,
Lest rune-lit swords be snuffed out.

Seven stars dispersing light,
Seven lamps a-burning bright,
Warriors sent into the fight
Before day ends and comes the night."

Saygus laid his toller aside. "It's imperative we maintain a close relationship with Logon, despite prolonged periods of inactivity, lest, as the warning declares, our swords grow dim and we get replaced by others who keep their zeal alive.

"Now, go and work on those runes; when you have them aglow, we'll discuss what each of you has learned. After that, we'll rehearse the seven stages of rescuing Carnalians, which are: first, talk about Logon; second, disarm any *kyllorn* surrounding them; third, explain

Logon's amnesty; fourth, answer questions and/or objections with swordrunes; fifth, draw attention to the superior workmanship of our weaponry; sixth, trust the Advisor to ready their heart; and when ready, seventh, plunge your sword into the heart.

"I'll want all of you to practice each maneuver until it flows like second nature."

A collective groan rose from the nine.

"Listen to me, when we get to Cosmopolis and are face to face with dronnets or skilled Cosmopolisian warriors—not to mention encountering a higher order *kyllorn*—you'll wish you'd spent more time rehearsing. The runes must immediately come to mind, as well as understanding the depth of their meaning. The skill of the soldiers and *kyllorn* you'll encounter in Cosmopolis will require you being totally familiar with your Child of the Stars, as well as being yielded to the Advisor's slightest hint. You'll likely meet few, if any, recruits there."

"If we ever get out of this endless circular current," muttered Fleb.

Saygus bounded across the gap between them and snipped his forefinger against Fleb's lips.

The others looked on, eyebrows raised.

"If you don't control that cusp whispering through you, I will! Either that or I'll be forced to remove you from the mission. The short time you carried that dagger lessened your ability to identify and resist enemy whispers. Now, I just barely touched your lips, Fleb, but this rebuke should evoke shame at spreading discouragement among us."

Tears welled in Fleb's eyes. "You're right, Saygus. I knew it was wrong before I spoke. It won't happen again."

"It better not. You need to converse with Logon." Saygus turned to the others. "Now, the rest of you . . . to your drills."

The men glanced sideways at each other but perfunctorily stroked tollers across their swords. Slowly, on each sword, a glow appeared on the first of the mystery runes revealing the message of that ancient brigade that had come under attack from one of the dreads. As that primitive Ecclessite brigade grew more numerous, the city's devotees to Psa, fearing loss of power and influence, raised false accusations against their former friends and neighbors who'd become kingsmen. Distrust had arisen among the citizenry, even to the point of attempting to murder kingsmen. The city's lucrative trade in merchandising images of Psa and other images of the dreads was threatened as multitudes were turning away from Lurcan to seek King Elyon's amnesty. As time went on, however, the kingsman brigade cooled in their ardor to rescue lives to Logon.

As the vessel rocked in the gentle waves, each of Saygus' warriors identified with that early brigade's waning devotion to Logon. Eventually, as Logon had warned, the glow had faded from that early brigade's swords; their tunics had become grungy; and they were disunited, scattering when attacked, forced to shelter in caves and woodlands. Their brigade eventually lost its influence and failed to rescue any more Carnalians.

Bismeta looked up from his study. "But, Saygus, I don't understand. What has this to do with us? This all happened long ago; and apart from the obvious lesson to keep our devotion and love for Logon vital, I don't see any other significance to learning these ancient runes."

"No, and neither did I, at first. But . . . " Saygus' eyes swept over his men as his hand beckoned for them to huddle close. "One night, my sword began to sing; and afterward, I understood. I hope to teach you to so love tolling your weapons that they, too, will sing and reveal insights Logon has embedded in them."

"Like what?" asked Benio, crawling near to Saygus. Saygus smiled as he remembered him as the one who had offered his own sword when Saygus came stumbling out of the night.

Saygus hunched over his sword and lowered his voice, as if uttering secrets. "Like, the seven brigades in the mystery runes are not merely seven ancient brigades: they're symbolic. Each of those seven brigades represents a different Ecclessite age, typifying the dominant nature of events in each era that has either already occurred in history or will soon appear, culminating when Logon sallies forth in the final age to gather all his rescued ones to Splendora and at the same time bring destruction and wrath upon rebellious mankind who hardened their hearts against his amnesty."

Saygus sat back. "I know that some of you—perhaps most of you—thought these runes too mystical, too mysterious to grasp, or else, since they happened so long ago, thought they have no bearing on us today. But their relevance is borne out by recent events. Take, for instance, the sudden glowing of the rune announcing the Second Trumpet of Doom that woke us from slumber. Now, down here in this underworld, we have no way of knowing what might be happening topside—except that our swords informed us that Logon is fulfilling his promises."

"I remember," said Schtor, "most of you were asleep. I was at the tiller keeping watch when suddenly my sword started glowing—everyone's did, all at the same time. You all awoke and grabbed your swords in an effort to understand what was happening. Saygus, you read it aloud to us:

'A great mountain burning, cast into the sea,
Bubbling and boiling a third of its beasts.

Roamer the second blows unhindered, free,
As ships and crews become death's feasts.'

I remember, most of us were afraid, thinking it meant us. But you assured us it meant merchant vessels and warships on oceans above, not us down here."

"We don't know what calamities might have happened up there." Saygus lifted his eyes to the cavernous ceiling. "But we can be sure Logon's plan is at work and that he's alerting us that the progression of the prophecies are being fulfilled."

Saygus paced to the fore of the raft. "Maybe we are drifting in circles; but if so, it's Logon's doing. Perhaps things aren't quite developed enough for our attack yet, or else we aren't as ready as we need to be." He shrugged and faced his men. "So, get to the drills. Select an opponent and rehearse the steps. Jemele, you duel with me."

The men paired off, touching swords in salute and, in the limited deck space, dodged, probed, circled, and lunged, practicing the moves of a warrior. An hour passed as the kingsmen harmlessly jostled each other, joking with each other, taking turns at playing obnoxious Carnalians. The activity gradually brightened their mood, and lively badinage again filled the air.

When they completed their drills to Saygus' satisfaction, they sat and talked again, exchanging what they had learned. Even as they shared, their tunics brightened; smiles again lit faces; hope again filled hearts. Finally, they tucked their swords away and prepared for sleep.

Schtor, who'd been gazing at the ripples along the sides of the raft, abruptly plunged his hand into the water and flipped a sizable *gringer* fish onto the deck. They descended *en masse* on the three-foot long, hapless fish, beheading, scooping out its entrails, sectioning, and finally searing the pale flesh under conjoined sword tips.

Saygus, smiling broadly, looked on as he received his portion. "See how Logon provides? He's not letting us go to sleep hungry after all, is he?"

The others nodded, their mouths too busy chewing to reply.

A buzzing sound caught their attention. Saygus stopped munching and retrieved Dread Bane.

The others turned to watch. "What is it, Saygus?" Jemele asked, grasping his own sword tightly.

Before Saygus answered, a bright, yellow light erupted from their swords in a splay of light and harmonious musical tones, surrounding and illuminating the rafts on the choppy current. The clinging algae slowing the rafts cleared away in the intense glare, freeing the encumbered vessels. But no one noticed. Instead, everyone's eyes were fixed on their swords. One of the mystery runes self-ignited, burning brightly:

> *A great meteor from the sky, bright as a thousand lamps,*
> *Fell churning and burning on rivers and streams.*
> *Third roamer has sounded, polluting all damps.*
> *Corrupter the worm-eaten brings death in its dreams.*

It resonated like a long-forgotten melody from ethereal realms long passed from mankind's memory. Though the language was an ancient tongue, each man grasped the essentials of the message. As suddenly as it had come, the light faded, the haunting melody, the archaic language gone in an instant, leaving the subterranean mariners blinking, baffled, their mouths full of half-chewed fish.

"That"—Bismeta was the first to find his voice—"was different!"

Jemele hurriedly gulped down his morsel. "What was that, Saygus? Surely you must know."

"It told us what it is . . . " Saygus examined his own sword as if for the very first time. "It's the Third Trumpet of Doom."

"D-d-does that mean it's happened, or is about to happen, or . . . or what?" Osk held his sword close to his face. "I mean, does it mean that for now? What in Splendora's name does it mean?" He stared at Saygus.

"I'm not sure." Saygus cocked his head to the side. "Shush! Do you hear that?"

The ten collectively held their breath.

Echoing over the waves rumbled a reverberation like a great gong, increasing in volume as it pulsated. "Bo—oo—oo—ng," till their insides trembled, their extremities tingled, and their ears and noses itched with the throbbing resonance.

Eyes wide, the ten glanced in every direction trying to discern the source of the sound. The sound wave passed, decreasing in volume until finally only the rippling of the waves slapping the edges of their raft were heard.

Then, from afar off came a voice: "Ahoy!"

Saygus stood motionless, trying to locate the source. They all rose to their feet and stood motionless as stone sentinels, swords at the ready, presenting a patch of blue lights adrift on a sea of green sparkles.

"Ahoy, ahoy!" repeated the voice.

Their eyes strained toward the sound wafting across the glittering waves—nothing.

Their rafts, no longer impeded by clumps of algae, were swept along in an increasingly turbulent current, propelling them toward the origin of the mysterious voice. The lead raft unexpectedly collided with a submerged object, spun around, and tilted high on one side, nearly dumping the crew into the water.

"A rock, Saygus, we hit a rock," Bismeta cried, clinging to one of the binding vines. "We must be near shore. The current is driving us at breakneck speed to shallows. If we hit any more rocks—"

"A boulder, on this side," Schtor shouted, using his sword to fend the raft safely aside.

"More rocks protruding out of the surf," Jemele warned.

"Ahoy, beware; rocks in the breakers," called the mysterious voice. "Heave to this away." A blue light appeared on the shore acting as a beacon, guiding them to the starboard.

Jemele called over, "Saygus, that's a Child of the Stars."

"Man the oars," Saygus commanded. "Our drifting nears an end. Heave to the starboard as our guide directs—and hope our guide isn't betraying us to shipwreck. In this rough surf, with those rocks— possibly coral-encrusted—we'd be battered and sliced to ribbons before reaching the beach. You forwards, use the oars or your swords to fend off outcropping rocks."

Saygus leaned his full weight into the tiller, straining against the rudder attempting to overcome the surging tide driving them hard to port and away from land. He cast his eyes shore-ward and saw the shadowy figure of a man vigorously waving a blue sword.

"Pull hard, men," Saygus shouted.

Breakers crashed and green sparkles sprayed high in the air. Greenish foam outlined the beach as waves retreated in rivulets.

Jemele's hand joined Saygus' on the tiller just in time to avert crashing headlong into a rock that was barely visible in the green caps. The underside of the raft scraped over it as a swell propelled the vessel higher and toward shore. An underwater obstruction sheared the rudder off with a loud crack, sending both Saygus and Jemele crashing to the deck. The raft, caught in the momentum of the roller, spun around in a circle headlong for the rock-strewn beach.

"Hang on, men," Saygus shouted above the crescendo of waves. "We've lost the rudder . . . hold fast to your swords."

The larger raft scrunched ashore, sending mariners sprawling, some washing up on the sandy beach while others fell flat on their faces aboard the raft. The second raft rammed into the first raft, toppling those who were just clambering to their feet.

Saygus rolled off the raft and found himself on the beach; he wiped grit off his face as he sat up. "Right, then," he said, taking stock of the situation, "Everyone, get ashore." He wobbled awkwardly, trying to stand. His men lined up before him, some feeling queasy at standing on firm footing that didn't roll under them. "I guess it'll take a while to re-adjust to walking on land, men."

"Yes, it'll be a while before you and your men acquire steady footing," intruded the stranger who'd flagged them ashore, arriving to assist in pulling men as well as whatever supplies they could salvage out of the waves.

Saygus eyed the man with a Child of the Stars in hand. "Well met, friend. I'm Saygus, and these intrepid shipwrecked mariners are my squad." Saygus swept his arm toward the crew.

The stranger seized Saygus' wrist and squeezed in typical Ecclessite greeting. "Frobasch." He then looked over Saygus' shoulder out to sea and asked, "Where are the others?"

"Others?" Saygus eyebrows rose. "I'm afraid we're all there is. You act as if you were expecting us."

Frobasch did a quick count. "Ten? This is all?"

"I wasn't aware anyone would be waiting for us. How many were you expecting?"

"A larger force than this, I assure you. And you're late."

"Late for what? Now see here, my men and I were just marooned upon your shore. We're wet, cold, hungry, not a little tired . . . and being on land again is, well, a bit awkward. We've been sent by Logon—"

"Yes, yes, I know, to launch a surprise attack on Lurcan's palace. But only ten of you?" Frobasch's left eyebrow rose. "My information said I was to meet you here and be your guide. I wasn't told how many to expect, but I assumed such a daunting task would require hundreds, at the least." He shrugged. "Well, anyway, follow me. I've got a fire going just over those dunes, where you can dry out and get warm. I've got some turtle soup warming."

Saygus fell into stride alongside Frobasch as the rest of his men followed in double rank. "How long have you been expecting us?"

"Months, actually—about half a year as close as I can reckon."

"Half a year! We hadn't even set sail that long ago. Why, I was still in the mountains with my family and brigade, and you've been here waiting for us since then?"

Frobasch led the troop over a sand dune and pointed to a cheery fire in a hollow between dunes. Alongside the fire was a stack of driftwood. Several turtle shells were strewn about, and one that was much larger contained gallons of simmering soup suspended over the coals on a tripod. "Fall to, lads. Help yourselves."

Jemele spoke for the others. "Saygus?"

Saygus nodded, whereupon his men clumsily raced down the dune, tumbling over themselves to get to the fire and the soup.

"Let me explain," said Frobasch as the two cautiously picked their way down the shifting sand. "A little more than a year ago, a rune began glowing on my *Blazingedge,* instructing me to temporarily leave my beloved wife and children in the highlands of Craniantium and go on a secret mission to Cosmopolis. Exactly what that mission was, I wasn't told. You know how the Advisor sometimes shows you things partially—and only after you've completed the first step does he reveal the next . . . Anyway, I only knew I was to go to Cosmopolis.

"Oh, yes, I was fully aware of the danger," he responded to Saygus' upraised eyebrows. "I wandered about the streets for two weeks until one evening, a girl running down a back street caught my attention; I immediately knew this girl was an Ecclessite. I did my best to catch up to her, but she was so swift, I lost track of her. I hung around that street for days, hoping to encounter her again to ask her for the location of a safehouse.

"Eventually, the local sharifs began noticing my presence and became suspicious. I avoided them for days; but having no permanent shelter and being low on funds, I got careless. Long tale lopped short, they caught me and took me into the castle for questioning; upon discovering my sword, they sent me to the interrogators."

Saygus regarded the man alongside him with a deep respect. "You escaped, I take it?"

"Not exactly. When they were through taking turns beating me, they dumped me down a hole in the floor of a rarely used tunnel, which landed me here. They expected me to die in the fall; but even if I survived, they figured I'd either drown, get eaten, or just die of my wounds or starvation. Thinking to mock me, they threw my sword down after me, taunting me to see what good it did me down here."

Saygus chuckled. "Little do they know the power of the Children of the Stars."

Frobasch nodded. "They tortured me to get information about some secret Ecclessite brigade thought to be in Cosmopolis. Between torture sessions, I again caught sight of the girl I'd previously seen running in the street. She seemed to be some sort of messenger, able to come and go at will in the dungeon with no one aware that she was an Ecclessite.

"Finally, an evil woman, Hod-ya kar something or other, took over questioning me. She was brutal; even just standing and staring at me with her cold eyes, she evoked such fear and loathing . . . I felt I'd reveal anything she wanted to know. I feared I'd break under her powers. Of course, her lackeys pummeled me, whipped me, hung me inverted by my elbows, beat the soles of my feet . . . But since I had no information to give, they were frustrated. But when she came into the room, such a powerful sense of evil dwelt with her . . . " Frobasch shuddered. "Just thinking about her gives me shivers. Thankfully, I never did contact any kingsmen in the city, or else I fear I'd have betrayed them."

"You were saying about the girl?"

"Oh yes, the only other time I saw the girl was when Hod-ya questioned me. Somehow, that sweet, innocent girl operates clandestinely under Hod-ya's nose as one of her messengers! How she manages to do it is beyond me. She tiptoed into the interrogation room when I was hanging by my elbows after Hod-ya stepped out into the corridor to berate some lackey, leaving us alone for a precious moment. I was sure my life was over and started to tell—Dancel, was her name—to let my family know what had happened to me. She put a finger to my lips and whispered, 'This is part of your mission. Have no fear; Logon is about to release you.'

"No sooner had she said that than Hod-ya reentered the room and circled me several times. I was afraid she sensed my hopes had revived; at any rate, her interrogation stopped abruptly. Dancel was sent on another errand, and Hod-ya told her guards to take me to 'the pit.' They cut me down and, after kicking me for a while, dragged my nearly unconscious body down several dark passages until we came down the middle of one particularly dark tunnel that had a hole stretching across the entire floor. I remember hurtling through the air . . . Fortunately, I landed in several feet of water—I've since learned that the tide was in. Had I landed head or feet first or when the tide was out, I'd have been severely injured, at the least, if not dead on the spot."

Frobasch and Saygus watched the others gather around the fire, warming themselves, chatting affably, sipping soup out of makeshift turtle-shell bowls. As Saygus and Frobasch entered the circle of firelight, the men welcomed them with smiles.

"Sure beats eatin' fish day 'n' night, night 'n' day," said Flonkry.

Frobasch offered Saygus a turtle shell of soup, took one for himself, and the two settled down as he finished his tale. The others leaned in, listening.

"Anyway, that was, close as I can reckon, nigh unto six months ago, maybe more. I could hear them laughing after they dropped me, though it seemed a fair distance 'tween me and them. I glimpsed my unlit sword and toller sailing down through the hole in the dark ceiling. One of them said, 'See if that can protect ya now.' They laughed some more; and when I didn't respond, they eventually left, probably thinking I'd died in the fall. Since then, I've kept busy just surviving, just *Blazingedge* and me. I quickly had to learn the patterns of creatures that live down here, catching what I could for food. Did you know there are fish with no eyes? I believe they're called *gringer*—"

"Yeah, we know all 'bout them blind fishies, all right." Flonkry groaned, holding his stomach in mock complaint. "'Bout ter got our bellies full o' 'em."

"They were our main supply of food after we lost most of our supplies," Saygus explained.

Frobasch nodded, then continued his story. "It took days to recover from the torture; when I felt stronger, I roamed the beach up and down, looking for a way to get back up to the surface world, but it's hopeless. We're on an island; I found no way to get back topside. I also discovered that there are beasts down here—not sure what or how dangerous, but my fires have kept them at bay. I've trapped several smaller varmints that come out of the jungle to drink from the shoreline, along with turtles that come ashore to lay eggs, and I also do some surf fishing. So, you can see I've managed to stay alive. I've about used up the available driftwood I could find. What you see stacked over there is the last unless I search the more remote areas of these small islands. If you don't mind, your rafts will come in handy resupplying my wood pile. Not much comes in on the tide anymore. I hoped Logon would soon send help.

"Then, about a month ago, a rune lit up of its own accord, letting me know help, which I presume is you, was on the way, and that an invasion of Lurcan's castle would soon follow." Frobasch sat back, crossed his arms and sighed. "I can see by your sword that you have rank, Saygus, so I submit to your authority. I attained the rank of lieutenant in my home brigade; but as you see, my sword is lit on just one edge, and only halfway, at that. Since being on my own down here, I've begun trying to toll the entire sword.

"By the way, what do you make of that flash of light and thundering boom just before you arrived? The surf never gets stirred up and rough like that."

Saygus stroked his beard and studied Frobasch's sword for a moment. "It's one of the mystery runes revealing the Trumpets of Doom, signaling the beginning of the end for Carnalia."

Frobasch let out a low whistle. "Tell me."

For the next hour, Saygus related how he'd come upon Artka and his comrades in the 'Beneath' and how that led to the formation of the Singing Sword Brigade, the liberation of the Daggerman Castle, and the undoing of the dread, Prive, at which Frobasch again let out a low whistle.

"And these men who are with me now were selected for this undersea voyage by the Advisor through the virtue of a glowing rune on each sword of theirs," Saygus concluded.

They all sat staring into the fire, each man pondering the string of events that had brought them individually here, beneath the earth's crust, to mount a surprise attack on the very gates of their enemy.

"And you've thoroughly explored this island," Bismeta asked, "finding no way back up?"

"Well, I stayed mainly to the beaches; not knowing what fierce creatures might live in the interior. I sometimes hear fierce growls from there when I lay down to sleep. Being on my own, I didn't want to chance venturing in . . . "

Saygus stood, stretched, then patted his clothing to see how dry it was. "Your fire has served us well, Frobasch; we're grateful for your hospitality."

"I'm grateful for your companionship; I've been alone such a long time."

Saygus smiled. "We need to acclimate our legs to *terra firma* again men. We'll start drills first thing after getting some sleep. Frobasch, as lieutenant, I expect you'll complement and assist Jemele, my second in command. Having been in the castle, perhaps you can help us plan our attack." Then, looking upward toward the ceiling reflecting the fire's faint glow, he mused, "I wonder if it's day or night up there."

CHAPTER EIGHT

SAYGUS' CREW STRETCHED OUT AROUND the fire and soon fell asleep, some snoring, others muttering in their dreams. Frobasch and Saygus sat beside the fire tolling their swords and discussing the mystery runes as they watched over the weary band.

"I never thought there was any significance to those runes, Saygus, so I never bothered to light them up."

Saygus nodded. "That's a prevalent attitude among many kingsman brigades."

"And it was your brigade years ago that got caught, disarmed, and slaughtered on the outskirts of Craniantium?"

Saygus' head hung low. "Yes, the Sharuner Brigade. I wasn't very knowledgeable in *kyllorn* warfare in those days. I failed to discern that my brigade was under a cusp attack. I kept appealing to my men with logical arguments, showing them rune after rune that supported my plan; I know now that I should have left off arguing with them and instead combated the cusps influencing their minds."

"It grieves me to admit that I'm one of those who attacked your men along that lonely stretch of road. Some weeks later, I discovered one of their swords that had fallen into a ditch along the roadside. And I wasn't the only one who found one of those discarded swords. Several of my friends from Sophista also found the abandoned Ecclessite swords along that road. Curious as to why the empire was so fearful of those swords, we met secretly to discover the power in them. Of course, we couldn't make them glow—or even achieve any kind of keen edge on them. We ruined many an iron file trying. It wasn't until a kingsman, traveling by on his lonesome through the wilds, boldly entered our campfire one night. Tren, I believe, was the soldier's name." Frobasch reached over and threw another chunk of wood on the fire.

Saygus' head lifted. "Tren? Are you sure that was the name?"

"Pretty sure. Why?"

Saygus' smile widened. "Wonder of wonders. Tren is the name of the warrior that rescued one of my trainees, Artka, from an Eroton brigade, that's all. Go on."

"Ah, if it's the same man, it seems your destiny and Tren's are intertwined in Logon's purposes then. Tren noted our ruined files and surmised what we'd been attempting. He brashly challenged the six of us to duel with him all at the same time, providing that we use only our newly found kingsman swords; he clearly expected Logon to give him the victory over all of us. We laughingly accepted. Needless to say, with his brightly glowing sword, he handily disarmed all six of us. We didn't as much as raise a welt on him when the sword in our hands touched him—which was rare. We were stupefied that he overcame us all so easily. He then offered to teach us how to acquire the powers in the swords and make them shine and reveal hidden runes."

"And of course, you said 'yes!'"

"Without hesitation. Within the hour, he'd pierced all our hearts and sent us off to Logon's Rock. A germ of a brigade was conceived that night. As a result, Logon's amnesty spread underground, as it were, throughout Sophista and even into Craniantium at large. So, take heart; your mission wasn't a failure, and your men didn't die in vain. Through those discarded swords, Logon's amnesty took root in Craniantium and spread outward from there. Tragic as the loss of your men was, it turned out for good, anyway."

A tear on Saygus' cheeks reflected in the flickering firelight.

Frobasch reached over and squeezed Saygus' shoulder. "Logon appointed my best friend to be captain of the Sophista brigade with me as his lieutenant. We persuaded our wives and children to be pierced; and likewise, they went to Logon's Rock . . . And the rest, as they say, is history."

Saygus cleared his throat, changing the subject. "So, in the six months you've been down here, since you expected help to arrive by sea, why haven't you built your fire on the beach so you could be seen by an approaching armada instead of concealing your camp behind these dunes?"

Frobasch stared at Saygus. "Because of the Gwollerbect! If it knew my location, it would've snuck up and eaten me as I slept."

"Gwollerbect?" Saygus' hands turned palm up as he shrugged.

Frobasch's lips parted. "You mean in all those weeks afloat you never encountered the Gwollerbect?"

"We battled varmints I dubbed *spidercats*—but only once. We fought boredom and sometimes each other . . . What's a Gwollerbect?"

Frobasch lowered himself off the rock to the sand, folded his arms, and leaned back. "I saw it twice—no, three times—twice up close, too close. It's a grayish color making it difficult to discern, blending in with the dark and all; it's almost as long as both your rafts end to end. Its open mouth can engulf a man standing up; its teeth are as long as your arm and curved inward so as to force prey down its gullet. It has four turtle-like pins on each side that act like legs on land and fins in the water; but it's almost as swift on land as in the sea."

"So, it has eight leg-fin-things to propel itself?"

Frobasch nodded. "I was exploring a stretch of the beach for driftwood by the light of my sword when all of a sudden, some fifty paces away, what I mistook for a wave rolled ashore and didn't recede. It would've devoured me had not a roamer come to my defense. I've since learned to be wary of any large waves that come crashing ashore, especially since there's no weather down here to produce large waves. That one particular wave caught my attention because it didn't stop or even slow down but, instead, kept rolling up out of the sea onto the shore. I stood stock-still, watching. The wave grew larger; then it seemed to sprout legs and charged directly at me."

"And that's when the roamer appeared?"

"Not at first. I ran—it was like those dreams when you try to run but your feet are stuck in something. Well, I was running all right—in place, digging a hole in the sand with my feet but getting nowhere. The Gwollerbect closed in, taunting me, chanting over and over:

'Run, run, run, fast as you can;
But I'll get you, you gringerfish man.'

"I collapsed as much from fear as exhaustion and cowered in the hollow my feet had scooped out. I looked up and saw a wide-open maw with huge teeth. I had no idea what it was chortling on about, except that it intended to swallow me alive. I shut my eyes to the horror. Then, even through closed eyelids, I saw a shining light; it was a roamer, big as a tree, straddling my ditch. It pointed a gleaming weapon at the beastie, threatening, 'Not tonight, Gwollerbect. Go find your meal elsewhere.' That's how I knew the thing was called a Gwollerbect, or maybe that's its given name . . . I'm not sure."

"And it obeyed the roamer and went back into the sea?"

Frobasch shook his head. "No, it closed its maw and backed off a few paces but menacingly stood at bay, slime slavering down its chin, looking greedily at me with its eyes. I was too stunned to move on my own, so the roamer nudged me out of the hole and inland over several dunes. After he deemed it safe, he set me down. It was hard to tell exactly how far I'd gone."

"What? The roamer didn't strike the monster? It just led you safely inland?"

"That's about the way of it. Anyway, before he left, the roamer warned me not to build fires along the shoreline nor dwell too long there, lest the Gwollerbect spot me."

"It doesn't make sense that he let it live," Saygus said with a snort. "Did he say why?"

"Something about pressing duties elsewhere . . . Anyway, I didn't see the Gwollerbect again until a week later. I was waist-deep in the surf out beyond the breakers, fishing for turtles and crabs by the light of my sword. Suddenly, I was inundated with clinging algae—"

"We were swamped in some of that, too, some days ago out on the sea, then just before we arrived here. It clung to our rafts thick as venison stew, nearly bringing us to a complete stop."

Frobasch smiled, his teeth gleaming in the firelight. "You can thank Logon it did. That's why the Gwollerbect didn't attack your rafts. It seems the beast is repelled by the algae. As I was saying, that algae soup surrounded me, inundating me, even to the point of impeding my ability to wade ashore. When the Gwollerbect saw me, it ripped across the tide, mouth agape until it got within several paces of me and halted as it encountered the edge of the algae mass. It got a good mouthful of the slimy stuff and immediately spat it out and backed away. It circled, hovering nearby in the surf for an hour or so, waiting for me to wade ashore where the algae couldn't protect me. But I wasn't about to go ashore; I kept begging Logon to keep the algae close. Finally, the beastie wandered on down the beach searching for easier prey.

"I saw it one other time, weeks later. It had beached itself and was munching on some deep-sea creature, the ones that glow, which is the only reason I saw it in this green semi-darkness. I saw a reddish-orange mist sprayed into the air as the Gwollerbect ripped it apart. I would have rambled right into the monster had it not been for its tearing and devouring its catch ashore. Fortunately, it was too engrossed with its meal to notice me."

"So, the algae we thought was a curse was really a blessing in that it kept the Gwollerbect from wrecking our rafts?"

Frobasch nodded.

Saygus shuddered. "I should've known there was a reason. In most of our journey, we never encountered anything like those algae, except once on the high seas and then again as we came ashore. I do recall a few weeks back espying something that appeared to be glowing red and blue—even some yellowish things way, way deep in the waters beneath our rafts—but had no idea what they could be." Saygus glanced over at his slumbering men. "Well, I'm for turning in." He scanned the ceiling above their heads. "Wish I knew if it was day or night. Sometime in the second week afloat, we lost track."

"I lost track of time in the interrogation room; so, my sleeping and waking cycles down here have been regulated by whether I'm sleepy or not. There are minor tides that keep to a regular daily rhythm, but I don't know which comes at evening—the ebb or flow—so I lost track."

"Should we set a watch?"

"Haven't needed one yet, on my own as it were. I stay far enough inland away from the haunts of the Gwollerbect, who seems content to patrol the shoreline, since his terrapins work best on wet sand and not so well on loose sand. As for any other beasties that dwell inland, the light of my fire keeps them at bay."

Saygus smiled. "So, there are other dangers besides the Gwollerbect?"

"I'm not sure. On the other side of a nearby island, I encountered some small waterdragons; but they stay confined to their area and rarely leave the water's edge, as far as I can tell. I think they fear the Gwollerbect. Upon occasion, I've heard growls when camping near the interior jungle on this, the largest of the archipelago. But fire keeps whatever creatures growl at a distance."

"A jungle, down here, with no daylight?"

Frobasch grinned. "I'm sorry. I didn't mean to mislead you. It's a fungus forest."

"Fungus?"

"Mushrooms, more precisely. Tall as trees—well, shorter than actual trees. All of it edible—at least as much of it as I've explored, which isn't very far inland, I'm afraid."

"Hmmm, I should like to investigate this mushroom forest on the morrow—or whatever portion of night or day it is."

Frobasch stretched out and rolled away to one side. "On the morrow, then."

Saygus laid his sword across his lap and traced the rune of the Third Trumpet with his finger, his lips moving imperceptibly.

~

"It's on the move again!" Artka whispered as he pointed. An entity a shade darker than the surrounding night slowly, silently slunk directly beneath them along the castle's outer wall toward the main gateway; much of it extended back to the forest's edge, seemingly uncoiling loop by loop to join the advancing head of the body surging forward.

Gulundur held his arms out for assistance. Artka and Hudge accommodated the captain, helping him to his feet. The trio peered down between the crenellations over the wall at the darkened, sloping field.

"You'd think we'd have a sense of evil pervading the atmosphere if it's a disembodied dread?" Reddy whispered as he watched the noiseless assailant.

"Maybe the stronger *kyllorn* can control their emanations," Harnet suggested. "I remember hearing about dronnet captains—"

"Sssss," hissed Gulundur. "This is no time for campfire ghost stories."

The foremost part of the shadow seemed to slither beneath the kingsmen, hugging the wall, making straight for the castle's entry. The shadowy tail end finally emerged from the shelter of the woods, strung out in impressive array.

"Cap'n," whispered Scang, "I kin chuck me sword an' stick it midways. I be's ready ter teach it what fer."

Gulundur's hand stayed the Eroton's rash plan. "You'll want your weapon in hand."

A rumbling, frustrated growl emitted from Scang.

"Maybe it's time we go down to defend the gate." Sajon stepped away from the crenellation. "That's where the battle will take place."

"Aye, we'll not be much use up here, will we?" replied Gulundur. "Softly now, lads. Make no noise."

Artka was reluctant to leave the rampart, fascinated yet full of trepidation at the unknown entity gliding noiselessly a mere fifty feet below their post.

"Coming, Artka?" Braxmore waited at the top stair.

Artka broke off his vigil and followed his companions down the spiral staircase to the main level.

The outer door was heavily bolted and triple-barred from the inside against whatever might assail them—from man-held battering rams to firedrakes breathing out flames. Armed ranks of soldiers waited inside, facing the door, ready to defend. Oddly, this fortress had been constructed more for welcoming rather than repelling. Wayfarers were encouraged to seek entry to Ecclessa through these portals; sojourners from Logon's Rock were welcomed here, processed, and sent into Ecclessa for training. Nevertheless, the runes foretold a day when not only this fortress but also the bridge itself would be besieged and fall into enemy hands, bringing an abrupt end to Elyon's offer of clemency.

"Captain"—Hudge's voice was hushed—"I'm afraid nobody thought to lower the portcullis after we entered."

"Well," Gulundur intoned, "little harm done; the grating would only delay the inevitable. Sometime or sooner, we must engage the foe."

A susurrus of whispers filled the keep's main chamber, kingsmen encouraging each other with runes or else sending whispered pleas to Logon. Fingers nervously clutched and re-clutched sword pommels; varying degrees of blue light emanated from the bristling line of swords held ready toward the portal. The frontline of kingsmen consisted of hale and hearty men, older lads, and skilled sword-maidens; behind them waited the elderly and those of somewhat less sword-shine. Next were the walking-wounded; and the last rank composed of children, mothers, and caretakers of those too feeble to engage in lively combat but were, nonetheless, able to send continuous appeals to King Elyon on behalf of those who bore the brunt of the fight.

A blazing fire in the hearth, along with torches ensconced on the walls, shed a soft, amber glow throughout the keep, providing a strangely comforting ambiance, despite the dreadful fray about to take place. If the entity turned out to be a dread's essence, Gulundur expected no survivors. If the enemy was a mixture of *kyllorn* and men, there was at least the hope that several invaders could be rescued before the castle was overrun.

Gulundur's forces defending Ecclessa's gateway were overmatched. The Trumpets of Doom had begun pealing dire warnings of impending destruction; a determined foe seemed certain to overrun this castle and destroy Logon's Bridge, bringing an end to Logon's amnesty. It was quite possible that no one within the keep would see another sunrise.

Thunka-thunka-thunka reverberated throughout the cavernous hall from outside the gateway.

The sudden pounding on the door brought an immediate halt to the whispered petitions. Instead, teeth clenched; eyes narrowed; nostrils flared as palms moistened . . .

Thunka-thunka-thunka.

Not a soul inside stirred as they braced to face whatever threatened to crash in from outside.

Gruff voices carried indecipherable words through the thick, wooden door—at least they were humans outside. *It wouldn't be all tophets, cusps, and who-knew-what-else,* Artka mused. More low-pitched, muffled voices bled through the oaken door panels.

Thunka-thunka-thunka! again echoed throughout the hall. Then a scraping sound like digging was heard. Several minutes of what could only be construed as scratching, grinding, gnawing, hewing, and chopping away at the door's foundation vibrated through the solid panels. The outside invaders, failing to break through the doors, turned to undermining the gate's threshold. Louder voices were succeeded by another series of pounding, then more scraping and chopping . . .

Anticipation that the door could give way at any moment took a toll on less-prepared warriors, but those with more light on their swords were primed and eager for battle. Win or lose, at least they'd be actively engaged. But for many, the building tension was maddening.

Bluskie, Ewert, and Skujj—their tunics now fresh and bright but their swords dull, except for the tiniest pinpoint of light on the tip—huddled close, eyes wide. Skujj wiped a sweaty hand on his legging. Ewert unconsciously massaged his bandaged thigh.

Sajon, also among the walking wounded, spied the three comrades' nervousness and gimped over to console them. "Just keep your swords pointed front. Who knows? You may have someone run upon your outstretched sword and pierce himself. Even that tiny bit of light is enough to rescue someone if the Advisor guides your sword." Sajon gripped Bluskie's shoulder and squeezed. "It's all in Logon's hands. You lads switched sides just in time."

Ewert looked up and smiled grimly.

"You'll do fine, men. No matter what happens, Logon wins."

Bluskie and Skujj nodded, their eyes fixed on the oaken door at the head of the hall.

"It's giving way . . . " a voice cried out.

Artka, Scang, Reddy, and Harnet rushed to bolster the door. Others joined them, but the force from without was too great. The bars bulged inward; crackling sounds pierced the air; then all three bars broke at once with a resounding *crack*! The disjointed jambs pitched inward; door panels bulged; the header broke free of its mooring; the dead bolts popped loose of their stays . . . Another loud *crunch* followed . . .

Dozens of kingsmen were repelled backward as the massive door crashed to the floor. A mighty gust of wind whistled through the breached doorway; wall torches flickered . . . A rousing shout rose above the clash of clanging swords: "Lives for the King!"

Blue flashing swords surged toward the breached doorway—and from outside the breached doorway, as well! Ringing, clamorous steel met steel, combining with shouts of "Logon," and "Lives for the King," swelling to an ear-splitting cacophony. The gust rushing through the breached doorway abated, and the flickering wall torches regained a steady flame, returning illumination to the keep.

"Metid! Is that you!"

"Gulundur . . . you hold the fort? Why did you lock us out? We thought sure the keep was in enemy hands, since we saw no light and found the gate barred."

"And we thought you were a dread's disembodied spirit creeping up on us . . ."

Laughter filled the hall; cheeks glistened with tears of relief and joy; and kingsmen hugged and welcomed each other, chagrined that they had been so worried at dueling a desperate foe.

Both battle groups quieted down as Metid's battalion entered the keep, making the castle crowded. Old friendships were renewed and new ones forged as the brigades that had been stationed on opposite sides of the Flaming Sword River merged. New recruits were happily surprised to find some of their old Carnalian mates had been to Logon's Rock since they'd last marched under the empire's banner.

Metid, Gulundur, Sajon, Hudge, and Evebryl made their way through the congestion and chatter to sequester themselves in Metid's office to convene a tri-consul. The three members of Saygus' family represented his voice; but only Sajon, as eldest son, could cast a vote in his father's stead.

"So, after we reclaimed the lost tunics and chased off Artka's former comrades-at-arms, we slogged back here and found the castle under Sajon's authority." Gulundur sat back, finished recounting the previous day's battles to Metid. "So, how'd it go with you?"

Metid sat in a great overstuffed chair before the fireplace stretching his legs toward the cheery fire. "Well, as you know, we left the fortress in a hurry. We could wait no longer; a rumor that dreads rampaged nearby caused our Sharpointers—the largest contingent we had—to abandon their positions. That clever bit of false propaganda unnerved many of our forces. They'd dealt with cusps, tophets, and even firedrakes—but the mere rumor of dreads spearheading the forefront of a new attack unnerved Tipsters and not a few Sharpointers. I had to send Ollo with several of his friends out to demonstrate Logon's authority even over dreads. They traversed the riverside up by the Wind Break Forest and had some success with only human foes; then I took the main body of castle defenders and headed straight for the grassy plains rolling down toward Swamp Tophet, where I assumed the Carnalian general, Phlugum, would muster his retreating forces. With Artka and Marn leading, a small but determined force regathered, emboldening our troops to join our somewhat limited attack force. I hoped to catch Carnalian forces off guard and drive those that were too hard-hearted for rescuing back toward the swamp. Along the way, we collected several of our troops who'd abandoned their positions."

Hudge tossed a log on the fire.

"It turns out that we didn't need them; most of the Carnalian forces drifted back to the swamp, anyway. We had a skirmish with a minor detachment and were about to head back to the castle when Gulundur showed up with Skujj and Bluskie . . . "

Metid continued, "Well, we encountered a task force, and were outnumbered at least five to one. But there were no major *kyllorn,* like tophets, to speak of; just a few cusps—funny, the cusps were partially visible, little *frog-like* shadows hopping around, whispering in Carnalians' ears. They approached us, thinking we couldn't see them; but since we discerned them as shadows, all we had to do was brandish our swords and utter Logon's name, and they fled like roaches from a torch.

"About that time, a runner from the shores of Lake Maniways reported that a fleet of corsairs was prepared to land at Tophet City to offload a few thousand hardened Eroton warriors, reinforcing Phlugum's forces. Phlugum's troops give a celebratory cheer, and we assumed they'd heard the news.

"Empire battlelines immediately formed and charged with renewed vigor, determined to overwhelm and push us back to Logon's bridge. They'd been repelled from the castle earlier and were embarrassed that we'd driven them back yet again, but their confidence surged when they heard that reinforcements were about to land."

Sajon, Hudge, Evebryl, and Gulundur leaned eagerly forward.

"We were attacked in strength. We thrust our Children of the Stars at them and spoke of Logon's amnesty. A few allowed the Advisor to move upon their hearts and put down their axes, spears, bows, halberds, and scimitars—whereupon, we immediately pierced them. But except for those few that were rescued, most of the Carnalian force laughed scornfully and regrouped to strategize their next assault."

Metid's head dipped low. "So many lives . . . so many bright, wonderful lives . . . " He raised his head. "We lost"—a tear rolled down his cheek—"too many on both sides. Men, women . . . At first, we rescued more than we lost. Eventually, though, we were forced to yield the field. They outflanked us; our escape was cut off; we were surrounded. We clustered together, chanting battle runesongs, expecting to find ourselves in Splendora at any moment. They pressed their advantage; every surviving kingsman and sword-maiden was engaged, dueling two or more deadly fighters at a time.

"Somehow, my *Pathfinder* fended off four determined soldiers; it was moving in my hand this way and that way, then back again, then down low. I've never in my life had runes come so swiftly to mind and shouted them with such authority. A fifth attacker joined my assailants; I was driven backward, where I stumbled and landed on my back. At such crucial moments, peculiar things happen; time slowed. I glanced about me while my sword kept parrying the blows raining down at me. Other kingsman had also been knocked flat on their backs, valiantly fending off blows intended to cleave them asunder."

Metid settled back against his cushion. For several moments, the only sound in the darkened room was the crackling fire.

Metid sighed, then continued, "That's when a powerful runesong filled the air, and a sword-rune flashed in a brilliant, white light that scorched the weapon-holding hands of our enemies:

J.M. MacLeod		125

'A great mountain burning, cast into the sea,
Bubbling and boiling a third of its beasts.
Roamer the second blows unhindered, free,
As ships and crews become death's feasts.'

"Like an iron hailstorm, Carnalian weapons dropped to the turf; our enemies' hands were blistered. All the Children of the Stars erupted with the same bright, shining rune, vibrating the song of triumph! We sang, shouted, and rose to our feet . . .

"Phlugum and his army fled in terror, running pell-mell in confusion and fear, hands over their ears, many unknowingly headed toward our castle. So, we gave chase, catching up to and piercing quite a few of them. This accounts for why we have as many—if not more—troops now than when we sallied forth, despite our casualties. But now, we have so many raw recruits to train and virtually no time to train them. It wasn't long until a messenger arrived announcing that the entire fleet of soldier-laden corsairs were swept out to the middle of Lake Maniways by a rogue wave with all hands, then swallowed by a towering wall of water twice as high as the ships' masts."

With a twinkle in his eye, he added, "That wave was caused, some reported, by a meteor falling from the sky and into the lake at the precise moment the runesong filled the air. I believe it announced the Second Trumpet of Doom."

Metid leaned forward, searching each face. "Now it remains for us to determine what's next. Do we stay here and guard the bridge? Or do we sally forth and attack Cosmopolis, leaving the bridge and the fort undefended? Bear in mind that at least half of our forces are raw recruits, just now rescued, with very little understanding or training in Logon's ways and warfare and, by most standards, unprepared to embark on a major campaign."

"Yes," ventured Sajon. "Foremost, we must dissuade them of any notions of injuring their opponents if it can at all be helped. They must be taught to allay all thought of retaliation or vengeance lest they fall back under Lurcan's spell. With this council's permission, I'd like to undertake training the new recruits."

"Are you sure Logon would have you do that, son?" posed Evebryl. "Your sword has a greater amount of light than many and would be useful at the front."

Sajon nodded. "I know; and that's not out of the question when the time comes. However, I sense a need to train these newly rescued soldiers in Logon's ways as soon as possible."

"Methinks the lad speaks wisdom, Evebryl," said Metid. "I have no doubt that in a short time, under his able guidance, a goodly number of trainees will gain enough of a glow on their edges—and possibly a rune or two—to make them capable rescuers, bolstering our forces. Besides, your son is still on the mend from that nasty sting he received. Mayhap, lad, that's why you sustained an injury, lest you dash away to the front with no one left to properly train recruits." Looking around, he asked, "What say all to that?"

Each looked to the others, nodding.

"That's settled, then," said Gulundur. "Next, we need to choose a leader to organize our defense as well as our offensive on Cosmopolis. Metid, you and I are brigade captains, trained well enough in tactical and strategic defense but not especially skilled at offense. Were Saygus here, I think there'd be no dispute that he should lead, having the rune-lore, as well as experience and wisdom to lead an assault. But he's not here."

"Evebryl and Hudge have greater light on their swords than either of us, Gulundur," responded Metid, his raised eyebrows silently asking if either one felt compelled to take leadership.

Evebryl broke her silence. "Saygus and I hold to the runes of Atel that say women, though valuable and able as sword-bearing warriors, are nevertheless not to take the reins of authority over men as far as brigade leadership goes." The determined look in her eye indicated the matter wasn't open for discussion. "I'll offer advice and counsel, which is my gift and calling. I've occasionally received words as a seer and will do whatever I can to help, but I decline to assume outright leadership."

Hudge plopped down cross-legged before the fireplace. "I'm too young; though my sword has light on both sides to the hilt and a second shine started, as Logon instructed Atel, leaders weren't to be selected from among the youthful and inexperienced. I feel this disqualifies me from leading a large battle group, but I have an opinion to offer to whomever is chosen as leader. I believe Logon would have the entire task force assembled here to march on Cosmopolis."

Gulundur and Metid held each other's gaze several seconds, neither saying a word.

Finally, Gulundur shifted in his seat. "Well, that leaves you and me. Somehow, I sense it's not a position either of us necessarily want."

Metid nodded. "Yet, at the same time, it falls to one of us. We could draw straws as when the ancient generals replaced Claygall."

"If I may," said Evebryl, "that method was used prior to the Advisor fully indwelling Ecclessites. Mature kingsmen should be able to hear the Advisor's voice and make decisions based on runes and the Advisor's counsel. We're to leave nothing to chance. And . . . I believe the Advisor has spoken to one of you."

Metid sighed. "I'd hoped I was imagining it, but yes, the Advisor is nudging me to take the mantle of leadership for now."

Gulundur grinned. "I concur."

A knock on the door drew their attention. Hudge rose from his seat near the fire and opened the door. Artka stood in the doorframe, sword in hand, sweat on his brow, hair mussed, eyes wide. "We've got trouble out here!"

CHAPTER NINE

METID PRECEDED THE OTHERS OUT the officer's chambers and found the great hall astir with arguing factions. Reasno—or Debator, as some called him—strutted back and forth atop a long table in the middle of the dining hall, lecturing several people gathered around. In his hand, he held a dagger that reflected torchlight off its highly polished surface, dazzling the eyes of recruits recently won from the fray.

"This isn't as difficult to sharpen, believe me," Debator's voice echoed off the overhead rafters. "I've been in this fortress several years but can barely keep the tip of my Child of the Stars aglow. What good is that against Carnalians, I ask you, not to mention the really hard-hearted Erotons? You remember how it was when you were a Carnalian, how you mocked the glowing sword points of Ecclessites who tried to pierce your armor with a half-inch of light on their sword—how you had such contempt for them. Yes, yes, I know that eventually someone with more light on their sword pierced your chest, but most kingsmen don't have that much power in their swords. And you, as brand new recruits, don't have the time to achieve the glow you need on your weapon. Yet kingsmen officers will thrust you into battle unprepared, and you'll likely end up a casualty because you're not properly armed. Unless"—he spun in a full circle, presenting an alternative weapon to the clustered recruits—"you receive one of these daggers. Swords get dull without even being used; daggers never get dull, even after days of non-use. Sharpen it today, and it will still be sharp the next time you want to use it, even if it's a month later . . . It's always ready when you need it. Those unwieldy swords require daily tolling, as they call it. I call it *toiling* because it requires hours of monotonous filing with that special file called a toller; and if you misplace your toller or miss a day or two of honing the blade, much of what you sharpened will grow dull, forcing you to waste more time tolling it over again just to get back what you once had aglow."

Metid pushed through young men crowding the table to where Reasno pranced back and forth prating his wares. Metid seized the collars of those nearest the table's edge, hauling them backward out of his way. "That's enough of that. Reasno, step down."

Hudge, Artka, and Sajon backed Metid, elbowing recruits aside.

Reasno glared down at Metid. "No, sir, I won't. They have a right to know what they're up against if they go out fighting with dull swords and no back-up—like a dagger."

"I said"—Metid reached out and grabbed Reasno's ankle—"come down, and I meant it!" Metid yanked Reasno's foot from under him.

Reasno landed heavily on his rump with a grunt. Hudge and Artka immediately seized Reasno by the armpits and hauled him off the table, ignoring the angry shouts of those clustered to hear Reasno.

"Hey, let him speak."

"I thought kingsmen were supposed to be open-minded—"

"He's helping us—"

"What's he done that deserves this treatment?"

Artka handed his share of Reasno to Sajon, then leaped top the table and raised his hands to quell the belligerent hubbub. "Listen to me, all of you. Hear me! This fellow, Reasno, once gave me a dagger."

The mob quieted.

"I admit, I, too, was enticed by its beauty and lured by the fact that it didn't get dull if not honed daily. Sure, it's a pretty little bauble—and yes, it stays sharp until used—but what Reasno didn't tell you is that it attracts *kyllorn*. Oh yes, in fact, because I kept my dagger a secret, I endangered my mission, my companions, and myself; a spitter-tophet sensed my dagger and was able to trail us through Ecclessa and nearly caught and devoured us."

Disgruntled recruits glared at Artka, even as Reasno, dragged away struggling and kicking, disappeared into Metid's office. Hudge stayed at the table, confirming Artka's words.

"What're they gonna do to him?" asked a scruffy-bearded recruit.

"Just verbally reprimand him would be my guess," ventured Artka. "Reasno has no authority here—and certainly no business addressing you, endangering your lives by tempting you with those counterfeits."

"How does having a back-up weapon for 'just in case' endanger us?" challenged another recruit.

"Because such things are useless in the king's work. Don't you understand? Logon's swords don't cause harm, but daggers do. Children of the Stars bring life and truth to those they pierce. Think, men: when you were wounded to the heart, did you feel any physical pain? Or was your discomfort something else, something deeper, something in your conscience? If a dagger had entered your heart, would you be standing here today? You must trust that Logon will provide only the best for you, else he wouldn't have rescued and healed your wound, would he?"

Artka stared at the cluster of puzzled, angry faces. "What's more, Logon even loves those who fight against him, not wanting them injured or killed. Daggers can only cause injury and death, not life.

It's the *kyllorn*, enemy phantasms like cusps, that deceive kingsmen into using daggers, discrediting Logon's offer of amnesty. I know some of you don't believe *kyllorn* exist; but I assure you, they do exist, as you'll soon enough find out. So, consider this: would you choose a dagger to defend yourself against a tophet or firedrake? And believe me, you will be wounded, even devoured, if you take a dagger into battle.

"Daggers are counterfeits of the Children of the Stars; they're not sanctioned by Logon; therefore, they can only bring harm and death. If you replace the worthy weapon Logon provided with a counterfeit, you can only expect hardness of heart, deception, and, eventually, madness." Artka paused, looking for any indication that his words were sinking in. "The Child of the Stars enters your inner being and changes you from within, but daggers will only render a mental indoctrination that changes nothing. You'd be well-advised to spend what time we have before our next battle in getting to know these marvelous swords Logon provided."

Several recruits looked bashfully at the swords tucked away in their belts and nodded, heeding Artka's appeal and drifting away. But a dozen or so of Reasno's core supporters clustered together, murmuring angrily amongst themselves as they crossed to the other side of the hall.

"I hope that ends that lunacy." Hudge extended a hand to assist Artka down from the tabletop.

Artka's eye stayed on the group that clung together like cockleburs. "I'm not so sure, Hudge."

"After the evening meal, Sajon will take all new recruits aside to teach them rune-warfare. I'll warn him about that crowd."

Hudge stood beside Artka as he rapped on Metid's chamber door. The door swung open, revealing Sajon, Metid, and Gulundur gathered around Reasno, who was seated in a comfy chair with his back to the window. Evebryl closed the door and ushered the two inside. Sajon rested his sword on Reasno's shoulder and leaned over the Daggerman, urging, "It has to be your choice to abandon that evil counterfeit. *Kyllorn* powers are drawn to it; they will dull your ability to hear Logon's voice, leaving you vulnerable to the enemy's lies."

Reasno shrugged in an attempt to knock Sajon's sword away. "I've never been accosted by *kyllorn* or anything of Lurcan, as you suggest. How could I dwell so long in this brigade if I wasn't in good standing with Logon?"

Gulundur and Metid glanced at each other.

"And I participated in battles with you, didn't I? Does that sound like someone under Lurcan's spell?"

"Where are the recruits you've won to Logon's amnesty?" Sajon challenged.

"Recruiting to Logon's Rock isn't my job; I'm to encourage and supply them with—"

"Yeah, we know," Gulundur muttered. "And therein lies the problem."

Reasno shot back, "Only because you refuse to accept that daggers were commissioned by Logon and are much easier to sharpen and wield. I believe one way; you believe another way, making me the outcast, a Claygall in your minds. You malign me just because I don't see things the way you do; meanwhile, new recruits are sent to their doom because you won't let me supply them with back-up weaponry. Shame! For shame on you, all of you!" Reasno pushed Sajon's sword away. "That—that weighed heavily on me."

Sajon stood erect and sighed. "Though you don't use a Child of the Stars, do you still believe the runes on it?"

"Yes, yes. The same runes that are etched on the daggers are on the swords, aren't they? Of course, I agree with the runes." Reasno folded his arms over his chest.

"Then what do you make of this rune?" Sajon tapped a brightly glowing rune on his own sword.

Reasno glanced at it briefly, then turned away.

"Did you read it?"

"I read it. So what?"

"What did it say?"

"You know what it said."

"I know that it said:

> *'Only one weapon to pierce man's heart,*
> *Not to destroy but new life impart.'*

"So, if, as you say, you believe that rune, where does that leave daggers? Only means *only*! No other weapon will accomplish Logon's purpose. And your daggers are another kind of weapon. Since every other type of cutlery—from knives to scimitars, rapiers, short-swords, sabers, and such—are banned from Logon's armies, doesn't that equally hold true for diverse types of weaponry like crossbows, spears, and daggers?"

"But this is an exact replica of a Child of the Stars; it's just reduced in size. It's every bit as reliable as a Child of the Stars."

"Is that so? Suppose I plunge a dagger into your chest. How, then? Will it impart new life like true Children of the Stars?"

Reasno's eyes grew round. "You . . . you wouldn't do that!"

Sajon plucked a dagger off the table. "Shall we see if this produces the same result?"

Reasno's face paled, his eyes fixed on the dagger in Sajon's hand. "Th-th-that would be murder, and you know it."

Gulundur spoke from behind. "So you don't really believe it's the same as a Child of the Stars, only compacted?"

"Well, it's almost the same . . . Something had to be left out in the smelting process; it's the runes that matter, not the actual piercing of the heart." Reasno twisted his neck around, hoping to catch a hint of sympathy from his interrogators. "Speaking the runes is what counts, isn't it? Yes, speaking the runes to persuade the enemy to lay down their arms and go to Logon's Rock."

Sajon brought the dagger within an inch of Reasno's chest.

"C-come now; be reasonable," Reasno muttered, staring wide-eyed at the advancing, sparkling tip.

"Reasonable?" Metid bent low and got face to face with Reasno. "Is it reasonable to replace a proven weapon with a farce? Is it reasonable to engage an enemy soldier and cause bodily harm, then expect him to believe that the runes declare Logon has his best interests at heart?"

Reasno burst into tears. "Why are you torturing me? I've done nothing wrong. I only mean to help."

"Who's torturing you?" Metid stood upright again. "We're only trying to help you recognize and escape the enemy's snare; your mind has obviously been taken captive to accomplish the enemy's purpose of misleading raw recruits."

"What? Are you insinuating I'm cusp-touched?" Reasno's eyes opened wide. His face flushed red, and the veins on his neck bulged as he grimaced. "If anyone is cusp-touched, it's all of you; clinging to outdated, ancient weapons and methods, claiming to hear the voice of some internal Advisor . . . I've about had enough of this treatment. You can't treat a fellow kingsmen like this." He strained against the hands pinning him to the chair. "Let me go!" he shouted loud enough to be heard clear out in the keep's hall.

"Well, I've heard enough." Gulundur leaned heavily on Reasno's shoulders, keeping him seated. "Appealing to his conscience won't do; forced extraction is necessary."

Sajon nodded in assent, as did Evebryl. Artka and Hudge looked on silently.

Reasno caught the non-verbal exchange among his restrainers. His face paled as suddenly as it had erupted in crimson moments prior. Beads of sweat popped out on his brow; his hands clenched into white-knuckled fists. He threw back his head and cried, "Nooooo," trailing off eerily into something akin to a wolf's howl.

For an instant, Artka saw a translucent visage of a wolf baring his fangs, lips curled in a snarl and yellowish, hate-filled eyes overlaying Reasno's features. Reasno inhaled and again erupted in a full-fledged howl.

Momentarily caught off-guard, the five stepped back but immediately regained their composure and clustered around Reasno's chair again.

A clamorous pounding came on the chamber door, accompanied with loud shouts, followed by a booming voice rising above the din. "'Ere now, yers best be a backin' off afore I begins bustin' heads!"

Artka grinned. "I'd better see what that's all about before Scang forgets himself."

Metid nodded. "Go." He then lifted his sword and pointed it at Reasno's chest. "Let's see if he even has a scar."

Artka paused long enough to see Gulundur slip his hand over Reasno's shoulder and part the rawhide lacing of his outer tunic, revealing unblemished skin.

"Why," remarked Evebryl, "there's no Logon tunic underneath, either!"

Artka opened the chamber door just enough to peek out. He beheld only the broad back of his Eroton companion pressed to the doorframe. "Scang? Everything all right?"

The huge Eroton, firmly grasping a recruit's head under each arm, turned and replied mischievously, "Ain't nobbut I cain't handle, laddie. Sorta reminds me o' the old days"—he winked—"when I hadda quiet the riot o' me mates arter extended bouts o' celebratin'."

"What's their problem?"

Clepy forced his way beside Scang, replying to Artka while Scang was occupied quelling one of his captives. "They, uh, heard the howling and thought Reasno was being tortured. Being fresh from Lurcan's armies, they dinnae yet ken Ecclessite ways eschew violence."

"How many are involved?"

"Hard to say." Clepy shrugged. "Seeing as a few hundred got rescued today, there's lots that could get agitated; but so far, only *aboot* thirty surged toward the door. Ye jest keep on a doing what ye was a-doing; we can handle any trouble out here." Clepy winked.

Artka smiled, closed the door, and returned to Reasno. "It's under control. His howling alarmed some recruits who thought we were using empire methods."

"See the division you've already brought into our midst, Reasno?" challenged Gulundur. "And you still don't think you're an unwitting agent of Lurcan? Wake up, man! As long as you've been here and sat under rune study, don't you realize yet how the enemy works?"

Head down, chin on his chest, Reasno wasn't communicative anymore. Instead, he muttered to himself as his eyelids fluttered, spittle dribbling down his beard.

Metid looked up at his companions. "We can't pierce his heart unless he agrees . . . "

"He's clearly in no state to make a logical, volitional choice at the moment," Evebryl mused.

Metid leaned close and looked into Reasno's eyes. "I trust you can hear me, Reasno; your mind has been commandeered by enemy *kyllorn*. We're going to remove them, but you need to cooperate. We need your permission to pierce your heart with a Child of the Stars, so you can receive Logon's amnesty. Do you understand?"

Reasno stared back blankly.

Artka and Hudge took positions on either side of Metid, bending low, searching Reasno's eyes for any flicker of comprehension. Metid gently laid his hand on Reasno's forehead.

Reasno jumped and howled as if he'd been touched with a firebrand, "Owwooo, you burned me. Have you no pity?"

"It's the presence of the Advisor that scalds you, *kyllorn*; Reasno is unhurt, and you know it. Who are you? Reveal your name, I command you in Logon's name."

Reasno cried aloud again, howling like a wolf, "No-oo, no-ooo, take it away; it burns."

Renewed clamor at the door showed the *kyllorn's* maneuver was having an effect.

Evebryl touched Metid's shoulder. "Maybe this ought to be done another time, another place?"

Gulundur clamped his hand over Reasno's mouth. "No, this is the time; this is the place. The *kyllorn* are stirred up and manifesting; now is the time to deal with them. If they're allowed to retreat back behind Reasno's personality, we may not get them to reveal themselves again so easily. We must deal with it now."

Reasno's furtive eyes darted from one person to another.

"Much as I hate to disagree with you, Mother, Captain Gulundur is right," said Hudge. "Now is the best time. We may not get another opportunity, especially if the fortress comes under attack."

"No-ooo," Reasno struggled against his captors. "I'll be good; I'll go talk to Logon by myself and ask him to rid me of any cusps or . . . or irks. Don't torture me anymore." Tears rimmed his eyes, and his lips quivered as he pled his cause.

"Ooh, that's very good, *kyllorn*, a very good imitation of contrition," chided Artka. "But we know who and what you are. You're not fooling anybody—except, perhaps, Reasno. Now tell us your name, so your nefarious work will be evident to even Reasno as you exit."

Reasno's demeanor reverted to sullen stubbornness. The eyes that had been so full of pleading moments before were now steely cold, his lips set in a thin, grim line covering clenched teeth, his brow furrowed, and his nose crinkled in a sneer.

"I command you, in the name of Logon, reveal your name." Metid held his sword inches from Reasno's face so that the glow of several runes reflected in his eyes.

Reasno tried turning his head away, but he couldn't escape the shimmer of the glowing runes. Even shutting his eyes brought no relief; the emblazoned runes flared through the eyelids and into the fallen *kyllorn's* memory, shaming him, reminding him from whence he fell in Brida's train long ages past.

"What is your—"

"Ahhhhhhh," the entity screeched with ear-splitting volume. "Kalodidasko." Then Reasno slumped; sweaty hair clumped on his forehead, and his chin rested on his chest.

"Of course," Evebryl murmured, *"Kalodidasko*—'False teacher,' a wolf among sheep!"

"With shiny fangs to savage the lambs of the flock." Artka bore down harder. "I've got scars from his thing's bite. Where's your stash of daggers?"

"Never mind that for now," Metid interposed. "We can ascertain that information once Reasno is in his right mind. The important thing is to set this man free and trundle him off to Logon."

The others nodded.

"Now, Kalodidasko, we adjure you, in the name of Logon Xychirion, come out of this man. You are defeated; you must obey when we speak with Logon's authority. Come out."

Reasno clamped his mouth shut. Strained noises arose in his throat.

"Come out," Metid reiterated.

Reasno's lips parted; his grunting increased in volume, setting off another round of clamor outside the door, which was immediately quelled by an indistinguishable Eroton-ish bellow.

"Come out."

Evebryl, Hudge, Artka, and Gulundur intently appealed to Logon on Reasno's behalf. Suddenly, a break in the tension brought peace to the room.

Reasno doubled over and regurgitated. Metid barely got out of the way as a ball of slime landed on the carpet. The earnest battlers smiled and knew the struggle was won—at least for the moment. Metid gently placed his hand on Reasno's neck. "Feeling better, son?"

Reasno sagged in his seat, his eyes downcast.

"Look!" Evebryl pointed to the slimy mass on the rug. "It's crawling!"

Dozens of irks slithered toward the edge of the rug, seeking a place to hide.

"Don't let them escape; they'll infect the recruits if they get out of this room," warned Evebryl.

Four shining swords simultaneously swept over the floor, driving the worms back into a tight-knit group around the slime, boxing them in. Gulundur got down on his knees and lay the flat of his sword over the clustered vermin. Tiny screeches rent the air as smoky puffs curled up and drafted to the fireplace, then up and out the chimney flue.

"We're not done." Hudge turned again to Reasno. "Those were weak *kyllorn* sent to trick us into thinking the job was done. The false teacher is still to be dealt with."

"Are you sure?" Metid asked. "He looks calm to me. I think we got them all."

Evebryl laid a hand on Meitd's arm. "Hudge has been given a gift from the Advisor of sensitivity to the presence of *kyllorn*; better heed his warning, Captain."

Metid's eyebrows arched, but he took a step back, gesturing with his hand for Hudge to resume.

Hudge moved in front of Reasno. "I can smell you, wolf."

Reasno averted his eyes.

Hudge grasped the man's chin, forcing eye contact. For a moment, their eyes locked; then Reasno's placid countenance evaporated, replaced with a hateful sneer. "And I smell the foul blood of a kingsman."

"It's the blood of our king who has defeated you by stealing away your right to assault us with guilt, for we are forgiven."

"Not Reasno! His guilt is too great. He stands condemned for all the evil in his heart and the evil he's done and the evil he's planning. Not even your liege can forgive all that."

"Reasno, Reasno, listen to me," Hudge insisted, "those words coming out of your mouth are lies. Logon's blood breaks every accusation leveled against you if you truly want to be forgiven and live a new life."

Reasno blinked, as if waking from a dream. "Wha—what? I can truly be forgiven?"

"Allow my Child of the Stars to penetrate your heart and send you to Logon's Rock. Is that what you want?"

"I—I guess so."

Artka tilted his head to the side and whispered to the others, "So, do we cast out the wolf first or pierce his heart?"

"Good question," said Gulundur. "Seems to me the *kyllorn* is still able to disrupt Reasno's understanding of what's taking place, so I think we ought to get rid of the enemy first."

"Right," agreed Metid. "Now, then, you false teacher, come out of this man right now."

Hudge added, "Reasno, you must tell it you want it to go. You don't want to believe lies, nor do you want to harm anyone else with lies. So, you must also resist."

Reasno made as if to resist this wicked thing that had invaded him. "Leave me alo—alooo—arrrgh!" but ended with a prolonged yawn, followed by a coughing spasm.

"Hudge?" Evebryl asked.

Hudge studied the man seated before him. "I sense no more *kyllorn*."

Metid re-opened Reasno's jerkin and applied his sword to the skin. "Are you ready?"

Reasno's eyes were large with fright. "Will it hurt?"

Metid smiled. "Not in the way you mean. Your conscience will briefly be a cause of concern, but that's a bearable pain. Logon will soon remedy that."

Reasno took a deep breath and nodded his assent.

Metid's sword slit the skin and entered beneath without drawing a drop of blood.

Reasno swooned.

CHAPTER TEN

"WELL, DID YOU MEET LOGON?" Artka probed. He parted Reasno's jerkin and doublet at the neck and sighed. "No Logon tunic. Did you touch the cliff?"

"I—I was afraid to. He said I'd die."

Metid leaned in. "But you must die to your old Carnalian life so Logon can fill you with his. This chest wound won't heal until you meet Logon atop his rock and he touches your heart's wound."

"It's too late now."

"What do you mean it's too late?" Hudge pressed.

"Logon disappeared, and a roamer was suddenly beside me. The roamer told me I'd have to brave many perils to find my own way back to the rock, since I wasn't yet ready to yield."

Artka stood upright and looked to the two captains. "I've never heard of such a thing—being at the base of the cliff and then denied."

"It happens sometimes when the recruit clings to unresolved loyalties," said Gulundur. "Logon, in his wisdom, assigns them tasks in which they must earnestly seek him. If they push their way through the obstacles placed in their path by the enemy, they'll emerge truly wanting Logon and not just his amnesty benefits. If they falter along the way—that is, if at some point they're beguiled to stop seeking—it reveals that they only wanted to escape judgment but not abandon their Carnalian lifestyle."

Reasno turned from one to another, following the conversation.

"What happens to them?" Artka asked.

Metid shrugged. "Any number of things. Some just forget the whole thing, no longer believing it's real, and go back to empire life. Others opt for an easier pathway that doesn't require trusting in promises and instead take up with one of the empire's counterfeit beliefs. Still others become hostile to Ecclessa and all it stands for."

"Such recruits usually need to struggle their way to Logon's Rock without first beholding him, like you did when Tren guided you, Artka, and were almost lost to Neask," said Evebryl.

Reasno turned white. "You mean, I'll have to face a dread?"

"No, no, not at all," Gulundur assured. "That was what Artka had to face to seal it in his soul that he really wanted Logon's forgiveness. Artka came from a place of utter hostility to Ecclessa, not believing in Logon or King Elyon. He had a lot to overcome. But you, already aware of Logon and his kingdom, shouldn't have near as much difficulty—if you stay to the path. And you ought not delay; there might not be much time to make the trek before the next trumpet sounds."

"But . . . where is this path? How far is it to Logon's Rock? Will someone come with me to guide me?"

The five Ecclessites looked from one to another.

"Well," Artka finally said, "I suppose I could—"

"Nay, Artka," said Gulundur, "you're too valuable to the battlefront. Too many depend on your leadership here. Your absence would create a vacancy, a vulnerability in our lines. No, I can't allow that. Nor can we spare you, Hudge. Both of you have much shine on your swords that ought not be squandered by trekking through the wilds as a guide."

Turning to Reasno, he spoke tenderly. "I'm sorry to have to tell you this, son; but if you want Logon's amnesty, you'll have to seek it by yourself, thus proving what you really want. You were at the brink of receiving all that Logon wants to give you, but you hesitated. Mayhap, fighting your way back to the same decision will settle it in your heart to fully commit to seeking Logon's will for your life."

"But what if I ask for someone in the castle to accompany me? I don't want to go alone. What if I get lost or something?"

"I'm afraid we can spare no one. Anyone who has even a modicum of light on their sword is sorely needed here; any recruit who'd go with you would be in greater jeopardy than you. Logon will protect you, since he's summoned you, as long as you stay to the pathway; but no one else has that assurance of protection. Their place is here, learning to toll their swords. You must trust Logon to guide you, lad. That's the whole purpose of making this journey alone, unarmed," said Metid. "This is how Logon teaches us to lean on him. It's how I had to come to him."

"Unarmed? Can't I at least take a sword?"

"You have no ability to put Logon's light on it yet. Not only would it be useless in your hands; it might be a liability. Since you were seduced by deception, it's likely you'll be beset by various deceivers along the trail who would use a dull Child of the Stars against you. Only after Logon heals your heart-wound and puts the Advisor in your heart and light on the sword will you be able to toll the blade and learn the runes. Consider how long you've been in this fortress, hearing lectures but not really listening, sitting in on rune studies, yet not learning because you'd not received the Advisor."

"And even then," Gulundur added, "you must take care not to receive instruction from questionable sources, such as Captain Sofista."

Reasno blushed at the mention of Sofista. But he nodded. "So, when should I leave?"

"Can you think of a better moment than now?" asked Metid.

"If you're ready, Reasno," said Evebryl, "I'll fetch a food sack and water-skin for your journey."

"And with the captains' permission," Artka said, "I'll accompany you as far as the bend in the road that turns toward the river. Along the way, you can tell me where your cache of daggers is hidden, so they can be destroyed."

Reasno grimaced as he stood. "Oooh! It's beginning to sting a little."

"Because you resisted his offer," said Artka. "When Tren pierced me, I had to overcome mistrusting Tren and an irrational desire to run away, deathly afraid of Logon rejecting me. Every time I decided to turn away, my bodily pains lessened; but the ache in my heart increased. You see, until your heart's wound is healed, your own body and mind will resist going to Logon because they're still under Lurcan's power. When my heart's pain became unbearable and I returned to seeking Logon, the grief in my heart lifted; but my body had all manner of aches and weakness in trying to dissuade me, not to mention a deep depression. You must resist the impulses of mind and body and set your face like a flint to find Logon's Rock, letting nothing deter you."

"Your heart's wound awakened awareness of King Elyon's laws and how you flaunted those laws all your life and are deserving of death. That's why your mind and body will try to overturn your decision; your Carnalian nature knows it's going to execution and is resisting," Metid explained. "But you're not a body that has a spirit; rather, you're a spirit that resides in a body. Long after your body has expired, your spirit will exist—I say 'exist' instead of 'live' because only in Elyon's presence is there life. The spirit of those who die without bending the knee to Logon Xychirion will be banished to nether realms, where there is no light or comfort but only a fiery inferno of dark flames occupied by hateful denizens trying to relieve their own agonies by tormenting others."

Reasno's eyes widened.

Metid continued, "So you see, it's imperative to see this journey through. I don't mean to scare you, son, but you must know the consequence of what awaits should you abandon your quest."

Artka, Metid, Hudge, and Gulundur walked Reasno out the doorway where they met Evebryl just returning with a food-sack and water-skin. Several dozen recruits were corralled by Scang, Clepy, Harnet, Reddy, and Braxmore off to one side of the hall.

Hudge whispered to Reasno, "You owe an explanation to your followers that you never really encountered Logon before and that you just now got pierced and are going to his rock to get healed."

"Is that necessary?" Reasno said. "I mean, it's embarrassing—"

"Only to your Carnalian self. These kingsmen have just been to Logon's Rock and had their wounds healed; you almost led them into deception with those cursed daggers because they hadn't had time to recognize the Advisor's voice or learn Logon's runes yet. These men would have followed you to their destruction. You need to make it clear you're not anybody's leader."

Reasno nodded and walked over to the group. "Uh, men—those of you who were concerned about what was happening to me inside there . . . " He pointed at Metid's chamber. "I, uh, want to say that I, uh, well it was decided that I needed to take a brief journey."

"To?" Hudge shot Reasno a stern look.

"Uh, yeah, uh, to Logon's Rock, where these men assure me that Logon has a special word for me." Then aside to Hudge, he whispered,

"Please let me keep a little dignity; they don't need to know that I've never been heart-pierced before. It might discourage them, please?"

Metid, emerging from his office, intruded in front of Hudge and grasped Reasno's arm to escort him to the door, brusquely urging, "You'd best get underway."

Hudge said, "But he didn't—"

"No time to waste, Hudge. We have urgent matters that need attention." Then to Reasno, he said, "Be on your way."

A handful of recruits grumbled under their breath as they watched Reasno guided none-too-gently out the gateway.

Meanwhile, Sajon had busily gathered several other recruits just outside the gate to demonstrate how to toll their swords and explain that runes might suddenly glow or vibrate in a musical tone.

Artka led through the group and down the trail with a reluctant Reasno, who kept looking behind as if hoping for either a reprieve or permission to take a sword along. He only saw new recruits drilling and unsmiling kingsmen officers watching his departure from the barbican.

"This," Artka instructed, "is how you'll discover Logon really loves you and wants you to become a kingsman discerning truth from error. You'll face dangers, sure; but since you have nothing with which to defend yourself, you'll have to rely only on Logon's promises."

Reasno turned front and double-timed to catch up to Artka. "But . . . but what if he doesn't?"

Artka withdrew his sword. "Here, can you read this?" He pointed to a rune halfway down the blade.

Reasno squinted. "Uh, it says:

'Be content with what you're given.
A warrior's lot is where he's driven.
Possessions—just a meager few
To keep distractions out of view.
Keep close your liege, and nigh he'll be.
He'll not forsake nor cut you free.
When direst need presses round,
No surer hope than he is found.'"

Reasno looked at his companion. "And that applies how?"

The corners of Artka's lips turned up ever so slightly. "By the expensive clothing you always wore, I surmise that you proudly owned many fine things. I would guess that you made no small profit from hawking daggers?"

Reasno made no reply.

"Well, no matter. That's between you and Logon. This rune declares that his followers ought to rely on nothing or no one except Logon. Until that's settled, he can't come to their aid because they're trying to rescue themselves with their own efforts instead of falling in surrender at his feet to live or die at his discretion. That's why you must take this journey, even though you're utterly defenseless. You must totally rely on the fact that he will never abandon anyone who is truly committed to seeking him."

"He asks a lot."

"He sacrificed a lot."

They walked in silence.

Then Artka asked, "So, where are they?"

"Who?"

"Not 'who.' 'What?'"

"I don't know what you mean."

Artka stopped. "Are you playing games? 'Cause if you are, I'm going back and will escort you no further."

Reasno turned to face Artka. "I really don't know—"

"The daggers!" Artka's eyes narrowed.

"Oh, those."

Artka's eyebrows arched.

Reasno scuffed the dirt beneath his feet. "Well, I hid them down in the lower end of the glacis of King's Gate Fortress by an outcrop of boulders. There's a hollow on the eastern side covered by thorn bushes. You'll find them in sacks."

"Sacks? How many sacks are there?"

"A few."

"And that's the only cache?"

Reasno's eyes avoided Artka, looking instead at the leafy canopy hanging over the road. "Uh, I believe so. Yes . . . I'm sure."

Artka continued alongside Reasno. "Any questions?"

"You're quite sure you won't come any farther with me?"

"Logon wants to be your source. Were I to go, you'd depend on me instead of him." Artka glanced sideways at his companion. "I know how you feel. I felt much the same when I was lost in the Valley of Shadows."

"What happened?"

"Well." Artka sighed. "First, Tren and I were attacked by tophets as we camped in a wooded tract. After we escaped them, I was beset by a swarm of cusps that caused me to doubt Tren's motives; I was tempted to quit searching for Logon and seek out my old Carnalian brigade. Those cusps had me convinced that Tren would betray me to be tortured and killed. A flood nearly swept me away when Tren finally found me—then we were beset upon by Neask, one of the Dreads of the Gates."

"And you escaped unscathed?"

"Not quite. I was so weak, I had to cling to Tren's belt as the floodwaters overran their banks. At first, I thought the flood was sent by Lurcan, but it turned out to be Logon's deliverance. What I deemed as a threat was meant to sweep my enemies away. A sudden swell lifted Tren right into the dread's face; and though severely wounded, Tren found the strength to ignore his pain and swing his sword at the boastful monster . . . Swish—and Neask's tongue went flying—a tasty morsel to his pet vulture. Neask fled howling; cusps were washed downstream, while, at the same time, Tren and I were carried on a riptide in the opposite direction to the base of Logon's Rock."

"Ah-ha, but you see, Tren's sword was necessary, wasn't it?"

Artka caught the mistrustful glint in Reasno's eye. "Yes, but I wasn't the one wielding it; my heart's wound was yet unhealed, and I had no sword of my own. It was Logon's strength through Tren, though wounded, that prevented the *kyllorn* from waylaying us. Tren was all but undone the minute Neask's chain-mace clashed with his sword, sending a shockwave that snapped his collarbone. Though Logon would let nothing interfere with my coming to him, I had to struggle, even to the base of the cliff when I realized it was necessary for me to die if I wanted Logon."

"I just don't know, Artka. It all seems so contrary to reality."

"It's a paradox, to be sure. The trail you're about to embark upon, alone and vulnerable, is meant to break you from trusting your senses, strengths, and reason. Such a drastic effort is necessary because

Lurcan's subjects make decisions based on his perverted rationale that rebels against King Elyon."

Artka halted. "Well, I hear the ripples of the Flaming Sword River; that means we're near the bend in the road, where I must take my leave."

Reasno turned. "Just a little farther? After all, you had Tren . . ."

"I can't. I'm needed back at the fort. Besides, we've encountered no enemies thus far; you'll be safe. Logon will see to that. Waste no time; you don't know how much time you have left before the next trumpet sounds, and you don't want to get caught without a lit sword when that happens. Stay to the pathway; don't get distracted. King's Road to you."

Reasno nodded but made no reply.

Artka put his hand on Reasno's shoulder. "Believe me, you're better off without a weapon or a guide. Just throw yourself upon Logon's mercy."

CHAPTER ELEVEN

REASNO STOOD ROOTED TO THE road, watching Artka recede into the shadow-dappled distance. As soon as Artka disappeared over a knoll, Reasno jumped the gulley running alongside the road and pushed his way through the shrubbery into the forest, muttering, "Tells me not to have a sword or a companion, while he had the luxury of both."

The thick undergrowth hampered his progress; it was thicker than he'd thought. It forced him to make small detours to stay abreast of Artka's course. Even so, he stayed close enough to monitor Artka's progress, yet kept hidden well within the brushy border. He broke into a sweat from the effort of pushing through the undergrowth, but he was determined to know Artka's intentions concerning "his" cache of daggers. One particularly dense patch of brambles sent him off course; and for a few minutes, he was disoriented and lost sight of Artka. In a panic, Reasno incautiously veered back toward the road, where he again caught sight of Artka in the distance walking nonchalantly, perusing some rune or another on his sword. Reasno swatted at insects buzzing around his face as he slunk behind another hedgerow. By now, his chest wound throbbed; but oddly, his limbs were invigorated. He'd been unaware of how weak he'd been until now, but his physical prowess was returning.

Artka's tale about his heart-wound intensifying or lessening in correlation to his pressing on toward Logon's Rock or shying away crossed Reasno's mind briefly; but a more "rational" thought occurred,

deathly throes. Time and age, or perhaps a violent storm, had toppled the great tree. Was this the elm he sought? Reasno scrambled up the bank to peer into the deep depression gouged out by the overturned root system. Ah, the burrow beneath the roots he'd excavated was still accessible. Reasno squinted in the dim light as he knelt and reached into the cavity. Was that . . . could it be?

A piece of a canvas bag poked out from under several rocks, roots, and soil. He lay flat on his belly and probed as far as he could stretch with his arm. The bulk of the fallen tree prevented him reaching any deeper. If only he had a shovel . . . Casting his eyes about, he spotted a long, thin, flat rock which had been churned up during the tree's upheaval. It would suffice. Reasno grabbed the improvisational spade and furiously attacked the loam, roots, and rocks barring his way. After several minutes of frenzied digging, he again stretched his hand down for the canvas sack. Not yet—he needed to delve just a little deeper.

Another five minutes and he achieved his goal. He snatched the bag with both hands and hauled it up. After all this time, he was delighted that the sack's opening was still secured by a leather drawstring. Brushing dirt away, Reasno anxiously tugged at the opening. He reached inside the sack and felt something cool and metallic.

"Ouch!"

He withdrew his hand and examined a half-inch slice in his index finger. Blood dripped on the canvas sack. He stuck his finger in his mouth to cleanse the wound and decided to dump the bag's contents onto the turf instead of risking any more punctures. Three daggers spilled out onto the moss, along with several coins imprinted with empire emblems, a couple of crude eating utensils, and a map scorched onto a fawn's hide depicting a coastal region.

A breeze shifted an overhead branch in the sunlight as a shadow rising out of the pit slipped beneath the sack.

Reasno threw his head back in laughter. "I remember that Sofista character charming me out of my horse and a warm cloak for these." He examined the coins and thought maybe they were valuable—if spent in the right places. Yes, he hadn't sold his horse cheaply. The man claimed he had been unjustly accused of heinous crimes and was now a fugitive needing to make a swift getaway. Reasno figured he could always buy another horse; besides, at the time, he was accepted at the kingsmen fortress and had no reason to leave. Sofista also bequeathed a cache of daggers to him that he'd hidden in the woods just before he hurried on his way.

Reasno relocated himself atop the fallen elm. In the intervening years, he'd almost forgotten this secret cache. He'd secretly moved most of the daggers night after night to the bottom of the glacis around the fortress so they'd be more convenient. Regarding Sofista, he'd heard rumors that the old rascal had become a captain somewhere over in Ecclessa. In the meantime, Reasno maintained a comfortable living dealing daggers to fresh recruits and spending the income in nearby Carnalian taverns whenever he left the fortress surreptitiously on solo "rescuing" missions.

Reasno stood up to full stature, pocketed the money, and slipped one dagger into each boot and lodged the third one in his belt. His chest suddenly throbbed. "Hunger. It'll pass," he promised himself and headed back toward the Flaming Sword River and the pathway to Logon's Rock.

An hour of pushing through the undergrowth brought him near where Artka had taken leave of him. He felt odd, as if divided against himself; but when he tried to purposely head for Logon's Rock, he was suddenly overcome with exhaustion—though his chest was relieved.

He sat on a large rock alongside the road with hands on both knees as he sighed deeply. He must take a moment and consider . . .

"You seem troubled."

Reasno jerked his head up in alarm. "Who said that?" He looked this way and that in a panic but saw no one.

"Fear not. I'm no threat." The top of a boulder just across the pathway suddenly shifted, revealing a tall man in a full-length gray robe and hooded cowl that shielded most of his face; only the light reflecting from his eyes was visible in the shadow eclipsing him.

"Do I know you?" Reasno challenged, trying to hide his fright at the man's sudden appearance.

"We've met, briefly."

Reasno cocked his head to the side and said, "I don't seem to recall . . . "

"No, I don't suppose you would. You were preoccupied. Now, is there a problem? I sense you're torn between two choices."

Reasno folded his arms across his chest, feeling as if his innermost thoughts were exposed. His right hand touched the dagger's handle in his belt.

The man turned north, toward Logon's Rock, his profile still obscured. "I was going that way; if you're heading there, too, perhaps we can make our journey shorter by keeping each other company. A little companionship helps make a dreary walk endurable, does it not?"

Reasno evaluated the stranger's prowess; it wouldn't do to fall prey to a highwayman, nor an over-exuberant kingsman. "Maybe I'm not going that way."

"Your *maybe* reveals you're not sure which direction to take. Both directions lead to death. One way, death is permanent; the other is but a brief death leading to life evermore. Which course will you choose?"

"Look here, I don't know who you are or why you think you know my dilemma—"

"Am I mistaken in saying that two paths lay before you and you're torn between your heart and your ability to rationalize? You were here not long ago with a companion. When he reversed course, you discretely followed him under cover of the woods."

"You're guessing. You . . . you observed me stumbling out of the forest and just assumed I couldn't make up my mind whether to continue my journey or return."

"I never make assumptions." The man slowly turned toward Reasno, his face still shadowed under his cowl. "Something clings to you, hardening your heart. Unless you summon the will to rid yourself of it, it will claim you. I heard you say you wanted a companion for your journey; I offer companionship. Citizenship in the kingdom of Elyon or citizenship in Lurcan's empire lay before you. One way is life, the other death. But I'll not tarry for you; make up your mind. Rebellion is beckoning. I cannot make this choice for you."

"Hah! You're just a crazy, old coot making wild guesses."

"I've been called worse. Your naïve rejection doesn't offend me, but your hesitation between two paths greatly concerns me."

"Why should you care?"

"I care more than you can understand." The stranger rose and began walking away. "Make your choice."

Reasno shrugged.

The stranger kept walking, not looking back.

"I'm tired from crawling through the brambles. I think I'll rest a bit. Maybe I'll catch up to you later."

"If you do, I doubt we'll be on such friendly terms. This is your moment of decision."

Reasno's hand swept the air toward the stranger as he muttered under his breath, "Crazy, old coot thinks he's a seer or something, trying to make me fearful."

Reasno awoke. It was dark; the sun had set, and a chill mist crept up from the river. He stood and gathered his cloak about him. Sleep had refreshed him; even his heart's discomfort was eased. Now, which way would he go? He looked the direction of Logon's Rock, then back toward the castle. He really had no reason to return there, where self-inflated officers would pester him about Logon's Rock. Yet did he really want to face death at the bottom of the cliff?

A dusky fog descended over the road as he deliberated. He shivered. There were dangerous creatures known to roam these wilds, especially at night. Even as the thought crossed his mind, he heard the snap of a branch in the nearby undergrowth. He swiveled his head toward the sound, extending a shaky dagger. He dared not take a step, lest he draw attention to his presence.

More crunching twigs and rustling leaves followed, disrupting the silence. A drifting fogbank rolled slowly down from an embankment not thirty feet away. Was it coming toward him? He sniffed the air. The echo of Artka's challenge came to mind: *Is a dagger what you'd choose to face a tophet?* Of course, he didn't believe in tophets. Nonetheless, surrounded by the growing night and watching a sinister fogbank approach . . . He'd been told that tophets emitted a vile odor.

He detected no such odor; but then, there wasn't any breeze to carry the scent. The twilight faded; to his horror, two barely visible, dark shadows came slinking out of the forest and slithering down the bank in the intensifying gray fog.

He backed away a few steps, bent over, and fumbled in his left boot for another dagger so he could fend off whatever approached with both hands. The two dark shapes landed on the road with a grunt.

"Hold! I-I-I warn you . . . I'm armed," Reasno managed though chattering teeth.

The two obscure forms halted. A long moment of increasing terror passed until a voice said, "Be's that yer, Reasno?"

Reasno blinked. "Who's asking?"

"It's me, Yumpik, and Frib is with me. We come out lookin' fer yer, expectin' yer must soon be returnin' from Logon's Rock. What took yer so long? It's got mighty dark . . . "

"Yumpik? Frib?"

"Yer promised usn's daggers ter use along wi' our swords, remember?"

"Oh, yes, now I remember you. Yes . . . "

"Usn's gots lost goin' off'n the pathway fer a spell lookin' fer a drink o' water. Lucky we come out whar we did, eh?"

Reasno just then noticed the small dots of light at the very tips of their swords swinging from their belts. "Uh, yeah, lucky. You, uh, you didn't happen to be there when I was, er, escorted from the castle?"

Frib answered, "Nah, we pulled guard duty and were on the parapets. Did we miss you giving out daggers? We each wanted one bad."

The dell darkened; Reasno's lips curled in a smile, and he forced the discomfort of his heart from his mind. He deftly flipped both daggers in his hands at once, proffering the hafts to the men. "Here, you can have these."

Even in the gloom, the dagger blades sparkled briefly as the men received them. They stared adoringly, quite taken with the beauty of the cutlery.

Reasno extracted the third dagger from his boot and tucked it in his belt. "Men, I believe it's best that we strike out to find some shelter where we can build a fire and make camp for the night, since both Logon's Rock and the castle are too far to go in this darkness."

"Eh? Logon's Rock? Ain't you been?"

Reasno's dilemma was resolved. "Sure, sure. So now we must find shelter and make plans. Tell me, before you left, were any soldiers toting bundles from the lower field up to the castle?"

"Come ter think on it, usn's did see summat strange happenin'," said Yumpik. "Usn's was jest comin' off'n guard duty an' thought we'd come an' find yer. Usn's wondered what thet be's all about."

"Well, I'll tell you; it seems not everyone has the same appreciation for daggers that we have. Can you believe they actually want to destroy such beautiful weapons just because they think only Logon's swords should be used?"

"No!" both men said in disbelief.

Frib continued, "Is that why they put the sacks atop firewood?"

"Did they set fire to them?" Reasno asked, drawing close to Frib.

"Not yet. Gulundur said something about waiting for another rainstorm, lest the flames set the field afire and it spread to the forest."

"Are the daggers guarded?"

"Doesn't kens," Yumpik said. "Whatcha gots in mind?"

As the trio conferred, complete darkness settled over the roadway. "Here's what we'll do: it's not really safe for me to go into the fortress anymore; they distrust me and will likely put me in irons just for having a dagger. But you aren't suspected of anything and can freely go in and out. First thing we do is raid the pile of daggers and remove a couple of sacks to a hideaway. Then tomorrow, you both return to the fort and carefully, secretly contact any other recruits who might want a dagger. Send them to our hideout. When sufficient numbers join up, we'll form a Daggerman Brigade."

Frib and Yumpik grinned at each other and nodded. "Them rules the kingsmen put on everybody was crimpin' our fun, anyway, eh, Frib?"

After discussing the best way to approach the pile of firewood and daggers without being seen, the three set off toward the King's Gate Fortress West.

Reasno's chest wound flared up in a stinging burst of pain. "Ahhh," he suddenly cried out and collapsed to his knees.

"What is it, Debator? What's wrong?" Frib asked, kneeling beside the stricken leader.

Reasno clasped his chest and flopped onto his side rolling over in a spasm. Had he heard a faint voice say, "You've made your choice, then?"

"Yes, yes! It's what I want! Leave me alone; pester me no more!"

"I'm sorry, Reasno, I only wanted to help," said Frib, springing back, looking wide-eyed at Yumpik.

"I doesn't ken he be's meanin' yer, Frib," said Yumpik. "Summat else be's a goin' on here thet we hain't privy ter."

Reasno sat up, breathing easier. "It's gone!" He probed beneath his jerkin and found there was no chest wound, no scar, and no pain. In fact, he felt marvelously refreshed.

Frib and Yumpik looked at each other, then back to Reasno. Then, noticing a strange, blue light near the ground, Yumpik muttered, "Hey, whazzat rune aglowin' on yer sword, Frib?"

"I dunno. I ain't tried to get none lit up yet. Lemme have a looksee . . . It says:

> *'And some seed fell on hardened path,*
> *So swift the bird that steals a life.*
> *Such crops will only harvest wrath*
> *And legacy reap of endless strife.'*

"Now whazzat s'posed ter mean?"

Reasno pondered for only a moment, then said, "Nothing. It means nothing, like most kingsmen adages intended to make us feel guilty about one thing or another."

The lighted rune flickered and went out, and the tips of both swords dimmed so as to be barely discernible.

CHAPTER TWELVE

WATER DROPLETS ECHOING DOWN A distant corridor blended with the scurry of rats' feet and the high-pitched squeaks of bats swooping erratically, snatching insects out of midair. Dancel's eyes strained to catch even the remotest hint of light, but the ubiquitous pitch-black was impenetrable. Chained with both feet and one hand to the cold stone wall, she shifted position trying to find comfort on the straw bedding that had been tossed at her.

Was it daylight yet? She'd lost track of time since confinement to the dungeon where the most notorious prisoners were kept. A tear rolled down her cheek and dropped to her shoulder. She'd been stripped of all garments except her Logon dress by Hod-ya's henchmen; but for some reason, they wouldn't—or couldn't—touch this garment. Hod-ya had demanded she remove it herself and seemed strangely impotent when Dancel refused.

Dancel lifted a knee, relieving pressure on the small of her back, but soon discovered another source of pain where truncheons had battered her ribcage. Her face and lips were swollen, no doubt bruised from the cuffing Hod-ya had bestowed on her. She'd been punched, slapped, kicked, and shoved in a circle from blackguard to blackguard, whipped across her back and legs, had her hair yanked, and then was sent round again to each dronnet until she staggered in a daze, her body numb, no longer registering pain from the individual blows.

When Hod-ya realized they were getting nowhere, she stopped the brutality; Dancel was nearly incoherent. Chains were clamped on her wrist and both ankles; then she was left alone.

Her mind wandered in and out of lucidity for uncounted hours until this most recent return to consciousness. She was now awake and slowly discovering the extent of her injuries—no bones broken; that was a wonder! She sensed bruises from head to foot with possible internal bleeding—at least, that's what it felt like. And worst of all, she couldn't remember if, in all her delirium, she'd revealed any information. There was no telling what she might have divulged. Why had Hod-ya left off bludgeoning her? Had Dancel revealed Flan's home as the secret meeting place? Had she betrayed her friends, her brigade, and, in so doing, her liege?

Another tear rolled down her cheek. She lifted her free hand to wipe it away. "Oh, Logon! I failed you. Oh, if only I'd pressed on to the next street instead of seeking shelter in that alcove!"

"Daughter, you've not failed me."

Dancel caught her breath. Had she actually heard those words? Or was it just what she wished Logon would say? And yet, the thought had come with such an unexpected sense of calm . . .

But no, she'd failed. Now members of the brigade were likely being hunted to extermination, and it was her fault. Just when there was a ray of hope by the visit of a brigade from Ra-Amawl seeking contact with their brigade, suggesting a battle plan, she'd betrayed them. Her trickle of tears turned into sobs—not for her suffering, significant as it was, but because she'd now become the source of torture and death to others who loved and trusted her.

"Was it my pride in eluding discovery as I sneaked in and out of the castle that caused my capture? Is that why I'm being punished? If so, I deserve this. But why let harm come to the others in the brigade for my mistakes? Why should they suffer for my arrogance? Oh, my liege, the children—I can't stand that they should suffer for my errors."

In the darkness, something furry with tiny, clawed feet dashed across her leg. She squealed, "Shoo! Get out of here!" She waved her free hand, hoping to ward off the vermin.

Through the open cell door, her eyes caught a faint glimmer of light reflecting off the walls of the corridor. Someone bearing a torch was coming. In its dim glow, she was finally able to make out her environs. She was chained securely at the farthest stanchion from the doorway at the end of a row of benches. Knowing there was no way she could escape, Hod-ya must have purposely left the cell door open to taunt the girl who had once had free run of the maze. Indeed, would she even be able to walk again after "interrogation" by Hod-ya's dronnets? This space had sometimes been used as a holding cell whenever the emperor enlarged the rank and file of his armies with captured lawbreakers. The "recruits" were coerced into taking an oath on pain of hanging if they refused. This was the foulest, deepest, most putrid cell in the dungeon. Only one criminal had been kept down here on a permanent basis, shut off from the rest of the world, chained one hand and both feet to the wall, as Dancel now was, occupying his place.

Increasing torchlight reflected off the walls. Muffled voices and several footfalls gave evidence that only a small group approached. Dancel shuddered. Dronnets coming to finish their work?

"Oh, Logon, please don't abandon me." She wept.

The torchlight, stopped a few paces short of the open doorway, illuminating the red and green mold-stained walls. The voices quieted as the echoing footsteps resumed.

Dancel slumped, feigning unconsciousness. Though her eyelids were closed, she knew when the torch entered the cell. The footsteps stopped directly in front of her.

"Do it," Hod-ya's unmistakable voice harshly commanded.

A bucketful of icy-cold water drenched Dancel, shocking her, causing her to inhale sharply. Hod-ya's eyes reflected the flaming torch. Behind her, in shadow, stood three dronnets and a girl. Was that Rissa?

"Are you awake now, wench?"

Dancel drooped her head again.

Hod-ya stooped and grasped Dancel's chin, forcing her to look up. "Awake enough. Unchain her."

The nearest dronnet bent to the task, unlocking first her feet, then her hand.

"Get her up."

Two dronnets seized Dancel by the underarms, hoisting her to her feet.

"Let's see if she can stand on her own."

The blackguards stepped away.

Dancel tottered. Aches that had previously been dull flared anew as blood coursed back into her limbs. "Oh, Logo—"

Hod-ya's open palm landed full on Dancel's cheek, nearly toppling her. "Do *not* speak that name!"

Dancel looked at Hod-ya out of the corner of her eye as her tongue probed the inside of her cheek for blood. "His name bothers you?"

"If you regard your tongue, you won't say that name in my presence again, understand? Or I'll have it removed."

Dancel glanced aside at Rissa, who stared at the floor.

"Look at me, child; don't go looking to her for pity. You'll find none there, I warrant."

"What do you want, Hod-ya? Haven't I given you enough information?" Dancel raised her eyes; the dizziness was clearing, even though the frigid dousing made her shiver.

"Mmmm. Yes, you've been quite helpful on that account," Hod-ya shot a sly, grin sideways to the dronnets. "Now I have another errand for you; you might say it's the last bit of service you can render for your emperor. If you perform it efficiently, I dare say he may be lenient and allow you a quick execution, instead of the prolonged, entertaining event that I planned."

"Oh? And what of your mother's claim on my remains?"

"So sweet of you to remember her." Hod-ya's eyes narrowed to slits. "Rest assured, she'll get her share. After all, she was instrumental in catching you. She'll not be denied her reward. No, my dearie, what I have in mind for you now is to take Rissa—I believe you are acquainted—and teach her the maze. She's your replacement—someone I can trust, unlike you. How you managed to deceive me so long, I'll never know; but I'm assured that this simple-minded girl will do only as she's told and not plot behind my back. My mistake in selecting you was thinking I could harness your cleverness to my own uses."

Rissa's eyes met Dancel's, an apologetic expression on her face.

"That will take weeks," Dancel said.

"You have four days."

"Impossible. It took me weeks to learn the maze door to door blindfolded—"

"You have four days. You'll find her a motivated learner." Hod-ya turned to Rissa. "Aren't you, girl? Besides, she'll have a torch."

Rissa looked steadily at Hod-ya, nodding her head ever so slightly.

"Four days or she'll lose her feet! And you will lose that rebellious tongue of yours. Need I say more?"

"And if I refuse?"

"Oh, please do." The pupils of Hod-ya's eyes flared with a violet light. "Having a messenger to run the maze is merely a convenience at this point—not really necessary. And you will provide such morale-building entertainment for the masses as they celebrate the coronation of their new ruler.

"Scrimmit, you know what to do. Oh, and wrap this around her. We can't have her traipsing about the palace in that rag, can we? And find some footwear for the girl; we don't want her coming up lame before she accomplishes her task."

The lead dronnet clicked his heels and slapped his chest armor. His raspy voice was barely audible as he opened his mouth, "Yes'm." He took the garment from Hod-ya's hand and passed it to Dancel, then cast his gaze about the guard station of the cell until he spied among various articles of clothing and what-not some old leather boots that had been abandoned by unfortunate former occupants. They looked a couple of sizes too large but would have to do.

Without another word, Hod-ya spun around and left with the other two dronnets trailing.

"Move." Scrimmit pointed toward the open door at the far end of the cell.

"What? Right now?" Dancel said, pulling the burlap work-dress down over her shoulders and smoothing out the skirt. "I can barely stand, let alone walk, thanks to the beating you gave me."

Scrimmit silently pointed at the doorway.

Rissa took Dancel by the arm. "We'd better do as he says. Hodya's not kidding about 'four days,' which means we really don't have much time to accomplish our assignment. I, for one, don't want to lose my feet."

Dancel tugged the worn, leather boots onto her feet. Her legs weren't quite as wobbly as they'd been a few minutes prior; and after a dozen paces, she was able to balance unaided. Scrimmit, holding a torch aloft, fell in behind the girls as they exited the cell and ascended the railing-less spiral stairway out of the dungeon's depths. It would be good to be in the fresh air and sunshine, even if it was only the courtyard and training fields. As they exited the dismal stairwell, instead of sunshine and warmth, snow flurries filled the air, though it was nearly mid-spring. Dancel shivered afresh.

Scrimmit led across the bailey and commons to an entry concealed under vines that led to the wall maze of the massive fortress.

Dancel appreciated the warm, dry garment over her damp Logon dress, as well as the ill-fitting boots on her feet.

"What's so special about four days?" Dancel whispered when Scrimmit turned to observe soldiers drilling on the field.

"Ssss, not now," Rissa whispered, giving a quick nod toward the dronnet. "Tell you later."

Dancel risked whispering once more, "Words of the word?"

Rissa tapped her skirt that swept almost to the ground.

Dancel bowed her head and smiled, despite her split, puffy lips. Hod-ya had been fooled again! Even so, the task of teaching Rissa the maze in only four days was daunting. Inside these castle walls were dozens of false doors and endless passages leading nowhere. These had to be memorized, or Rissa would become hopelessly lost, possibly even perish in those musty confines of the wall maze devised to ensnare invaders. The only other person who knew the entire labyrinth well was Hod-ya herself.

The three entered under a black-stone archway to a secluded section of wall, where a faint outline of a door was barely visible behind the tangled vines. The girls turned to Scrimmit. "Do you have the keys?" Dancel asked.

"Oh, wait . . . " Rissa said, "I think I do. Hod-ya gave me this key ring before you were interrogated. She withdrew a ring of some sixty keys from her pocket. "I-I'm afraid I don't know which one to use . . . " She handed them to Dancel.

Dancel took the key ring and selected the largest one. "This one opens all doors that lead outside the castle walls. The others are etched to match raised markings found in the beginning of each significant passageway." Seeing Rissa's puzzlement, Dancel paused. "Don't worry, I'll show you how to recognize which keys open which doors in each tunnel as we get to them. The hardest part is learning which portals and passages are false, leading to confusing, circuitous routes or deadly unseen traps and pitfalls. By the way"—she turned to Scrimmit—"are you allowed to know these secrets?"

Scrimmit made a noise that was a cross between a growl and a hiss.

Rissa asked, "Was that a yes or a no?"

"Girls, attend to business; obey Hod-ya."

"Wow, I bet that's more words than he's spoken all year," taunted Dancel.

A low growl emitted from the dronnet, followed by, "Open door."

"Please don't rile him," Rissa said. "I need to learn this; and if he's agitated, I won't be able to keep my mind on what I'm doing."

Dancel nodded. She leaned her body's full weight against the door. Its rusty hinges groaned open. The passage was in absolute darkness until Scrimmit's torch entered. The ceiling and walls were overhung with cobwebs as far down the corridor as they could see.

Rissa drew back. Dancel took her elbow, saying, "Don't be afraid. I learned long ago that as long as you have a torch—or some other source of light—you won't be bothered."

"Really?" Rissa's round eyes studied Dancel's face.

"Trust me. Here, Scrimmit, let me have that torch, since I know where I'm going."

Scrimmit reluctantly handed the torch to Dancel. "No tricks."

Dancel rasped in mock imitation, "No tricks."

Scrimmit partially withdrew his scimitar from its scabbard.

Rissa looked nervously from the dronnet to Dancel.

Dancel tugged Rissa's arm as she led down the tunnel. "Come on. This is the main entry that, more or less, goes around inside the castle's perimeter walls, turning only where walls join."

"What about these doors?" Rissa pointed left and right as they passed a dozen closed doors on either side.

"False trails leading to pitfalls and traps. In fact, down the first leg of this corridor, none of these doors lead anywhere, except to snares and traps."

The trio traipsed down the corridor until they came to a "T."

"Which way?" Rissa asked.

"Well, we'll go to the right first. Each way leads to different parts of the castle, but we'll start with the right side. None of these doorways are significant until we reach the end. The door at the very end opens to a steep ramp that descends into the bowels of the palace, where the lower kitchen serves food to the unfortunate inmates. I guess we'd better go all the way down and let Caldon know you're taking over my position."

"Is that necessary?" Rissa asked.

"I think so. Since you've been there, it will help you get oriented, so you can plot other locations from that point. We won't return the same way."

Dancel led off, holding the torch high enough to burn through the cobwebs draped across their path. Their visit to the lower kitchen was brief; then they passed through other dingy passages of the castle's foundation. Dancel tried to teach Rissa her memorization system—which doors led to "safe" chambers and which led to a vast underground labyrinth of unending false trails. Such trails, Dancel told her, could lead wanderers to get lost and die a lingering death of dehydration or else tumble blindly into spiked pits or waterdragon dens.

It was late afternoon by the time Dancel opened a secret panel that led into the womens' dormitory. The two weary girls slipped out of the tunnel and plopped down on the nearest cots. "Always check through that little spy hole to make sure no one is present when you use this entry."

Rissa nodded.

"Let me quiz you now," said Dancel, "to see how much you've retained and what we need to rehearse tomorrow."

"Not waste time," Scrimmit rasped as he followed the girls through the secret panel. "Three days left."

"If I don't know what she remembers, it will all be wasted time. Don't you understand?" Dancel fearlessly stared into the dronnet's half-masked visage. Somehow, knowing she was slated to die when her task was completed settled her fears. And she had an abiding sense of Logon's reassurance. What could man, a dronnet, or Hod-ya do to her that couldn't be undone when Logon rode forth to claim his kingdom? "We're tired and need to rest. If she does well, I'll show her the upper tier of tunnels after supper; that shouldn't take much time. Then we can get a fresh start tomorrow. Now leave us alone. Don't you have to report to your mistress or something? We'll be right here, reviewing."

Scrimmit stared for a moment at Dancel, then extended a gloved hand and demanded, "Keys."

"I need them to make sure Rissa knows which ones we've covered and where they go, not to mention going to the upper tier after the evening meal."

Scrimmit stood resolute. "Keys."

Dancel bit her lip. "Oh, all right; but don't blame me if she gets confused and her training takes longer—it'll be your fault." She handed the key ring over.

Scrimmit pointed a finger at Dancel and said, "No tricks."

Dancel mimicked his raspy voice. "No tricks."

The back of Scrimmit's hand landed on Dancel's cheek. The room spun around as a dark pall momentarily blurred Dancel's vision as she hit the floor.

"Hod-ya say, 'Keep girl alive.' You alive, for now." Scrimmit turned and headed for the doorway at the far end of the dorm, keys jangling from his hand.

Rissa knelt beside Dancel and cradled her head. "Dancel, are you all right? Let me help you up."

Dancel spat out some blood. "That . . . was foolish. I'm okay. Wait till the room stops spinning."

"Well, then, let me try to recount the keys you showed me." Rissa counted off on her left hand with her index finger. "The smallest set belongs to the galley just above the lower kitchen, with only doors five and seven active; the rest are deadly traps. Then there's the thick keys. Uh . . . they go to, uh—"

"The soldiers' barrack immediately behind the walls. Almost all of them open to important places in the military compound. If you make a mistake, you can always dodge back into the tunnels and try the next one. There are no traps in that section—just in case any soldiers or sharifs wander into the maze, they won't get killed or lost. The doors that don't open are just sealed and have nothing behind them."

"Right, I remember."

"And the long tunnel? Do you remember the key for that tunnel?"

"Did we go down that tunnel? I don't seem to recall . . ."

"No, we didn't; we passed by its opening. I pointed down the dark corridor and told you it was rarely used. I was hardly ever sent there; in fact"—Dancel checked the dormitory around them to make sure they were alone—"I sometimes went down there to talk to Logon and toll my sword. But until you get more familiar with the lay of the maze, I advise you to avoid that tunnel. There's only one special key that opens one door at the end of that tunnel to the outside. Every time I went down there, I got a creepy feeling, as if tophets or cusps were watching. Oh, and there's a wide hole in the floor that stretches nearly wall to wall. I don't know what's down below; but sometimes, an eerie, luminous green mist rises out of the hole. Other times, it's blacker than midnight; and I hear things growling as if rising up from the bowels of the earth. Whatever the emperor keeps down there, it sounds quite fierce."

"And you're the only one besides Hod-ya that has the run of these tunnels?"

"Well, not quite. Various officials and some dronnets have limited permission to use certain sections of the wall maze that pertain to their stations; however, they're restricted from other parts of the maze. Only you will have keys to the entire maze—and, of course, Hod-ya."

"And those keys with the tiny, embossed white dot on the top? I forget—where do they lead?"

"Ah, those lead to the catwalk high above the foundry and to the outside doorway on the other side. I didn't take you all the way there because I was afraid Scrimmit would suspect that's how I sneak out of the castle. If you go that way, you must be brave. At any moment, someone working the furnaces and bellows below could look up and see you, especially if you make any noise. And then there are huge bats that roost in the rafters over the catwalk that might swoop down at you out of curiosity. Don't worry, though. They're harmless."

Rissa shivered. "Ooh, I despise bats."

"They're not so bad. Better company than most of the people in the palace." Dancel giggled.

Rissa laughed, covering her mouth.

The door at the end of the dorm opened; and Marga, chief of the kitchen crew, barged in, towing some poor girl by the ear and berating her with every step. "And if I ever catch you stuffing your face with those dainties again, I'll do more than put you in stocks; I'll slice off your nose and make you eat it. Do you understand me?"

Rissa and Dancel tried to stifle their laughter because they knew Marga didn't mean a word of it.

"And what are you two doing, lollygagging about in the middle of the day? Oh, it's you Dancel—and Rissa. Dancel, what happened to you?"

"Haven't you heard? I had a little disagreement with Hod-ya."

Marga let loose of the girl's ear lobe and instead cuffed her lightly on top of the head. "Now, get back to work before I follow through with my threats." The girl scampered back into the kitchen without a backward glance. Marga sat and examined Dancel's bruised face and arms. "Ntch, ntch, I warned you, didn't I? I said this secret-sword thing you insisted on doing was going to get you in trouble. And you'll come to the same end, Rissa, if you don't learn from her mistakes."

Rissa's eyes widened. "You know?"

"Of course, I know. Nothing goes on in my kitchen that I don't know."

"You didn't know about Jeda."

Marga looked penetratingly at Dancel. "No, no, I didn't know about Jeda. She pulled a fast one on me there. Say, you aren't cooking up something like that are you? If you are, I'll have to report you; or I'll face Hod-ya's wrath myself."

"Not to worry, Marga," said Dancel. "I'm training Rissa to take over my duties."

"And then what?" Marga's face drew close to Dancel's. She frowned, and the flour embedded in Marga's forehead cracked into furrows.

Dancel lowered her eyes to the bed's coverlet. "Well, if I'm successful in teaching Rissa in the next three days, I'm promised a swift, relatively painless execution. If not . . . "

Marga sat back. "I see." Turning to Rissa, she said, "And are you learning?"

"I . . . I hope so."

"She has a rudimentary understanding," said Dancel. "By the time our days are up, she'll know enough to figure the rest out for herself."

"But, three more days? That's all she's giving you—three days?" Marga stood, hands on hips. "That's ridiculous. The maze can't be learned in three days! Not even a rudimentary grasp of it." Marga's face reddened.

"It's under control, Marga." Dancel stood. "Like I keep telling you, Logon will work it out."

Rissa's mouth dropped open. "You . . . you speak openly to her about Logon?"

Dancel looked over at Rissa. "She has to know, too. Everyone needs to be confronted with the truth, or they'll perish—especially now that the prophecies are coming true."

"Well, your Logon has let you get in a fine stew now, hasn't he?"

"Please, let us pierce your heart, Marga. Then you'll see."

"I'm too set in my ways, child. Not that I don't believe you, but I'd never fit in with you kingsmen. No, I'll take my chances."

"Then you have no chance."

"For sure, I'll have no chance if Hod-ya catches us talking like this!" Marga shook her head and retreated to the kitchen to find someone to berate.

Dancel and Rissa sat silently for several moments, staring at the floor. Then Rissa lifted her eyes. "Aren't you afraid?"

Dancel nodded. "I'd be liar if I said no. Though I loathe the pain, I trust Logon will help me bear it."

Tears brimmed in Rissa's eyes. "I fear getting revealed as Ecclessite, too, and will suffer the same or a worse fate."

Dancel laid a hand on Rissa's shoulder. "When the time comes, you'll find the strength. Who knows, mayhap Logon will effect your escape before that happens."

CHAPTER THIRTEEN

AT THE DAWN'S FIRST GRAY rays, Scrimmit intruded into the scullery maid's dormitory and stood as a silent sentinel over Dancel and Rissa as they slept side by side in separate cots. Outside, a crow winged past the dorm window croaking to the advent of day, upon which Scrimmit reached down and yanked a tress of each girl's hair, bringing them instantly awake and not in the best of moods.

"Not waste time. Teach maze." He thrust the key ring at Rissa.

Thus, Dancel and Rissa were in the tunnels even before breakfast was served anywhere in the castle—indeed, even before Marga rousted her kitchen staff from their slumber.

"Now, these tunnels," Dancel instructed, "are color-coded with the keys. Of course, if you've been dispatched without permission to use torchlight, you'll have to identify the keys by the way they feel, like you did in the other tunnels. Match them with the embossed codes where I showed you, just above the floor on the inside of each doorjamb."

"Oh, Dancel, I'll never be able to distinguish so many keys by the way they feel."

"Yes, you will. You must."

"But they all feel exactly the same." Rissa fretfully rubbed several keys between her thumb and fingers.

Dancel's hand closed over Rissa's. "That's because you're trying to learn them all at once. One tunnel at a time, one passage at a time, one doorway at a time." Then Dancel leaned close and whispered, "Don't forget to ask the Advisor."

Scrimmit seized Dancel by the throat, lifting and pinning her against the mold-splotched wall. "No secrets, no tricks." He held her suspended for a full minute, her ill-fitting boots threatening to fall off before he finally let her drop and catch her breath.

Rissa froze, eyes wide.

Dancel sank to her knees, massaging her throat, rasping for breath. Her eyes filled with tears, and her body trembled. For several minutes, she was unable to speak.

Rissa bent to assist. "Dancel, are you all right?" She grasped Dancel's wrists and hoisted her to her feet.

Dancel sputtered, coughed twice, and drew a deep breath. "Yes, I'm okay." Then turning to Scrimmit, she narrowed her eyes and rasped, "If you ever touch me again, I'll lead you to the hall of turnstones; and the two of us will slip away from you—and I know just how to do it, too, leaving you to wander lost and alone with no hope of ever finding your way out. Do you hear me?"

Scrimmit responded with a deep growl but made no aggressive moves.

"How would we just disappear?" Rissa whispered.

Dancel nodded at Scrimmit as he stood at bay. "He knows what I'm talking about. There are stone slabs that reach from floor to ceiling, balanced on pivots comprising an entire section of wall in certain interior passages. When slight pressure is applied in the right spot, they open to another passage, leaving whoever was with you in a dead-end passageway all alone with no way out."

The dronnet bent down till he was face to face with Dancel. His breath stank like rotted meat. "Breakneck. No tricks. Who Advisor?"

"I was just reminding her to ask *advice* before entering a section of the maze if she felt unsure of her way; that's all. Next time I see Hod-ya, I'm reporting your lack of restraint."

Scrimmit hissed in the blackguards' weird manner of laughing. "Teach maze."

The girls went down the passageway discussing various doorways and alternate tunnels with Scrimmit tagging along behind, staying closer than usual, just in case Dancel meant to follow through on her threat of abandoning him in some darkened tunnel. Darkness wouldn't normally be a problem, for dronnets develop a *"second sight"* during their conditioning; however, even that *second sight* needs a minimum of natural light. These maze tunnels were completely void of even the minutest hint of light; if Dancel disappeared, he'd be as blind as the proverbial eyeless *gringer* fish occasionally caught along the outer coasts by the seaside caves.

After an hour of reviewing doorways in a particularly long tunnel, Dancel turned to face Scrimmit. "We're hungry. We haven't eaten yet, as you might have a care to remember."

Scrimmit stood motionless; even by the light of the torch, the girls saw only dark slits where eyes should've been.

"Come on, Rissa." Dancel grabbed her friend's wrist. "This way to the lower kitchen." Still holding the torch, the pair trotted down the tunnel, leaving Scrimmit a few paces behind before he gave chase.

There was enough distance between themselves and the dronnet that Dancel felt safe whispering, "I've got to make my escape today, Riss. The way he choked me back there shows I will no longer be needed once I've taught you the main pathways. You have enough basic knowledge to explore and learn the other sections on your own.

Hod-ya probably thinks you'll be able to figure out the seldom-used tunnels later."

"Oh, Dancel, I'm frightened . . . What if he—"

"He won't. We'll be at Caldon's kitchen in a few turns. When we get our bowls of mush, I need you to create a diversion by 'accidently' spilling yours on one of the workers. Can you do that?"

Rissa, trotting alongside, nodded.

"Good. Prolong the commotion as long as you can," Dancel instructed. "Goodbye. I doubt we'll meet again this side of Splendora. Remember the pattern I've shown you; you'll figure the rest of the maze out."

Tears welled in Rissa's eyes as she inadvertently sobbed, trying to cover it up with a fake cough. She dropped a step behind Dancel, wiped the tears from her face, and whispered, "King's road to you."

Dancel came to a halt at a nondescript portion of stone wall, pressed her hand along a rough seam, and stood back as the stone swung silently inward. Scrimmit arrived, lividly threatening Dancel for leaving him behind, but did nothing to follow up on his threats.

"Bet you didn't know this portal to the lower kitchen existed, did you, Scrimmit?" Dancel stepped inside, followed closely by Rissa and Scrimmit. The torch lit the narrow tunnel, revealing gobs of cobwebs dangling from ceiling to floor. Dancel swiped the torch back and forth, up and down, burning away as much of the gossamer webbing as she could, ducking her head, covering her hair with her free hand. Rissa did the same with both hands, scrunching her face in disgust. Occasionally, a spider sizzled as it was caught in the torch's flame. Scrimmit followed in the girls' wake, not quite reaping the benefit of the cleared path due to his height. They traveled thus for several score paces until Dancel paused again and pressed her hand on an inlaid, hand-sized rock in the wall. A stone panel swung open, revealing a torch-lit room with a nonplused Caldon staring blankly at them and holding a dipper over a tray of empty bowls.

"Are we in time for breakfast?" Dancel waltzed into the steamy kitchen.

Caldon, head of the lower kitchen staff, recovered quickly. "Hmmph! Come bustin' in here any time yer pleases, 'spectin ter git fed wi'out helpin' do any work." Caldon plopped her dipper into a bowl of mush. "Me thought yer was outta sorts wi' the powers thet be's." She slopped the dipper of mush into a bowl. "S'posin' he wants ter et, too?" she nodded at the dronnet. If she was amazed at their discovering her kitchen had a secret entry, she didn't let on.

Two other helpers staring open-mouthed stood nearby, dippers hovering over bowls on the rack.

"Git back ter work, yer nitwits. Aincha ne'er seen dronnets come through a wall afore?" Caldon snapped. Then to Dancel and Rissa, she said, "Help yerselves; ain't nobbut gonna wait on yers."

"Thank you very much, m'lady," Dancel did a sarcastic curtsy with a wink in her eye directed at Rissa. "I believe I'll have the eggs grandee and some of those croissants with some butter and elderberry jam. What'll you have, Rissa?"

Rissa, apprehensively anticipating her role in Dancel's escape, replied, "Uh, I . . . I'll have the . . . the s-s-s-same, I guess."

"Izzat right? Eggs grandee an' croissants, eh? Yer kens right well all yer'll git is mush." Caldon turned back to her duties. "Fruity as bats, all o' yers," she muttered.

Dancel handed the torch over to Rissa, picked a bowl of mush off the racks, and slipped past Caldon, flitting toward the far end of the kitchen. "Spoons still kept down here?" she called over her shoulder.

Rissa blocked the aisle as she picked up a bowl of steaming mush from the rack. "I thought the spoons were up here," she said, spinning around and colliding with Scrimmit as he tried to force his way around her to keep near Dancel. But Dancel had already reached the far recesses of the kitchen and was rooting through the lower drawers.

Rissa's steaming bowl of mush was knocked out of her hand and splashed all over the dronnet's jerkin, soaking through to his skin. The bowl clattered to the floor and spun on its rim for several seconds, making a *wuka-wuka-wuka* noise.

Scrimmit yelped like a scalded hog as he pulled his shirt away from his blistering chest. He staggered backward, caught his heel on an edge of the table leg, and fell into a huge, bubbling pot of mush. The pot tipped over taking Scrimmit with it, feet kicking in the air, arms flailing wildly.

Rissa turned just in time to see a stone panel in the cookery's shadowy end close, leaving only a featureless, stone wall.

"Gaaah!" Scrimmit's anguished cry resounded down into the lower prison as he extricated himself and scraped off the seething mush.

Caldon stepped between Rissa and the dronnet, brandishing her dipper menacingly as she said over her shoulder, "Best yer makes yerself scarce, girl."

Rissa didn't need to be told twice. She gripped the key ring tightly in her hand and headed down the tunnel into the lower prison. She fairly flew past cellblock after cellblock of curious inmates wondering what had caused the painful bellow they'd heard and if they'd be fed on time.

Rissa remembered this path from when she'd been assigned to dole out the contents of the cart to these hopeless denizens of Lurcan's dungeon. She was able to cope with the stench and squalor, though she'd never get used to it. She racked her mind trying to remember which key Dancel had used to open the portal on the second level. Was it this one or one of those? She had dropped the torch in her collision with Scrimmit, so the only light she now had was from the smoky candle-sconces placed every dozen paces along the wall. How was she going to find the right key before Scrimmit came hunting for her? She must hide in some secret tunnel before he recovered enough to pursue her. Surely, he must suspect that she was a willing participant in Dancel's escape. Rissa shuddered; Hod-ya would be merciless.

Something gently bumped her shin as she rounded a corner. Her Child of the Stars! A wave of calm swept over her at remembering its presence. She could use the light from her blade to sort out which key was which when she reached the stairwell where no one—neither prisoners nor guards nor kitchen servers—would see as she consulted her oracle-sword.

Halfway to the second level, she paused on the spiral staircase and listened for telltale footfalls of pursuers. When confident she was alone, she withdrew the sword from her skirts and held the keys close to the glowing sword tip. The key she wanted, as she recalled, was to a doorway seldom used on the second tier of cells. That key had a peculiar nick in the top—Dancel had emphasized that—for it was the only mark that set that key apart from several others that fitted doorways elsewhere. After shuffling through a score of keys, she found the one she sought. Gasping, she clutched it to her heart, letting the other keys dangle and jingle like tiny bells as she scampered up the steps.

She located the obscure doorframe, groped for the keyhole, and inserted the key. Tumblers clicked into place as she twisted the key.

She heaved her slight frame against the door; and after second and third attempts, it gave way, opening to a lightless void. She closed the door behind, leaning against it to maintain equilibrium; there was enough light from her sword to illumine her environs. She was safe, at least for the moment.

~

Dancel slipped through the gap in the wall, glancing over her shoulder one last time at the commotion in the kitchen as she stepped inside the lightless tunnel and released the counterweight shutting the stone portal.

"Logon, please protect Rissa."

Then she was off at a trot down the familiar path, having often come to this portion of the maze for a rendezvous with Logon. She'd never before entered through this portal but knew of the entry's existence and that it led to where she so often went to toll her sword and commune with her liege. But now she had no sword. She knew this passage well enough even without light; she could identify her location by lightly feeling for the wall's cracks and crannies as she went, but now she had no keys. She was restricted to main-trunk tunnels connected to other tunnels inside the wall that eventually led to the labyrinth. Without keys, she wouldn't be able to slip in and out of the palace for food and water—except for that one remote tunnel that extended into the farthest reaches of the outer wall, the one with a gaping hole in the middle of the floor and the mysterious green mist that occasionally rose up through it. She could perhaps collect some of the discarded crockery scattered about in various tunnels to collect and condense the mist that arose from that hole to quench her thirst, but what about food? Dancel slumped against the wall and slid to the floor, trying to recollect in her mind's eye the turns and bends of various tunnels.

She sighed. "Oh, Logon, I'm in a fix now."

Her hand went instinctively to the folds under her skirts, where she usually stowed her sword. She tilted her head back and sighed again. "What am I to do without my sword? No keys, no light . . . " She closed her eyes for just a moment.

~

Rissa, hiding inside the doorway on the second tier of the dungeon, had barely moved since coming into this dark, silent haven, unsure where to go or what to do. It was possible, in her stunned state of mind, that she'd been there for hours. They must be searching for her by now. She uncovered her sword, and her finger touched a faint rune:

In the Valley of Death, shadows surrounding,
When all seems lost, enemies pursuing,
Your Captain is near, His presence abounding.
Quake not, nor fear, His love is ensuing.
Deliverance will come with feasting unending.
Ointment will flow, eternally blessing.
So look up and trust and know his attending.
His own hear his voice and onward go pressing.

Rissa laid her toller on her lap. Calm embraced her, despite the dire circumstances. She had her sword and the keys to the maze, but she didn't know the lay of the tunnels. Wandering about, she might just suddenly pop into Hod-ya's own rooms or offices of other high officials who were, undoubtedly, combing the castle and dungeon for

Dancel and her at this very moment. She got to her feet, tucked her toller away, and let just enough sword point poke from beneath her skirt to illuminate a path for her feet; she'd hide until hunger drove her out to seek sustenance. Perhaps by then, the furor over Dancel's escape would have died down . . . Only then would she emerge and risk capture.

Before she took a dozen steps, however, the door latch behind her clicked; and the heavy, wooden door swung open, filling the tunnel with reddish-orange torch light. There in the glare stood Hod-ya and two dronnets. "Ah-ha! There you are!"

Rissa's knees went weak, and she collapsed. Her sword retracted back into her skirts, seemingly of its own accord.

The two dronnets stepped instantly to her side, dragging her to the entry.

"Gently, m'lads, gently," purred Hod-ya. "She's been through a harrowing experience and is, no doubt, scared half out of her mind." Hod-ya put a hand under Rissa's chin and lifted her face. "I don't blame you for that crafty girl's escape or Scrimmit's clumsiness. Caldon told me how Dancel took advantage of an opportunity created by that oaf of a dronnet. And you, poor thing . . . you do have the keyring, don't you?"

Rissa found herself unable to speak, so she just nodded.

"Good." Hod-ya's voice turned syrupy. "Probably thought I'd blame you, so you came here and hid. Well, I'm aware of the stress you're under, trying to learn the maze in such a short time; and I understand why you felt the need to run. But I assure you, I attach no blame to you. Rest assured that Scrimmit will pay for his carelessness." She released Rissa's chin. "I have the only other set of keys to the maze. There was another set once; but unfortunately, they got lost somewhere. I suppose I'll have to take some time myself to instruct you. But you've had enough excitement for today. Go to your dorm and rest. We'll start early in the morning. There's been a setback in the coronation plans, anyway, so I have a few extra days to help you."

Rissa's face paled. "M'lady?"

"Tut, tut, don't you worry. We'll come across that ungrateful wench as we go from tunnel to tunnel. After all, where can she go but to the few non-keyed portals that lead nowhere? When we find her, I'll let you choose the exact mode of revenge for abandoning you."

Rissa nodded politely but was nonetheless stunned at Hod-ya's change of character. What was she up to? The runesong crossed her mind, and she was again comforted.

Hod-ya didn't notice Rissa's positive attitude, for she was already outside the tunnel on the stairway, instructing her dronnets to extend the search for Dancel.

CHAPTER FOURTEEN

LED BY SAYGUS AND FROBASCH, the kingsmen formed a grid pattern "V" and ventured into the mushroom forest—or, as Frobasch, referred to it, the *"fungal jungle."* The men fanned out to either side ten paces apart so as not to lose sight of each other in the darkness amid the thick stalks. Upon entering, Frobasch demonstrated harvesting the tender parts of fungus stalks that hadn't yet turned *woody*, thus they foraged as they explored the forest.

For several "afternoons," they systematically ranged up and down the coastline to learn the lay of the land. They were indeed stranded on an archipelago of sandbars and small islands that were easily accessed by wading, as Frobasch had related. But the island where Saygus and his crew had landed was the largest and, therefore, their primary campsite. A couple of men fashioned stone-slingers with which to bring down any smaller, fur-bearing creatures that lived in ground burrows or scampered on the domed tops of "mushroom trees," thereby supplementing their diet of edible fungi, turtles, and fish with small "critters." They also found that a form of sea kelp that drifted from the deeper waters off the outermost island, when prepared with turtle meat, was quite tasty.

"We're not far from the hole I was dropped through," said Frobasch.

"I'd like to see it," Saygus replied, "since it's the only connection to the upper world we seem to have at this point."

"Like I said, I thought there was no other way back up except by sea; and since I've no means of constructing a vessel that would stay afloat, I felt that that hole in the ceiling must be the sally port through which kingsmen forces would invade Lurcan's palace. After exploring these islands more thoroughly, I'm convinced there's no alternative; we must find a way to get up to that hole."

Saygus studied the vaulted ceiling above as it dimly reflected the flickering green of the luminescent algae-laden waves. "Can we even locate the hole in this darkness?"

"It took me a while; I often retreated here during the first weeks of my banishment, hoping they'd throw something down the hole that I could use. I guess that tunnel is rarely used. Anyway, I lay on my back and stared for long hours until I noticed a small void where the flickering green light doesn't reflect. It's difficult to tell how high it is or precisely the size of the hole. About twice a day, the tide rolls in, sometimes bringing with it a fog that obscures the ceiling. Once I thought I saw torchlight; but it was so brief, I wasn't sure if it was a torch or just wishful thinking."

"Take me there," Saygus said. Then he turned to his crew and ordered, "You men, continue scouring the forest for food. We'll meet later back at the campfire."

Frobasch led Saygus through the stand of mushroom-like trees until they heard the lapping of waves on the shore. The sloshing waves grew louder as they drew near, and Saygus noted a faint green glow from sea algae flashing through the fungi stalks. Frobasch trotted ahead along the shoreline, staying well back from the water. "Not much farther," he called over his shoulder.

Saygus scanned the *greencaps*, watching for the mysterious, still unseen Gwollerbect. The two weeks he and his men had spent with Frobasch had failed to yield any sightings of the monster or even his footprints.

"It's up there, somewhere," Frobasch pointed. "If we sit long enough, our eyes will adjust; and we'll be able to spot a very dark area. That'll be the hole I was dropped through." Frobasch sat on the pebbly beach, craning his neck upward.

Saygus started to withdraw his Child of the Stars.

Frobasch laid his hand on Saygus' wrist. "No, don't do that. Your eyes won't adjust if the light of your sword is shining in them."

"Trust me." Saygus winked. He withdrew his sword and held it aloft. Its blue light reflected off the choppy sea and somewhat less off the distant ceiling. "Is that it, over there?" Saygus pointed to a ceiling section farther down from where Frobasch had first indicated. "Get your sword out and lay its tip on mine."

"Wha—"

"Just do it."

Frobasch leaned to the side and reluctantly drew his sword. "You're aware, of course, that this light will act like a beacon for the Gwollerbect if he's nearby."

"We haven't seen it since we've been here, have we? If it even knows about us, it's probably afraid to tackle two or more armed men at once. Now, lay your sword tip on mine."

Frobasch joined his sword to Saygus'. For a moment, nothing happened; then a beam of blue light flared from their conjoined swords.

"Tilt the sword with mine so the beam shines up yonder—that's it, more to the right, more, more . . . There, hold it." A black spot loomed in the center of a round beam of light. "Is that the hole?"

"It . . . it must be. I've never seen it this clearly before, but this is definitely the area where I was dropped."

"How deep is the water directly underneath?"

"Uh, when the tide is in, about six or seven feet." Frobasch was awed by the sight of the portal through which he'd been dropped to this forsaken underworld.

"And the footing beneath—is it sandy, stony, muddy . . . "

"It's sand with some scattered stones. What are you thinking? That hole must be seventy feet high. How would we ever get up there?"

"Let's set a marker on the beach, so we don't waste time looking for this exact spot whenever we come back. Let's pile stones into a pyramid."

Frobasch and Saygus bent to the task of gathering and stacking stones into a mound. "I don't like this, Saygus. It leaves a marker for the you-know-what."

"It won't know what it's for, even if it does come across it. Now, what building materials have you come across down here?"

"Why, what do you want build?"

Saygus looked upward. "We need a framework tower to climb up to the hole; and since that hole is in one of the fortress tunnels, that will be our invasion point."

"A tower? That high? Won't the sand underneath shift under the weight of it?" Frobasch rubbed his chin.

"Not if we anchor it on a firm base, like those larger rocks along the shore and in the shallows. Now, what building materials have you come across? Have you tried constructing anything out of mushroom stalks?"

Frobasch shook his head. "No."

"Well, we need to try," Saygus remarked as the two tucked their swords away after finishing the foot-high pebble mound. "Back to camp. We'll start experimenting right away with tough mushroom stalks."

Upon reaching camp, Saygus appointed different squads to various tasks: The first team was to cut down rigid mushroom stalks for constructing the upper levels of the tower; the second team was to haul the stalks to the worksite; and another group was to shape the stalks at the worksite into length and width of usable lumber.

"Search for older, thinner stalks that have turned *woody*," Saygus advised. "Jemele, Frobasch, and I will explore the coastline for long, tough strands of kelp to use for binding the mushroom-stalk logs together. Everything will have to be cured and tested, but I think we can find enough suitable materials to build a tower high enough to reach the hole. Tomorrow, we'll go to the beach and dismantle what's left of our rafts and portage the poon logs and any usable vines to the work site to serve as our tower base. Those logs should still withstand water well enough to provide a solid foundation against the tides. We'll want to keep the mushroom stalks well out of the water, lest they get soggy."

"What about me?" asked Fleb. "You haven't assigned me to a squad."

Saygus placed his hand on Fleb's shoulder. "You guard the camp, keep the fire going, generally tidy up, prepare our meals, and relay communications should any teams report in with a progress report."

As planned, shortly after sword drills and a breakfast of select seaweed, mushroom chunks, turtle eggs, crabs, and fish, the eleven trekked to their landing site on the beach and set about dismantling the rafts. Afterward, they split up into their appointed teams and dispersed to their diverse tasks. Frobasch led Saygus and Jemele through the dunes parallel to the waterline behind long-running dunes to the far end of the island, where kelp beds flourished offshore.

"The longest kelp stalks are out in deep water," Frobasch pointed out at the sea. "I suggest we take turns leaving one of us ashore to keep watch here while two of us swim out and harvest the kelp."

"Maybe you should stand guard permanently while we dive," suggested Saygus, "since you alone know what to watch for. Your Gwollerbect encounters indicate he's a sly creature able to disguise his presence."

Frobasch nodded. "I'll keep my sword hidden and will only bring it out in the open and strike the water's surface if I see any sign of you-know-who; hopefully, you'll see the blue flash on the waves."

"We won't be out there long, and we'll keep our eyes turned toward shore. Any suggestion as to what manner of kelp we should harvest?"

Frobasch answered with a grin, "We can catch two fish with one pole; the 'leaves' we strip off the long, thin stalks will go nicely into the stewpot, while the stalks themselves will dry out in a couple of days if we keep working them to make them supple enough to use for bindings. They have a tough, stringy consistency as it is and only need to be dried and worked. But avoid stalks thicker than your thumb; they're too hard to work. You want the long, slender ones."

"Right," said Jemele. "The sooner we get started, the sooner we can get back to camp."

Saygus winked. "Let's go."

The two waded side by side chest-deep into the gentle waves. They came upon the front edge of the kelp forest, where the current sent the kelp stipes undulating toward the shore. Saygus and Jemele pulled themselves under water using the strands of the plant bases and found that with a hard tug, the holdfasts loosened. Soon, a dozen plants floated free, drifting shore-ward. Saygus and Jemele followed, only too glad to let the tide do the work.

Frobasch was surprised when his friends re-surfaced after such a short a time. "Couldn't hold your breath?" he called.

"We're done for now—don't want to harvest more than we can carry at any given time." Saygus waded ashore. "Now, the hard labor begins as we drag these twenty-foot-long plants to the campsite."

Saygus and Jemele splashed through the shallows and hoisted the thick end of the stalks to their shoulders. Frobasch garnered his share of the bounty, and the three trudged to base camp across the rises and hollows of the dunes, mindfully keeping out of sight of the shores.

"Strange flora and fauna in this underworld," said Jemele. "I always thought kelp needed sunlight to grow."

"Well, up on the surface, I guess it does," remarked Saygus. "But down here, who knows what resources King Elyon has created to sustain subterranean life. You'll notice that this kelp isn't green but orange, suggesting it's sustained by something other than light. At any rate, it meets our needs."

~

As the three continued across the dunes, a large, dark gray form silently glided some thirty yards offshore, passing the beach the men had just departed. It barely broke the water's surface as it swam the opposite way, as oblivious to the kingsmen that had just exited the waters as they were to it. But something had disturbed one of his feeding lairs. He had sensed unusual vibrations in the waters; some creature was tearing away the front lining of his kelp bed and would soon come to rue the deed.

~

A day later, while the men wrestled their salvaged poon logs beneath the hole into position for the tower's base, Osk's eyes caught the glint of something sparkly underwater. "Hullo, what's this?" He reached his hand into the water and withdrew the object from the rippling current, bringing it to his sword's tip for a fuller examination. "Hey, Saygus, look what I found."

"Hold on, just a minute, wait till I get this tied off." Saygus finished lashing a piece of cured kelp around an upright support connected to the second course of mushroom braces on the tower's base.

Osk waded out to the foursquare structure with its poon log struts wedged between rocks of the surf. "Here, take a look at this." He lifted the metallic item for Saygus to examine.

Saygus finished tying off another three-fold strand of kelp, wrapped his arms around the jointure, and tugged. "Guess that'll hold. Good thing there's no storms down here; this makeshift tower would never withstand a gale. Now, what are you babbling about, Osk?"

"What do you make of this?" He tossed the item up to Saygus.

Saygus caught it and sidled out on the beam where his affixed sword provided light for the workers. He held the object close to his blade. "Seems to be a key of some sort. Where'd you find it?"

"Yonder in the knee-deep shallows."

Saygus climbed down off the scaffolding and waded into the surf, taking his sword with him. "Let's look around and see if there are any more. Keep working on the tower, men; I'll be right back."

Osk showed Saygus where he'd found the key. The two men swept their weapons back and forth, examining the sandy bottom. "Hey! Here's another!" Osk stood upright displaying it for Saygus.

"I've got one too," Saygus plunged his hand into the surf to scoop up another key. "No, wait, there's two, three of them!" He looked over at Osk laughing, dangling the keys for others to see.

Others abandoned their tasks and joined in the search.

"Frobasch, you ever come across anything like these since you've been down here?" Saygus asked.

"No, I never came across anything man-made. Of course, I wasn't really looking either."

"What does it mean?" Jemele asked, splashing knee-deep in the search area, bending over and dipping his arms up to his elbows in water, sifting wet sand through his fingers.

"I haven't any idea." Saygus stood erect to stretch his back.

"So why waste precious time grubbing about in the sand if there's no purpose?" Fleb called from the shoreline.

Saygus twisted side to side. "I didn't say there was no purpose; I said I didn't know of any purpose. However, earlier today in my rune-tolling, while most of you were still asleep, I lit up a rune that posed a curious riddle."

"Got another," Bismeta said, triumphantly hold his find aloft.

"I've got two more," chimed in Benio.

"Riddle?" Flonkry probed. "I be's a riddle-solver extree-ordinaire. Tell me. Bet I guesses it afore anyone else."

"It's not that kind of riddle, Flonkry, though it will take some ciphering to grasp the meaning." Saygus thrust his hands back into the water and raked his fingers through the sand again. "If the riddle means what I think, we'll need all the keys we can find—and anything else we might dredge up. All hands, quit what you're doing on the tower and search this area thoroughly." He glanced overhead at the hole in the ceiling. "Unless I miss my guess, these keys weren't supposed to be down here."

For the next hour, the men combed the sandy bottom from tower to shore and back again, widening out to either side, making sure they hadn't missed anything of importance. By the end of the work period, they had found sixty-six keys, two key rings, and a kitchen knife with a broken blade.

"You want I should put these keys on the rings?" Jemele asked.

"Umm, I don't think so. We don't know much of anything about these keys; and if we mix them up, we may run into problems that'll take even more time to straighten out. Better wait and see what we can learn about them first, if anything," Saygus advised.

"Now, then, Gen'l," Flonkry reminded, "what about thet riddle?"

Saygus gave Flonkry a stern look for mentioning his rank, then said, "Tonight—we'll have a rune study about 'the riddle.'"

"Time for our study," Saygus announced as they cleaned up after their meal.

"And thet riddle? All day long, I been a hankerin' ter git my mind a workin' on it."

Saygus smiled and surveyed the eager faces of those pulling out swords and tollers. He hefted his own sword aloft, so the others could see where he was going to toll. "These runes, halfway down the blade, contain the sayings of the ancients. Logon whispered secrets to the seers and generals of old that weren't intended to be understood by casual seekers."

"Why would Logon do that?" Benio touched his toller to his sword's edge.

Saygus lay his sword across his lap and held the toller just above the runes he'd indicated. "King Elyon, his son Logon, and the Advisor are unfathomable in their being. Their ways, likewise, are inscrutable. He's allowed us to know that he is one being in three persons, but to understand . . . " He shrugged. "On the same token, though his ways and his plans are beyond our comprehension, he has deigned to reveal some of his secrets to his most trusted soldiers. Those secrets could be dangerous in the hands of raw recruits and non-committed warriors."

"Why is that?" Bismeta asked.

"Those secrets can unleash mighty, unseen weapons meant only to be used against enemies. Such power must not be divulged to unproven or unreliable men, who, for lack of dedication, might revert to Lurcanish ways, men such as Claygall. Use of such deep knowledge could cause severe harm, even among Logon's own armies—as in the case of Captain Sofista—because once given, that knowledge cannot be rescinded. It's like a river flooding its banks; the water rushes out, causes its effect, and cannot be recalled. Unless those who receive such power are utterly reliable, those powers could be put to selfish, nefarious uses. That's why Logon often taught in fables—so only those the Advisor enlightened could perceive his meaning. Many that follow Logon aren't yet totally committed to doing his will. Casual tollers of the runes will only glean what applies to them personally and to everyone generally. But the deeper plans of Elyon are held in reserve for those devoted enough to commit their entire life and being to seek and serve him. One of my favorite runes says:

Elyon, in his glory, has hidden secrets deep.
Kingly warriors only are given them to keep.

The more time you spend tolling your blade in communion with Logon, the more secrets the Advisor will reveal. So then, let's take a look at the enigma that lit up on my sword early this morning."

The squad applied tollers to the runes under study and slowly guided their files across the edge. For most of them, nothing happened; but Jemele's and Frobasch's runes began glowing a little brighter.

"Keep tolling; I never said it would be easy," Saygus encouraged.

The men struggled, honing their blades for half an hour without much change. Even the two lieutenants couldn't coax brighter light out of their swords.

"I be's readin' the runes but gits nobbut unnerstandin'," Flonkry groaned to no one in particular.

"That's because you're trying to grasp it with your mind." Saygus grinned. "You need not strive so hard; but at the same time, be on guard, lest any cusps whisper lies to your thoughts. If you keep your mind on Logon and trust the Advisor to guide your understanding, you'll be safe. That's why so many captains of various brigades read the same runes but get contradictory understandings. They think the will of Elyon can be apprehended by strenuously applying their minds to learning, but it's the Advisor's function to instruct. When Logon dictated runes to the original generals and the ancients, his meaning was precise and specific—often with various applications but only one meaning. Brigade leaders get into trouble when they put away the meaning Logon intended and alter it or unknowingly modify it. And that's why many deeper truths are kept from them; for if they disrespect what Logon and the Advisor breathed upon the swords, they're obviously not reliable enough to handle the mysterious runes."

The men bent back to their task again.

After several more moments, Saygus said, "Okay, put up your tollers. I see you're not getting anywhere. I'll give you as much insight as I'm at liberty to share. The first stanza goes:

'First comes a letter.
Second comes a word.
Third comes a sentence.
Then a paragraph is heard.
Fifth is a story,
Be it logic or absurd.'

Tell me what you discern from that." Saygus studied his charges. "Come on, venture your ideas."

"Well," Jemele drawled, "I see a progression from small to large to larger."

"Seems to be about learning your letters and writing," Osk observed.

"And counting, leastways to five," Bismeta shyly offered.

"Doesn't make any sense to me," Fleb said, laying his toller on the sand.

"Do the next stanza," Saygus urged, casting a disdainful eye at Fleb. "You're beginning to grasp the method of looking intently into Logon's words and seeing beyond what you would ordinarily see."

Frobasch read aloud:

'One is a key.
Two is a lock.
Three is a door,
Then a room full of stock.
Five is a passage,
A den-full who mock."

"All right." Flonkry stretched out his legs. "Here be's the same pergression from small ter large, an' I now kin see how yer linked usn's findin' them keys wi' yer earlier rune study an' all, but—"

"I see that fourths aren't specifically mentioned." Frobasch tapped the rune. "I mean, they're implied but not specifically mentioned. Is that significant?"

Saygus smiled. "Is it?"

Benio commented, "All this thinking makes me dizzy. Won't you just explain it?"

"I wish I could. Fact is, I have only a bare understanding myself. But we're at the first step. We have a key—or rather a set of keys—and there is a letter on each key."

"So, the two stanzas are connected." Jemele rubbed his chin. "I thought they were unrelated, obscure sayings of . . . I don't know what."

"The keys are marked? I didn't see any marks." Osk held a key up to his eyes.

"I did; my sword's blue light lit them up, revealing an ancient alphabet."

Frobasch held another key close to his sword. "I don't see any letters." Others gathered around peering at the keys in his hand, murmuring that they, likewise, saw no markings.

Saygus scooted over and lifted a key. Holding it up by the shank and tapping a jagged line on the bow he said, "Here, on the bow—the part you hold with your thumb and forefinger—is a mark intended to look like a scratch, but it's really a letter. I only know that because before I went to Logon's Rock, I studied ancient Carnalian cultures and came across relics of the culture that used this language."

"Do you understand the language?" Bismeta almost put his nose on the key searching for the mark.

"I think so," Saygus replied. "It's a very simple, even primitive form of communication. And"—he tilted his head upward to stretch his neck—"I wouldn't be surprised if we found that all sixty-six letters in that alphabet are on these sixty-six keys."

"Well, let's find out," Jemele said, taking a key and peering at the bow. After a few minutes, he put the key down and looked to Saygus. "I don't know what to look for. I can't find anything that even remotely resembles a letter. I guess you'll have to interpret it by yourself."

"I will tomorrow, as all of you get back to work on the tower."

"That reminds me." Osk rose to his feet. "We need more strands of kelp."

Saygus nodded. "How are the vines from our rafts holding up?"

"Well enough; below the water line, they work better than dried kelp," Bismeta answered. "Tomorrow, we should finish securing the poon-log foundation. Those logs have resisted the water well and are firmly set and bolstered by the large rocks we found. The absence of serious tides helps a lot."

Saygus, Frobasch, and Fleb trudged along the sandy trail heading toward the kelp beds, mindfully ducking well below the brow of the dunes lest they be spotted from the sea. "Okay, we're close to water now, so tuck your swords away," Saygus instructed. "When we top the ridge, we'll have sufficient light from the algae in the water."

They crawled on hands and knees to the top of the last dune before the water's edge and peered out at the sea.

"All clear," Frobasch whispered. "I say we make a quick work of it."

"I'm all for that," agreed Fleb. "I get goosebumps just thinking about that Gwollerbect. The sooner we get back to constructing the tower, the better."

"It can just as easily show up there as here, you know," said Saygus.

"Like I needed to hear that," Fleb groaned.

"Yes, Fleb, you did need to hear that. Your attitude borders on endangering the mission. I thought you dealt with that after the *spidercats'* attack, but your moodiness is affecting your work and everyone else's morale. You'd better straighten up; or else, you'll likely be the first casualty."

Fleb bowed his head. "I know. I know, Saygus. I just can't seem to shake this gloominess."

"Keep your mind on Logon, recite runes you've memorized, consciously thank Logon for all his benefits. That's the only way any of us will defeat the cusps that muddle our minds."

"I'll try harder, Saygus."

"We'd better go," Frobasch urged. "The reaping field is further out since we've depleted the nearby kelp beds; it'll take us longer, especially since the tide won't help float our harvested stalks to shore from that far out, due to an off-shore current."

"Fleb, stay alert."

~

In the quiet darkness, disturbed only by the gentle lap of waves on the shore, Fleb selected a position offering a wide view of the coastline. Saygus and Frobasch had been gone a quarter of an hour, vanishing into the dim green illumination. Fleb faintly heard their splashes as they swam away. Then, all trace of them was gone. Fleb reached beneath his tunic and grasped his sword handle, keeping the lit part of his blade below the dune, lest it reveal his position.

Time dragged. Fleb strained his eyes into the greenish glow, looking for something to focus his eyes upon against the faint green background. He attuned his ears for the first hint of his fellow kingsmen returning from kelp harvest. Neither eye nor ear was rewarded. Another quarter of an hour inched past. A tingle at the base of his spine made him feel like he was being watched. His features scrunched; he turned side to side, checking the immediate area. Nothing. Yet his uneasiness continued; no matter which way he turned, he felt vulnerable.

"They should've been back by now," he muttered. "They must be on their way. Maybe they got disoriented so far from shore. Should I flash my sword to show my location? Dare I risk calling out? Oh, Logon . . . "

A large wave rolled ashore down past his lookout—unusual in this underworld environment, according to Frobasch. The hair on the back of Fleb's neck stood erect.

Several yards up the beach, there was a sudden crackling sound. Then some fifty feet to his left shimmering sparkles of yellow and red shot into the air. "Gwollerbect!" Fleb flipped over backwards behind the dune. At the same time, voices floated from the other side of the beach, accompanied by the slosh of someone wading through the surf.

"Fleb?" a voice called softly.

Fleb gritted his teeth. No, they mustn't call out. They mustn't alert the Gwollerbect to their presence . . .

CHAPTER FIFTEEN

DANCEL WENDED HER WAY ALONG the cavern, her fingertips brushing cobwebs away from the wall as she probed for features known only to her. This was the second day of her escape; she'd had no food nor water and had only slept in brief snatches curled up on the cold stone floor. She'd wandered the hallways and tunnels she thought she knew so well, only to discover that without her keyring and light from her sword she was almost as helpless as Rissa. Rissa . . . the thought of her friend's peril welled up in her mind, forcing aside all thought of her own jeopardy. How could Hod-ya not suspect Rissa's part in the escape? Had Scrimmit retaliated for blistering him with hot, steaming mush? Was Rissa at this very moment languishing in chains or undergoing unspeakable torture to answer for Dancel's whereabouts?

"Oh, Logon, let her not suffer for my mistakes." Her fingers found the bulge in the wall she sought, the one approaching the remote tunnel with the gaping hole in the center of the floor—the tunnel with the greenish, misty glow that mysteriously rose from time to time. Her other hand clutched a vase. She'd quite forgotten that she'd left it long ago in a passageway outside the lower kitchen, when she had been learning the maze; that was even before she'd met Logon. Hopefully, the vessel could collect enough condensation from the mists that arose through the floor's opening to assuage her thirst.

Despite being engulfed in pitch-blackness, Dancel noted a physical change in the atmosphere, the yawning maw of the tunnel lay just ahead. Cool air flowed from it into these stuffy passages; she sensed the open space from that seemingly pointless passage. Though it connected to another tunnel, there was only one other portal connected to it, and that was at the very end where it opened outside the walls of the palace on a nondescript alley via a small doorway. Dancel smiled as she turned into the cavern, still groping the walls to discern telltale bumps and hollows that preceded the pitfall. This was connected to the tunnel she and Jeda had once used when sneaking back into the castle after attending an underground kingsman meeting in the city. She'd tricked the guard into thinking he'd seen ghosts disappear when the two of them slipped inside the hidden portal.

The pit was still some ways off; nevertheless, in this jet-black darkness, it would be all too easy to lose sense of time and distance, especially famished and parched as she was, and not fully aware. The first time she encountered the gaping hole she had nearly tumbled into it. She'd been trying to learn the maze without light. Had it not been for faintly visible, green sparkles way down below . . .

Dancel had advanced down the tunnel thirty paces when she heard a distinct *click* echoing in the tunnel she'd just vacated. She dropped face down to the floor and held her breath, squeezing tightly into the juncture of floor and wall. The opening scrape of an ill-hung door followed, accompanied by a soft, reddish-orange torch light reflecting off stone walls. Who was in the tunnel? The nearest alcove where she might hide was still a hundred paces away. Dare she break and run for it and risk a commotion, no matter how slight?

Voices carried down the tubular passage. A soft, girlish voice droned indistinguishably, rising in pitch as if posing a question.

The voice that answered sent chills down Dancel's spine.

"That doesn't concern you, child," snapped Hod-ya. "You need only know this tunnel is here; it's seldom used except to dispose of . . . refuse." Hod-ya's cackling reverberated down the cavern as she laughed at her private joke, which echoed back in an eerie, grotesque, fading dissonance. "You're doing just fine, girl. Whatever that wench taught you seems to have served you well."

The pair stopped at the entry to the tunnel where Dancel lay on the floor hard-pressed against the passage wall. Hod-ya poked her torch arm's length into the tunnel but only looked at Rissa.

"Be careful if you ever go down there; a portion of the floor gave way decades ago after an earthquake and was never repaired. It's difficult to see even with a torch; if you're not careful, you could fall through."

"What lies beneath?"

"You don't want to know, trust me. But don't concern yourself; you'll have little reason to come this way."

Rissa stared into the passage.

Dancel feared she might be seen cringing against the wall in the flickering torchlight like a frightened mouse. As of now, Hod-ya was intent upon continuing down the main corridor; but if Rissa kept staring down the passage, it might draw Hod-ya's attention.

Dancel scarcely breathed.

"Come, girl, don't linger. There's nothing to see down there." Hod-ya tugged Rissa's sleeve, pulling her from the entry. "Now, this next section opens to various secret chambers of . . . " The echoing words became indistinguishable as they moved on down the corridor.

Dancel scarce dared move until all trace of light reflecting off the tunnel walls disappeared, and no more footfalls or echoing voices were heard. Only then did she rise to her feet. Her sudden getting to her feet combined with lack of food and water caused her to swoon. She braced her hand against the wall and inhaled deeply until the spell passed. She took a tentative step, then another and another. Her equilibrium, however, didn't fully return, sending her veering back and forth across the tunnel, caroming wall to wall.

Rapid footfalls echoed again in the main tunnel, bringing Dancel back to her senses in a rush. Someone was racing down the connecting tunnel—though from which direction, she couldn't tell, since all sounds entered her tunnel from the mouth of the "T." Dancel froze in the middle of the pathway, her mind clear but her body unable to obey as her mind screamed, "Run!"

The hurrying of footsteps approached the tunnel entry. There was the slightest hint of a rosy glow off the wall in the outer tunnel; and in the gloom, Dancel made out a dark, shadowy form coming to a halt in the adit.

"Dancel," a whisper carried down the passage, "it's me. Catch." An object landed softly near Dancel's feet. "If you're still there . . . it's a couple of biscuits in a napkin I was saving for later. I told Hod-ya I dropped something and had to retrieve it but that I'd be right back. Can you hear me? I hope you're still there."

Dancel stooped over and picked up the packet. "Got it, thanks," she called back softly. "Doesn't Hod-ya suspect you?"

"Apparently not, incredible as that seems. I'd best get back and tell her I couldn't find what I dropped—my lunch."

"Something doesn't seem right, Riss; have a care."

"I will. King's road to you, Dancel."

"And to you."

Rissa took to her heels and headed back toward her loathsome guide, leaving Dancel to open the pinned napkin and ravenously devour the purloined biscuits. They were the most delicious biscuits she'd ever eaten—moist and buttery and with two kinds of cheese tucked between the halves. Gradually, renewed strength flowed into her limbs. Surprisingly, she had enough saliva to swallow her feast; but after the last crumbs went down her throat, her mouth felt like gauze. She must get something to drink. Her dizzy spell quite vanished, she remembered how far she was from her destination where she'd hole up and collect moisture until . . . until what? Without keys, there was no way to sneak into the castle and scavenge food, nor could she escape these castle precincts to the outside world. She would likely starve or thirst to death camped out by the hole in the floor . . .

In vain does feeble man toil so hard to stock
Sweetmeats and many grains stored under key and lock
In hope against that forlorn day when calamity will mock
And does not see that the king feeds all his needy flock.

The rune sprang unbidden to mind. It was one of Logon's instructions to his original generals before launching their first campaign into Carnalia. They were to have no care regarding their supplies as they went forth to rescue lives; they were to demonstrate the provision of the king by simply trusting that their necessaries would be met at the moment of need.

Dare Dancel claim that promise here and now in this ominous situation? Could King Elyon find a way to send sustenance even to this dark, forsaken labyrinth?

"Haven't I just supplied for your need?"

Dancel whirled about, fully expecting to behold her liege. But no face greeted her searching eyes; instead, the gloom was just as pervasive as ever. "Logon?"

"Dire as your situation seems, daughter, you are accomplishing my will. Walls of solid stone cannot prevent my hand from meeting your need as you do my bidding."

Dancel blushed. Of course, Logon would supply if it was his desire to do so; and if not, then dying for lack of food or water beside a hole in the floor of a dark tunnel would be the best of outcomes. "I'm ashamed that I even allowed such a doubt to enter my mind, Logon. Forgive me."

"You are forgiven, but guard your heart. A cloak of evil enshrouds Carnalia and is growing stronger. Twilight fades; deep night comes. You need to know the light is with you, even though all that your eyes behold is only dark. You cannot see my face now, child, but I am, nonetheless, right beside you. Your help will arise unexpected; on that day, many foes will be routed and many friends encouraged."

Tears rolled down Dancel's cheeks. The immediate sense of his presence was suddenly gone, but the hope he'd brought lingered. She smiled, wiped away her tears, and pressed onward. The rest of the rune sprang to mind:

Vainest garb of all man's pomp and power
Lies fallen in the dust before the humblest flower.

Beauty oft goes unseen midst faith's unheeded bower,
But man and beast will only reap wine's vintage turned sour.

Dancel smiled; she was "wrapped" in a common work dress too large for her and forced to slog about in boots way too big. Yet underneath it all, her Logon dress was clean; and she was clothed in a simple elegance that put Carnalia's "upper crust" with all their jewelry, frilly lace, and gaudy apparel to shame. She confidently trod the darkened corridor with a renewed hope; her liege would provide.

CHAPTER SIXTEEN

BONU SLOWLY PARTED THE BUSHES, listening, casting his eyes this side and that. On his left, Scung, wincing as thorns poked his palms, crept behind a bramble bush. The calm surface of the marsh reflected the late rays of the afternoon sun. The rare absence of overspreading trees in the marsh itself made it one of the few places in Ra-Amawl where sunshine reached ground. The gray, rocky cliffs towering above the jungle floor across the swamp were pock-marked with caves and niches concealing recesses from which either friend or foe might be spying on them.

"Be's awful quiet." Scung settled into a hollow.

Bonu turned around to observe the warriors who had escaped Pitland and were stealthily creeping into the undergrowth behind Tren and Ollo, watching for his signal to approach the cliff fortress.

"I dunno, Bonu," whispered Scung, "summat seems amiss. It even looks different. I dunno how, but summat be's amiss."

"Looks deserted," Bonu mused. "Where are the brigades we sent here? There should at least be some sign in the surrounding jungle of foraging patrols coming and going."

Tren sidled in on the other side of Bonu and peered across the marshy expanse. "Problem?"

"Not sure. Seems like nobody's around—leastways, not Ecclessites. A settlement containing so many various brigades couldn't possibly hide from experienced trackers. Yet there's no indication of recent foraging, outposts, or even patrols. It's as if no one was ever here."

"You think they were attacked?"

"That's a possibility." Bonu rose to his knees. "I'm going to *hop-frog* the stone path across the marsh and scout it out."

"Belay thet thought, laddie," Scung said. "If'n empire forces be's hereabouts, yer kin bet Mileer left nuff o' troops, mebbe even dronnets, ter keep out a watch fer usn's."

"We have to know, Scung; we're out of provisions, and Tren's corps has been too long afield without supplies, barely scraping a living off the land as we traveled. Even if Varter has left, there should still be food stores in the cave complex."

"Then lemme go instead o' yer. Yer be's too valuable ter lose if'n the enemy be's lyin' in wait. Yer kens the lay o' the land an' kin lead these troops ter safety. I be's expendable, an' I kens the stone path acrost the marsh."

Scung rose to his knees and prepared to push through the veil of shrubs.

Bonu grabbed Scung's sleeve, staying him. "Aren't you forgetting something?"

"Whazzat?"

"The roamer guarding the wights—or did you forget?"

Scung growled lowly and settled back down beside Bonu. "Yer had ter mention the roamer, dincha?"

"I'll go," said Tren, rising to his knees. "Tell me where to find the stepping-stone pathway."

Scung growled again, then muttered, "Nay, I ain't gonna let no roamer deter me from me duty. Besides, yer won't likely find the stone path acrost on account o' it bein' tricky."

Tren patted Scung's shoulder. "Well said. But if you don't mind, I'll tag along. Roamers often seem intimidating due to the solemnity of their duty. And unless I miss my guess, guarding these marshland wights is nigh the gravest responsibility which any roamer can have as his assignment."

"You know something about these wights?" Bonu ventured. "Tell me."

Tren shook his head. "I'd rather not. I may be wrong."

"It has something to do with the trumpets we found, doesn't it?"

Tren winked at Bonu then addressed Scung, "Ready?"

Scung blinked, gulped and, sword in hand, stood. "Ready."

"Lead on."

"This way, Genr'l." Scung skirted inside the shoreline shrubbery to the embankment where the stepping-stones started a pathway across the swamp. "Best ter keep yer eyes off'n the water. There be's quare critturs down below what'd like ter snatch an' drag yer in ter drown if'n yer looks at 'em."

"I'm sure they would, though they have no power over kingsmen who know how to immediately expel any projected thoughts from Lurcan's agents. But make no mistake, when they're finally released, they'll be a scourge."

Scung landed on the first stone, then hesitantly proceeded to the second, then third and so on, calling back over his shoulder, "Git in a rhythm, kinda like a kid skippin' down the street."

Tren followed, noting the Eroton's touchdowns. "It doesn't seem as if your roamer is on duty today, Scung." Tren teetered precariously on one foot before leaping to the next stone.

"Aye, an' thet be's mighty quare, too. O' course, it be's broad daylight . . . an' it might be a-hoverin' anywhere out here, invisible-like. They be's hard nuff ter see in dim light."

Tren bit his lip. "So I've heard." As a recruit, Scung's recent experiences made him more aware of cusps and tophets than many other kingsmen, yet the Eroton couldn't begin to understand the depth and scope of supernatural things Tren had experienced in his years of service to Logon.

~

Hidden in the bushes back along the shore, Bonu studied the cliff face through the light of his sword's glow. He noted with a smile that Scung had bravely taken the lead.

Ollo crawled up beside Bonu. "Still no sign of life?"

Bonu shook his head. "I don't understand." He watched as Scung and Tren reached the halfway point across the watery marsh when, unexpectedly, a low-pitched trumpet blared from the sky.

Bonu's sword vibrated.

Ollo's Child of the Stars also vibrated, as did the swords of those skulking behind in the bushes.

Even Scung and Tren, in the midst of crossing, had stopped leaping rock to rock and withdrawn their swords.

The mystery runes on all kingsmen blades erupted in a bright golden glow that pierced the surrounding forest's shade. The trumpet call changed into a haunting melody; words resounded in each kingsman's mind and heart:

> "Sun and moon and stars, all a third part
> Have they lost of what they once had.
> Dim and short, day and night at this word,
> Fades all hope—for Lurcan, bodes bad.
> Then rose up roamer, the sounder of fourth,
> And flying discreetly o'er all the earth,

Cried a message of worse woes to come forth,
Three judgments more cruel, spewing wrath in their birth."

A shadow descended on the wetland, dimming the sun's light as if some dragon on the wing swooped across the sun and blocked the light. The sun was eclipsed as if an opaque shade had been drawn across its face. The jungle surrounding the hidden kingsmen darkened to nighttime shades; the sparkling reflections off the watery marsh were extinguished.

The Ecclessites lying scattered about in the flora behind Bonu, peered wonderingly about them, murmuring nervously.

Without warning, the glowing runes on their swords receded to only the ones they had tolled. As the brief, joyous surge of light faded from their swords, all that remained was a murky atmosphere hanging over the jungle and marsh and the knowledge that somewhere behind them in Ra-Amawl empire forces stalked.

~

A breeze rustled behind Scung and Tren and a column of twinkling lights suddenly hovered beside them.

"Time is short," said the roamer. "Beckon your companions to cross now. They must merge with Varter's forces. My goalkeeper duties will shortly come to an end; this intermission until the next trumpet won't tarry. The evil beings bound here since before man walked the earth will be loosed at the next trumpet, bringing unbearable suffering and grief. You would do well to be in a safe place before then."

A breeze rippled the water's surface; waves lapped against the stones as frightening entities sped up from the depths to roil the surface then return to the muck of the bottom. Tren sensed these imprisoned wights eagerly anticipated the Fifth Trumpet's blast.

~

Scung stared down into the waters, mesmerized.

"Scung, let's get over to Varter." Tren nudged the Eroton with his sword.

At the unexpected touch, Scung started; and his foot slipped, plunging him headfirst into the water. Grasping claws immediately stretched toward Scung, entangling his hair, tugging him downward. Horrible faces leered at him. Words entered his mind, unintelligible, angry phrases of a defiled language. Bony fingers splayed wide to pierce him; reptilian eyes narrowed as sharp, fang-filled maws expanded . . .

A bright blue sword swiped before Scung's eyes. The wights receded even as Scung's hulk was plucked from the water by the back of his belt. Water and swamp scum drained from his face and beard as he coughed out a mouthful of slimy water, uttering between gasps, "Thanks, Tren, I thought I be's a goner."

"Don't thank me, all I did was poke my sword into the drink. Thank your roamer friend."

Still suspended in mid-air by his belt, Scung twisted around and beheld the roamer holding him. "Y-y-yer done saved me?" His face blanched, and he nearly lost consciousness.

The roamer set Scung down on a rock, and an almost invisible hand appeared and smacked Scung's cheek. "No time to faint. Summon Bonu to the caves. When the fifth roamer sounds, these wights will be released and create havoc."

Scung's vision cleared. He looked to the shore where Bonu and those with him emerged from hiding. Then he peered to the opposite shore. The cliffs were crumbling from the top down and appeared to swarming with creatures. "Whut in thunder?"

Tren laughed, pointing at the cliff face. "Behold the missing brigade! Brilliant! Camouflaged themselves with dun clothing and clay to blend right into the rock face! Bonu told me about Varter's concealment skills, erecting foliage walls in the jungle and making campsites invisible, but this . . . this is genius!"

"So, thet be's why the cliff looked different," Scung rubbed his cheek where a fading red mark had been and stroked his beard wringing water out of it. He turned and waved to Bonu. "It be's safe. Come over," he said as he proceeded to the next stepping-stone.

Bonu led the procession single file out onto the marsh, revealing the whereabouts of the stones for Pitland's escapees to form a *hop-frog* line across the marsh.

Drawing nearer, Scung recognized Vawella waiting on the far side. She was covered in clay head to foot and urgently beckoning them to hurry. Beside her, leaning on a rustic tree-branch crutch, was Captain Varter. He waved anxiously, wanting to sequester the new arrivals in the honey-combed caverns as soon as possible.

~

The next evening, a heavy rain pelted the cliff's exterior with blustery wind gusts, occasionally splattering droplets inside the opening where Bonu sat cross-legged beside a campfire in the topmost cave portal with Generals Tren, Ollo, Leton, and Marn. They had spent much of the day organizing the various kingsmen brigades into squads and companies appointing rank and file leaders over their swollen ranks. Across each officer's lap rested a glowing sword; under scrutiny were the mystery runes.

A deerskin curtain was pulled aside, admitting Captain Varter hobbling in on his crotched-oak crutch. "Your detachment seems to have settled in, Tren," said Varter, last of the war council to arrive. With some difficulty, Varter lowered himself to a log and extended his hands toward the fire.

"So, we are in agreement that fulfillment of the mystery runes has begun?" Leton looked around the circle of faces.

"You accept our understanding of the trumpets and the role they play in these days?" Tren probed, his eyes unblinking, looking directly at his friend.

Leton nodded sheepishly. "Too many coincidences to ignore, especially since the devastation of Pitland. I now believe that we're soon to face the long-anticipated *Tremendum.*"

"But you couldn't just take our word for it?" Bonu cast a twig he'd been fiddling with to the stone floor. "Or the fulfilled prophecies accompanying the trumpet blasts we've all heard?"

Captain Varter tapped Bonu's wrist. "It's not for you to criticize another man's servant; nor the method and timing Logon chooses to enlighten him. Mind your rank and place, *Lieutenant.*"

Bonu gazed into the fire, muttering, "I apologize, Leton. I sometimes speak out of frustration."

After a moment, Leton nodded at Bonu. "Apology accepted."

"Nevertheless," said Tren, "if what Captain Varter says is accurate about the emperor tattooing every man, woman, and child, then it's also certain that the end of this age has fallen upon our generation. It's imperative we be of one mind concerning tactics and strategy; there must be no division of opinion among us."

"Tell us again, if you don't mind, Captain, how you learned of this mandatory marking the empire's entire population with a mystical tattoo." Marn stretched his legs.

"Perhaps my daughter, Vawella, ought to relate the story. She's the one who found the refugees."

"Is that necessary? This is an officers' meeting," Marn crossed his arms. "I mean, there's a reason our decisions, plans, and discussions are kept from the rank and file until they need to know."

"Vawella is a key member of my brigade." A flush of red rose to Varter's cheeks. "If anyone has a right—nay, a *need*—to know our intentions, it's her. She's familiar with the surrounding territory better than anyone here and, thus, is needed to guide us through the tangle of Ra-Amawl. I trust her implicitly."

Tren laid a hand on Varter's shoulder. "Invite your daughter to join us, Captain. Her input will, no doubt, be invaluable." He looked around the circle at his fellow officers and asked, "Any objections?"

"None from me." Bonu shrugged. "I'm not even sure why I'm allowed to sit in on this council, seeing I'm just a junior officer. Vawella has certainly distinguished herself as a warrior who can handle her sword among the best, as well as demonstrate Logon's compassion. If I'm permitted to be here, so ought she."

Varter screed like a nighthawk, summoning an aide from outside the deerskin covering the entry.

It took half an hour to locate Vawella. She was finally found stashing away woodland bounty in the storage caverns from her latest foraging patrol. The arrival of Tren's task force nearly tripled the population of the Cliff Brigade, putting a strain on supplies.

Vawella cautiously drew the deerskin curtain aside that separated the "conference room" from the other chambers of the cave and entered. "You wanted to see me?" Her usually smiling lips were set in a thin, grim line. "Have I done something wrong?"

"Not at all, daughter." Varter patted a vacant space on the log beside him. "Here, come sit beside me. They want to hear about the girls you found wandering the wilds and what they told you."

Vawella scanned the room before nestling in between Bonu and her father. "Well, about a week ago, I led a foraging patrol farther afield than usual. We'd heard rumors of a large military force somewhere in the jungle and didn't want to leave any telltale signs near our encampment here, so we went farther afield than was our custom. We headed toward the main road, out past where our camouflage camp used to be—if you know where that is."

"We're not familiar with Ra-Amawl, other than the main road running through," Leton said.

"She means away north by northwest toward Cosmopolis." Bonu shifted his weight to relieve pressure off his all-but-healed leg wound.

"Ah, so you ventured dangerously close to the seat of those who seek to exterminate us," Marn stroked his beard. "And what happened?"

"Well, it's not as if we went anywhere near the actual roads leading to Cosmopolis or anything. The capital of Carnalia is many leagues beyond, a few days' travel under the best of conditions. The ten of us spread out to forage but kept within hailing distance of each other. As we found a good supply of mushrooms, roots, nuts, berries, cattails, and such—we uncovered a root system of tubers growing alongside a stream and were digging them out—when Trembu, one of our team, sounded a hawk's cry, warning us of strangers nearby. I answered with the countersign for the foraging party to rendezvous and quietly withdraw.

"It was fortunate that Glend, Jeda's friend from Cosmopolis, was on detail with us. Trembu said he'd spotted movement across a large briar patch, which was why he sounded the danger signal. He was about to head to the rendezvous when Glend stopped him. Four girls in tattered garments had gotten themselves enmeshed in a patch of brambles and were having a difficult time. They were bemired with mud from traipsing about the wilds for days, scratched and bleeding, bug-bitten, hungry, and thirsty. It was a wonder that lions, gorrils, or other beasts hadn't come upon them before we found them. They would've soon died of exposure if we'd left them there, which is what Trembu suggested at first. Don't misunderstand; Trembu is a valiant warrior and has a kind heart, but the safety of the camp was foremost in his thinking."

"I'll vouch for Trembu." Varter thumped his crutch on the floor. "He and Vawella slew a Craniantium lion as we moved our camp here."

"Hear, hear!" said Leton. "Well done, Vawella. I know of few men who would dare such a feat."

"Yeah, she's our representative dronnet," Bonu teased.

Vawella blushed, casting a baleful eye at Bonu, but quickly resumed her narrative. "Anyway, Glend stood up, revealing her presence and frightening the forlorn stragglers. She recognized them. One was a scullery maid, Rissa, a secret follower of Logon, conscripted as a bond-slave in Cosmopolis, as Jeda also had been. So Trembu and Glend picked their way through the thicket to free the frightened girls, doing as little damage as possible to the vegetation, lest they leave a trail to be followed. When Rissa recognized Glend, she encouraged her companions by telling them that they'd found safety.

"They were led to the rendezvous. Rissa already was Ecclessite, but the other girls—Flanner, Daddetta, and Scranner—weren't. We tended their wounds and gave them water and food before questioning them. We didn't dare bring them to our cliffs until we could trust their loyalty, remembering the tussle we'd had with Glend."

"Wisdom, that," said Marn. "And?"

"Rissa told us how she'd fled the castle without her sword; she had been trying to explain to her companions the necessity of getting their hearts pierced and going to Logon's Rock. Even though the others didn't know what she meant, they were nonetheless anxious to escape from Cosmopolis.

"They related that a coronation of a human emperor, a Feuhr, was in planning stages, after which every person in the empire will be required to receive some sort of tattoo as proof of fealty to the new regime. Rissa got wind of it before it was put into practice. Working inside the castle as she did, she overheard Hod-ya and General Mileer discuss the mass branding of hundreds of thousands in Cosmopolis, the rest of Carnalia and other countries soon following."

Tren whistled lowly. "Prophecies are moving apace, indeed! Do you know who this new emperor is to be? What this tattoo looks like?"

Vawella shook her head. "I only know that, according to Rissa, a mysterious prisoner who'd been confined to the deepest, darkest recesses of the dungeon was not only rehabilitated but especially conditioned by Hod-ya to be indwelt by the wraith of Lurcan himself during the coronation. Lurcan will then indwell the visible leader, or Feuhr, of the empire."

"Well, we know who the invisible head of Carnalia is, don't we?" Tren looked around the circle of officers. "And that leaves no doubt that this mysterious prisoner will be the flesh-and-blood vehicle of Lurcan ruling through the flesh of that wretched man, whoever he is."

"Uh, if I may offer a conjecture?" Bonu raised his hand. "I was tolling the mystery runes this morning and, uh, well this rune sort of lit up as my sword vibrated just a little when I honed the edge. I think it describes the tattoo."

The others stared at the brash lieutenant daring to instruct senior officers—all that is, except Tren.

Ollo's eyebrows arched. "So, show us."

Bonu gulped, lifted his toller, and stroked the edge of his sword. A hum gently filled the granite-walled enclosure, becoming a dirge that filled the hearers with somber words coursing through their minds:

> *Deep in the heart of the earth sits a man.*
> *Deep in the heart of the man bides a lie.*
> *Deep in the heart of the lie grows a plan.*
> *Deep in the heart of the plan they will die.*
>
> *Festering hatred will rise with the man.*
> *Bloodshed of innocents rise with the lie.*
> *Despairing of life will rise with the plan.*
> *An ancient numeral insulting the sky.*
>
> *Now triple the rage in tri-part man,*
> *And triple the crime that comes with the lie.*
> *And triple the grief in tri-part plan,*
> *And triple the mark that bids them die!*

"And you get a sense of who this man is or what his tattoo will look like from that?" Marn shook his head.

"Didn't you hear the whispered numbers during the hum of the musical tones?" Bonu asked, his eyes wide, lips parted.

"I did," said Vawella.

"So did I," said Tren.

"And I," agreed Leton, Varter, and Ollo.

"Marn, ye must be hard o' hearing," said Ollo. "Ye will just have to take our word for it that it was there."

"What was there?" Marn extended his hands.

"The ancient numeral the rune referred to—the number of the day Mada and Ivi were created, the number prophetically assigned to humanity; the Treblesix." Tren leaned back and studied their faces in the fire's glow. "So, we seek the identity of a man given great power that has three 'T's' in his name—'T' standing for twain, thus three T's equaling Treblesix."

"And that's the number you all heard?" Marn eyes were wide.

Each one nodded silently, soberly.

"So that would mean exactly what, then?"

"That the tattoo," Bonu whispered as he stared into the fire, "is either a man's name or some configuration of the Treblesix numeral itself."

"Or both," added Tren. "And possibly disguised in a variety of designs so as to confuse anyone expecting the fulfillment of the Treblesix prophecy."

"There's one more thing I feel I ought to mention." Vawella broke in on the discussion. "Rissa clearly heard Mileer say that anyone who resists receiving the tattoo will be—"

"Beheaded." Tren tapped a rune on his sword.

The council sat in silence for several minutes.

Ollo broke the contemplation. "Well, I guess that ends all speculation about fulfilled prophecy happening in our day. What became of the girls accompanying Rissa?"

Vawella smiled. "Trembu showed them this same rune and explained its meaning. That convinced them that Logon was their only hope. They each yielded to Glend's sword as it penetrated their hearts and took them instantly in their mind's eye to Logon's Rock."

Varter poked an errant log back into the flames with his crutch. "There's a kingsman brigade in Cosmopolis. I sent Trembu and Knarsh with some others to contact them and let them know we're prepared to coordinate an assault on Cosmopolis if they would be so inclined as to support our attack."

"What? Even before we took council?" Marn objected.

"You weren't here; I got orders from Logon." Varter crossed his arms and smiled.

"And wisely so," said Tren, arching his back. "Now we need some good maps of Ra-Amawl, roads to and from Cosmopolis, and whatever we can learn of the emperor's palace and its defenses."

CHAPTER SEVENTEEN

ARTKA FLAPPED HIS ARMS ACROSS his chest to stay awake as he kept watch from atop a parapet. The morning's foggy damps on the glacis had dissipated long before creeping to the battle zone near the wall that had been the scene of many heated skirmishes a week prior. The distant mists that floated slowly uphill and vanished into thin air had created a mesmerizing effect that, combined with the twelve-hour shifts he'd been pulling, left him drowsy. But his duty was nearly at an end. The dawn's light rising behind the fort made things visible. Artka arched his back and rotated his neck side to side. He needed sleep.

The blockhouse door at the end of the walkway creaked as Reddy shuffled through, munching a muffin and wrapping a cloak around his shoulders as he approached. "Good morning, Artka. Anything seem to be happening?"

"Nary a thing, except the gloom covering the western sky. Was foggy this morning, but a fresh breeze is evaporating the mists before they get close to the castle. You my relief?"

"Umm-umf." Reddy stuffed the last bite of muffin into his mouth.

"Good, I could sleep for days." Artka gathered his kit and water-skin and turned toward the blockhouse.

"Oh, I almost forgot," Reddy said, "there's going to be a general meeting in about three hours; I was told to make sure you knew."

Artka groaned.

"I know; I know. We all feel that way. We spend so much time on duty that we're too weary to do much of anything else." Reddy looked out across the field. "It's not as if any patrols found the slightest sign of Carnalian activity nearby. Seems like they've retreated and there's only been a trickle of recruits coming our way. It seems as if the war is almost over."

"Well, we know it isn't, it's just the calm before the storm." Artka made for the doorway, then turned back before passing through, "Make sure to toll your sword while you stand watch; some intriguing runes lit up for me. Let's compare runes later and see if the same ones light up for you."

"Which runes?"

"You'll know if they light up for you." Artka replied over his shoulder as he disappeared into the blockhouse. He paused a moment at the long table overspread with foodstuffs and grabbed a couple of muffins, cramming them into his haversack before descending the spiral stair down to the main hall.

Harnet and Braxmore were waiting at the bottom to greet him. "Here he comes now." Harnet wrapped an arm around Artka's shoulder. "Have you heard there's a meeting in a couple of hours?"

"Reddy told me. What's it about?" Artka took a bite of muffin.

"Nobody's saying." Braxmore leaned close and lowered his voice. "Whatever the officers are planning is a well-kept secret."

"Aye, it be's the secret-est secret I ever heered 'bout." Scang joined them as they strolled toward the sleeping quarters on the main floor. "Sajon, Hudge, Metid, an' Gulundur hain't droppin' no hints a-tall. Yer got's any idees what it be's, Artka?"

"Just one—sleep. Wake me when they start." Artka fairly stumbled through the doorway, where he fell face down on the nearest vacant cot in what previously had been the junior officer's quarters. He closed his eyes and breathed deeply. His three companions watched from the doorway before turning back to the main room, letting the exhausted watchman slumber.

"Artka, lad, it be's time."

Artka opened his eyes a mere slit and beheld the shaggy visage of Scang. "Can't be time already. I just fell asleep."

"Thet was four hours since. While yer been sleepin', a messenger come from a kingsman brigade in Cosmopolis wi' important news."

Artka rolled over, put his feet on the floor, and supported his head in his hands. Then, taking a breath and pushing off his knees, he rose and stretched the kinks out of his back. He rummaged in his kit for the other muffin and took a bite. "All right, let's get on with it so I can get back to sleep."

"I wish it was going to be that easy." Sajon leaned against the doorframe. "The captains invited you to sit with them during the meeting." Sajon looked over his shoulder at the roomful of Ecclessites awaiting the last member of the task force. "It seems that immediately after this meeting, we're evacuating the fortress. Your name has been suggested as leading a mission."

"What?" Artka, shook his head trying to make sense of Sajon's words.

"Come, you'll see." Sajon barely leaned on his crutch anymore as he led into the murmuring crowd.

The throng of Ecclessites parted as Sajon and Artka ambled toward the officers who were seated on an impromptu dais of hastily arranged tables at the front of the assembly. Seated alongside Gulundur, Metid, Hudge, and Evebryl was a stranger garbed in house-servant's attire. Two seats beside the stranger were vacant.

Artka rubbed bleariness from his eyes as he neared the platform— but wait! There was something familiar about the stranger. His lean face and body, sinewy hands, sparkling eyes, and cropped shock of gray hair were familiar; yet there was an added air of authority to his demeanor that had almost prevented recognition. "Smid? Is that you? Wha—what are you doing here?"

Smid stood and greeted Artka, smiling broadly. "Yes, Master Artka, it's me. And right glad am I to find you amidst this lot, too."

"How long have you been an Ecclessite?" Artka was hoisted by several hands atop the makeshift dais. Sajon also was lifted up and took a seat among the leaders of what was the final brigade to defend the King's Gate Fortress West.

"Longer than should've been, without telling you and your sisters about my true allegiance."

"You mean, all the time I was in my father's house, you were—"

"Yes."

"And Gwinnid, your wife?"

Smid grinned sheepishly. "Yes, her, too."

Artka was now wide awake, stunned that this seemingly innocuous servant of his father's household was secretly a kingsman. "And . . . and anybody else among the staff?"

"No, I'm afraid not. But I have good news. Your sister, Jeda—"

"Jeda! You and Gwinnid escorted her to Logon's Rock?" Tears brimmed in Artka's eyes. "And what of Velnu and Cornil? Did they meet Logon, too? Or my parents?"

Smid momentarily lowered his gaze to the floor. "No, Master Artka, I'm afraid not. Besides you, only Jeda has encountered Logon so far. Gwinnid and I revealed what we were to her just before she was sent to the emperor's palace. We offered her an opportunity to meet Logon, but she declined. Nevertheless, Logon sought her out and drew her to himself, though she's had a rough go of it, I'm afraid."

"Is she all right? What happened?"

"Ahem," Metid interrupted. "You two can catch up later. Right now, we need to settle on preliminary plans for invading Cosmopolis, of which you, Artka, we are hoping will consent to lead a dangerous but extremely important mission, if you will."

Artka settled into his seat and surveyed the eager faces looking upward at him. Among them were Sejisca and Cocee, with Hudge, Harnet, Brendle, Braxmore, Clepy, and Scang in the very front, with rank after rank of people he'd met during his odyssey—such as Chahan, the bugler from Sofista's castle, Darfe', Gronch, and Wertie, among the former lion poachers, the father and son team of Fram and Flegg who'd assisted him in the Daggerman keep when the dread's spirit attacked . . . So many who had already lived through much carnage. Yet, the war was far from over. Artka sighed and suddenly realized that Captain Metid had directed a question at him. Everyone was waiting his response.

"Uh, I'm sorry, what did you say?" Artka turned to Metid and Gulundur.

"We wanted to know if you feel fit enough and are willing to embark on that dangerous course," Metid reiterated. "You've been through a lot; much has been demanded of you. You've generously given of yourself, even to the point of exhaustion. That's why we ask rather than assign this task. Only you can know if you're able to carry on another challenging assignment. We don't ask lightly because you—and whoever accompanies you—will be pushed to the limits of endurance and courage. Otherwise, we'll appoint someone else. There are others reluctant but willing to undertake the mission, so don't feel obligated. Indeed, you should only accept if, in your heart, you bear witness that Logon wants you to do it. We could certainly use your abilities in the main attack force, should you defer this special mission."

"Why offer it to me first?"

Metid and Gulundur exchanged glances, as did Hudge and Sajon. Smid smiled and kept his eyes unwaveringly on Artka.

Evebryl extended her hand, touching Artka's shoulder. "Saygus saw potential in you. And beyond that, during the past winter when you and your friends and the lion poachers trained, Logon sent specific instructions to prepare you for a certain risky mission. At the time, we thought that mission was to accompany Saygus on an underground sea voyage, with all its unique perils; but the mission before you is equally fraught with danger and just as necessary."

Artka furrowed his brow. "I don't recall any special training."

Evebryl smiled. "You didn't know—neither did those you're probably going to choose to accompany you—but in addition to rescuing Carnalians, your training focused on discerning and combating *kyllorn*. Saygus took extra pains to make you aware of the invisible battle that rages against Ecclessites. The runes foretell that before the death knell falls on Carnalia and the rest of the empire, Lurcan will summon all his forces from the natural realm, as well as the ethereal realm, to engage in fierce battle for their plain—but not against roamers, against rescued kingsmen."

Artka's face drained of blood; the memory of waiting in the antechamber of Lurcan's Womb for Blist and his cronies to attack flashed before his mind's eye. All too overwhelming was the stench, not to mention the sheer horror of encountering evil beings face to face from the *kyllorn* realm as they surged into the cavern, the waves of hatred emanating from the tophets overpowering their stench, being slammed against the wall like a toy doll as the monsters struggled against each other trying to get at him, the fiery sting to his shoulder and accompanying paralysis from traces of venom that flowed into his veins, and the nightmares that followed . . .

But there was also the joyous wonder of his sword finding its mark and slashing open the great scorpion's venom sac, the awareness of Logon's presence, the exhilarating dash down the tunnel, the giddy sidling out on the merest of ledges, the daring rescue by Scang swinging out over the bottomless pit, and the waking up in Saygus' lodge looking into the faces of Saygus' lovely daughters.

"I accept."

"Gor along now, thar be's a true kingsman fer ye." The giant Eroton elbowed the crowd aside as he approached the dais and slapped Artka on the back, nearly sending him over the edge. "Cain't hardly wait ter git started, laddie."

The others on the tabletop dais breathed a sigh of relief. A sense of swelling excitement permeated the gathering. That was the last issue to be settled. There was no turning back now. The summons of the

Trumpets of Doom would be joined by this contingent of Logon's forces marching on the very gates of the empire's stronghold, Lurcan's throne in Cosmopolis.

Rising, Metid stood beside Artka, laying a fatherly hand on the young warrior's shoulder. Then, looking up to the rafters of the keep and extending the other hand aloft, he spoke aloud for the entire hall to hear, "O Logon Xychirion, our plans are laid; our lives are in your hands. We have our orders from you and march our separate paths until we gather together again, either within the gates of a defeated Cosmopolis or else in Splendora. May your guidance direct all our paths to victory in your name and to the establishment of your throne over all lands. So say we all!"

"So say we all!" echoed the entire gathering.

The solemn oath reverberated off the walls covered with various heraldic mementos, brigade banners, and tapestries depicting stories from the sword runes.

Metid paused, tears in his eyes as he peered around the room at those who zealously joined in dedicating life and limb to Logon's glory. Finally, he instructed, "We sally forth within the hour. Officers and noncoms, see to your charges." He then bent over and whispered into Artka's ear, "Come with me."

The meeting broke up. In every corner of the keep men equipped themselves for travel, strapping on sword sheaths; tucking tollers in their belts; and filling packs, various pockets, and pouches with other essentials in preparation for prolonged stages of march.

Women, children, and the elderly gathered extra food and supplies in order to provision the main army. Physicians and attendants bundled essential medical gear, surgical implements, and various dried medicinal plants, along with bandages, stretchers, and tents; the kitchen crew sorted through pots, pans, and utensils, deciding what they could do without and what was necessary for meal preparation.

Artka hopped off the tabletop and followed Metid and Gulundur into the captain's chambers. Harnet, Scang, Braxmore, Brendle, and Clepy, along with Reddy who was just returning from sentry duty, trailed after Artka at a distance and stopped respectfully outside when Artka was admitted into the inner sanctum of the officer's quarters. Artka closed the door at Gulundur's nod.

"Have a seat, Artka." Metid pointed to a chair in front of the desk. "We'll be brief." He then settled into an overstuffed chair behind the mahogany desk. Gulundur, nodding his head, hovered behind and off to the left of Metid. "Artka, we believe that the Advisor would have us bestow the rank of journey lieutenant on you for this mission. We're only acting in response to his leading; it's not our own thinking. In fact, some of us have expressed doubts about thusly promoting you due to your youth, but then Evebryl approached us out of the blue and confirmed that she'd received an oracle from the Advisor to the effect that you were to be commissioned. At that, we could no longer doubt it is Logon's will for you."

"I'm not sure I'm ready for such responsibility. Besides, though I accepted the mission, you've kept the details vague. What's the objective? Where do I go? Who's to come with me? Who or what will we face?"

"We don't fully know what you'll face, son." Gulundur patted the back of Metid's seat. "We only know that you can choose your own patrol and as many as you like."

"Well, within reason, that is," Metid interrupted. "No more than twenty or thirty fighting men. We'll need all the manpower we can muster for our assault on the main gates. Even so, we'll be vastly outnumbered."

Gulundur added, "As to the enemy you'll be facing—"

Artka leaned forward. "Tophets and cusps, I should guess. That's what Saygus trained us to fight. I've had some limited experience with the likes."

"No doubt, Artka, no doubt. But"—Metid looked to Gulundur for support—"we think you and your squad might encounter firedrakes . . . and possibly dreads, in force."

"D-dreads . . . in force?" Artka's stomach lurched; he gripped the arms of the chair to steady himself. "I-I don't know . . . I was nearly done in by the smoke-daemon of the dread we encountered in the Daggerman's castle, the one Saygus disembodied."

"We're not unaware of how that Chimeree affected everyone that it touched; however, through all that, you learned not to trust your own abilities. Only Logon, manifesting through you and the other members of your company, will be able to confront the powers supporting the evil reign of Cosmopolis."

"Which will most likely not be anywhere near the actual gates of the castle or even the city but away in an obscure place, since a couple of their number have already proven vulnerable," said Gulundur. "Our force will assail the main gates of Cosmopolis and various other positions around the wall. Logon willing, we'll be joined by other Ecclessite bands from surrounding regions to the west. We won't have the numerical advantage to overcome Lurcan's armies, which will be massed in regimental strength. The assault we wage likely won't last long, I'm afraid; and many will find themselves in Splendora once the attack is underway, unless you locate and bind the *kyllorn* dukes of darkness and interfere with their incantations supporting Lurcan and his flesh and blood minions."

"On a hopeful note," intruded Metid, "another of the ten dreads has been disembodied, thanks to Saygus; and there are rumors that another one has been injured. You yourself know that Tren's sword sliced off Neask's tongue, so he won't be able to cast any verbal imprecations."

"Oh, well, that's better then; we only have to deal with seven healthy dreads and a mute." Artka feigned bravado to mask his trepidation.

Metid and Gulundur looked on soberly.

Metid finally spoke. "We know it's a daunting task—one that we don't set lightly before you—but Logon indicates that you're prime for this responsibility, even if you don't feel ready. Evebryl insists that your recent battle experience, combined with Saygus' training, will stand you in good stead. Now, do you have any idea how many men you'll need?"

"This is so reminiscent of the first time I was sent from this very castle into Ecclessa with Reddy, Harnet, and Scang, remember? Only this time, it's the other way, back to Carnalia."

"I remember," said Metid with a twinkle in his eyes. "Little did we know then what would befall any of us in so short a season."

"I'd like to take Scang, Reddy, Harnet, Clepy, Brendle, and Braxmore, if I may. Oh, and Hudge and Sajon, too. That's all I think I'll need. Nine of us to meet eight well-armored dreads—sounds like a fair fight!"

The captains chuckled.

Metid said, "I'm sorry Artka, Sajon and Hudge are needed as battalion leaders here with us. The others, however, are yours, and I'm sure they'd have it no other way. Is there anyone else you'd like to take in Sajon's and Hudge's place?"

Artka lowered his gaze to the scattered papers on Metid's desktop. Then looking up, he said, "No, our little band started with four and was joined by two more, then Braxmore last of all; I think that's the squad Logon would give me, providing they'll come once they hear the objective."

"Be's yer joshin'? We would'na miss thet action fer all the rum in Eroton, would we lads?"

Artka spun around. Scang and the others had unobtrusively been admitted to the consultation by Evebryl, while Artka and the captains were intently focused on the mission.

"Nay, nor for all the codices and scrolls in Craniantium," added Clepy, smiling broadly and leading the surge to embrace Artka.

"Dreads?" asked Brendle. "Why not? Lead on." His pale face, however, belied his undaunted words.

CHAPTER EIGHTEEN

Reasno, damp from the night's rainstorm, squatted by a fire and warmed his hands while the squirrels they'd snared earlier roasted over a low fire on a spit. Nearby, Yumpik and Frib played mumbly-peg with their daggers, seeing how close to each other's feet they could stick the dagger without actually nicking the other's foot.

"Thar! Beat thet!" Yumpik boasted as his blade nudged the instep of Frib's boot. "Thet's a three-pointer. Score be's ten ter seven, my favor."

"You don't get three points for that—only one," Frib challenged, anger in his tone.

"I do, too; it touched."

"But it made a slice; that disqualifies the touch, making it only one point."

"Whar? Thet slice been there afore."

Frib lifted the foot in question, balancing awkwardly on one foot while pointing out the merest of scrapes on his instep. "There, it's a fresh slice, not old."

"Thet? It been there afore—"

"Knock it off, you two," Reasno growled. "You'll dull your daggers, throwing them into the dirt like that. Come over here and eat; these tree rats are done. Then we have work to do, and I don't need you two squabbling with each other."

The three fell to devouring the squirrels and kept quiet as they gnawed the meager, nutty-tasting meat off the bones. When finished,

Reasno stood. "Now, we have to get the daggers out of the field without anyone from the fortress seeing us."

Wiping greasy hands on breeches, the trio kicked dirt on the fire. "Let's go," Reasno barked like a drill sergeant. Frib and Yumpik fell in line. "This is going to be easier than I thought," Reasno mumbled under his breath as a grin overspread his face.

"Yer say summat, Debator?" Yumpik asked.

"Er, just thinking out loud; we need to enlist more men to our cause, is all."

"Why don't we go back to the road?" Frib swatted at a deerfly buzzing around his face. "I mean, we're going back to the fortress anyway, right? So why not take an easier path?"

"If you must know, we're a mere hundred paces parallel to the road. I just don't want to bump into—hush! Hide. Somebody's coming."

Reasno, Frib, and Yumpik dropped to their bellies and crawled beneath the shrubbery toward the source of the noise. Sounds consistent with a large company marching down the pike from King's Gate Fortress West filled the forest. The trio cautiously crept forward, taking extra pains to stay concealed the closer they drew to the road. Through gaps in the underbrush, they observed the kingsmen martial column marching four abreast in unison without aid of a drum, faces stern, eyes fixed forward, jaws firm, brows furrowed, swords swinging from belts in perfectly timed arcs with each step. Recruits were intermingled amongst veterans, their relatively un-lit swords a contrast to the greater shine of seasoned warriors. The army of men in clean, bright tunics and women in bright Logon dresses included a fair number of older adolescents interspersed among them, all marching with determination.

It took half an hour for the military procession to pass before Reasno and his conscripts, which was then followed by less organized medical, mess hall, and other various support staff lugging equipment and supplies packed on their backs or in handcarts. Following them were the walking wounded, the infirm, the elderly, and the very young toted by their mothers. All in all, the entire parade took over an hour and a half to pass.

Reasno whispered, "Did they leave no one behind at the fortress?"

After the kingsmen were a good distance down the road, Reasno crawled out of the shrubbery to watch until the tail end of the column passed from sight. When reasonably sure no stragglers would be coming down the road, the trio brushed off their clothes and scampered down the embankment to the pike.

"Thet musta been everybody whut was left in the fort, eh Reasno?"

"Looks likely."

"You mean, they left the castle undefended and abandoned?" Frib stared down the road after the departing kingsmen army.

"I don't know." Reasno stroked his chin whiskers. "Where do you suppose they were going?"

"Logon's Rock?" Frib suggested.

"Maybe, but for what purpose?"

"Mebbe they be's a goin' ter Splendora, like we was told when they pierced usn's."

"No, Yumpik, I heard enough kingsman legends to know it's not going to happen like that. First, there has to be a great battle—" Reasno's face reddened. "They think they're marching to the final battle— attacking the very gates of Cosmopolis and the emperor himself! This is an all-out, do-or-die attack to invade the capital of Carnalia."

"With only a few thousand warriors fit to fight?" Frib said. "That defies reason." Frib pulled out his sword and examined the point. "So many that were rescued the other day in the battle, like us, have nothing more than just a pinprick of light on their swords. How can they hope to defeat Lurcan's multitudes?"

Reasno coughed up a wad of phlegm and spat. "If you ask me, almost everything they do is irrational. Anyway, there are more Ecclessites in other places that will come to the summons. More than likely, they're marching off to their own destruction. The fools!"

"Lucky thet usn's came lookin' fer yer, Debator, else me an' Frib woulda been a goin' wi' 'em." Yumpik examined his sword's point. "Good thing yer gave usn's these here daggers ter defend ourselves wi'."

"Daggers!" Reasno spun on his heel and looked up the road in the direction of the fortress. "We've got to see if they destroyed my cache of daggers before they left."

"But what if somebody was left behind?" Frib asked. "You know, to keep the bridge open?"

"Well, if there's anyone left, they won't likely bother with us. Let's hide there and see just what the situation is. Chances are we'll own the place and whatever they left behind. Why, we can headquarter our newly formed Daggerman brigade there."

"Sounds good ter me," Yumpik enthused. "But what if'n they returns?"

"That's not likely. When they engage the might of Lurcan's forces, there'll be no one left to return."

"And we'll have sole possession of the fort." Frib clapped his hands.

"Right! Let's go." Reasno trotted up the trail.

The two followed, daggers in hand, swords on both tucked in their belts and bouncing erratically as they jogged. An hour later, they drew within sight of King's Gate Fortress West's ramparts. The portcullis was raised; and the door, showing signs of recent repair, had been left ajar.

"They just plumb up and abandoned it, Reasno," said Frib. "They wouldn't have left the door open if someone was inside, would they?"

The trio slowed to a walk. "No, I suppose not," Reasno replied. "Nevertheless, we need have a care. It's possible empire troops are inside or savage beasts prowling about drawn by the scent of leftover foodstuffs."

Frib extracted his sword and held it before him as they advanced on the archway.

Reasno sneered disdainfully. "What do you think you're going to do with that dull thing?" He brandished his dagger in Frib's face. "Get used to using this."

"Well I—" Frib's voice trailed off, and he sheepishly slipped his sword back into his belt and drew his dagger.

Reasno nodded, then turned his attention back to the doorway and the shadowed keep beyond. He stepped cautiously inside. "Hello? Anybody here?"

Debator proceeded into the shadowed room and scrutinized the keep. Frib and Yumpik came close on his heels. Wordlessly, Reasno pointed his dagger to the right as he tilted his head at Yumpik; then with the other hand, he pointed left and tilted his head at Frib. The two peeled off to their assignments, quietly treading the stone floor to reconnoiter the various side chambers, archways, vestibules, and portals.

Reasno went straight for Captain Metid's chambers where he'd so recently been humiliated by those smug, self-important officers. He nudged the door open and paused. The room had been put back in order since he'd been restrained in a chair against his will, brow-beaten, shamed, forced to invent confessions . . . Anger smoldered in his chest.

He went to Metid's desk and spread the papers that were neatly piled in the center. The topmost sheet read:

Having decided upon leadership for the main army from the eastern marches, we also consigned a small detail to a promising young warrior (temporarily commissioned as a Journey Lieutenant) for a secret mission. The war council in King's Gate Fortress West has convened with a determination to cast ourselves upon the swords, spears, and halberds of Carnalia. We trust that our liege will coordinate roamers from Splendora and any other kingsmen brigades he summoned to join with our attack on Cosmopolis. We hope that by our willing sacrifice, many more Carnalians will forsake loyalty to the empire and find amnesty with Logon Xychirion.

Signed,
Captain F. Metid, Sr. officer, KGFW

Reasno shook his head. "Defies all human logic."

Frib and Yumpik knocked on the door. "May we enter?"

Reasno looked up from the papers on the desk. "Yes, yes, do come in." He held the sheet aloft for them to see. "They've gone and done it; they've marched off to their own suicide in the vain hope that Logon will rescue them at the last minute. Sofista was right; illuminating the ancient runes on the swords and expecting them to work in our day is mentally unstable. I advise you both to cast off those burdensome weapons like I did some time ago, forget about them, and devote your time and effort to sharpening your daggers."

Yumpik immediately pulled his sword from his belt and tossed it unceremoniously across the room, where it slid with a clattering noise across the stone floor until it hit the wall with a loud clang. "Glad ter be rid o' it, always bumpin' inter me shins an' causin' grief."

Frib half-extracted his Child of the Stars, then paused. "But, Reasno, I was bested in a fair fight by a young warrior who had barely a few inches shining. He learned to use his sword effectively, even with just a small portion alight. And I'm no slouch when it comes to sword-fighting, being among the top ten in the Razorback Brigade. I'd like to keep mine."

Reasno narrowed his eyes and gritted his teeth. "Well, if that's what you want. But you'll soon discover it's nigh impossible to sharpen, and it won't stay sharp either. You'll have to keep redoing the same edge time after time, but if that's what you want . . . "

Frib replaced the sword in his belt. "I'll be careful."

"Just don't neglect your dagger. It has basically the same message as the swords, or so I've been told. Now, we need to find out what happened to my stash of daggers down in the bottom field. Follow me."

Frib and Yumpik trotted on Reasno's heels, out the doorway, down across the field of waist-high grasses, and to a pile of brush and tree limbs stacked at the very bottom of the glacis.

"This is where they took the burlap sacks they dug up from under the rock pile yonder." Frib pointed up the hillside. "Then they cut branches off the trees and piled them here."

Yumpik knelt at the edge of the pile and sifted a handful of ashes through his fingers. "Looks like them tried ter burn it, too, only last night's rainstorm musta doused the brush pile afore it caught."

Reasno lunged at the topmost charred branches of the pyre, tossing them helter-skelter, probing beneath boughs and saplings with his hands for the burlap sacks. After several minutes, he paused to bark at his companions, "Don't just stand there; give a hand."

Frib and Yumpik fell to, scattering branches and half-burnt saplings around the extinct bonfire until Reasno cried out in relief and tugged on a large sack, freeing it from its confines under a tangle of twigs and roots. "They're safe." Reasno laughed, flinging another branch aside. "I see, three . . . no, more. Four, five sacks. We have enough to arm a brigade!" he cried aloud as he furiously tore at the impeding network of interlaced branches, vines, and stems.

Showered with litter from Reasno's maniacal digging, Frib and Yumpik stepped out of the way of the flying debris. Finally, when the rain of twigs and limbs ceased, they assisted Reasno in lugging the sacks out from under the pile.

Reasno mused, "They must have expected the daggers to melt into one big, molten lump and lie in the bottom of a hole, buried forever under ashes. Well, we just might have something to say about that, mightn't we, lads?"

"Right yer be's, Cap'n," Yumpik enthusiastically enjoined.

Frib agreed as he absentmindedly rubbed his recent chest scar. "Ah, strange, I felt a sting . . . " He looked down inside his jerkin but, seeing nothing of note, went back to work and dragged another sack from under the firewood.

"Five sacks." Reasno smiled, opening one and peering inside. "At least forty daggers per sack—that adds up to some two-hundred or more daggers. Let's drag these three sacks up to the fortress; then you two come back down for the other two while I strategize our defense. Tomorrow, we'll start combing the wilds for deserters from either army as well as those who got confused in battle and wandered off aimlessly. Who knows, we may even meet new recruits coming from the battlefront and persuade them to join us." Reasno's eyes moistened as he adoringly held a dagger before his face.

Later that night, the threesome sat around the fireplace in Metid's office, imbibing the captain's store of fine brandy and guzzling foodstuffs that had been abandoned.

"Yessiree, men." Reasno leaned back in Metid's favorite overstuffed chair and propped his feet on an ottoman. "This here's the life. All we have to do now is seek out stragglers and show them the wisdom of joining us. I hereby promote you two to be my lieutenants. I'll conduct classes on dagger warfare and tactics, and you two will drill them into fighting shape."

"Who we gonna fight?" Frib asked. "I mean, if all other Ecclessites are fighting the empire's forces, who's left for us to engage?"

"You just let that little detail to me. I'm the captain; that kind of decision is best left to me. You just concern yourself with learning your daggers well enough to train others, eh?" Reasno popped a confectionary into his mouth and wiped the icing off his lips. "Have you picked your bunks yet? There's a whole keep full of choice bedding, you know. Better select yours before we gather recruits. Tomorrow, you'll start seeking in the nearby woods and trails for wanderers. I'll check out the other side of the bridge to see if anyone has been left over there."

~

As morning sunshine broke through the mists, Frib and Yumpik set out in search of stragglers, splitting up and heading toward the previous week's battle zones. Frib wandered along the trail over which Artka and his friends had retreated after setting the field afire. Yumpik went the other way, finding remnants of the battle that had taken place on the edge of Lake Maniways. It was there where the empire's fleet was driven back out to sea, all ships capsized by a rogue wave that accompanied the ominous tone resounding from the skies.

Reasno had watched his two henchmen exit beneath the portcullis; then he exited out the back way through the empty stables toward the bridge that spanned the Flaming Sword River. The livestock had been sent across the bridge into Ecclessa in the event the castle was besieged, lest the animals be captured and subjected to the cruelty of Carnalian troops.

Reasno slid down the bank and stood upon the easternmost ledge of ground on the Carnalian side of the river. He wanted to cross over and search for supplies and round up any possible latecomers that might have filtered down from the remote hills of Ecclessa in the last few days. He stared at the narrow bridge spanning the waterway to where it disappeared in the morning mists. Across the river were the ramparts of the King's Gate Fortress East rising above the mists, presenting various pennants on the watchtowers fluttering in the breeze. He lifted his foot to place it on the bridge. A sudden, irrational trembling seized him. He broke into a cold sweat; try as he might, he was unable to lower his foot to the planking. Captain Metid's voice echoed in his memory, "Only those who've been to Logon's Rock dare venture upon that straight and narrow conduit."

As many years as he'd inhabited the kingsmen fortress on the Carnalian banks of the river, enjoying the benefits as if he were a true recruit—eating, attending lectures, associating with and making friends, not to forget enjoying the security and protection—he'd never come this close to actually crossing the river. Now, here he was, on the fringe of entering Ecclessa, legs aquiver, palms sweating, unable to take the first step.

A harsh, buzzing sound burst from the sky. The vibration intensified; Reasno's vision blurred; vertigo overtook him; his stomach turned queasy like he was being spun in circles. The bridge in front of him vibrated with the tone, pulsating to the melody. Fearful words flowed unbidden through his mind:

> *Sun, and moon, and stars, all a third part*
> *Have they lost of what they once had.*
> *Dim and short, days and nights at this word,*
> *Fades all hope—for Lurcan, 'tis bad.*

Reasno put his hands over his ears and shouted, "Stop! Stop that awful sound!" He collapsed to his knees.

~

In Captain Metid's office, a sword lying in the corner against the wall had several runes suddenly blaze bright amber and resonate with the ubiquitous tone drowning out all other sounds.

~

Miles away, Yumpik, nearing the shoreline and espying several kingsmen weapons scattered over the battleground, was stunned by the hum; his eyes frantically searched his surroundings. He winced at the increasing volume and covered his ears as he crumpled, nauseous, whimpering, wanting the horrible noise from the sky to stop.

~

On the opposite side of the mountain, Frib felt a vibration pulsing through the sword in his belt. He instinctively grabbed the hilt, and a tingle ran up his arm. Had he just heard a voice say, "It's not too late," as a humming tone washed over him? Unbidden words ran through his mind accompanying the song but made no sense. An amber light beamed from his sword even as a shroud of darkness over-swept the sky and land, dimming the sun.

~

At the ramp to Logon's Bridge, Reasno collapsed onto his backside and stared stupidly in front of him. How long the tone lasted, he didn't know; but when his senses returned, it felt like hours had passed. The bridge and its environs had become dark as twilight. Rolling mists rose up from the river and encroached on and around the bridge; it was as if the foggy billows had minds of their own and were intentionally surging at him.

Fragments of an argument with Artka about invisible tophet creatures, enshrouded in fogbanks who were voracious devourers of human flesh, played over in his mind. Reasno shook his head as he struggled to regain his feet as he reached for his dagger. He trembled as he kept his eyes riveted on the approaching fogbanks. In his haste, he accidently grabbed the exposed blade. He looked at the slice in his hand in horror; blood-scent filled the air.

Swirling mists swarmed closer. Color drained from his face. Reasno folded his arms across his chest and opened his mouth to scream, but there was no breath in him.

The first murky wave engulfed him. It was just a dense, rolling mist—nothing more.

A voice floated to his ears as if from the next wave of oncoming fog banks. "Hello, is someone there?"

Reasno caught his breath and replied, "Heh—hello? Who's there?'

Several shadowy forms coming across the bridge emerged out of the fog. "I'm Rarn. With me are some kingsmen who missed the general muster."

Reasno's pulse slowed. "Advance and be recognized."

Rarn, followed by nearly a score of men and women, dismounted from the bridge and lined up in front of Reasno. Most, but not all, had tip-lit swords, either in sheaths or dangling from belts; only the very tips of these swords twinkled with the merest speck of blue light, including Rarn's. Some carried various other implements—such as pitchforks, axes, and shovels—presumably to use as weapons. Some had left their swords behind.

"There are more of us back on the other side—a few hundred or so who've migrated down from the hills over the last couple of days."

Putting on a false bravado, Reasno threw back his shoulders, arched his spine, and strutted back and forth in front of the arrivals. "I'm Debator—er, that is, Captain Debator. I'm in charge of re-establishing defenses here at King's Gate Fortress West, since the main force has marched off to attack Carnalia. I presume you've come hither with the intention of defending the castle and bridge?"

"Well, actually"—Rarn glanced behind at his comrades—"we just sort of meandered around wondering what to do ever since everyone else left to join the muster. We felt it'd be safer to stay behind and get prepared—you know, sharpen our weapons." He sheepishly held up his sword. "Seeing as we weren't really prepared for this final battle to come just yet."

"I see. Well, I have good news for you. I can supply you with a weapon that doesn't require hours of laborious tolling and is easier to use. Rarn, is it?"

Rarn nodded.

"Yes, well, I see characteristics of leadership in you. What's your present rank?"

"Barely a recruit, sir. The officers kept urging me to light up my sword if I wanted to advance in rank."

"Yes, yes, I know. Such officers only regard activity connected with their precious swords worthy of promotion, whereas I can see qualities apart from mindless dedication to ancient inscriptions on an obsolete weapon. Rarn, I commission you here and now as a sergeant in this Daggerman Brigade."

Rarn grinned and clicked his heels.

"Sergeant, your first duty is to designate two men to return across the bridge and summon everyone left over there to come here to this fortress. Tell them they're now part of this Daggerman Brigade; they're to bring as many supplies as they can tote. Oh, and leave posted messages for any others who might yet wander down out of the hinterlands to come across and join us."

Rarn turned to the two men standing immediately behind him and sent them off with Reasno's instructions.

"And hurry," Reasno called after the departing messengers, "since it's so late in the day."

"But, Captain, it's still forenoon," said Rarn.

"That can't be . . . look how dark it is."

"Aye, Captain, but t'was merely minutes ago that trumpeting call made our swords glow strangely, and then the atmosphere suddenly darkened. At first, we thought it was due to thickening fog; but it came on so rapid like—and with the bridge shaking so—it like to 'ave toss us into the torrents below. As soon as the shaking stopped, we found ourselves here at this end of the bridge. What made you think the day was far spent?"

"Eh? Oh, I must've fallen into some sort of spell, I guess, when that awful trumpet blast shook the bridge. Anyway, let's get your people into the castle. Are you hungry?"

"Well, we ate this morning from the kitchen on t'other side. We figured it was all right, since no one was there anyway and the food was just going to spoil."

"Didn't I recognize leadership qualities in you? Well done, Rarn, well done. Now, come along."

Reasno led the new arrivals up a series of elongated steps that had been designed to accommodate horses, all the while chatting excitedly with Rarn about advancing in rank and authority in the King's Gate Daggerman Brigade. He led through empty stables into the dimly lighted keep as he encouraged his newfound followers to settle into the quarters of their liking and, once settled, to reassemble in the keep's hall for a lecture on dagger-warfare.

CHAPTER NINETEEN

"GET DOWN!" FROBASCH WHISPERED WITH such intensity that Saygus didn't even consider the jagged seashells that might be under water. The two men dropped into the knee-deep surf, leaving only noses, eyes, and foreheads above water. The kelp strands they'd harvested undulated in the choppy waves around them like sea serpents. Looking ashore, Saygus spotted a luminous, crimson spray mixed with amber-hued sparkles shooting into the air against the dark environs. Intervening dunes obscured the view of the green-flecked sea and whatever was behind those dunes causing that spray; but there was no doubt that the sights and sounds, faint as they were, indicated that some pitiful victim had been seized by the Gwollerbect.

Saygus nudged close to Frobasch and cupped his hand over the other's ear. "Do you think it caught Fleb?"

Frobasch shook his head and pointed. "Not likely—we left Fleb over there, somewhere in those dunes; and that commotion is along the shoreline. Probably caught one of those deep-sea creatures. I think we'll be safe if we backtrack and circle out around."

"Dare we take our harvest with us?"

Frobasch shook his head. "If we don't get this kelp onshore, it'll float away. We can store it ashore, then come back later to get it."

"What about Fleb?"

"I'll go collect him once you get safely hidden in the dunes."

Saygus nodded.

The two propelled themselves backward through the lapping waves with their hands on the pebbly bottom, getting tangled in the kelp they'd towed from deeper waters. After a hundred paces, they rose, disentangled themselves, and heaped their catch above the tide line ashore. Then they crawled a hundred paces inland.

Frobasch whispered, "Wait here. I'll fetch Fleb."

Saygus nodded. "Hurry."

~

Fleb grimaced at every crunch and snap he heard coming over the dunes. He lay with face buried in sand, too terrified to move. The happy chatter of his friends returning from harvesting kelp stopped so abruptly that Fleb was sure they'd fallen prey to the beast. What would he tell the others back at camp? What would they do without Saygus? He groaned unintentionally.

The Gwollerbect might seek him out next; it could even be searching for him now. He had no idea which direction to flee. It was only a matter of time—wait, what was that?

Something slithered over the sand dune from behind and was creeping up on his blind side. If he drew his sword in defense and it wasn't the Gwollerbect, he'd give himself away; but if he hid like a frightened rabbit and it was the Gwollerbect, he'd be taken before he could defend himself. The bone-crunching sounds no longer emanated from the breakers. Had the beastie abandoned his meal to come for him? Fleb held his breath, afraid the Gwollerbect could hear his breathing and thumping heart.

There it was again; something was definitely sneaking up behind him! He seized the hilt of his sword, preparing to fend off the Gwollerbect as best he could.

There was a sudden tug on his collar hauling him backward. Fleb gasped and nearly fainted.

A soft voice whispered, "Come."

It was Frobasch. Fleb exhaled and went limp in relief.

"Why are you dallying? We need to git."

Fleb obediently scrambled on all fours after the lieutenant. After ascending and descending several dunes, he grabbed Frobasch's foot and whispered, "Where's Saygus? Did it get him?"

Frobasch turned around. "Did you hear a battle? Do you think Saygus would go down without a fight?" He stood. "Come on now. Get up; we need to make haste."

Fleb rose and stumbled behind Frobasch, nearly pitching headfirst down a steep dune where Saygus waited at the bottom. The three then set out for camp on a roundabout path, constantly checking every few moments to make sure they weren't followed.

Upon reaching camp, they found the others warming themselves around the fire, impatiently waiting for Benio to stop fussing over the ingredients and just prepare the meal. Jemele looked up as the three entered the hollow. "Where's the kelp?"

Frobasch and Saygus squatted close to the fire, drying their damp clothing while Fleb watched over their back trail. "Had to leave it on the shore," Saygus answered.

"Gwollerbect," Frobasch added.

Heads snapped up in alert, hands on sword hafts.

"Is—is it following you?" Jemele voiced for all.

"Doubtful," Frobasch said. "In all the time I've been down here, it never pursued me inland, even though it seems to know the general vicinity I inhabit. I think its fin-legs can maneuver on wet sand but might have difficulty on dry, shifting sand."

Furrowed brows relaxed, and the men resumed their former postures around the fire.

"Come on down, Fleb," Saygus called. "It won't trail us. Even if it did, I doubt it would want to take on eleven warriors at once." He turned to the group. "So, how'd tower building go today?"

Skitter replied, "Just fine. We've got most of the woody mushroom stalks cut to length and began constructing the first story atop the poon-log base. By the way, we found some large stones inland and reinforced the base against shifting in case a storm causes the tides to swell."

Saygus nodded. "A wise precaution, though I doubt it's necessary, considering the gentle nature of the tides in this underground ocean." Then turning around, he said, "Frobasch, how long does the Gwollerbect hang about its kill?"

"From what I've observed, it immediately wanders off after it's had enough."

"Tomorrow, we'll go back to retrieve our harvest. I see no need to get it any sooner."

Frobasch nodded and squeezed a few drops of seawater out of his shirttail before spreading it out to dry on a tortoise shell.

Saygus continued, "And when we've eaten and had some rune study, we'll sleep. Tomorrow, you'll go back and start the second story of the tower while we fetch the kelp. Do you have enough cured kelp on hand for the bindings?"

"Enough to go at least to the third story," said Schtor, who had assumed oversight of the actual construction since his prior occupation had been a builder. "I figure five stories will almost reach, needing only a small, sixth-flight platform to support a ladder which ought to reach the hole. A full-scale sixth story would be unnecessary and might prove too heavy for the lower stages to support."

"Saygus," voiced Bismeta, "I'm not sure that the timbers we cut from the mushroom stalks are rigid enough."

"I told you they'll do!" snapped Schtor. "It's not as if we're building a complete tower with walls and floors and supports; we only need a basic framework that can be climbed."

"Easy, men." Saygus crossed over between Schtor and Bismeta. "We don't need to get peevish with each other, nor be in any hurry. We can take our time to assure the tower's stability. I'll go have a look tomorrow, after we retrieve the kelp. Is that chow ready yet, Benio?"

After the meal, they gathered fireside as Saygus regaled them with rune lore of ancient battles. He spoke of the impossible odds stacked against kingsmen, of unexpected help arising suddenly, and of surprise tactics revealed by the Advisor that brought about victory from what threatened to bring sure defeat. Eventually, one by one, they drifted off to sleep.

After hours of restful slumber, the camp stirred and breakfasted on dried gringer fish, mushroom stalks, seaweed, and turtle eggs; cleanup chores were soon finished and Saygus and Frobasch hiked a meandering course over the inland dunes to retrieve their abandoned kelp stash.

Meanwhile, Schtor and the construction crew traipsed through the fungus jungle to the tower site, lugging more building materials to complete the second and begin the third levels. Fleb stayed behind, minding the fire.

The kelp-harvesters trudged up and down steep dunes, heading unerringly for the kelp they'd left on the beach. Frobasch searched for their own footprints on the downside of the dune. "We're close now. Should we douse the light of our swords?"

"There's not much algae-glow from the sea here. I don't think we need hide our swords—especially if, as you said, the Gwollerbect leaves his kill when he's done."

Frobasch nodded and scampered over the next dune. "Here we are; our kelp hasn't been disturbed."

Saygus shouldered the holdfasts of half a dozen plants, letting the thirty-foot stalks trail down his shoulders extending back as they dragged the stalks along. He paused and turned around. "I'd like to investigate the spot where the Gwollerbect devoured his prey. Do you mind?"

"I don't know if that's a good idea, Saygus; the Gwollerbect might return to eat any remains." Frobasch scratched his nose. "Oughtn't we get these stalks back as soon as possible?"

"Nah! A little side trip won't take much time; besides, we might learn something. Before I set forth on this undersea journey, I was advised to seek to understand any new or unusual dangers I might encounter."

"So, does that mean you have to go looking for danger?"

Saygus chuckled. "Better I learn what I can about my enemy before it discovers what it can learn about me."

Frobasch shook his head. "I've told you everything you need to know; it's huge, moves fast on wet sand, is quite agile in the sea, has gigantic teeth, and is always hungry. What more do you need to know?"

"I'm not sure. Nevertheless, I believe the Advisor is nudging me to study its kill zone, traits, and abilities, such as how it eats."

"Chomp, chomp, chomp, swallow, belch; that's about it!"

Saygus laughed. "Come, my friend; it's not wise to ignore the Advisor's prompting, especially since I'm sure this prompting is from the Advisor."

Frobasch shrugged. "Lead on."

"Which way?" Saygus asked.

"About fifty to a hundred paces or so over that way, we ought to find the remains of the poor creature it caught."

The two ditched their kelp strands once again and jogged with swords flashing back to the shoreline, alert for telltale signs of struggle or discarded creature fragments. They weren't disappointed. Almost immediately, high on the beach, they found a pile of innards, fins, a tail, and a bashed-in fish head out of the tide's reach. A luminous, sticky, yellowish-orange fluid was splattered over the sand. Surrounding the gory mess were several deep impressions that couldn't have been made by anything resembling a foot or paw. Saygus knelt and placed his fist into one of the sand depressions.

"Fin print," Frobasch confirmed.

"He's a heavy rascal, isn't he?" Saygus said, probing the depth of the print. "And how long is its body?"

"A good twenty or more paces—with mouth wide open, it can swallow a tall man standing on tiptoe. And its teeth"—he held his hands shoulder-width apart—"are this long, and—"

"I get the picture." Saygus swiveled his head side to side, scanning for more sign. "I guess I've seen enough."

"Good! Now, did you learn anything you didn't know before?"

"I'll have to think on it."

"Wake up, Fleb." Saygus nudged the fire-minder with a foot. "You might consider spending time tolling your Child of the Stars, rather than napping." Saygus and Frobasch dumped their payload of kelp beside Fleb. "Start stretching these so they don't dry out and become brittle. We'll be back after checking progress on the tower."

Saygus and Frobasch trudged half an hour through the fungus growths to the tower site. Upon arrival, they met Schtor and Bismeta handing pre-cut notched planks to workers on the framework where they were then fitted and secured to the mainstays with cured kelp bindings.

"What ho!" Jemele hailed the officers entering the worksite.

Saygus returned the greeting and, through the light of his sword, observed the progress. "Looks sturdy enough, men. I see you've made good time in lashing the third story tight. Are you ready to begin the fourth stage?"

"Just need some more cured kelp-rope." Schtor swung down from a higher level. "We found it best to twist three dried kelp strands together instead of just two—makes it more durable."

"Which also means we'll need more kelp," said Bismeta, sitting on the shoreline braiding kelp fibers into a finger-thick cord. "We're running low."

"We left more stalks back at camp to cure," Frobasch said. "But that won't be enough, will it?"

"Not unless they're twice as long as these were." Bismeta coiled the rope he was working around his elbow and shoulder, placed it on the ground atop other cured lengths, and began twisting other fibers into a knot.

Saygus sighed. "I suppose we need more. Jemele, have you cut enough struts?"

"Will have soon. Skitter and Flonkry are in the *fungal jungle* as we speak, chopping more stalks. After Osk notches these lengths to fit, I'll send him to help haul planks over here. Main thing we need right now is more kelp-rope."

"You've taken all the vine-cordage from the rafts?"

"All that was usable."

Saygus nodded. "Well, completion of the tower will have to wait a few more days, so the bindings will be trustworthy. Let's knock off for now, men. It's been a long, tiring day. After our meal, we'll study rune-lore and do sword drills to prepare for the battles ahead. Someone fetch Flonkry and Skitter."

"I'll go; I know where they're logging," Jemele said.

Jemele chugged over the high dunes toward the mushroom jungle, while the others trailed Frobasch and Saygus back to camp.

The next day, Saygus left Jemele in charge of the building crew and then assigned Skitter, Flonkry, and Osk to the jungle logging crew. Saygus went with Frobasch and Fleb to the kelp fields. Fleb nervously kept checking all around as he wordlessly trudged over the dunes.

Though Saygus said nothing, Fleb interpreted his commander's actions as if there was an urgency in building the tower and time was becoming a factor.

"Wait here, Fleb." Saygus indicated a hollow of a ridge under the last dune overlooking the shoreline. "We have to swim farther out this time; the nearest kelp beds are depleted. So, don't panic if we're out longer than usual, okay?"

"Just be careful coming in; last time, you almost stumbled into . . . you know."

"Promise." Saygus touched his hand to his chest. "We'll be careful. Don't forget to toll your sword while you wait, but keep it below the crest of the dunes, lest it be seen."

Fleb nodded and withdrew his Child of the Stars as the two officers waded out into the surf's pale green glow. He seated himself cross-legged in the sand, sighed, and laid his sword across his lap, placing his toller on the middle of the blade and giving it a gentle push. The soft scraping sound produced a sense of calm; everything would be all right. He relaxed as he honed the blade; memories of past lessons taught by former brigade leaders stirred in his mind. Though he and the men he was with were in surreal circumstances, the risks unknown, the mission impossible, and the dangers such that not even Saygus had any previous experience, the runes impressed the message that Logon wasn't unaware. Nothing caught Logon by surprise; nothing surprised or brought fear to Logon's heart.

Fleb was in such a state of bliss that he didn't notice an hour had passed as he eagerly lit up three previously undiscovered runes. He smiled, embarrassed that he'd allowed fear to get the better of him. The runes comforted him, but what was it Saygus had said during their voyage? "Beware upon receiving joyous revelations from tolling the runes, for that exuberant experience is often preparation for a severe trial or battle."

Fleb's smile disappeared; he craned his neck around. All seemed quiet enough—no Gwollerbect on the prowl, no splashing of waves, no disruption of any kind . . . and no Saygus and Frobasch returning from harvest! Fleb clambered to his feet. How long had it been? He descended the dune and anxiously paced the waterline, searching the green sparkles for some sign of his friends' return.

How long had he been absorbed in rune study? With three new runes aglow, it must have been quite a while. They should've been back already. Had he been so absorbed in tolling that he had missed their signal, seeking where to land? Once again, his irresponsibility put everyone, and the mission itself, in jeopardy. He plopped down on his backside, head in his hands. They must have desperately flashed their swords above the waves, seeking to locate him; but he'd been so engrossed in rune discovery, he'd failed them. Now they were adrift somewhere up or down the coast, treading water, packing kelp stalks, fatigued, unsure where to come ashore. It was all his fault! They would perish at sea! Who would lead the assault now? Saygus, gone. Frobasch gone. Due to his folly! "Oh, Logon, what am I going to do now?"

One of the runes he'd just illuminated flashed briefly across his mind:

> For those committed to serve Elyon,
> What e'er mayhap, to portend grief,
> Be nature, beast, or human hellion,
> Logon's own will know relief.

Fleb studied the rune, then started to stow his sword away. He felt inclined to glance seaward one more time; and as he did, a sense of calm flooded his heart. Logon knew. That was enough. Logon could easily have prodded him to look up in time to signal his friends, especially since it was Logon's sword he'd been so focused upon. He tucked his weapon away.

"Fleb," a hoarse whisper carried over the dunes from behind.

Fleb spun around. "Saygus? Is that you?" he called back in a hushed voice. "I thought I'd lost you—"

"No, it's me, Benio. I've been sent to retrieve the three of you immediately. Something's happened to the tower." A shadowy head and shoulders appeared on top of a sandy ridge. "Come quickly."

"Alas, Saygus and Frobasch"—Fleb's voice cracked—"are lost at sea."

"What?" Benio slid down the dune and landed alongside Fleb. "What are you talking about?" His voice rose in panic. "What do you mean, 'lost at sea'?"

"I—I wasn't paying attention. I failed to signal them."

Several yards offshore, something splashed in the waves. Both men backed away, fumbling in their belts for their sword hafts.

"And did you think, Fleb, that we wouldn't be able to find our own way ashore?" The large form emerging from the waves appeared as a dark spot for a moment, then dissolved into two men: Frobasch and Saygus. They were hauling a kelp harvest between them on some sort of implement, which turned out to be both their Children of the Stars crisscrossed between them, draped in kelp, revealing why the light of their swords went unseen as the two emerged from the sea.

"Saygus! Frobasch! I thought I missed signaling you."

"Are you jesting? The bright light of your sword glimmered clear out to the farthest kelp beds. What were you thinking? The Gwollerbect would surely have been drawn to your beacon had it been in the vicinity."

Fleb gulped and looked down at his sword. "I guess it looks kind of bright after all, doesn't it?" The beach surrounding Fleb and Benio was alight with the blue glow of Fleb's weapon.

Saygus laughed. "Well, if you're going to attract the enemy, it's best that it be by the light from a Child of the Stars. Nevertheless, a little caution is advisable, especially when this deep in enemy territory."

"Saygus, I was sent to fetch the three of you, no matter what part of harvesting you're engaged in. Something's happened to the tower," Benio intruded, his eyes sparkling in the light of Fleb's sword.

"What happened?" Saygus demanded, tugging the seaweed ashore.

"I don't know. I was at camp when Bismeta suddenly burst in from the worksite telling me to fetch you, that something had happened to the tower. I dropped the cords I was braiding and ran straight here."

"And hasten we shall, but we'll not abandon this load like last time. It's too abundant a harvest to risk losing. Besides, it's the last we'll be able to collect from this farm for a while. We've depleted the bed of all useful kelp. So, both of you, fall to and lend us a hand."

Fleb and Benio grabbed several strands each, lugging the plants out of the lapping surf and dragging them through the dunes behind Saygus and Frobasch. They made good time with four sharing the load, though Benio kept urging haste.

Upon depositing the kelp at camp, they headed straightway to the tower site. Along the way, they encountered Demunt descending a dune. "Well met, Saygus." Demunt stopped abruptly. "I was just looking for you. The tower—"

"We're on our way now. But tell me, what about the tower?" Saygus' eyes bored into Demunt's.

Demunt's features scrunched together. "Well, you'll see." He extended his hands in front and then twisted them around and back to his left shoulder. "Somehow, it got all tangled up and twisted and caved in. Just come; you'll see."

"Did the Gwollerbect do it?" Frobasch's teeth gritted.

"Gwollerbect? Maybe." Demunt shrugged.

"We'll know more when we get there." Saygus led the way back, following Demunt's trail. The five trotted across the ground until they arrived at the small pyramid of stones and shells marking the way to the worksite.

They found the building crew sitting on the bank along the shore, dangling their feet just above the waterline, peering at what remained of the tower. The poon-log base still appeared secure, fortified by the rocks that had been placed in the turf. The planking taken from the rafts to build the first platform as well as the cured kelp bindings still seemed firm; but the fungi studs of the second floor were warped, bowed over, and collapsed under the weight of the upper framework. Several days' work bobbed along the shoreline in ruins. The hole in the ceiling seemed more unreachable than ever.

CHAPTER TWENTY

A DENSE, GREEN MIST SWIRLED around Saygus' and Frobasch's knees. The mist drifted overtop the water and seemed drawn by some atmospheric phenomenon to rise up the tower framework and vent through the gap in the ceiling, their entry into the castle precincts. Saygus and Frobasch inspected the studs bobbing in the breakers. Jemele and the others remained on shore, watching.

Frobasch plucked a stud from the water that had bumped against his shin. "Water-logged." He poked a hole through the stud with his finger. "Turned to mush."

Saygus climbed aboard the poon-log base as high as the first platform to probe the dangling, twisted fungi studs with his sword. It immediately disintegrated to chunks. "This one's not water-logged, nor are any of the others up here; but the mist has softened them to pith!" He grabbed the dangling end. "It's flexible, rubbery." He twisted it in his hands. "These sodden mushroom studs won't even bear their own weight, let alone the weight of ten men on the tower, even if we went up one at a time. Once exposed to the atmosphere, they lose integrity and crumble."

Frobasch, knee-deep in the surf, looked up at Saygus. "This fog comes along at odd times, saturating the beach environs. I could detect no regularity to it; it just comes and inundates the area for hours . . . sometimes a whole day or two. Then, just as suddenly, it vanishes."

"Well"—Jemele gave voice to the concern the others felt—"what are we going to replace those studs with? How are we going to reach that hole in the ceiling?"

Saygus studied their faces in the soft glow of their swords and the luminescent foam breaking on shore. He felt the weight of their trust. They'd followed him across uncharted waters, believing he'd had a revelation from Logon. And then there was Frobasch, who believed Logon had sent him as an advance to lead the force invading Cosmopolis.

Saygus tugged absentmindedly on his beard. What could he say? He had no answers. The first solution that presented itself—studs cut from fibrous "mushroom trees"—seemed to be Logon's provision. It was so timely and easily put into effect—but now so useless. There was no alternative construction material sturdy enough to do the job. Frobasch had scouted the chain of islets during his six-months banishment but didn't remember coming across anything suitable as building material other than fibrous mushroom stalks. Unless Saygus came up with a new and innovative solution, his crew would lose heart. Indeed, he himself was tempted to doubt the validity of their mission if access to the palace through the ceiling aperture was impossible.

But he couldn't be wrong; he'd been led to this point step by step. He was neither deceived nor misinterpreting the runes . . . or was he?

Discovering the underground sea was the serendipitous result of stumbling into Artka and his companions, confirming to him that the runes foretold of a surprise attack on the fortress of Cosmopolis via an underground sea. Then, after the battle of the Daggermen Castle and the dread's demise, he had seen runes shining brightly on the swords of the men who were to accompany him. Finding Frobasch was another confirmation . . .

Or were those just coincidences? Had he concocted a "mission" for himself in his desire to be useful and significant? Had he commandeered needed warriors away from the battle at the gates of Cosmopolis? Was he uselessly wandering about beneath the surface of the world, instead of offering Logon's amnesty to Carnalians? Had he been sidetracked by the enemy, marooned himself and his men here, with no way to join the fight up above, which must surely be about to be joined?

Saygus sat on a poon log of the base, head in his hands, softly groaning, "Oh, Logon, what have I done? Has my pride, my ambition to achieve great things, caused me to deceive myself and lead these valiant warriors astray?"

"Saygus?" Jemele waded out to the tower base and peered into his mentor's eyes. "What's wrong? Surely, there's another way."

"Yeah, we'll find some sterner building material," Bismeta called from the shoreline, "something that will hold up, like rocks. We could dig up lots of rocks—"

"No, my friends; we'd never gather—let alone stack—a pyramid of rocks high enough to accomplish our purposes. I'm afraid I've led you all astray. There's just no way to achieve entry into the castle from here."

The group on shore looked glumly at one another.

"I refuse to believe this venture is in vain, Saygus, and neither do they," Jemele argued. "I've benefited much on this voyage due to our training; this has to be Logon's plan."

"Aye." Flonkry waded out beside Jemele at the base of the tower. "This here be's nobbut jest 'nuther challenge ter overcome. Dinnae be losin' heart, genr'l."

"Uhh, Saygus," Demunt, still ashore, called timidly, "I don't know if this means anything, but . . . Well, the city of Sophista suddenly came to mind. I tried to dismiss the thought, but I keep feeling urged to mention it. Do you think that means anything?"

"Sophista?" Saygus lifted his head. "You would remind me of my worst defeat?"

"But it wasn't a defeat, though it seemed to be at the time, remember?" enjoined Frobasch. "Kingsman brigades were birthed by that 'misadventure,' if you'll recall. Though a dear price was paid, Logon achieved a great victory in those mountain passes through you."

"In spite of me, you mean."

Skitter rose. "You told us betimes on the voyage, 'Feelings don't matter as long as you obey Logon's runes and know you heard the Advisor's voice.'"

Saygus jumped knee-deep into the surf and waded ashore. "How'd you guys get so stalwart all of a sudden?"

"Must be summat in the algae-water what makes us'ns thataway," Flonkry jibed. "Surely t'warn't summat yer tried drummin' inter usn's day after day after day."

Saygus chuckled and put his arm around the Eroton's shoulders. "No, I'm sure it isn't anything I drummed into you." Then, turning to Frobasch, he said, "Have you really searched the islands thoroughly? Maybe there's some kind of rigid plant somewhere you haven't found?"

"Well, like I said, I never investigated the far side of the largest island because of the ominous howls and growls I heard over there."

"Well, it's time we searched the unknown parts of this island and see if there isn't something we can use to accomplish our objective. Back to camp now for a meal and a good rest. On the morrow, we'll establish a search grid into the unknown precincts of the isle, agreed?"

"Agreed," said all in unison.

Frobasch took point leading into the unknown sectors of the isle; the others flanked him in an inverted "V" formation, each man spaced ten paces from each other on either side. Saygus was second in line to Frobasch. All swords pointed forward, illuminating a path through boulders, decomposing matter, odd growths, and various forms of fungi that flourished all around. There were mushrooms of all shapes: puff balls as large as buckets that launched volumes of spores into the air when bumped; slender, pale stalks a few inches high with tops bowed over resembling a smoker's pipe; small cup-shaped growths extending into fairy-rings; luminescent fungi that ran along the ground for yards in blue and green strips, eventually curling inward upon themselves. It was a veritable cornucopia of unknown species through which the kingsmen searched, but nothing met their need.

"Saygus—" Bismeta cupped his hand to his mouth—"there's some sort of animal track here."

"Hold up," Saygus raised his hand. "Let's have a look." He circumspectly stepped over a line of "creeping" fungus and stood beside Bismeta, who held his sword above the impression. "I've seen similar, though this is a lot smaller." He knelt and probed the depression with his fingers. "From these tracks, I'd say that some kind of predatory feline made this mark. You were wise not to venture into these parts alone, Frobasch. Though smaller than lions, the size of this breed of feline looks quite capable of killing humans." He stood and peered into the darkness ahead. "No doubt they can see in this infernal darkness—might even be observing us now."

The troop of kingsmen nervously looked around, gripping their swords. Saygus resumed his position and okayed Frobasch to proceed. Wordlessly, they moved onward, carefully checking the ground for potential snares or den holes before each step, eyes straining ahead into the murk, ears attuned to the slightest sound.

An hour later, they reached the water's edge on the far side of the isle. "This is Land's End, lads. Now, we swing back a little deeper in." Saygus indicated with his sword. They swung in a wide arc and wheeled off at an angle, wading through thigh-high fungi stalks. Upon returning to their original embarkation point, they made another sweep on a different trajectory, and then a return, continuing the search pattern until the greater part of the unknown region was covered. They found no usable construction material.

"Well, that's it, men." Saygus turned toward the campsite. "There's nothing in all this Beneath that we can use for building our tower." He scratched his head and sighed.

"Now what?" Jemele asked.

"Back to camp to consult our swords. Frobasch, I hope you know the way back."

Frobasch grinned. "I do. This isn't far from one of my first exploratory ventures."

The kingsmen traipsed back to camp single file, arriving at camp weary, hungry, and frustrated from their futile exploration of the island. They tossed the odd pieces of driftwood gathered on their return journey onto the dying embers of the fire or on the woodpile, then fell out sitting cross-legged around the fire.

Saygus noted discouragement in their downcast eyes. He was discouraged, too; and he was the one supposed to know what to do next—or, at least, keep their spirits up. He stared into the flames spewing sparks into the air.

Flonkry was the first to begin tolling his sword.

"At least, we didn't encounter any of those wildcats," Benio said to no one in particular.

"Nah, them's wouldnae dare ter attack all of usn's at oncet," Flonkry said, looking up. "It be's when yer all alone thet them attacks."

"What rune is that?" Saygus rose from his seat, eyeing Flonkry's sword.

"Eh?" the Eroton examined his weapon. Sure enough, a small rune was brightly glowing inches away from his toller.

"Read it," Saygus urged.

"Read it? Er, it be's sayin':

> 'Stone foundation, stern of form,
> Stands secure midst the storm.
> Let builders care for what they add;
> Weak supports will prove bad.
> To raise the wall safe and sound,
> Strong resource must be found.
> Where the struts expected least,
> Guarded by voracious beast,
> Conquered foes become your meat
> To have at the Grim Lord's seat.'"

"Well done, Flonkry—and without an Eroton accent!" teased Jemele as he rubbed the Eroton's shaggy head.

"But what does it mean?" Frobasch tossed another piece of driftwood on the fire. "Do we have to fight vicious beasts like the wildcats lurking in the area we just searched in order to find suitable building materials?"

"Yeah, Saygus, there's nothing in there that we can use." Bismeta nudged an errant branch back onto the fire with his foot. "We searched far and wide, water to water each way, and there's nothing."

Others murmured in agreement.

Saygus raised his hands. "I know; I know. But . . . let's get our swords and toll the rune together and see if we receive insight from the Advisor. Remember, we're soldiers of the sword. We live and die by the sword's runes, not conjecture, nor prevailing conditions. Logon drew our attention to this rune by causing it to light up, so he'll give understanding if we patiently seek." So saying, he returned to his place and began tolling. "All right, let's take this stanza by stanza:

> 'Stone foundation, stern of form,
> Stands secure midst the storm . . . '

"Originally, this rune is about forming brigades by using the metaphor of castle-building. But, as with many runes, secondary meanings can be derived when and if specific conditions apply."

"And does this condition apply?" Fleb fixed his eyes on Saygus.

"Are we not building something? Something that, when completed, will allow us to 'have at the Grim Lord's seat?' And is our tower's base not set firmly amidst stones?"

The men nodded.

"Right. The storm, then, could be the battle we're preparing for. The next line—'*Let builders care for what they add; / Weak supports will prove bad. / To raise the wall safe and sound, / Strong resource must be found*'—might well apply to the ruined fungi studs we tried."

"But how does it apply to brigade building?" Demunt scrutinized the rune beneath his toller. "I mean, I'd like to know that, too, not just what it means specifically here and now to us."

Saygus smiled. "That's a wise question, Demunt. Originally, it meant that Logon's officers were to only teach troopers truths that are clearly explained by the runes on the swords; otherwise, brigades could unknowingly get led astray. Falsehoods prove unreliable and useless in battle, even dangerous. When you apply yourself to learn the runes, seek not only what directly applies to you but also learn what you can about the original meaning. Knowing the primary truth will help keep you from deception, and you'll be able to see if the new application fits without applying a proverbial shoehorn."

"Yeah, all right, we get that part; it's the next lines that are confusing." Skitter tapped his sword and read, '*Where the struts expected least, / Guarded by voracious beast.*' If that don't mean to go hunting those wildcats, what does it mean? They are, after all the only 'vicious' creatures we have come across."

"Maybe that part of the rune doesn't apply to our situation?" suggested Osk.

Saygus shook his head. "No, I think it does, Osk. Since the rune lit up, we should seek the fullest application."

"But how, Saygus? We've exhausted every avenue. Other than this flimsy driftwood, there's not a sturdy thing on any of these forsaken isles to use for construction. We've cannibalized our rafts till there's nothing left, and we're still a couple dozen feet short of our objective." Schtor leaned back on his elbows, letting the sword slide partly off his lap.

Saygus exhaled slowly. "I don't know how yet."

Skitter mumbled under his breath and stroked his sword once more:

> 'Where the struts expected least,
> Guarded by voracious beast.'

"That's it!" Saygus stood to his feet clapping his hands. "We've been thinking of 'vicious beasts'; but the rune says, 'voracious beast.'"

The others stared, brows furrowed, mouths slightly open. First Frobasch, followed by Jemele, then Bismeta, nodded.

"What?" Fleb challenged, his nostrils flaring.

"The most voracious creature down here," said Frobasch, "is—"

"The Gwollerbect!" Demunt, Skitter, and Osk chorused together.

Fleb whistled a prolonged note.

"The Gwollerbect." Saygus smiled at his squad.

Jemele hunched forward. "Frobasch, do you know where the Gwollerbect's lair is?"

"No idea. Never wanted to know. I stayed as far away as possible."

"So, let me understand." Skitter rose to his feet. "You're saying that the Gwollerbect has a hidden treasure trove of building struts somewhere, and our mission is to sneak into his lair while he's out marauding and steal them so we can finish our tower? Do I have that correct?"

Saygus pursed his lips. "Almost."

Skitter flung his arms wide. "Almost? Almost? What, by Pitland, do you mean 'almost'? We find his lair, steal the supplies we need, and hie back and finish the tower. What's 'almost' about that?"

"I don't believe the Gwollerbect has a lair. In fact, I believe he rarely, if ever, sleeps—if he does, it's while on the prowl. No, I think the building material we need stays with the Gwollerbect wherever he goes."

"That's crazy, Saygus! Why would the Gwollerbect drag a lot of cumbersome logs around with him as he hunts?" Benio extended his arms behind his head and leaned back.

"Ah." Frobasch, bent forward re-examining his sword. "I think I see. Yes, Mr. Gwollerbect will protect these building materials quite fiercely."

"You mean, it knows why we're building a tower?" Demunt scratched his head in frustration. "How could it know? Why would it care?"

"Yeah, from what Frobasch told us, it's just a beast, with a beast's instincts for survival, isn't it?" Fleb added.

Jemele sidled in next to Saygus and examined his leader's sword to see if perhaps another rune had lit up which his sword hadn't revealed. "I don't understand, Saygus."

Several others voiced the same sentiment.

"All right, consider this: what would the Gwollerbect value more than anything?"

"His treasure trove, if he has one," ventured Benio.

"We've already established it's not likely he has such a thing, due to his roving nature. But even if he did, isn't there something he would value and fight to protect even more?" Saygus tantalized.

Scrunched brows and pursed lips from his squad greeted his riddle. Then Osk spoke almost too softly to hear. "Is it . . . his life?"

Saygus smiled broadly and pointed at Osk. "You were the one to find the keys in the sand; and now, you find the key unlocking this enigmatic rune."

The others stared blankly.

"And how are we to take the Gwollerbect's life?" Saygus held his hands palm-up and twitched all his fingers.

"With our swords?" Demunt shouted.

"Yes." Saygus smiled. "and just what do we do to him with our swords?"

Flonkry jumped to his feet and pantomimed. "Arrgh, we hacks an' stabs an slices an' sticks an' slits him wide open, we does."

Laughter filled the campsite; the tension was broken, and fear of the Gwollerbect was diminished by the Eroton's antics.

They settled down, and Saygus continued drawing answers out of them. "And when we slit him open, what do we find?"

"Innards!" Flonkry gleefully responded.

More laughter.

"And what else do we find after the innards are removed?"

"None of us, hopefully," ventured Fleb.

Again, the warriors laughed.

"All right, but seriously, what else do we find inside the Gwollerbect that we might find useful for construction?"

Again, the kingsmen looked blankly at each other.

"Come on, men, think. This isn't alchemy."

Bismeta shrugged and sheepishly said, "Steaks and spareribs?"

Saygus stared at the overhead blackness and gasped. "And ribs are made of . . ."

"Bone!" shouted several, jumping to their feet.

Saygus leaned back with a sigh. "Finally!"

Skitter crawled over to Saygus. "What are you hinting at—that we have to kill the Gwollerbect, skin him, and collect his bones to finish our tower?"

Saygus smiled at Frobasch, who smiled back.

"An 'ere I thot we be's gonna hafta do summat difficult," said Flonkry.

A few men groaned.

Saygus read aloud, "*Conquered foes become your meat, / To have at the Grim Lord's seat.*" Then he added, "Killing the Gwollerbect is the last phase of our training for the battles we'll encounter in Lurcan's lair."

The kingsmen settled back into their hollowed-out nooks and stared into the fire, swords upon their laps, tollers motionless in their hands.

"We're not ready," muttered Jemele. "We need lots more training."

"And rune study," said Demunt. "At least, I know I do."

Several others murmured in agreement.

"After we sleep, we resume training." Saygus stretched. "We've let training go lax for the purpose of building the tower. We—that is, I—got priorities out of order. Obviously, Logon knows we're not as ready as we—as I—thought, to encounter whatever battles await us in Lurcan's palace. If the Gwollerbect is a lesser foe than the shock troops we'll encounter, we have much work to do."

"I'm not looking forward to that tussle," said Frobasch, his face noticeably pale even in the diminished light of their surroundings.

Even Flonkry was subdued by the realization of meeting the alpha predator of the underworld. "Hey, Saygus"—he leaned back on his elbows—"what if'n there be's a Mrs. Gwollerbect? Or what if it gots a momma an' a poppa? I mean, every crittur comes from a family, don't it?"

Saygus massaged his brow. "You had to take us there, didn't you? Just when we're trying to cope with taking down one Gwollerbect, you had to suggest there may be more."

Demunt and Benio threw handfuls of sand at Flonkry. "We didn't need to hear that brilliant bit of insight."

"Actually, we did," said Saygus. "What we don't need is to get surprised by any Gwollerbect kith and kin. We need a plan, a comprehensive plan for any and all possibilities. But proceed without delay, we must; for without the bones of a Gwollerbect, we'll not be able to complete the tower."

CHAPTER TWENTY-ONE

JORNA LOOKED INTO HER HUSBAND'S eyes, then to the sword on the table. The shaking stopped. The house quieted, and the sword runes faded; candlelight mainly illumined the room.

The dominant trumpet blare that had reverberated through the streets and alleys of Cosmopolis pervaded every building, but the call-to-arms was comprehended only by kingsmen. Flan arose to his feet and surveyed the roomful of assembled Ecclessite leaders. "Well, that ought to affirm our decision. We'll send Knarsh and the others back to the Ra-Amawl brigade with tidings of all that transpired during this confab with our brigade. Cleese, I appoint you to go along and speak on my behalf should an official word be required."

Knarsh and the Ra-Amawl personnel lodged with Flan and Jorna for the next two days, sitting up late at night comparing runic insights each brigade had discovered. They were told how the city brigade survived under the very noses of Carnalian spies who constantly tried to ferret out kingsmen. In return, the forest brigaders explained how they avoided detection by camouflage techniques and dodging Carnalian patrols in the wilds.

They basked in the fellowship of fellow kingsmen from another place and delighted in discovering that both brigades, remote as they were from each other, were led to the same conclusions about the weighty times the world had entered upon.

Knarsh, however, felt an urgency to return to the jungle brigade. "Flan, we need to inform Captain Varter and coordinate the timing of our attack with your strategy on the assault of the fortified palace."

Jorna looked imploringly to her husband. "I'd hoped the Ra-Amawl squad could tarry a few days longer."

Flan held his wife's gaze a moment. "I respect your opinion, dear, but have you any reason as to why?"

Jorna looked eye to eye at the visitors clustered around the table. "I can't say why, perhaps it has to do with—"

Flan raised a hand, interrupting his wife. "Look, we just experienced the fourth trumpet blast. Knarsh, I believe this is why Logon had you linger as long as you did—so that you might witness the sounding of the fourth trumpet safely with us before returning. The days of our exile in a hostile world are drawing to a close. Very soon, cataclysmic events will engulf the planet; and many of us will be gathered to Splendora. But first, we must offer amnesty to as many Carnalians as possible before the fifth, sixth, and final trumpet sounds. I believe Logon wanted you here so you could relate to Captain Varter that we believe this fourth trumpet signifies the fulfillment of yet another foretold event."

"I agree," Jorna said. "The next trumpet, the fifth, will unleash a horrendous evil across the empire. You'll need to be safely secure in your own brigade before that happens."

Knarsh leaned forward, pressing his knuckles on the tabletop, nodding in agreement. "Do you know what form the evil will take?"

Flan retrieved his sword from the table and read:

> "'Sun, and moon, and stars, all a third
> Have they lost of what they once had.

Dim and short, days and nights at this word,
Fades all hope—for Lurcan, 'tis bad.

Then rose up roamer, the sounder of fourth,
And flying discreetly o'er all the earth
Cried a message of worse woes come forth,
Three judgments more cruel about to have birth.

At the fifth roamer's sound,
A power from great height
Fell toward the ground
And released the fell wight
From waters undrowned,
Rising darker than night,
As smoke pours unbound,
And vapors take sight,
Tormenting those found,
Void of Logon's renown
And victims of fallen bright.'"

"Ever since the third trumpet sounded, the sun's light has been dimmed, as well as the darkness of night diminished. What all this means . . . " Flan shrugged. "But the trumpets clearly augur evil curses falling on the inhabitants of Lurcan's domain. The next trumpet will release tormenting wights. And they'll wreak havoc. I strongly advise you to be safely embedded in your brigade by then."

Dacey tugged Knarsh's sleeve. "The phantoms under the marsh waters where our brigade sequesters—didn't Captain Varter call them wights?"

Knarsh studied Dacey's face. "Yes, I believe so. Legend has it that they were imprisoned by King Elyon in a watery crypt due to their heinous cruelty shortly after the dawn of creation. They'll be allowed to roam free for a short season prior to the end of the age. Do you think those hideous faces glaring up out of the swampy depths are the wights mentioned in the rune?"

"Seems likely," Flan agreed.

"I think so, too," added Jorna. "And now, with all Cosmopolis in a stir over the impending coronation and its prophetic ramifications, time is indeed growing short. You must leave as soon as possible in order to get there before . . . "

"Before those wights are released." Flan slipped his sword into its stays underneath the tabletop. "Jorna's right; there's no time to waste. How soon can you pack and be on your way?"

"Soon as it's dark enough," said Knarsh. "It's been a privilege being here, meeting all of you, gleaning your knowledge of the runes."

Cleese lifted a window curtain and peered out. "Streets are astir—probably caused by the trumpet blast. And I see more citizens sporting tattoos on their foreheads in preparation for the coronation. Sharifs on patrol look askew at anyone who hasn't taken the *treblesix* venerating the Feuhr. If we go out in daylight without the mark, I'm afraid we'll arouse suspicion."

"No more suspicion than if we were caught in a house-to-house search." Trembu joined him at the window. "And it's imperative we deliver the battle plans to Varter so he'll know when and how to mobilize his forces."

"So speaks the bold lion killer," jibed Knarsh. "Always ready for the dangerous mission."

Flan looked up. "Lion killer?"

Glend spoke up. "Oh yes, he was very brave. When our campsite was relocating, a huge, black lion—"

"Craniantium lion," interrupted Dacey.

"Er, right, a Craniantium lion attacked Jeda," Glend resumed, "when she was at the rear of the column. It stalked us from behind, burst through the rear guards, and made straight for Jeda. But Trembu stabbed the beast, saving her."

The assembled Cosmopolisian brigade members perused Trembu afresh.

"Well, actually"—Trembu blushed—"the captain's daughter, Vawella, struck the fatal blow, splitting its skull. I only slowed it down. Truth be told, it had previously been wounded, and a roamer was there, too. The roamer seized the great cat and held it suspended in mid-air for a moment, allowing me to gather my wits and stab at it, delaying it until Vawella was ready to strike."

Flan grinned. "Well, I see our little brigade has linked up with mighty warriors. I think we need not worry about you getting back to your brigade safely. Even so, Cleese, lead them by safe routes where sharifs rarely patrol in the city."

Cleese nodded.

Knarsh placed his arm around Cleese's shoulder. "We're comforted he's accompanying us, Flan. Who knows what we might encounter, as unfamiliar as we are with this city's streets? It seems like the whole world has turned darker since we've ventured from Ra-Amawl: the fourth trumpet has sounded; a heinous villain is about to ascend the highest throne in the empire; and by coercion, citizens are branded like so many cattle. Worst of all, we hear of Ecclessites from various locales mercilessly hunted down and exterminated as if they were a plague."

"Sharifs heading this way." Hanell let the curtain drop and backed away from the window.

~

"Quick, into the secret hall behind the tapestry, everybody." Jorna spread her arms like a mother hen huddling her brood. Before closing the door and letting the tapestry fall into place, Jorna added, "King's road to you," aware she wouldn't likely see them for a long time, if ever.

The very next moment, a fierce pounding battered the exterior door. "Open up in the name of the empire."

Jorna's eyes widened as she went and stood beside Flan as he answered the door. He smiled briefly to give her confidence, then raised his hand to the latch bar.

Ruthless pounding again rattled the door's frame. "Open up!"

Spying her sword on the tabletop where she had left it—and since there was no time to cover it in one of the baskets along the far wall—she dashed to the table and in one fluid motion placed her sword underneath the tabletop in its stays beside Flan's.

Seeing the sword secured, Flan lifted the bar and swung the door open, brazenly blocking the doorway. "May I help you, sharifs?"

At the forefront of the sharifs was a tall, black-garbed dronnet. Despite his half-mask and uniform identical to every other dronnet, Jorna recognized Flarg from his visits to the Boar's Tusk Inn; he was often in the company of various commanders and government officials. Flarg jabbed his index finger into Flan's chest, forcing him backward as he and his squad of sharifs entered.

"May *you* help *us*?" bellowed a short, plump lieutenant prominently sporting a badge of authority on his chest as he pushed his way around the dronnet and barged into the middle of the room. "Here's how *you* may help *me*: you can tell me why you haven't reported to receive your loyalty tats!" Ten armed sharifs streamed into the room behind the lieutenant.

Flan and Jorna were forcibly pressed backward against the table at the back wall. "As I understand the decree"—Flan grabbed the dronnet's hand and vainly tried to move it off his chest—"we have several days until we must decide whether to take the oath and tattoo."

"Not for you," snapped the lieutenant. "Your time has run out." Turning to his men, he ordered, "Turn the house inside-out."

Out of the corner of her eye, Jorna spied her toller on the table behind Flan; she gasped and bit her lip. She then unobtrusively edged herself in front of it and leaned backward against the table, ostensibly for balance while maneuvering the file behind her into a fold of her skirt.

The sharifs ransacked the house, overturning the hutch; pulling cabinets away from walls; flipping chairs, settees, trunks; rummaging through desk drawers and even storage baskets, strewing the contents across the floor—everything except pulling down the wall hangings and flipping the table Jorna and Flan leaned against. Sharifs charged into the adjacent sleeping quarters making a loud commotion, banging and throwing Flan's and Jorna's possessions around with disdain. They finally emerged several minutes later, one of them reporting, "Nothing incriminating, sir."

"Hmmm," the lieutenant narrowed his eyes and stared at Flan, then Jorna. "Search them."

"Now see here," Flan protested, "we're honest citizens with rights. We've done nothing to deserve this treatment."

The dronnet put his face an inch from Jorna's and rasped, "Honest? Hod-ya say different." His putrid breath washed over Jorna, nearly causing her to swoon. Blood drained from her face, and she shuddered as a wave of nausea convulsed her stomach, making bile rise in her throat. Flan, noting her distress, slipped his arm around her waist, supporting her. She caught her breath, and her stomach calmed. She looked thankfully up into Flan's eyes.

Flan's jaw muscles flexed, however; and his brows furrowed, shadowing the anger in his eyes.

Jorna had seldom seen him this angry. Would he, in her defense, go for his sword under the table? Such a move, with this many sharifs and a dronnet in the room, could only end in disaster.

"I'm all right, Flan," she whispered, putting her hand to her mouth.

~

On the other side of the tapestry, ears tight to the door panels, Knarsh and Cleese listened intently. Face to face, each anticipated having to burst through the door to their hosts' rescue. They read in each other's eyes that if they launched an attack, there was little doubt they'd have to battle their way down every street in the city, diminishing their chances of getting back to Varter to relay the tactical information of the campaign. Yet if they didn't intervene . . . that option was likewise unthinkable. Knarsh turned and observed the others huddled close behind and knew at a glance they also were willing to make the sacrifice in an attempt to rescue their fellow kingsmen.

~

Rough, groping hands pressed, squeezed, and tugged at every article of clothing Jorna wore. Flan tried to grab the sharif's hands from humiliatingly pawing his wife and was rewarded with a gut-punch from the dronnet. Flan bent over gasping for breath.

"Stop it! Let him alone!" Jorna pled.

"'Ere now, what's this?" The sharif detected a lump in Jorna's skirt.

The toller Jorna concealed in her skirt was dislodged by the rough frisking and slowly slid down her leg to her calf. She bent her knee slightly, so the implement would catch her shoe's heel, hoping it would roll off her ankle and go under the table without making a clunk. In all the commotion, no one paid any attention to the slight thump as it slid across the floor and fell into a crevice in the molding.

Jorna reached into a side pocket, drew out a bunched handkerchief, and shoved it under the sharif's nose. "Is this what you mean?"

The sharif's mouth opened briefly and then shut. "I thought . . . I thought I felt a knife or something." He looked toward his lieutenant and shrugged.

The lieutenant shook his head and commented aside to the dronnet, "Look what I have to work with, Flarg. It's no wonder I'm still a lieutenant with commanding melon-headed dolts like these? Gimme that!" He grabbed the handkerchief. "Can't tell a handkerchief from a knife!"

"Both clean, lieutenant," reported the other sharif, who finished frisking his subjects.

"Satisfied?" Flan glared at the intruders. "We've done nothing wrong and don't deserve this treatment."

"So, you're honest citizens, eh? Well, now you'll have a chance to prove it. Bind their hands."

Flan said, "Why are we being arrested? You've found no evidence to accuse us."

"And what makes you think we need evidence?" sneered the lieutenant. "But relax; this isn't an arrest. These bonds are merely to guarantee your safety as we escort you to the palace to receive your loyalty tats." Then to his men, he said, "Take 'em away. I'll be along shortly."

The sharifs filed out into the street with Flan and Jorna in tow. As she was hustled out the door, Jorna dared a quick peek at the floor under the table and the tapestry behind concealing the secret chamber. All was secure.

~

Two Carnalians yet remained in the room.

"Flarg, employ those flaunted dronnet skills you're supposed to have," ordered the lieutenant turning a full circle to examine the room, "and find something. I don't know how they did it, but they've managed to conceal any evidence of this being a secret Ecclessite gathering house. This place has been under observation for weeks. People go in and seemingly disappear, then mystically reappear elsewhere in the city. There must be a doorway to a hidden basement, tunnels, or at least a secret room. Find it."

Flarg went to a corner, got down on all fours, and systematically navigated the room's floor boards for a secret entry to a supposed subterranean room. He then searched the perimeter walls, sniffing like a hound and occasionally pausing to taste the air. At times, he put an ear to the wall, listened, then crawled on. After circumnavigating the room, he returned to the lieutenant resting his backside against the table.

"Under here, too," said Lieutenant Glimp, tapping the table.

Flarg visibly bristled at the upstart lieutenant ordering him about, a dronnet of the second order; but he grudgingly yielded and crawled beneath. He scarcely checked the baseboard molding and thereby missed discovery of the toller, nor did he bother to glance up at the table's underside and thus failed to note the swords mere inches above his head. He exited from under the table, sniffed the tapestry, and sneezed.

"Bah!" He spat in disgust and sneezed out years of dust accumulated in the wall-hanging.

The lieutenant bit his lip to keep from laughing.

Flarg stood erect and stretched a hand toward the lieutenant's throat. But his grasping fingers stopped inches short as the dronnet rasped, "Not laugh, Glimp. Not funny."

"Get over yourself, Flarg. I meant nothing by it. Go check the other rooms. I'll wait here."

~

Knarsh and Cleese, on the other side of the concealed door, had their swords drawn and ready, just in case the dronnet discovered the lever that opened the panel to the hidden room. They would resist if discovered, no matter what followed; Varter must be apprised of Flan's strategy to attack the palace. They waited breathlessly, ears tight against the door.

Several minutes turned into half an hour of waiting for fading footsteps that would indicate Flarg and Glimp had quit the premises. Glend, Dacey, Hanell, Etel, Plenk, and Trembu knelt patiently behind Knarsh and Cleese, swords in hand, prepared to respond to the slightest indication that the game was up. All they heard was Glimp tunelessly humming as he waited for the dronnet to finish his inspection.

The slightest of footsteps finally echoed from the other rooms.

Flarg rasped, "Nothing."

"Are you sure? Not even a hint?" There was a pause; then Glimp muttered, "Well, I don't know how they do it, but this house is the center of kingsman activity in the region. I'm sure of it. I'm going to petition Hod-ya to have you and another dronnet stakeout this house. Until then, I'll post a couple of my dunderheaded sharifs to lay in wait for any Ecclessites that might show up. Come, I've wasted enough time here."

The Carnalians' footfalls padded away, and the front door thudded shut.

Cleese said, "We can't wait till nightfall; we must leave now. Those sharifs will be back within minutes, and we'll be trapped."

"But what if this is a trap?" asked Glend, her eyes wide with fright. "I know how they work; they pretend to vacate a place, hoping their quarry will come out of hiding. Then they pounce."

"That's a chance we'll have to take," said Knarsh. "No matter how risky it is, if we don't leave now, it's certain we won't get another chance after they station dronnets here."

"I agree." Trembu nodded. "If fight we must, let's get to it."

Knarsh looked each member of his squad in the eye, nodded his head, and stood. "Ready? Let's go."

A bolt slid from its stay with a loud click. Knarsh nudged the door open an inch and peered out at the room.

"No point in being cautious." Trembu pushed past Knarsh and leaped into the room. "If they didn't hear that lockbolt click, then they aren't here. Let's move."

They passed into the front room single file. "Stash your swords away," Dacey reminded.

Cleese went to the window and drew the curtain aside, peeking out. "Seems clear."

"Should we go all at once, in small groups, or one at a time?" Etel asked, securing his sword.

"Eight of us walking in one group, without tattoos, will surely draw attention," Hanell advised.

"As would two groups of four." Plenk slid his toller into its hiding place. "And one by one would make us too vulnerable. Two at a time seems best."

"Agreed." Knarsh stepped away from the window. "But stay within sight of each other—say, fifty paces between each pair?"

"And on alternate sides of the street?" suggested Dacey.

"However we go, it must be now." Cleese went to the doorway. "Those sharifs will be back at any moment."

"Right." Knarsh pointed at Cleese. "Cleese, you and Glend go out first. The rest of you team up as you like, leaving only when the pair before you reaches that second lamppost down the street. Etel and I will follow last. Once we're clear of city limits, we'll join up again. Now, go!"

Cleese and Glend slipped out the door and scurried up the street.

"Too fast! They're walking too fast and will draw attention to themselves," Knarsh moaned to no one in particular. He turned to Hanell and Dacey. "Keep them in sight but slow the pace; act natural. Hopefully, at some point, they'll see you've fallen way behind and will slow down. Ready . . . go!"

Dacey stepped out the doorway with Hanell taking her arm in his, appearing as a couple. When they reached the designated spot, Knarsh nodded. Plenk and Trembu exited, strolling carelessly, talking in quiet tones, gesturing from time to time in the hopes that anyone seeing them in deep conversation with each other wouldn't interrupt.

They'd barely reached the first lamppost when four sharifs sallied around the corner.

"Gotta go now." Knarsh nudged Etel into the street and followed, firmly closing the door behind, hoping the sharifs hadn't noticed them leave the building.

Several paces ahead, Trembu and Plenk broke into a loud argument. They pushed and shoved each other into the middle of the road, shouting and shaking fists. Trembu gave a quick glance backward at Knarsh and Etel, winked, and turned back to his mock argument with Plenk.

"They're diverting attention away from us," Knarsh whispered. "Quick, cut down this street, then over on the first side street we come to. We'll double back on a parallel street to catch up to the others." The two did an about-face, crossed the street, and trotted to the next corner, where they paused just long enough to see how things fared with their companions.

Four sharifs surrounded Plenk and Trembu, trying to calm their argument before it evolved into a fight.

"I told him we should get branded today." Trembu's angry voice carried down the avenue as he gesticulated wildly. "But he wants to wait."

The four sharifs gathered around Plenk, who, after some discussion, slumped his shoulders and nodded. The sharifs congratulated him, patting him on the back as Trembu and Plenk shook hands. The sharifs turned up the street and made straight for Flan's house.

"They're safe." Knarsh sighed. "And they drew attention away from us." The pair quick-stepped to the next corner and turned right on what they expected was a parallel path.

~

"Eh, what've we got here?" A gruff guard at the gateway lowered his halberd, blocking the palace entry.

One of the sharifs pushing Flan under the portcullis mumbled, "A couple of reluctant Feuhr supporters, volunteerin' to get their loyalty tats."

Flan glanced sideways at his wife.

Tears filled her eyes.

His vision blurred, too. There was no way either of them would willingly accept the mark. "Logon," he uttered under his breath, "is this our time? Or do you have a plan to deliver us?" Flan blinked away tears, clearing his vision. He then noted Jorna's lips quivering . . . or was she silently talking to Logon? He scanned the gateway entrance and beheld nothing but unfriendly faces. A dozen guards stood nearby in idle stances, some leaning against the stone wall, others grouped in tight circles as if sharing some bawdy story; but now all eyes watched the reluctant newcomers hustled into the courtyard to see if they would put up a struggle.

"Take 'em on in." The guard raised his halberd and stood aside. "The 'skin artiste' is ready to perform his service to the Feuhr." He bowed, mockingly extending his free hand in a grandiose sweep toward the inner courtyard. "Your lordship, your ladyship."

The other guards snickered. "Flemkoff," said one, "you always know how to make the day entertaining."

Flemkoff bowed low, garnering another round of chuckles.

Flan and Jorna were brusquely hustled off to a side where a long table abutted an outer wall. Several men and women stood in line along the table.

"Where you want it?" grunted the tattooist to the person across the table. "Forehead or back of the hand?"

A freshly marked man and wife received hearty congratulations from an official who handed them a scroll. "This indicates you have willingly and gladly proved your loyalty to the empire, the emperor, and the Feuhr," proclaimed the decorated official to the couple. "It's also a receipt for your taxes; your next year's levies are remitted in full." The man and his wife accepted the scroll, bowed before the official, and left sporting wide smiles.

Flan watched the pair exit the castle.

The sharifs, nudging Fran and Jorna forward, skirted around the queue of some thirty people, putting them at the front of the line. Muckle, one of the sharifs, loudly declared, "These two have priority; they're suspected of being in league with enemies of the empire. By receiving this mark, they'll prove their innocence in the matter. If not . . . " He drew his forefinger across his throat and smiled wickedly.

Flan was shoved to the table, forced to bend over at the waist, and had his face pinned down by a sharif's hand on the back of his neck. "Do this 'un first."

"Aren't you going to undo their hands? They are to be given their choice where the mark goes, you know." The tattooist stared at Flan's and Jorna's bonds. "Maybe they'd like it on their hand. I mean, after all, we're under strict orders not to force anyone . . . "

"They forfeited their choice by not coming of their own free will. Put it on their foreheads for all the world to see."

The tattooist shrugged. "If you say so."

"I says so; these two are likely the first of many we'll bring, requiring the same treatment. We've uncovered a whole rat's nest of 'em living amongst decent, law-abiding civilians right here in Cosmopolis, spreading lies about the Feuhr and distorting what we know about the evil Ecclessite King. The branding these rebels get must be vividly displayed on their foreheads, proclaiming that they no longer believe Ecclessa's lies."

The tattooist shrugged again. His associate pulled a blank scroll from the pile on the table and said, "Name?"

"Flan," the sharif replied for Flan.

An assistant wrote at the top of the page. "Where do you live?"

"Ward Street—never mind the number; Ward Street is sufficient." The sharif spat a wad of phlegm into the dust.

The tattooist's assistant scribbled on the paper, then raised his head to look at Flan full in the face before reading the contents of the scroll. "Do you hereby and forthwith declare your fealty to the realm of Carnalia, its emperor, and the soon-to-be coronated Feuhr, Turit Tyrannus, and the *treblesix* insignia of his Divine superiority, to live and die by his decrees? And do you furthermore denounce any and all allegiance to every other leader, ruler, prince, king, potentate, or whatever, on pain of death and eternal, fiery torment?"

"I do not!"

A vise-like grip painfully squeezed Flan's neck. "Wrong answer. Try again."

Flan winced. "Ahh!" White spots floated before his eyes.

"Stop it! You're hurting him!" Jorna cried, lunging against her captor's restraints.

The other sharif cuffed Jorna across the mouth with the back of his hand, drawing blood from her lower lip. Jorna's knees buckled from the blow, but her guard had a firm grip on her waist and hoisted her back to full stature.

Flan, in a vain effort to protect his wife, elbowed the sharif, compressing his neck.

In response, Flan's head slammed down hard on the tabletop. "Here now, that's enough of that!" Then to the tattooist, he said, "Mark him."

"You know I can't unless he willingly accepts it. For some curious reason, the mark won't take unless he agrees to it."

The sharif growled and again squeezed Flan's neck, knowing the precise pressure points to induce maximum pain. "Tell him you'll take it."

Flan shut his eyes and gasped, "Never!"

"Stop it!" screamed Jorna.

Jorna crumpled under another blow, this time to her temple. She dangled limply in the arms of the guard.

Flan noted the amazement of people watching from the queue as he and Jorna resisted the tattoo and its benefits, choosing instead to suffer pain, embarrassment, and rejection. Murmurs ran down the line like a grassfire. Why was the empire so insistent on forcing people to take the *treblesix*? Wasn't it a matter of free choice, as the town criers announced? So why this brutality?

"You don't understand," Jorna whimpered, hanging in her captor's arms. "He can't, and neither can I. Everyone taking the *treblesix* takes a curse unto themselves."

The queue grew restive; some murmured to their spouse, seemingly reconsidering their decision.

A highly decorated official overseeing the proceedings strode out from under a sheltered doorway toward the sharifs holding Flan and Jorna, hissing in a low voice, "Get them out of here. They're unnerving everybody. Take them to Hod-ya; she'll know how to deal with them."

The sharifs nodded respectfully. "Yes, Lord Kway, as you wish."

Flan's eyes locked on the official as the sharifs dragged the couple across the bailey. Lord Kway turned to the people in line, raised his hands, and apologized. "Sorry for the disruption, good citizens. We are sometimes forced to deal harshly with rogue malcontents, lest they foment an uprising against good, honest citizens like yourselves. We can't let them ruin our fair empire nor the freedoms our leaders bless us with, can we? No need for alarm; the situation is well in hand. So, step up and get your tax remittances that's a reward for your loyalty to the empire and our new Feuhr."

Flan's boot-toes scored lines in the dust as he was dragged face down, elevated at the waist by a pair of guards. Jorna was aware enough to stumble along between the sharifs who held her up by her arms. Though dazed, Flan comprehended the sharifs' conversation. One of them spoke barely above a whisper, "Hain't thet Lord Kekinor Kway, high muckity-muck or summat? What's he doin' supervisin' a lowly operation like this'n?"

"Shhh! Fool! Do you want a demotion?" whispered the stouter of the ones hauling Flan.

"Nah, yer needn't be's worryin', Flacht. His lordship got's busted on account o' his son bein' a traitor an' runnin' off ter join the enemy," said another unceremoniously toting Jorna.

"I heered it was summat more than jest thet," said another. "I heered—jest a rumor, mind yers—but I heered Lord Kekinor's daughter be's the one what brung down the White Priestess and burnt up all o' Pitland."

"Nay, yer says!"

"Yep. The way I heared it, Lord Kway be's not only demoted from his position and assigned a common one but, along with his wife and two remaining daughters, is forced to live in the palace amongst the servant staff instead o' on his own estate outside o' town. Seems the Lady Hod-ya wants ter keep an eye on him an' his family, jest in case there be's any more o' 'em about ter high-tail it over ter the enemy. Shh, we's comin' ter the interrogatin' cells now. Best keep shut-mouthed 'bout all this."

Flan watched Jorna's head bob up and down with each stride her captors took. She was smiling at him wanly. He, too, smiled. So, it was true; Jeda had succeeded in her mission. An army of men couldn't have accomplished what Logon did through a simple girl's trusting obedience.

CHAPTER TWENTY-TWO

SIX WAYFARERS GROUPED BEHIND A waist-high stone wall anxiously searching for the prodigal members of their party along the road they'd just traveled.

"I'm sure they got away," mused Plenk.

Trembu nodded. "Happily, our ruse distracted the sharifs long enough for them to slip down a side street so they could circle out and around."

"So, where are they?" asked Hanell. "It's been half an hour, and there's no sign of them."

"Maybe the sharifs weren't fooled by your sham argument and pursued them." Glend sidled in between Hanell and Plenk.

"No, the sharifs went immediately to Flan's house. They had no clue that Knarsh and Etel had even been in Flan's home, much less have any reason to pursue them."

"Cleese, you know the lay of Cosmopolis' streets," posed Dacey. "Might they have veered off on a tangent and gotten lost instead of taking a street parallel to our course?"

"Which way did you say they went, Trembu?" Using his hand as a visor, Cleese shielded his eyes and kept staring down the road.

"They doubled back downhill to the next street."

"Was it a crossroads or just a side street?"

"Side street."

"Uh-oh. If they turned on that side street, they're headed for the center of Cosmopolis instead of this way." Cleese drew imaginary streets in the air. "The streets on that side of the city are confusing; most of them lead in concentric arcs that eventually spiral down to the palace."

"Should we go back and search for them?" Glend was already a few steps down the road before turning to see if anyone followed.

"If we go looking for them"—Hanell leaned against the stone wall—"and they do find their way here, we'll miss meeting up with them."

"Maybe we should split up." Plenk came alongside Glend. "A pair of us can stay here, the others divide into search teams; we'll all meet back here in, say . . . an hour."

"Too risky." Trembu shook his head. "Lingering here any longer will only draw unwanted attention. In fact, we've tarried too long as it is. Passersby have been eyeballing us standing idly beside this wall. Knarsh knows the way through Ra-Amawl to the cliffs. I say we strike for home and leave Knarsh and Etel to fend for themselves."

"That's cold, Trembu." Glend tilted her face upward and narrowed her eyes. "You know Knarsh would wait for any of us who got lost."

"Well," Cleese moved beside Plenk and Glend. "I could go look, since I know the streets."

Trembu sighed. "It's important that you, out of all of us, meet with Captain Varter. Besides, you're a known associate of Flan; if they forced him to talk . . . There's too much danger; you'll be recognized."

"So, you think Knarsh and Etel got caught?" Dacey's eyebrows rose.

"We should consider that a possibility. At any rate, we should resume our journey. If Knarsh is at liberty, he'll find his way back. If not, the less time we hang around Cosmopolis, the better."

"Let's wait just a little longer," pleaded Glend.

"No, Trembu is right," Plenk acknowledged. "Waiting here or going back into Cosmopolis will only increase our chances of arrest. I say we go."

Dacey and Glend stood staunchly with arms crossed but said nothing. The others nodded assent to Trembu's suggestion and hoisted their packs.

Trembu gently lifted Glend's chin, "It's for the best. We've tarried too long in Cosmopolis as it is; we must make haste. I'm sure Knarsh would agree."

Cleese adjusted the hood on Glend's cape, took her by the hand, and said, "Let's go." Then looking at Trembu, Cleese asked, "In pairs, like before?"

Trembu smiled. "Same distance apart but keep tabs on each other. And not too fast, lest you draw attention. Once safely beyond city limits, we might dare group up again."

As before, Cleese and Glend led, followed at forty paces by Dacey and Hanell. Trembu and Plenk delayed their departure as long as they dared, anxiously watching the road in hope that Knarsh and Etel would make a last-minute appearance. It was not to be, however, and the final twosome departed the stonewall, trailing after their companions.

Houses and various other wooden structures and out-buildings—along with diverse clay, brick, and stone storefronts—dwindled the farther they ventured from the city. The kingsmen drank in the welcome sight of open green fields, hills, and distant mountains, instead of the gray, stodgy, huddled edifices of Cosmopolis and its outskirts. The pastoral scenes revived their spirits after their time of hiding in the city's stuffy, cluttered, gray atmosphere. Even Cleese, who was used to the oppressive character of Cosmopolis, experienced gladness of heart engendered by sunshine—even as dim as it had become since the fourth trumpet—with fresh breezes, birdsongs, and buzzing insects. He turned his gaze from the glory of nature to the pretty lass at his side, admiring her dainty little nose and curly blonde hair that framed her face. "I wish we could just keep walking like this forever. I mean, it's so peaceful, refreshing."

Glend's cheeks flushed as she looked up with a slight curl of her lips. "Me, too. This airy, open part of our journey to Ra-Amawl is so enjoyable."

"Is Ra-Amawl as dark and oppressive as I've heard?"

"Oh, it's not so bad once you adjust. At first, I was really spooked; but then again, my initial experiences were as a Carnalian and a prisoner. The threat that they might just abandon me to be devoured by wild beasts was very real. It wasn't the best introduction to Ra-Amawl. Add to that discovering that Jeda was secretly an Ecclessite made me feel so betrayed. It wasn't until after I was freed from the cusps that clung to me that I began to see the advantages of wilderness living."

"Someday, you'll have to tell me all about it."

Glend gave him a curious smile and turned her head. "Maybe, someday."

Cleese checked the progress of the pair behind. "I think we'll be able to safely bunch up soon." He faced back around front. "Although pairing off like this has allowed me to get to know you better."

If Glend caught the hint, it didn't show; for she suddenly stopped and pointed at the ground. "Look!"

Cleese, two paces ahead, turned around. "What?"

"Don't you see the track?"

Cleese bent over and studied the ground. "A track, where? I don't see it."

Glend stooped and described a wide circle a few inches above the road. "Look, take it all in. It's not small; expand your view and look at the larger imprint."

"What are you looking at?" Hanell and Dacey trotted up to see what had caused Glend and Cleese to stop.

Glend pointed again.

Dacey paled; Hanell stood erect and drew his sword halfway out of its sheath as his eyes scanned the road ahead.

Trembu and Plenk arrived moments later, studied the ground, and likewise grabbed their swords, forming a defensive perimeter.

"Will someone please tell me . . . " Cleese's eyes darted face to face.

Glend knelt, picked up a twig, and circumscribed a foot-and-a-half circle around the paw print in the loose dirt. "Craniantium lion. Open your eyes, Cleese; your vision is too limited to see the larger print of the beasts that inhabit Ra-Amawl. It seems this one has traveled beyond his usual haunts. Would you agree, Trembu?"

Trembu grunted an affirmative.

Cleese's eyes widened as the oversized pawprint came into view. "That's all just one paw print?"

"Mm-mm," affirmed Glend. "Imagine the size of the creature that made it."

"There's another here," called Plenk who scouted further afield. "And I think this track was made by a different lion."

Trembu sprang across the roadway to check the newfound spoor. "I believe you're right, Plenk. This one is slightly smaller." He waded into the grassy paddock. "They slept here just last night, right along the roadside. I see three, four, possibly five bedding spaces with the grass all matted down." He lifted his gaze to the distant mountains dominating the landscape off to the right. "Appears that this pride ventured down out of those foothills."

They all gathered around Trembu and studied the flattened grass. "Now, that's odd." Hanell plucked a shaft of grass and put it between his teeth. "They never venture this close to human populations; they prefer the anonymity of deep, dark forests."

"Perhaps the dimness of the daylight hours and increased twilight has disturbed their instinctive sense of time." Plenk knelt and put a hand to the crumpled grass.

"And possibly, the coronation of Turit?" Glend sounded wistful, far-away. "All the empire is astir the closer that event draws. All the evil, hurtful, violent, and dangerous elements of Carnalia seem to be roused out of their usual haunts and dens as if drawn by the emperor's bidding."

Cleese took Glend by the shoulders and turned her face toward him. "Are you all right?"

Glend blinked, then turned her gaze toward the mountains. "I'm all right, but I sense trouble lies in our path. And twilight creeps across the land, even as we stand here. Evil is waxing stronger in this unnatural semi-darkness."

"Where's the trouble from: before or behind us?" Trembu's face was inches from Glend's. "Does it stalk us or lay in ambush?"

Plenk drew his sword completely out of its scabbard. "How does it even know who we are or where we're going?"

"Is it a whole pride of lions?" Dacey urgently pressed.

"I don't know; I don't know the answer to any of your questions." Glend shook her head. "All I know is what the Advisor just told me, and now I've told you."

"Well, you're right about it being unnaturally dark," Trembu mused. "We shan't make much progress tonight unless we use the light of our swords to guide us, which is risky due to Carnalian patrols, not to mention the good citizens of Carnalia that would turn us in for a bounty."

"Bounty?" said Dacey, Cleese, and Glend at the same time.

"Haven't you noticed the posters on trees and fence posts lining the turnpike?" Trembu chided. "Or were you too busy chatting?" He peered at Glend and Cleese, then Dacey and Hanell. "Are you too busy getting to know each other instead of keeping a watchful eye?" The sternness in his eyes was softened by a slight smile. "Posters have warned people to beware of strangers without the loyalty mark, offering a reward of one hundred silver coins for information that results in capture."

"Well, that definitely rules out traveling by the light of our swords." Plenk replaced his in its scabbard.

"But neither dare we make camp this far from the cover of the jungle." Dacey wrung her hands. "A campfire will surely draw attention. But a camp without a fire, with lions and who-knows-what all prowling about, is unthinkable. If only we were closer to Ra-Amawl, we could press on till we were under its dense bowers that would conceal our campfire."

"Meanwhile, the twilight deepens," said Hanell, "and there are lions about. We've got to decide—and quickly."

~

Knarsh grabbed Etel's sleeve, pulling him backward into a side alley. The pair flattened themselves against a merchant's brick wall, counting the seconds, waiting for the patrol to pass.

The Carnalians chatted as they strode past the alleyway and on down the street. "Seems ter me they gots the whole city in a uproar over nuthin', Trunch."

"I dunno, Glumpus, yer warn't thar when Pitland like ter melted underfoot," the other the sharif replied. "Them 'Clessites be's trickier than they looks. Why, jest afore the whole Scrarth 'n' Avangar happent, I be's in Pitland an' seen me ol' pal, Scung—Terror o' the Southlands we used ter call him. He went an' turned hisself over ter become a kingsmen! Howlin' banshees if'n he warn't one o' the 'Clessites what plotted Pitland's overthrow! If'n the Magician casts sich a powerful spell on Scung, it could happen ter anybody! Soon as Mileer's regiment climbed outta the fiery lava pits—wi' barely the leathers on our backs, mind yer—and come through the beastie-filled jungles, I decided ter transfer outta the regular army an' switch over ter bein' a sharif. Cap'n Blassher done give me no grief over it, neither; said he unnerstood perfectly an' signed me transfer then an' thar."

"But this here be's Cosmopolis, Trunch, the seat o' the emperor. Even as usn's speaks, the empire be's preparin' to coronate a Feuhr, what nobbut kin wage war agin' cause o' his bein' the mortal body what Lurcan hisself be's gonna inhabit. No force on earth kin stand agin' him."

"Yeah, well, the White Priestess twarn't no blushing lily, but thet slip o' a 'Clessite girl undone both Hod-ya an' Bablo-ya right in the middle o' their glory an' power, wi' cusps an' dreads an' all assistin' 'em. If'n a slip o' a 'Clessite girl done thet, imagine what a corps o' dedicated kingsmen warriors kin do!"

"Yer talkin' treason, Trunch—"

"I be's talkin' reason, Glumpus. An' the way them strange sounds keep on a comin' from the skies, makin' all the higher-ups nervous . . . I dunno; it don't bode well, I'm a thinkin'."

The sharifs passed beyond hearing. Knarsh exhaled in relief. Etel grinned ear to ear. "Looks like Logon has the enemy shook-up, eh?"

"Uh-huh. I'd even go so far as to venture Logon has the hearts of many of our foes ready to be pierced. Did you notice how tense that Trunch fellow was?"

Etel nodded. "Well, they may be shook up, but we're still lost. I think we've been traveling the wrong direction. These streets just don't run in a logical pattern. The sun ought to be over there instead of where it is. And what's more, it's dimming; and soon, it'll be twilight and full dark not long after. Didn't Flan say something about a curfew? How are we going to evade capture, let alone catch up to the others?"

"I expect they had enough sense to keep going after they realized we were misdirected." Knarsh eased out of the alleyway into the street, checking both ways for sharifs. "Come on; it's clear. At any rate, we can find Ra-Amawl on our own once we slip this infernal city."

"Y-you think they just abandoned us?" Etel's voice rose in pitch.

"I hope they did. You wouldn't want them caught dawdling around waiting for us, would you?"

"No, of course not. It's just that with only the two of us . . . There are so many dangers, not only in Cosmopolis but along the way and even when we reach the jungle."

"Once we escape the city, we'll be fine." Knarsh tapped the hilt of his concealed sword. "Besides, it's not just the two of us, is it?"

Etel's cheeks flushed. He knew what Knarsh meant; even so, that didn't garner much comfort. Ecclessites were often caught, interrogated, imprisoned, and worse. He plodded alongside his companion, casting his eyes about, studying every group of people they passed in the hopes of spotting their friends. He only saw a benighted people desperately scurrying about, lacking knowledge of Logon's amnesty, not knowing judgment was about to befall the empire because of the bondage Lurcan induced upon hapless, rebellious humanity.

The pair hustled down the street hoping one of the avenues would turn the direction they needed before total darkness enveloped the byways and left them nowhere to shelter for the night. They hurried down a promising-looking boulevard, only to be confounded yet again by an obtuse corner at the end of the street leading away from the pathway they wanted.

"It's gotten darker, Knarsh," said Etel. "There's hardly anyone on the streets except patrols; everyone's gone home. We'll stick out like glowworms in a cave if we don't soon find our way out of the city."

Knarsh silently nodded, quickening his pace. Even now, his hidden sword's light reflected off the cobble-stoned road from under his cape.

"How now, Gents," a soft, feminine voice hailed from the shadows. "'Tis late to be wandering the streets of our fair city looking for all the world like you've lost your way."

The kingsmen stopped and scrutinized the doorway alcove whence the voice emitted. Silhouetted against the amber light of the room behind her stood an old woman, bent with age. Her face was obscured, and her head and shoulders were draped with a knitted shawl as she leaned on her cane.

Before either Knarsh or Etel recovered from their surprise, she added, "'Tisn't safe for anyone to be found in the open this late, especially from the direction of Ward Street. Your 'glow' betrays you . . . " She pointed to the wet cobblestones beneath their feet. The deepening twilight enhanced the contrasting shine from their swords. "If I may offer my humble home for the night and a bite of food?" She extended her hand toward the softly lit, welcoming inner room.

Knarsh glanced at Etel. "Very hospitable of you, old mother. I assume your allegiance is, ah, shall we say, same as ours?"

The old woman's face turned to the light, and she winked and cupped her hand to her lips, whispering, "Don't the runes promise reward to those who accommodate roamers unawares? Now, don't dally; come in before the next patrol passes by."

The kingsmen crossed the threshold into the warm environs of a neatly kept room. A wardrobe, two bureaus, a mirrored chest of drawers, and a coat rack lined the near wall on the left. Directly ahead blazed a cozy fire in the hearth with a kettle spouting a jet of steam into the air. Two stuffed chairs and a rocker were situated in front of the fireplace just near enough to benefit occupants with warmth but not so close as to be uncomfortable. The rest of the old woman's home was concealed behind a richly brocaded tapestry shielding off an unused portion of the house for the sake of concentrating heat in the main room.

"Very kind of you, ma'am, to take such a risk in providing aid to strangers, though I assume you trust us, since you weren't frightened by the glow of our swords."

The old woman closed the door and limped behind the tapestry leaning on her cane, calling over a shoulder, "Of course, I do. What did you think? I'd invite just anyone into my home from off the street?" She made a funny noise like a cackle, then coughed and said, "I'll just get you a crust of bread, a slab of bacon, and something to drink. I'm sorry I don't have more to offer. I'm an old woman with limited resources. But whatever I have, I'll gladly share with you. I'll be right out. Just make yourselves at home by the fire while I prepare you a bite to eat."

Knarsh and Etel settled into the stuffed chairs, smiling at the good fortune of finding an Ecclessite in the nick of time.

The old woman shuffled out from behind the tapestry bearing a plateful of food in each hand, having left her cane behind. "Here you go, lads; eat hearty."

Knarsh and Etel received their platters with a smile and a nod. Then Etel said, "We thank Logon for this provision."

Knarsh along with the old woman responded, "So be it."

The old woman then settled into her rocker by the fireside and stared dreamily into the flames.

Knarsh chewed and swallowed a tasty mouthful. "How is it we've not seen you at any meetings?"

The old woman's shawl was again atop her head, shadowing her forehead and eyes as she explained, "I get such a chill, even with a good fire going. Getting old isn't an easy burden to bear. I used to go to Flan's house. But then it got to be such a taxing journey crossing the city, so I just stopped going."

"Didn't they send someone to bring you to meeting—or, at least, have someone look in on you?" Etel asked.

"Oh, who bothers to look after an old woman? Besides, I don't mind. There was that one girl who used to come semi-regular and look in on me—er, Dancel, I believe was her name. She kept me abreast of goings on. But she hasn't been to see me in . . . must be months now."

Knarsh and Etel eagerly turned full attention back to their meals, complimenting the tasty provisions. Their last meal had been early morning in Flan's and Jorna's home.

Finishing first, Knarsh put his plate on the floor beside his chair. "Forgive us for being so impolite. It's been a rather long, stressful day. I'm Knarsh, and this is Etel."

Etel nodded courteously. "We came from a brigade in Ra-Amawl to arrange a rendezvous with your brigade here in Cosmopolis."

"Indeed?" The old woman turned from the fire to her guests. "Ra-Amawl? There's a brigade in Ra-Amawl? I wasn't aware of that." She tugged on her shawl so that her face remained shadowed.

"Not many people know."

"No, I guess not." She turned back to the fire. "And the purpose of such a rendezvous?"

"Our captain contacted your captain in order to coordinate an attack on Cosmopolis' palace gates."

A small dog crawled out from under a bureau along the wall and started licking Knarsh's plate. Knarsh smiled and reached down to scratch the dog behind the ears as he continued, "We believe that this upcoming coronation will bring about the end of the empire to great loss of life unless we can crash the gates and restore Elyon's law and order as well as offer Logon's amnesty to the empire at large. It's the only hope for a reprieve, lest Elyon send utter desolation."

Another small dog wriggled out from under the other bureau and growled at the first dog as he licked Knarsh's plate. The first dog growled back, baring his teeth.

"Here, little fella, you can lick my plate." Etel lowered his plate to the floor. The second dog spun around and pounced on the offering, greedily drooling and smacking his lips.

"Ach, they act like I never feed them." The old woman rose from her seat, raised her voice, and said, "Now, now, Clovis, Cinnamon, get away," and clapped her hands. The dogs scurried back under their respective bureaus.

The men laughed, picked their plates up off the floor, and then handed them to the old woman. She wordlessly received the dishes and shuffled behind the tapestry. The sound of rattling dishes and silverware mixed with splashes of water soon came from the direction she had gone.

Etel yawned, raised his hands overhead, and stretched his legs out straight. "I'm bushed, Knarsh."

"Me, too," said Knarsh, resting his chin on his chest. "I'm so embarrassed," he said through a yawn, "to be such a poor houseguest, ma'am, but I feel the need to take a bit of a nap."

The old woman, finished with her chores, walked briskly back into the room. "Now don't you never-mind about that. Just take a little nap if you need. I'll just let my 'little wolves' go outside for their last romp of the day. You both just nestle in and have a good snooze. I'll be right here if you need anything." She placed an ottoman before each of her guests, then went to the doorway and called, "Clovis, Cinnamon, I have a little chore for you."

They poked their noses out and came eagerly wagging their tails.

She picked Clovis up and whispered in his ear. She then held him at arms-length forcing eye-contact. "Understand?"

The little dog gave a quiet yip.

She put him on the floor and opened the door, and both pooches trotted outside. After closing the door, she again went behind the tapestry and brought out two blankets. "Here you go, lads, these will keep you comfy. I'm going to let the fire die down now and ready myself for bed." She went behind the tapestry.

Knarsh stirred from his sleepy dizziness to ask, "What about your pups? Aren't they going to want in before long?"

"Oh, they'll be all right. They stay out for hours sometimes."

A firm hand seized Knarsh's shoulder. He opened his eyes and saw the old woman standing before him. "Wake up, kingsman! There's someone wants to talk to you."

Etel was likewise just being roused, still groggy. The room was crowded with a dronnet and at least ten sharifs.

"Well done, Tiladith," rasped the dronnet. "The sleeping powders worked?"

"Like they were charmed." The old woman smiled as the two captives were hauled to their feet and had their hands bound. She drew back her shawl from covering her face, revealing a *treblesix* mark on her forehead.

CHAPTER TWENTY-THREE

"Captain Reasno, sir," called a guard knocking on the commandant's door.

Reasno stirred, threw back the coverlet, and swung his bare feet to the cold stone floor. "What is it? What time is it? Who's banging on my door at this infernal hour? It's not even full daylight yet."

"Uh, no, sir," said the Daggerman, answering nervously through the door. "It's Sergeant Rarn, sir, duty officer of the third watch."

"Rarn? Why are you disturbing my sleep?" Reasno grabbed a fur-lined robe that he'd discovered in Captain Metid's closet, draped it over his shoulders, shuffled across the floor, and cracked the door open. "Well?" His bleary eyes peered out at the newly appointed sergeant. Tarrying a little too long at the aged bubbly the previous evening had rendered Reasno a bit under the weather; his vision was blurred, and his temples throbbed.

"I was up on the parapets overseeing the changing of the guard, sir, when I glanced down the road—"

"Road? Which road? Speak up, man, which road?"

"The one leading to Logon's Rock."

"What of it?"

"I saw several blue lights headed this way along the pike. I thought you ought to know."

"B-blue lights? Coming this way? Are you sure? How many? How bright? What configuration did they take?" Reasno opened the door and pulled the sergeant inside. "Quick, man, speak up."

"I'm not sure, sir. Maybe half-a-dozen or more fully lit swords. I couldn't be sure. They're still some fifteen minutes distant, if that's any indication of how bright they appeared. I came down immediately to inform you."

Reasno slumped. This was bound to happen eventually, but so soon? He'd barely begun to get a taste for command. He blearily eyed the sergeant. "You did right, Rarn. Send Yumpik and Frib to me and put the fort on alert. Oh, and barricade the main entry as best you can."

"Barricade it, sir?"

"Isn't that what I said? Now, step lively."

Within ten minutes, the keep was an anthill of frenzied activity as several soldiers wedged furniture against the mended gateway.

Reasno dressed and entered the main hall, barking orders to various individuals, pointing out weak spots in the barricade, frantically ordering the redoubt to be reinforced with whatever heavy furniture or other weighty things they could find. If anyone wondered why Reasno was ordering defenses to be put in place against kingsmen—what else could those shining blue lights be but kingsmen swords heading for the fortress?—no one said anything.

Yumpik and Frib scurried across the keep and reported to Reasno on their activities, then received instructions and turned on their heels to set about distributing any available weaponry that previously decorated the walls, such as broadaxes, halberds, spears, and especially daggers hauled up from the cache in the lower end of the field. Nothing was said about Ecclessite swords.

Rarn paced back and forth between squads, pointing out vulnerable spots an enemy might breach, though he also never questioned Reasno why the approaching kingsmen were regarded as enemies. The barely functional blockade was, more or less, stabilized to the best of their ability.

"All is in readiness, sir." Rarn saluted and clicked his heels.

"Good, good." Reasno paced along the line of defenders, his hands clasped behind his back. "All right now, you men, when they arrive, they'll demand we open up; no one is to respond, understand? I'll do the parlaying. Their kind must be firmly dealt with, and only I have the experience to know how. Their views are dangerously radical. They're probably all that remains of that foolhardy attack on Cosmopolis, now coming back whimpering to hide and reclaim the fort as their presidio. I warn you, if they get inside, the insanity that drove the task force to its demise will play on your minds, goading the non-discerning among you to follow them to utter destruction in another insane attempt to breach Cosmopolis' walls. So, let me deal with their spokesman. If they trick any one of you to answer, you'll be mesmerized as surely as if the Magician had done it."

Frib's brow furrowed. "But, Reasno, the Magician is a myth invented by the empire to frighten the populace away from seeking King Elyon and Logon Xychirion. Why are you using the same ploy?"

Reasno only glared at his sergeant.

The daggermen at the barricade calmed and waited silently as the minutes passed, all ears straining for the sound of approaching footfalls.

The tension increased again when faint voices were heard from the other side of the barrier.

"What ho, brothers-in-arms, there's no need for this blockage. We're all on the same side, aren't we?"

Several thumps and scrapes indicated the barricade was being dismantled from the outside. The outsiders were swiftly breaking through the mended gate and Reasno's hastily assembled breastworks that bolstered the gateway defenses.

"Go away! This is no longer your base!" Reasno snarled. "Finders owners, losers donors. You abandoned it; now we're in possession. Go away. You and your sword-wielding kind aren't welcome here."

All external work on the makeshift redoubt ceased. Indistinct murmurs and fragments of conversation seeped through the jumble of piled-up desks, chairs, bureaus, and wardrobes that had been clumsily nailed together by a few spikes and reinforced with cords.

Reasno rubbed his stubbly chin whiskers. There was complete silence. Had they given up?

All remained still for several more minutes on both sides of the barricade; then Artka's voice penetrated through the barricade warning. "If you don't dismantle this blockage and let us in immediately, what happens next will be very unpleasant for you."

Yumpik, Rarn, and Frib turned around, staring wide-eyed at their commander.

Reasno's jaw was set. He shook his head, scrunched his eyebrows, and snarled, "Bluffing! They're bluffing."

Yumpik, Rarn, and Frib glanced once more at each other before returning to watch the barricade, their faces pale, jaws clenched.

"Last warning," Artka called.

Reasno touched a forefinger to his lips, ordering his defenders to be silent.

A *whump* was followed by a series of crackles and snaps. Then the acrid smell of smoke drafted into the keep's interior, stopping short of the alcoves where the women and children sheltered before spiraling up to the second story. Daggerman eyes teared up, and some were taken with fits of coughing as they retreated from the greedy smoke and flames spreading inward throughout the blockade.

"Stand steady!" Reasno commanded, but to no effect. Many of his troops fell back.

Thicker smoke billowed in, choking the strongest defenders as they, too, broke ranks to seek fresh air in hallways and antechambers. A column of smoke wafted up the spiral staircase and vented out the upper-level doorways, flowing along the walkway and tumbling over the crenellations, where it down-drafted and spread out across the grassy glacis before the castle.

Soon the flames at the barricade engulfed the piled-up furniture, driving the most stalwart of defenders back from the heat to huddle among the women and children. Reasno perceived that he hadn't taken command of the bravest of brigades but, rather, was the leader of a pitiful bunch of reluctant misfits who'd deferred even to show up for Metid's call to arms.

Sparks and cinders from the conflagration flew into the great hall's foyer as the barricade itself crumbled to glowing chunks of wood and ash. Even Reasno at last backed away from the bonfire's intensifying heat.

An hour later, the blaze finally abated, and the charred rubble disintegrated to glowing cinders. Seven bright swords on the outside shone brightly through the smoke and dwindling flames of the ruined gateway.

Realizing that the only protective barricade between himself and the determined blue-blades was a smoldering pile of ashes, Reasno physically grabbed his fighters and hustled them in front of and to either side of him. "Remember, don't answer if they address you; your sole duty is to protect your captain. Frib, Yumpik, stand to and secure the flanks. Rarn, position yourself in front of me."

Rarn faced his commander. "Them glowing swords can't hurt Ecclessites, right? I mean, it's all safe, right?"

"Turn around and protect your commanding officer."

"Yessir, but I mean, if we hold up our swords, unlit as they are, they'll still ward off any blows from brighter swords, right?"

Before Reasno answered, a crash resounded throughout the keep as the last pile of charred furniture cascaded to the floor spewing sparks and ashes everywhere. A giant of a man bounded through the ash cloud, sweeping glowing coals out of his way with a low-slung sword, clearing a pathway for his fellow warriors. Strangely enough, Reasno noted, whenever the sword touched a coal, the coal went out like a snuffed candle. The other blue-blades traipsed single-file behind the huge kingsman warrior. Upon entering the keep proper, the swordsmen fanned out to either side of him, facing what was left of the trembling, defensive line of Daggermen. The man who'd led the procession was obviously an Eroton, engendering even more trepidation among Reasno's forces.

Reasno's face drained of color.

Frib replaced his dagger in his belt and withdrew a meagerly lit sword; but, Reasno noted, Frib tried to keep it concealed from him by hiding it behind his leg.

Artka approached Reasno, his sword out straight as he apprised the bristling line of daggers and poleaxes pointed at him. "Ntch, ntch," his tongue clicked, "you should lower your weapons before you harm yourselves. After all, Scang here doesn't like needles, especially the dagger kind!"

Scang stomped his foot, sending a flume of ash and sparks off the floor, then leaned forward and growled.

Several defenders flinched and lowered their weapons.

"Yeah, that's what I thought." Artka waved his sword slowly along the line of Daggermen. "Now put those useless things away . . . Better yet, discard them altogether."

"Now hold on there," Reasno found his voice. "Wh-what right do you have, forcing your way in here, giving orders to my brigade?"

"Your brigade? Don't you mean Sofista's brigade?" Artka stepped closer to the line of defenders and, with a swift swipe of *Sky Saber*, slapped four daggers out of their holders' hands and sent them skittering across the floor. The four men backed away, rubbing their wrists. "These foul daggers were hawked by that deceiver, Sofista, who paid the price for introducing such lies into Ecclessa." Artka advanced another step, even as Reasno's defensive line fell back until they could retreat no farther. Artka stood face to face with Rarn. "Don't I know you? I've seen you somewhere."

Rarn cocked his head to the side, looked at Artka, and in a barely audible voice said, "No, I don't think so. I never encountered anyone with a sword as bright as yours."

Artka snapped his fingers. "Yes, yes, I saw you after the battle of the Windbreak Forest, where Poppitt nicked you; you bled all over yourself. Sadly, you didn't take your friend's advice and apply yourself to your Child of the Stars instead of that corrupt article of cutlery."

Rarn's jaw fell open.

Artka chuckled. "Yes, you nearly sat on me when the kingsmen brigade you were with searched the lower grasslands by Swamp Tophet. I was in the Roaring Lion's brigade back then, hiding in the grass as I overheard you complain how difficult it was to sharpen your sword. Looks like you chose the easier, but wrong, path. Well, you can see how that turned out."

Rarn hung his head, his dagger dipping toward the floor. A sword hung loosely from his belt with only the very tip barely alight. Artka effortlessly brushed him aside and stepped face-to-face with Reasno.

Reasno screeched, "Rarn, what are you doing?" Then he backed off a step from Artka. "Leave us. What business do you have here, anyway? Aren't you and your fellows supposed to be off molesting people about harboring cusps or tophets?"

Ignoring Reasno's insolence, Artka grabbed the man's tunic at the throat and ripped it open, exposing the self-appointed commandant's chest. "Where's your scar, Debator?"

Reasno quickly pulled his tunic closed.

Eyebrows rose, and jaws went slack as members of Reasno's brigade stared. They'd assumed he bore the usual kingsman scar.

"Yes, take a good look at what you chose to follow, instead of answering Logon's summons to battle," chided Artka. "He still claims to be a kingsman like he did over a year ago when I first met him. He also bestowed a dagger to me, which nearly cost me my life. A little over a week ago, I accompanied him partway to Logon's Rock with a wound in his chest and the understanding that he'd seek Logon to get his heart healed. Instead, he turned away from admitting the depth of his decay and need for Logon's amnesty, all the while continuing the pretense of being a kingsman. I thought we had destroyed your daggers. Where you found another stash of them and how you convinced these people to take them and follow you, I can't fathom. But even though you appear to be kingsmen, you have, nonetheless, let your Child of the Stars go dull and invented excuses to not report for duty when the king called. That left all of you"—he pointed his sword in a semi-circular motion at the line of defenders—"wide open to deception by the likes of Debator.

"Now, my companions and I need to be elsewhere about the king's business. We don't have time to shape you into a viable brigade. We only came here to retrieve certain documents from the keep and be on our way. Neither I nor my companions have any time to spare outfitting you for battle, apprise you of recent events, nor let you know the details of what's about to happen to this fortress."

Reasno, fuming in disgrace, watched Frib step up to Artka. "Why? What's going to happen here? In the name of decency, you must let us know if we're in danger."

"What be's gonna happen here 'bouts be's written plain enough on yer swords," Scang scolded, striding through a flank of defenders, knocking them aside as he headed for several shelves along a wall. "Yers might still have summat o' time left ter sharpen them swords and learn a thing or two afore it comes. Now, get outta me way," he growled at the men in his path. "I needs ter have at them there scrolls."

"The first thing you must do is depose this pretender, Debator," Artka said to the group now attending his every word. "Second thing is to throw all your daggers into the river before they draw a thousand tophets down on you. Then use your tollers as they were intended—to sharpen your swords. It won't be easy, but even a quarter inch of light is better than a barely glowing tip."

Frib stepped forward. "Will you show us?" He held a sword in one hand and a toller in the other. "I confess, I led Reasno to the daggers stashed in the field. The bonfire you people set to destroy them never caught. He offered me a dagger and related his intentions of starting a brigade."

"I've no time to instruct you, even if I was so inclined." Artka brushed Frib aside. "Our mission is already delayed far too long. We need some specific scrolls, maps, and charts."

Clepy laid a hand on Artka's forearm. "Perhaps the real reason we came back was to provide counsel to these misguided soldiers. We can't just turn them loose with no instruction and woefully unlit swords."

"Especially not with a corps of dronnets headed this way," added Reddy.

"Dronnets?" Frib shuddered. "Hod-ya's blackguards?"

"You know of them?" Artka paused.

Frib answered, "I almost joined them but was put into service elsewhere before my training began. You must help us; we're in a desperate state, as you see."

"He's right, Artka," Harnet whispered in Artka's ear. "I don't believe Logon would just abandon them."

Artka hung his head and sighed. "Yes, you're right. We must do something, but what? There's no time to sharpen their swords or even train them in tactical maneuvers."

"Only thing we can do is to send them back across the river where they'll be safer than here," Reddy suggested.

"Yeah! They'll at least be safe there, though I don't know how Logon will receive them after they ignored his call to arms." Braxmore shrugged.

"That's a consequence they'll have to face." Artka turned from Reddy to Braxmore. "After all, they did bring this miserable state upon themselves."

"How bad will it get before Logon comes?" Rarn held his sword up and touched he unlighted mystery runes.

"I don't ken." Clepy shrugged. "I warrant it'll not be pleasant, and they'll be no honors won in battle to lay at Logon's feet in thankful adoration, which in my estimation, will be shameful in and of itself."

"But . . . but what should I do?" cried Reasno. "I've tried, but I can't cross the bridge; something prevents me."

"It's because you haven't died at Logon's Rock," said Harnet. "Only resurrected life can actually enter Ecclessa. Even so, some who have been there still fall back into their old Carnalian lifestyle instead of heeding the Advisor and become defiled again."

"What about me?" Yumpik grabbed Reddy's arm. "I hain't ne'er been ter Logon's Rock neither."

Brendle stepped up. "The only chance for both of you is to hightail it to Logon's Rock and seek his amnesty before it's too late. And hope you don't encounter any dronnets heading this way. You may live a while longer if Logon, who knows your heart's true intentions, doesn't intervene; but after that, you'll suffer the same fate as every other Lurcan follower. Now, off with you; you haven't a moment to spare." Brendle shooed them with his hands.

Reasno and Yumpik dashed through the smoking pile of cinders for the outer pathway, scurrying down the road like foxes with singed tails.

"And get rid of those daggers!" Clepy called after them.

"Now, the rest of you," Artka announced, "gather up your things now and make for the bridge. We'll stand watch as long as we dare, so waste not a minute. Mothers with children, the wounded, and elderly go first. Where's that man who kept his sword and toller?"

"Here." Frib stepped out from behind several men.

"What's your name?"

"Frib."

"Okay, Frib, you're in charge; lead them across. Once on the other side, you'll need to organize watchmen, fighters, kitchen help, and so on. Understand?"

"Watchmen and fighters in Ecclessa?"

"Dronnets and regulars aren't the only agents with which Lurcan and his soon-appearing emperor, Turit, will inundate the world. In Ecclessa, you'll undoubtedly be attacked by cusps, tophets, and who-knows-what-else that can navigate the river's torrents. We've even encountered ancient firedrakes on that side of the river, so be on your guard. And waste no time sharpening your swords, every man, woman, and child of you."

"Turit, the infamous criminal? What's he got to do with all this?"

People formed a line and filed to the bridge as Artka continued his explanation, "Those wanted posters of Turit spread all over the empire were a hoax. He was never on the loose; he was held captive in Lurcan's lowest dungeon while everyone thought he was at large. Turit was being conditioned—I believe that is the word they use—for the past decade to be a pipeline for Lurcan's hate-filled thoughts and directives to his phantoms, cusps, even the depraved musings of the dreads. Turit was selected at birth to fulfill Lurcan's ultimate desire of being worshipped by inhabiting a man so lawless, so evil, so contrary to everything Elyon wants for mankind. Lurcan is so perverted that he'll never hesitate to commit the vilest acts and torment humanity so hideously that even roamers shrink back in horror.

"Turit is almost ready to assume the throne. During the upcoming coronation ritual, with the help of incantations and benedictions from the empire's fraudulent ritualistic leaders, Turit will be inhabited by

Lurcan himself. Then comes the final war, the Tremendum. News of Logon's amnesty has been heard in every land and language, yet so many refuse his mercy or remain undecided. That's why the combined Ecclessite battle force now risks everything to attack Cosmopolis, hoping to disrupt the proceedings and buy a little more time and one last chance for those who haven't yet responded to Logon.

"Meanwhile, my squad is assigned to assail and bind the ethereal brutes behind the empire's human forces. Nevertheless, the runes foretell that Logon's Bridge will collapse when the last Carnalian finds his way to Logon's Rock and crosses this bridge into Ecclessa. At that precise moment, the empire will appear invincible, sweeping across lands with all manner of evil intent. Lurcan will rage mercilessly against not only Ecclessites but also his own subjects, knowing that he has a short time to vent his hatred for Elyon with vicious acts of cruelty on those who bear Elyon's image: humanity.

"Just before the very end, Logon will sally forth from Splendora with wrathful roamers to rescue his own that are still in the fight and to wreak vengeance on Lurcan and his followers, kyllorn or human, condemning them eternally for the torment they perpetrated against kingsmen."

Frib's eyes widened. "I never knew."

"Of course, you didn't know; you didn't toll the sword runes. Nevertheless, do what you can now for these under your charge. If you earnestly seek Logon with all your heart, he may allow himself to be found by you."

Artka turned toward his squad members waiting beside the smoldering pile of ashes. "Find them, Scang?"

"Most o' 'em." Scang had several scrolls tucked under his arm. "These here be's the important ones."

Harnet took it upon himself to tuck the maps into a rucksack, slinging it over his shoulder.

"Right then, let's go." With a wave of his hand, Artka motioned his squad to precede him out the doorway.

Scang took the lead, and the others followed at the giant's heels, staying to the clear path through the ashes.

Artka gave one last look at the disillusioned Daggermen. The women, children, wounded, and infirm had already departed the castle and were down at the bridge. Frib instructed Rarn to lead them across the bridge and secure a defensive position on the other side. The enemies they would face could come from any direction, and the eastern fortress only had walls along the riverbank.

"Logon," Artka whispered, "we trust them to your keeping." He trotted past the caved-in doorway, ducked under the portcullis, and sallied out across the meadow grasses to catch up to his companions.

The seven chatted little, saving their breath to maintain a rapid pace that would consume leagues. They trotted single file with their heads down, avoiding snags and pitfalls as they cruised through the savannah, a sense of urgency growing with each passing mile. After three or four leagues, Artka slowed the pace to a complete stop.

Harnet presented one of the scrolls from his sack for Artka to study, but he had difficulty keeping his finger on a mark and at the same time preventing the scroll from rolling back into a coil.

Seeing Harnet's predicament, Reddy seized a corner of the scroll. "Let me give you a hand."

"Have you located the doorway to our destination?" Artka drew alongside his friends and took hold of another corner of the map.

"Not quite"—Harnet bent closer—"but I think this dotted line reveals the crack in the earth's crust that descends to their cavern pathway."

Reddy released his corner of the scroll, causing it to slip from Artka's grasp and roll up in Harnet's hand again. "I-I'm sorry, I just didn't realize that we'd have to go underground again."

"What's the matter, little fella, still got the screamin' meemies about facin' them dreads?" Scang chuckled. "Doncher ken they hain't but critturs made by King Elyon, too? Logon gots authority over 'em. Yer'll see, thems won't put up much o' a fight. Arter all, if'n Artka goin' ter Logon's Rock caused Neask ter lose his tongue, how tough kin dreads be?"

"Tough enough," muttered Artka as he spread the chart open again. "Don't forget, Tren suffered severe injury; and if Logon hadn't intervened—"

"But Logon whar there, warn't he?" Scang challenged.

Clepy joined, "We're only going because we're assured of Logon's power and authority, not our own. We all accepted this assignment, knowing the risks, but also trusting Elyon's strength. And, might I add, we signed on knowing it could cost us dearly. Even so, what's the worst that can happen? We find ourselves in Splendora gazing into Logon's face! And besides that, we just might create enough of a ruckus to disturb Lurcan's castle defenses."

Harnet retraced the line on the scroll with his finger, then looked up from the parchment and stared straight ahead.

"What are you looking at?" Artka turned to follow Harnet's gaze.

In a faraway tone of voice, Harnet pointed. "First we have to go up—way up—before we can go down."

A mountain range loomed in the distance. "Gentlemen, our first objective: Skull Peak, doorway leading to the trail to the dreads."

CHAPTER TWENTY-FOUR

W<small>ITH ELONGATED STRIDES</small>, H<small>OD-YA STOMPED</small> down the corridor, leaving the precincts of the prison in fulminating dark words of wrath and promising excruciating vengeance on the absent victims of her ire when she found them. "Dared cross me again . . . *again*! Wretched wench! Somehow, Dancel got to her while teaching her the keys. I'll see that they roast slowly . . . " She wiped her drool-covered lips at the thought of spiting the girls over an open fire. "And where was the dread Mambu when needed? Everything is falling apart—the powers of the dreads are dwindling; Ecclessites are crawling out of the woodwork like roaches; our navies are sunk by strange, violent outbursts of weather on all coasts; armies are driven from battlefields with blistered hands, unable to wield their weapons . . . " She spun around abruptly and shouted toward the ceiling, "What in the name of Pitland is going on here?"

Mileer, following close behind, nearly collided into her. "Did you think it was going to be easy? Coronate Turit, tattoo every living person with Lurcan's curse, swarm the enemy's castle, destroy Logon's Bridge, and put an end to Ecclessa? You're the one who reminded me about the powers our enemy possesses. Sure, sure, it seemed we had everything under control—"

"Shut up, you fool! I wasn't talking to you." She turned to the fore again and resumed her rapid pace down the corridor, growling all the way.

Mileer rolled his eyes as he trotted in her wake; a dozen dronnets wordlessly followed. Hod-ya had led them into every nook and cranny of the maze, places no one else knew existed, searching for Dancel, Rissa—the newly appointed keeper of the keys—and three other missing serving girls, to no avail. There wasn't a tunnel or passage they hadn't thoroughly inspected from end to end except the slimy, mold-encrusted shaft that had no exit other than a small doorway that opened onto some back street of Cosmopolis.

Hod-ya bypassed that passage, commenting, "If they went that way, they fell through the breach in the floor and are beyond our grasp. No sense wasting time traipsing down that tunnel to have a look." The posse moved on, fruitlessly examining other tunnels, passages, and even crawlways of the wall maze—anywhere the girls might even remotely be hiding.

Hod-ya turned sharply to the right, pulled a keyring from her pouch, and slipped a passkey into a wall niche. A door instantly appeared where a blank wall had been, allowing entry into the dimly lit kitchen where Caldon and a few serving girls ladled a steaming, foul-smelling effluent into bowls and carefully placed the bowls onto multi-tiered shelves of wheeled carts.

Caldon's glower disappeared the moment she recognized the emperor's overseer-mistress of the castle. A polite curtsy from the rest of the kitchen staff was forthcoming, which Hod-ya ignored.

"M'lady Hod-ya." Caldon bowed, not deigning to lift her eyes to the domineering woman invading her kitchen. "How may I be of service?"

Hod-ya squinted at her. "You could start by telling me where those missing wenches are."

Caldon trembled. "Would that I could, Madam. I sorely needs them here, meself; as you can see, we're short-handed and way behind in our tasks."

Hod-ya strode into the kitchen proper, trailing a fingernail along the counter and leaving a fine line in the thin veneer of flour covering the top. Mileer and the dronnets stood idly just inside the entry. "Would that you could," Hod-ya mocked. She turned to face the lower kitchen's chief. "The more I think about Dancel's escape, not to mention Rissa's clumsiness, the more I wonder how that happened right under your nose." Hod-ya's eyes glared at the short, stout woman, as if challenging her to deny the suspicion.

"A-as I told you, m'lady, it all happened—"

Hod-ya held her palm menacingly in front of Caldon's face. "I know, it all happened so fast, you had no time to react."

Caldon lowered her gaze to the floor.

"If I ever"—she broke away from the table and headed for the thick, wooden door that opened to the ramp leading upward to the main kitchen—"discover you assisted them . . . " With a toss of her head, she signaled her entourage to follow as she undid the bars and latches. Hod-ya then shouted through the aperture to guards on the other side to remove the stays. Hearing the last one undone, Hod-ya pushed open the door. Mileer and the dronnets obediently trotted through the portal in her wake. She was in no mood for lag-behinds. Not today.

"Hod-ya"—Mileer huffed keeping close behind the emperor's lady of the palace as she set a demanding uphill pace—"do we need all these dronnets anymore? Couldn't they be put to better use elsewhere?"

Hod-ya rigorously pressed onward.

"Hod-ya?"

"I heard you," she said without turning, continuing her rapid ascent. As she neared the middle landing, however, her pace slowed, then came to a complete stop. "Of course! Why was that hidden from me?" She resumed her uphill pace, leaving the puzzled Mileer and the trailing dronnets scurrying to catch up.

"What? What is it, Hod-ya?"

She called back over her shoulder as she attained the top of the ramp, "Mileer, prepare your regular troops to saturate the city, turning out every citizen. The tattooing of every citizen in the city must be accomplished by the end of today. Anyone without the mark is to be immediately remanded to the castle and forcibly tattooed, understand?"

"T-today?" Mileer sputtered. "I mean, that'll take thousands of sharifs and troopers away from their other details, not to mention—"

"Do it!" Hod-ya glanced down at Mileer who was still chugging uphill. "The outlying districts and the rest of the empire can wait until the end of the week, but no longer. This phase must be accelerated, or we risk falling behind schedule and losing it all."

Mileer slowed his steps; his brow furrowed as he pondered Hod-ya's order. The dronnets passed by on either side, keeping pace with their mistress. "Wait, Hod-ya, wait. What do you mean, 'risk losing it all'?"

From the top of the ramp, Hod-ya called over her shoulder, "Can't you figure that out, imbecile? You just make sure to do as I said. Now I have other matters to attend that I've neglected far too long, so quit bothering me with your foolish questions." At that, she spun around sharply and stormed through the pantry and into the main kitchen, bellowing, "Out of my way, toads!"

Hapless scullery maids scurried out of her path. Pans clattering and the *thunk* of broomsticks and mophandles bouncing off the floor echoed down the tunnel ramp.

~

Mileer came to a standstill on the ramp's landing, fingers stroking his whiskered chin. He was all alone in the dark and damp, free to think on his own without her probing his private thoughts. It almost seemed as if . . . as if Hod-ya was afraid. Even terrified. Of what? She was perpetually in a bad mood—and nasty—but of late, she was even more testy.

"What if Lurcan isn't as powerful . . . " He sharply inhaled and covered his mouth as if trying to force the words back in. It was treason of the highest order to even entertain such a thought, much less speak it aloud. Mileer glanced about the dim tunnel lit only by a lone, smoky torch flickering wanly in a wall sconce. A cold sweat broke out on his brow. He was sure he was alone; no one had heard his gaffe. Well, he would do Hod-ya's bidding—for now, at any rate. He'd muster all available troops and sharifs to accomplish the mega-task dumped on him. Strategizing how to go about the next step, Mileer ascended the remainder of the ramp and passed through the bustling kitchen staff that was cleaning up after Hod-ya's tornadic passage.

~

Meanwhile, Hod-ya, with the double file of dronnets dogging her heels, marched determinedly out of the palace gates and down the main promenade toward the massive facade of the Hall of Belief where Virac, the steward and propagator of sham superstitions and meaningless rituals, dwelt in luxury at her expense. Well, it was time to cash in on her investments. She was two days overdue for this meeting due to searching for the missing girls, but Virac wouldn't complain.

What could he say? What dare he say? And the chief inquisitor, Spand, had better not have grown lax in his skills during his recent years of being idle, either. It was time for their expertise in extracting information from the imprisoned kingsmen and forcing recantation so she could again take up her nefarious work.

~

Flan sat on the stone floor, one hand and one foot bound to an iron ring embedded in the granite wall. He had been roused by shuffling feet outside the heavy oaken door that isolated his cell from the outer corridor. Gruff, garbled voices filtered through the panels; a jingling was followed by a click as tumblers fell into place. The door swung open, revealing several guards, one of them bearing a torch. Flan squinted in the torch's glare. It had been two or three days, by his reckoning, since his eyes had seen any light. He squinted against the stab of light and observed as two new prisoners were clapped in chains as they were shoved into his cell alongside Flan. The men's feet were knocked out from under them, and their buttocks hit the stone floor hard amidst the straw and sawdust mixture covering the floor. Then each had a hand and a foot chained to the same ring holding Flan's shackles.

Both men's chins rested on their chests; they'd been beaten within a breath of their lives and were barely conscious, as Flan had been the day he'd been deposited here. The guards joked crudely about tophet bait as they finished their task and exited, taking the torch with them. In that fleeting flare of light, Flan tried to identify his new cellmates, but to no avail. Their disfigured, bloodied faces and matted hair defied recognition. The door slammed to, and the cell was again devoid of light.

"Hello." Flan ventured a whisper. It wouldn't do to have the guards—who might be listening outside the door—hear them conversing. There was no response from either prisoner. In fact, though prevented by the pitch blackness, Flan sensed that the man farthest away was slowly tilting sideways, suspended only by the chain on his wrist, preventing him from slumping all the way to the floor, where his body might find a modicum of relief.

Flan sighed. Without a doubt, these prisoners were kingsmen, possibly members of his own brigade. He'd hoped they might have heard some scrap of information concerning Jorna during their sessions of torture. Tears rimmed his eyes. What must Jorna be going through? What they'd put him through was bad enough, but his wife . . . What atrocities were they capable of committing?

"Mmmmph!" uttered the prisoner nearest Flan.

"Are you awake?" Flan whispered.

"I hope not," the man croaked through puffy lips. "I'd hate to be awake and feel like this."

"Who are you?"

The man groaned and shifted his position, finally answering, "Knarsh."

Flan's eyes closed, and tears welled over onto his cheeks. "Then, you were captured before you escaped the city?"

"A-as far as I know," Knarsh mumbled. "I think only Etel and I were captured."

"The others got away, then?"

"Let us hope. And you are . . . "

"Flan. I'm Flan. You stayed in my house."

"Ah, yes, I know you . . . I was in hiding when you were taken. Did your wife escape?"

"Both of us were brought to the castle and threatened to take the mark. I was hoping you might have heard something about her."

"Sorry. We were hustled directly into the dungeon, where the machinations of torture were employed to the full extent of their design. They didn't even try to get information out of us. They just"—Knarsh sobbed—"just bent to their task of inflicting pain." He fell silent. "They didn't even try very hard to make us take the tattoo."

Flan reached over with his free hand and patted his companion's shoulder, whispering, "I know; I know."

Knarsh sniffed, calmed himself, and laid his hand over Flan's for the comfort of human touch. "Must have beat us nonstop for the better part of two days."

"And nothing was said about a woman they'd brought in?"

"Nothing was said at all. Blackguards—or dronnets, as some call them—rarely speak, especially when they're enjoying their work. Never asked us a question. Then this tall, thin woman all in black—I'm guessing she was this Hod-ya we've been hearing about—comes in and tells them, 'Enough.' Then we were dragged down here."

"If you were captured the same day that you left my house, it's probably been three days, rather than two."

Etel, his head dangling inches off the floor, suspended only by his arm, groaned, and tried to sit upright. "This can't be Splendora," he said through gritted teeth.

"Not hardly," Knarsh returned. "But take heart, Flan is here with us."

"Captain Flan? Of Ward Street?"

"The same," Knarsh answered.

"Come with a brigade to our aid, has he?"

Neither spoke for a couple of moments.

Then Flan said, "Afraid not, I'm in the same condition as both of you."

"Any others in here besides us?" asked Etel.

Flan answered, "Just the three of us."

"Oh?" said a very quiet voice from a far corner.

Flan froze, his eyes widening despite the ubiquitous darkness.

Knarsh and Etel cocked their ears, unsure if their beatings weren't causing delirium.

"Did . . . did you hear something?" Knarsh asked, a tremor in his tone.

Flan held his breath. Finally, he admitted, "I thought I heard . . . something. All this time, I thought I was in here alone." Raising his voice, he challenged, "Is anyone else in here?"

"Have I not promised to share in your sufferings if you shared in my rejection?"

Flan barely found the breath to exclaim, "Logon?"

A recessed corner began to glow with a soft, blue light, gradually revealing the silhouette of a man garbed in a robe and cowl, hunched over as if warming himself beside a campfire. He lifted his head, and his eyes shone out like beams of light from an otherwise shadowed face.

The cell brightened as Logon rose and approached the battered men. He stood just out of reach. "All you had to do was deny me, and your tormentors would have stopped. But you chose to honor me by willfully suffering for my reputation's sake. My father and all Splendora observed your great loyalty with profound joy. Many have likewise been tested and likewise, found true; but there were also those who dishonored me by denouncing me for temporary relief, not realizing that in their self-preserving denial of me, they proclaimed Lurcan as the regent they preferred above me. All who endure mistreatment for my name, foregoing the fleeting pleasures of Carnalia, openly declare their choice to suffer instead of renouncing me." He moved closer to the three and extended his hand, first touching Etel, then Knarsh, and finally Flan.

At Logon's touch, a warmth coursed inside as well as outside Flan's body; simultaneously, the shackles on his wrist and ankle opened and clanked to the floor, as did the irons of his companions.

The three rubbed their wrists, scarcely daring believe they weren't just dreaming.

"Come." Logon walked to the massive wooden locked door and paused, extending his hand toward the three.

Flan rose first and assisted Knarsh and Etel to get up. As they made the effort to stand, each man's aches and pains dissipated; and renewed strength coursed through their limbs. Smiling, they approached Logon, waiting for him to undo the door locks. Instead, Logon walked into and disappeared through the door.

The three kingsmen stood at the door baffled, groping about in the pitch black.

"Logon?" Flan called, a quiver in his voice.

"Come." Logon's voice resounded through the door.

"Wha—" Etel blurted. "We can't walk through a solid door."

"Have you ever tried?" Logon's voice filtered through the oaken panels. "Here, take my hand—"

Logon's arm glowed up to the elbow and was extended through the door, his outstretched fingers splayed open, spreading beams of light into the room.

Flan immediately grabbed Logon's hand and turned to the others. "Take my hand."

Knarsh and Etel each took hold of Flan's other hand. Flan gritted his teeth, closed his eyes, and stepped into the door.

They found themselves outside the cell, just the three of them, alone in the torch-lit corridor. The door was barred and locked behind them.

"Where did he—" Knarsh looked up and down the corridor.

Flan laughed. "We should have known Logon would never send us somewhere unless he would make the way."

"Even mystically, it would appear," Knarsh enjoined, also laughing.

"Flan? Is that you?" a woman's voice echoed from down the corridor.

"Jorna! I'm here. Where are you? Did you escape?" Flan took off trotting toward the sound of her voice, followed closely by Knarsh and Etel. Though the tunnels were lit by dim, smoky wall torches, no one else was seen. The three trotted on, pausing only to glance down side corridors for a brief listen as they passed.

"Jorna?"

"I hear you, Flan; you're much closer. I hear footsteps. Keep coming. I'm afraid to move. It's all dark where I am."

Flan skidded to a halt. "Listen." He held up his hand. "Sounds as if she's right here. Jorna?"

"You're so close," Jorna replied. "Why can't I see you?"

"Why can't I see you? Your voice sounds like it's . . . here." Flan touched both hands to the wall.

Knarsh nodded. "Her voice seems to be coming from inside the wall. Are you trapped in the wall?"

"No, I'm in some kind of tunnel, but it seems as if you're in the wall."

Knarsh tugged Flan's sleeve, pulling him aside. "There's more here than meets the eye, Flan. Is it possible that her voice might be a deception luring us into a trap?"

A momentary chill ran down Flan's spine. "No, I reject that. Logon wouldn't release us to be immediately captured again. Nor would he set us free and not Jorna."

Etel stepped back from the wall, eyeing it curiously, then stepped up to it touching its rough surface.

"Flan, please, get me out of here. I've wandered around for what seems like hours, seeking a way out. I fear I'm going to be recaptured."

Flan bit the inside of his cheek. His beloved wife was imprisoned just out of reach, and he was helpless to do aught about it.

"I remember," Knarsh said. "I heard something about a maze inside the walls of the palace, a labyrinth to ensnare invaders and would-be-escapees so they'd wander futilely searching a way out until they starved."

"Well, that's helpful. Thanks for that little tidbit of hope." Flan placed both hands on the wall again and sighed.

"But aren't there keys that unlock doorways of that maze?" Etel said. "Rissa said there was a pattern to it all if one took the time to learn—and besides that, she also said there were some sections of wall that needed no key to open but instead turned on some sort of pivot?"

Flan stepped back to examine the wall before him. Then he stepped close again and probed up, down, and all around for a seam or pressure point. "Help me." He glanced over his shoulder. "You men try that way. Jorna," he called through the wall, "feel around for a chink in the wall. There may be a pressure point on your side that will open the wall."

"I have been—oops!" A soft grinding sound accompanied the movement of a huge segment of the stone wall swinging perpendicular out into the tunnel. Jorna wasted no time leaping out of the dark tunnel to fall into the arms of her husband. Then, stepping back, the couple examined each other at arm's length. "Ntch, ntch," she chided. "Just look what becomes of you when left on your own. You're a mess." She again embraced Flan, burrowing her head into his shoulder.

"You don't look so kempt yourself," he teased. Then with concerned eyes and furrowed brow, he asked, "What did they do to you?" He lightly kissed her forehead.

"They only buffeted me for a short while. I was surprised they didn't do more. I was left alone shortly after they dragged us out of the courtyard. They took you off somewhere but left me in that first interrogation room. Then Hod-ya—"

"Hod-ya?" Flan winced. "I encountered her, too. What did she do?"

"Just studied me for several long minutes after her dronnets slapped me around. She sent them away, studied me some more, then abruptly left the room. That's when Logon appeared and led me out into the torch-lit tunnel. He pointed down a tunnel; and I went, asking no questions. Finally, after hours and hours of exhausting wandering, I sat against the wall and fell asleep. When I woke, I was no longer in a lighted tunnel but in a dark chamber, or cave or . . . or . . . Anyway, I've meandered blindly since then until I heard your voices."

"Well, thankfully, we're together again." He hugged Jorna tightly.

"Now what?" Etel probed another section of wall with his fingers.

"Find a way out, I guess," ventured Knarsh. "Only, how? From what Rissa told us, there's no escape to the outside without a key."

Flan smiled. "Have you ever tried walking through a solid, wooden door?"

Knarsh and Etel laughed.

"What are you laughing about?" Jorna's frown declared she was not a little peeved at the men for not taking the situation more seriously.

"I'll tell you later." Flan chuckled.

"Shh . . . voices coming from down yonder." Etel pointed.

"What'll we do?" Jorna's voice was tense.

Flan looked up and down the tunnel. "Get back in there and hide, where Jorna was."

The four stepped through the yawning opening. "Where did you touch it to make it open, Jorna?"

"Me? I thought one of you touched the spot."

The approaching voices became louder.

"Oh, hurry, try touching everywhere," Jorna implored.

Standing where Jorna had previously been, the four frantically passed their hands over the rough-hewn stonework from top to bottom and side to side. Without warning, the rumble started again; and the stone slab closed, leaving the foursome in dark obscurity.

"Remember that spot, whoever touched it," Flan whispered.

"I thought you touched it," said Knarsh.

"I thought you found it," said Etel.

"Great, no one knows who touched it," Jorna moaned.

"It was found before; we'll find it again," Flan encouraged. "Shh now, they'll be passing right where we stood a moment ago."

Holding their breaths, the four leaned their ears against the cool stone wall.

The footpads of several passersby were heard. Then a low-toned but unmistakable female voice said, "Locked them up together, the three of them. Two weren't from Cosmopolis; but the first one, the mate of that woman who escaped—Falm or Frum or whatever his name is—he's the leader of the local ring of kingsmen. Break him first in the sight of the other two—whatever it takes: fire, dismemberment, flaying, whatever. Once he's broken or dead, they'll crack. We have a good line on the whereabouts of the locals; but I need to know about the visitors: where they are from, which road they used to enter the city, how many they are, what weaponry they possess . . . "

"Hod-ya, it's highly unlikely there's more than a handful of kingsmen out in the wilderness. How could any sizable force even survive the wilds any length of time, much less go undetected?" posed an unfamiliar voice.

"Virac is right, Hod-ya. Besides, Cosmopolis is too well-defended. We have the dreads, the armies, the sharifs—not to mention several corps of firedrakes and tophets assembling in Swamp Tophet for a final assault on that obnoxious fortress and bridge. Once that collapses, any that are left will melt away like a late spring snowfall."

"Hah! Dreads, you say?" Hod-ya sneered back. "Spand, I've trusted them to my own undoing. Sure, they have power, but you can never depend on them to do what you want. As for the other defenses you rely on, if Ecclessites discovered the chicanery of daggers and rejected them, instead having learned their swords well, not even dreads and firedrakes can resist for long. Our best defense is to keep kingsmen discouraged by believing it is too daunting a task to sharpen their swords or else get them so bored or frightened so that they ignore their swords and remain virtually weaponless. Believe me, I learned that through harsh trials."

"But surely the dreads are almost as powerful as Lurcan himself."

"Shh, you'll remind her of what happened to Pitland," whispered one of the other voices.

"I heard that! You think I forgot? That's precisely why it's imperative we break these captives and get information from them. I don't want to be surprised by another secret army arising out of nowhere, get it?"

The voices wandered out of range and were soon obliterated by the tramp of dozens more feet. The four hiding behind the wall's partition collectively released their breath. Moments passed. Only when the echoes of marching feet were no longer heard did they dare relax.

Distinct clicks, as of a lock opening, and bars being shifted out of their stays echoed down to them. There was a long moment of silence, then an anguished wail resounding down the corridor. "Not again! Gone! Disappeared from a locked and barred door? No trace? No clues? How is that possible? What in the name of Pitland is happening?"

"But m'lady, Pitland is gone," said Virac. A loud smack echoed down the corridor.

CHAPTER TWENTY-FIVE

IN THE ONCOMING DUSK, BLUSKIE, Ewert, and Skujj crawled on hands and knees to the top of a knoll overlooking the pike to Cosmopolis. Upon attaining the overlook, the three lay side by side on their bellies peering down into the vale from a rock ledge. Far below was a road snaking like a meandering river through the thinning forest. They had earlier identified the banners and insignias of Carnalian, Eroton, and Craniantium brigades that had been summoned from remote corners of the empire. The forces had met up together and were marching in six files, obstructing all other traffic, pushing them aside to wait along the shoulders of the road until the martial columns had passed. They were obviously heading toward a massive muster in Cosmopolis. The kingsmen scouts watched in silence, keeping their vigil until the twilight deepened. But still the *tramp, tramp, tramp* of hob-nailed boots reverberated through the benighted, wooded hillsides as torches lit the outer columns passing through the forest.

Ewert rolled over to his back and sighed. He checked his deerskin overwrap, making sure it covered his white Logon tunic, lest the garment reveal their position to Carnalian out-flankers who might be scouting the countryside.

Bluskie slid down beside Ewert, asking, "How's your wound?"

"Gone, totally healed."

"Never saw the like—'specially not in the empire's service," Bluskie added wistfully. "When them girls poured oil on your leg, then simply

352

said, 'Logon heals you,' I thought to meself they was jest simple-minded maidens what meant well. I smiled at their naïveté . . . But when you suddenly stood up and did a jig, I about fell off me stool."

"Yeah, that was somethin', warn't it? And then them three girls went to anyone else what was wounded and done the same thing, healing any what had a heart to join the fight and finish the mission. Not a lame leg nor feeble arm be's left in the brigade."

Skujj slid down and joined his companions. "That's the last of 'em. I figures around twenty-thousand afoot; they'll reach Cosmopolis bolstering the empire's forces, arrivin' 'bout daybreak."

"Well, we'd better make our report. This influx of troops, plus the multitude already in Cosmopolis preparing for battle, will make our task force of five thousand seem like a puny feint rather than an earnest all-out attack."

"But Logon works miracles, and the emperor don't," said Ewert. "So, how can the emperor succeed? When his soldiers get wounded, they stay wounded; when kingsmen get wounded, them girls can just pour healing balm on them and, *presto,* back to the fray."

"Whether that's the way of it or not, rumors abound that another kingsman army will join Metid's army when we assail the palace walls." Skujj rose to his feet. "That'll help even the odds some."

"And don't forget Saygus' secret mission; come to think of it, isn't there supposed to be some kind of Ecclessite task force bivouacked somewhere in Ra-Amawl?" Bluskie said. "I remember trampling through thick brush and primal forests when we were with Captain Mileer and Hod-ya, looking for the escaped Scrarth and Avangar girls."

Skujj rose to his feet and preceded his companions down the mountainside trail toward the Ecclessite outpost some miles distant.

"Yes, and there's supposedly a rag-tag bunch of escaped Ecclessite prisoners from Pitland making their way north, too."

"Well, what little I've heard about the mystery runes certainly seems to be coming to a head," mused Bluskie. "We should toll our blades to be ready before the assault begins." He observed the tiny blue light on Skujj's sword as it barely lit the pathway ahead and exposed his own difficulty in getting the sword to yield up its secrets. It wasn't for lack of trying; he'd spent hours trying to get the toller to interact with his sword, to meager effect.

The trio found the trail and set off at a trot toward the scout outpost. There was no longer any need to slink noiselessly between bole and bush; the enemy had made no attempt to conceal their movements as they progressed to Cosmopolis, which meant they would waste no more time searching the wilderness for kingsmen.

"I even heard rumors of a kingsmen brigade in Cosmopolis itself," ventured Ewert, breaking his silence.

"Little use they'll be." Bluskie waved his hand to shoo a mosquito buzzing near his ear. "Likely too timid to even show themselves openly. Can't say as I blame them for hiding, though, surrounded and outnumbered as they are."

"Way I see it," posed Skujj, "if they do exist, they're brave enough to not forsake their Logon tunics when threatened." He stopped beside a tall larch tree and cupped his hands to his lips. "Words of the word."

"Advance and be recognized," returned a voice out of the darkness.

"Three scouts returning from reconnoitering Carnalian troop movements." Skujj stepped forward, showing his sword, flanked by the other two.

Bushes surrounding the trio parted, revealing a squad of kingsmen with varying amounts of shine upon their swords.

A corporal stated, "About time you returned. The sergeant's as nervous as a hare in a fox den awaiting your report. Follow me."

The sentries blended into the underbrush again, ready to screen any other passersby as the corporal led the trio of scouts past several busy tent sites.

The small scouting campsite resonated with the sound of tollers rasping on metal and sergeants conducting small groups in mock combat drills, demonstrating finesse in their swordplay maneuvers all in preparation for a full-scale assault. They were ushered directly into the command tent, where another sergeant presided over a gathering of scouts. The sergeant's attention was drawn to the tent flap as the corporal announced, "Last of the scouts reporting in from the perimeter, sir."

Skujj stepped forward and saluted. "We watched the tail of the column disappear down Seven Bridge Pike, heading for Cosmopolis: no out-runners, no delayed search parties. They marched with purpose. We figure upward of twenty thousand afoot and a couple of hundred mounted—mostly officers."

The sergeant pressed his fingertips into a pyramid as he mused, "Twenty thousand, you say; and with the ten thousand or so mixed dronnets and elite troops returning from Ra-Amawl . . . that makes near fifty thousand, counting those already in and around the palace."

"Don't forget the masses of Eroton troops rumored to be gathering on the northern border," the corporal interjected. "They may be disorderly and uncouth, but they're fierce fighters; and it seems, they've been summoned to Carnalia's defense as well. Their hearts will be as difficult to pierce as any dronnet. What was the last count we had on them?"

"Hard to say. They're so disorganized and mill about so much that our scouts couldn't tell those they had counted from those they hadn't counted. Best guess is about fifteen thousand. And then there's Craniantiumites from the southern border who only move under cover of night, making it impossible to reckon their numbers. Probably upward of twenty thousand judging from the trail they left behind."

"So, what's our best guess at a tally?" The sergeant scribbled figures on a piece of parchment. "What kind of force are we up against? We need to report these estimates to Metid and Gulundur by messenger as soon as possible, leaving tonight posthaste. Who's the swiftest runner?"

A soldier sitting cross-legged in a corner rose and stood before the table of non-commissioned officers. He displayed his sword for all to see. "What matter the numbers we face? All we need to know is whether Logon sends us forth or not. All else is irrelevant." He ran his finger along the edge of his sword. "The Advisor tells me that this battle must be waged, despite the odds." He leaned forward, placing both hands on the table and staring into the sergeant's eyes. "I ask leave to carry this report; I'm rested and can set out immediately."

The sergeant glanced at the corporal seated beside him. "I don't know. What do you think?"

The corporal shrugged. "I see no reason not to send him."

Ewert, Bluskie, and Skujj, not having been dismissed, stood just inside the tent-door flap, curious to know details of what would take place when the entire Ecclessite Strike Force stormed Lurcan's palace. They had all-too-recently been in Cosmopolis and knew the impregnability of the fortress. Carnalian war machines were designed not only to kill but also to cruelly maim and cripple and were deceptively placed to effect great devastation on any adversary foolish enough to attempt scaling the outer walls.

CHAPTER TWENTY-SIX

SAJON AND HUDGE FOLLOWED METID out of the command tent after assuring the general they were flexible to their assignments.

"Was there anything else, Captain?" Evebryl tucked a wisp of hair back under her snood.

Metid's head shook ever so slightly. "No, I think not. As distaff members of this task force, do you and your daughters understand you're not required to participate in the fray?"

"Of course, but with our hearts lit by Logon's light, as are our swords, how can we refrain? The end of the age is come, Captain Metid," Evebryl asserted. "Carnalian lives will be forever lost to eternal torment—trophies for that usurper—something that Lurcan, even in his agonies, will gloat over while he himself suffers the just punishment of the corrupt. We must do all we can to rescue fellow humans from that horrible fate, even if it means they might kill us."

Evebryl, Sejisca, and Cocee exited the command tent, leaving Gulundur, Metid, and their aides-de-camp under the shelter of the canvas roof.

"Well, that's that," said Metid. "Nothing left but to draw the order of battle, eh?"

"Well, at least that answered the question of who should spearhead the attack against the gates." Gulundur sighed. "I doubt we'll see them again this side of Splendora. My heart is heavy, yet I couldn't find it in my heart to deny their wish."

"It's likely they'll meet Saygus in Splendora before we do, seeing as his task is even more daunting than assailing the front gates of Cosmopolis. I hope he holds no grudge against us for letting his family take the lead."

"I think he'd be miffed if we denied them that privilege." Gulundur managed a wry smile. "Now, about the other units and where they can best give a good account . . ."

~

The Generals Tren, Marn, Ollo, and Leton strode through the campsite seeking Captain Varter. He was a hard man to keep tabs on, ever since the night of wondrous events back in the cliffs when many wounded and infirm were miraculously made whole as they tolled their weapons. The common report was that particular runes started glowing from nearly everyone's sword, accompanied by a brilliant light, followed by delighted cries of surprise as people found themselves strong and healthy once again.

Varter was one of those recipients. His wounded leg had been instantaneously restored; only a scar remained where a grievous, festering gash had been. Since then, he wandered continuously round and round the encampment giving encouragement to all. Now, however, it was imperative that he parley with the generals, sketching out the various approaches to Cosmopolis and Lurcan's fortress.

Tren grabbed the arm of a soldier who was going the opposite way. "Have you seen Captain Varter?"

The startled private gasped upon realizing who had seized him and finally stuttered, "I s-s-saw him just a moment ago, sir, over there." He indicated a grove where a cheery fire lit the night with several troopers gathered around singing a runesong that echoed faintly through the trees.

Tren released the man and headed toward the campsite. Ollo, following on Tren's heels, thanked the private, then urged the others, "Let's go."

"Varter, we've been searching all over for you," Tren chided, adding a grin to show he wasn't scolding him. "It's time we drew aside and agreed on the order of battle." Tren was joined seconds later by the other generals.

"The very thing, General." Varter sighed. "I was thinking to delay this discussion until we heard from the delegation that was sent to Cosmopolis; but for whatever reason, they haven't shown up. We might as well get to it. Until we hear a definite word, we'd best not count on coordinating our attack with the Cosmopolisian kingsmen brigade."

"To my tent, then." Tren pointed *Starsplinter* at a pathway through a thicket. Captain Varter followed close behind with the other officers. "Would you like to invite the brigade leaders that Bonu delegated to this war council?"

"It would be wise." Varter nodded. "And we might as well include Lieutenant Bonu. He's as responsible for this army assembling out of nowhere as anybody. He thought his mission was to rescue his beloved; but as it turns out, that was just a side benefit of Logon's intentions."

"Indeed." Tren winked at the other generals. "Our ambitions are sometimes just the incentive Logon allows us, so we follow his purposes. Without Bonu directing those 'lost' brigades to your cliff cantonment, we would've had a very small army to confront Lurcan. As it is, we're still vastly outnumbered by Carnalian, Eroton, Dronnet, and Craniantium forces, not to mention various battalions summoned from lesser duchies and territories bordering Carnalia."

"Don't forget cusps, tophets, firedrakes, dreads, and such," added Ollo, last in line.

"I even heard rumors," said Marn, "that wild beasts may play a part in the havoc as well. Craniantium lions, wolf packs, water-dragons, half-men—all rising to defend the usurper Lurcan and his achievement of producing the ultimate man of rebellion, Turit Tyrannus."

"Where did you hear such rumors?" challenged Leton. "I mean, the human foes we'll face are overwhelming enough without you adding all sorts of unnatural animal behaviors."

"Nevertheless, it's quite possible," said Captain Varter. "Kyleah had a vision the other night as she and her husband, Throll, tolled their swords. She saw some kind of plant creeping along the ground as a battle raged in the background, and following with those plants came animals, fierce and feral. Though in her oracle, their objective seemed unclear."

"A vision? Really? Tren, do you buy into all this hokum?" Leton stubbed the toe of his boot on an unseen root.

"Gifts of the Advisor are the proof that our rescuer arose from the house of the dead and lives, even after being sacrificed. Special abilities to the wise are a demonstration of those gifts—meaning dreams and visions from Logon, as long as the message conforms to the runes on our swords."

"But man-eating plants creeping along the ground? Wild animals joining in concert with evil forces?"

Tren paused, allowing those following to catch up. "You've lit up your entire sword, Leton, else you wouldn't be a general. Yet you've never taken the runes literally for what they actually say; instead, you treat them as metaphorical, a lesson to be learned but not lived. Unless and until you know the reality of the truth that's inscribed on those blades, you'll always be wondering how and why. Questions of whether manu really exists—those who never search will never find. Visions and dreams can be of Logon, especially when they come through a yielded servant such as Kyleah, who has a proven record. We'd be fools to ignore any message she believes is from Logon."

"But aren't the runes on our swords enough to know Logon's instructions?" Leton stepped directly in front of Tren pleading his case, hands extended to either side.

Tren smiled. "Usually, yes. But there are times—intense times of need and danger— when immediate, specific instructions are required."

"Such as?" Leton persisted.

"Such as when we captured and pierced the dronnet, Gragnold, to his heart," reminded Tren. "You were out of the room getting those jester outfits; but when you came back, you saw that Gragnold had met with Logon. No rune on the blade told us that of all the other dronnets who'd been knocked oblivious, only Gragnold's chest would be pierced. That was a word of knowing Logon's desire through the indwelling Advisor—a gift, if you will—of Logon to assist and guide us in our warfare."

Leton shook his head. "I don't know. It's true. So many runes I'd taken figuratively have come literally alive before my eyes, yet . . . "

"If the ancient generals actually performed the actions described on our swords, why would you think the tools and weapons Ecclessites needed at the beginning of rescuing lives for the king are any less necessary in these final days of rampant evil?" Ollo waved his hand in agitation at his companion's obstinacy.

"Sooner or later, Leton, you must trust Logon's runes and follow the trail of our liege," urged Tren, nudging Ollo gently aside. "Unless you're fully committed to expect Logon's intervention and follow his supernatural manifestations, I'm afraid we must leave you out of the planning, the attack—everything. This ultimate battle of all battles requires unshakable confidence in Logon's power to overcome Lurcan and Turit and the empire under their control."

Leton regarded Tren, studying his features in the shadowy light of glowing swords and the surrounding campfires. Then turning to his fellow officers, he nodded. "I'll try."

"Not good enough," Tren intoned. "You must fully commit."

"But I don't know how to make myself believe more than what I already believe."

"Your sword is fully lit, but your runes lack the intensity of light ours exhibit," noted Marn. "In fact, your blade, though it glows from tip to haft, appears almost dull alongside ours. Even Captain Varter's three-fourths glow shines brighter than yours. You know the facts but lack experiencing the reality of those facts."

Leton shrugged. "So, rather than belittle me, do you have any suggestions? I've done all I know to do."

Tren put an arm around Leton's shoulders. "Simply ask Logon."

"What good is that?"

Tren placed a forefinger on Leton's lips, silencing him, then tapped a rune that was aglow on Leton's own sword.

Leton read aloud:

"'Let those that understanding lack,
Gently ask and not be slack.
For wall betwixt lore and fact
Must surely yield to op'ning crack
And truth no longer seem abstract.'"

Leton scrunched his features.

"You look puzzled. You can't bridge that gap between real and unreal on your own, Leton. No amount of tolling alone will reveal what you need to know," Tren counseled. "You can only ask Elyon to merge what you know with what you must realize is living truth. Simply ask."

Leton looked from face to face. Finally, he said, "Okay, so I'll ask."

"But he who asks must believe what he asks for is in accordance with Elyon's will and believes he will receive it." Tren smiled. "Are you ready?"

"I need to think it over, on my own. I need time."

"Now is the moment of truth," Ollo pressed.

"No, Leton's right," Tren responded. "Such decisions must come from honest seeking, not coercion. We, too, must trust Elyon to perform his word without us applying pressure. Our king is well able to do his work without us. King Elyon allows us to participate in his plans for our benefit but doesn't need us." Tren turned and headed for his tent again. "Leton, do what you must do. We'll be somewhere around my tent if and when you're inclined to join us."

Ollo and Marn trailed after Tren to the command tent.

~

Leton wandered off a little way and sat on a fallen tree. He laid his sword across his lap, then took toller in hand but hesitated before applying it to his blade's edge. With head bowed, he sat unmoving for several minutes.

~

"Sentry." Tren summoned the guard as he and the other generals drew near his tent. "Find Bonu and tell him he's needed."

The sentry clicked his heels. "I know right where he is, sir. Have him here in a trice." And he was off.

"What about the other brigade leaders, Tren?" asked Ollo. "I know they're mostly junior officers or captains, but didn't we agree to include them?"

"And so we shall, Ollo, so we shall. All in good time. Bonu will aid us in accomplishing that detail, since he's maintained contact with them, providing a liaison between the various brigade backgrounds." Before entering his quarters, he glanced back and observed Leton sitting on a fallen tree trunk in the distance. "We need Leton's assistance to consolidate unity among some of the factions we've inherited. Many of the newcomers think and feel as he does. His arriving at a deeper understanding will encourage others. If the various brigades don't come into unity, our differences over how to sharpen and apply Logon's swords will imperil our entire campaign with divisiveness that Lurcan will surely exploit."

Marn placed a hand on Tren's shoulder. "He's a man of integrity. He'll come. Logon wouldn't have included him in this group unless he was going to come into agreement."

Tren nodded and entered the tent, followed by the others.

The tent easily accommodated twenty to thirty people at a time; and more, if all, stood and bunched close together. Its ceiling was higher than most military tents, having a vent allowing heat to escape lest the atmosphere become stuffy. The group they were expecting would be the largest gathering of Ecclessite officers Ra-Amawl had ever witnessed, even overflowing outside the tent into the immediate environs.

Tren grabbed a rustic camp stool and moved it to the back of the tent, indicating for Varter, Ollo, and Marn to do likewise. Marn picked up the remaining fifth stool and set it beside himself. The four sat with their backs against the tent wall, chatting quietly, waiting for Bonu and Leton.

"Sir." Bonu entered, lifting the tent flap. "You sent for me?"

"Come in, Lieutenant," Tren welcomed. "We have a task for you, one of the most important details we could assign. The various brigades that you and Scung encountered—yes, Scung, I see your shadow lingering at the door flap, even though you weren't summoned—you may as well come in, too, for this assignment involves you as well."

A shaggy head with a gnarled beard poked into the sanctum of the tent. "Me? Yers be askin' for me?"

"I told you they'd know you were there," Bonu chided softly. "Now look at the trouble your curiosity has brought upon you."

Scung entered, obliterating the doorway behind him as he stood to full height. "Hey, I kin stand tall in here." He grinned. "Hain't like them tunnels in the cliff, nor the teeny deer-hide things yer calls a tent, Bonu."

"Ahem! As I was saying," Tren continued, "regarding the various brigades you and Scung encountered on your outward trek to Pitland, we need you to contact each leader—leaders mainly, mind you." He glared sternly at Scung. "And summon them here to my tent for a special meeting. Can you do that?"

Bonu saluted, but Scung blurted out, "Why sure we kin, Gen'rl. Taint no problem a-tall."

"That means when Bonu—who is invited to attend the council, as well—returns, you are included, though we haven't specifically invited you, Scung." Tren stood, emphasizing his point.

Scung's face fell, and his head drooped. "I be's hangin' around outside like, jest in case yer be's needin' the Eroton perspective?"

"I doubt very much we'll need the Eroton perspective, Scung," Tren intoned.

"But what if'n yer comes across a knotty problem, only me an' Bonu kin solve since we been ter Pitland an' back an' kens the peculiarities o' the wilds an' the critters what lurks there an'—"

"Nay, man." Ollo stood and rebuked Scung loudly. "Decisions are only for officers, don't ye ken?"

Scung glowered at the general but closed his mouth, mumbling through closed lips, "Amongst Erotons, I be's the nearest thing ter a junior officer."

"But you're not among Erotons anymore, are you?" Marn smiled calmly, seemingly amused at the exchange. "So, your status as 'almost a junior officer' doesn't really qualify for anything here, does it?"

Captain Varter leaned back silently, observing the discussion, biting the inside of his cheek to keep from chuckling, as if, knowing the Eroton's persistent temperament, how this was likely to end.

Scung puckered his lower lip. "No, I s'pose not."

"Stand aside, you great hulk" came a voice from directly behind Scung. "You're blocking the entry." A soft tap on Scung's buttocks with a sword reinforced the request.

"'Ere now, who dares assault the Scourge of the Southlands?" Scung whirled about, hand on his sword hilt, an irritated glint in his eye.

"General Leton dares, you big lummox. Now, get out of my way. I've business with those inside." A fully shining and much-brightened sword was pressed flat against Scung's nose.

The giant Eroton backed down, his jaw agape and eyes wide as Leton pushed past. Bonu tugged his friend to the side and whispered, "You'd better apologize for your unbecoming actions."

"Leton," Tren noted, "your sword glows brighter?"

"And so does my expectation of Logon to perform his runes. I simply asked; and he filled my heart and mind with such glorious runes, thoughts, and images." He turned and looked at Bonu. "One of which concerns this young man. Tren, I believe Logon would have—"

"Hold that thought, Leton," said Tren.

"Well, you have changed," stated Ollo. "And right glad I am of it."

"All these years, I've studied the runes, never realizing the impact they could have if I took them not only at surface value." Leton grabbed the vacant stool at the back of the tent and sat with the other generals, his sword glowing brightly. "Thank you for confronting me."

"'Instruct a wise man, and wiser will he be,'" quoted Marn.

"'Try to instruct a fool and receive bruises for your trouble.'" Tren finished the adage, staring at Scung.

"Yer be's right Tren, I be's a fool. I asks yer pardon, an' am willin' ter betake any discipline yer deems proper." The Eroton slumped and bowed his head. "I 'poligizes ter yer, Leton fer barkin' at yer when yer whacked me backside. I desarved it."

"Furthermore, Scung, when you and Bonu finish assembling the 'wandering brigade leaders,' come back; and we'll decree your punishment. Now, off with you both. And Bonu, leave no brigade leader out that you encountered on your way through Ra-Amawl."

"Aye, sir." Bonu ducked and went out with Scung hard on his heels.

Tren wheeled about and faced the generals. "I assume, Leton, that what you were about to say concerning Bonu is that he should be promoted—but not be merely made captain at large but captain over all those brigades he and Scung brought to the cliffs and that Scung should be appointed his adjutant?"

Leton smiled.

Varter looked up. "Truly? This is what you intend? I've oft considered the deed but lacked confirmation. But the Eroton . . . I'm not so sure."

Ollo and Marn nodded at each other.

Marn said, "We received that word from Logon earlier today, from a specific rune we each uncovered individually; but it was needful that all of us be in agreement. We weren't allowed to even share it with anyone else except each other until you, Leton, gave confirmation. When you went aside and simply asked and received understanding from the Advisor . . . well, it showed that Logon has, indeed, included you in the planning and confirmed Bonu's promotion to higher rank."

Ollo added, "As well as confirmed our battle plans."

Tren returned to his stool, his jaw set, brows knitted as he stared out the tent doorway. The tent's interior was illumined by the glow of soft lanterns hanging in advantageous spots as well as the blue glow from the five officers' bright swords. "Well, whatever comes of it now, we at least know that we truly perceived Logon's intentions."

"Aye, whether victory or defeat, Logon's decree is that we follow the plan he's revealed," said Marn.

"And we generals are united at last." Ollo crossed his arms, leaned back, and smiled.

"And I'm in total agreement. Bonu has proven reliable and capable as a junior officer," added Varter. "And I suppose Scung, if nothing else, is faithful to Bonu his captain."

~

Bonu and Scung went campsite to campsite rounding up the various officers they'd encountered in the jungle, even though the task would have taken half the time if they'd split up. Fortunately, the groups camped close beside each other, so locating them wasn't difficult. Added to that, the brigades that had been sequestered in the cliffs were clustered alongside each other as they bivouacked, making for familiarity and friendships among the brigades. Nevertheless, the thought of the impending battle hung heavily in the air, causing warriors to want to be with loved ones and friends.

At each campsite, the leader dropped what he was doing and complied when Bonu invited them to the council, as if they'd been expecting the summons. Every man, woman, and older adolescent knew that very soon, they would face overwhelming masses of cruel enemies. It was for their oppressor's sake that they imperiled their own lives, offering to sacrifice themselves in an attempt to rescue their enemies; this was Logon's way.

"What kinda punishment be's them genr'l's gonna dish out ter me, thinks yer, eh, Bonu?" They had just informed the remotest brigade leader and had turned back toward the command tent.

"I don't know, Scung; your actions were outrageous. I don't ever remember seeing you act like that. What got into you?"

"I dunno, Bonu. Somethin' jest come over me all at oncet wi'out warnin'. I ain't been thet angry since . . . since—"

"Bend down, let me have a look. Uh-huh! There it is . . . " Bonu swung his sword up and lightly touched the nape of the Eroton's neck. A brief sizzle and a tiny screech resulted.

"Boar's breath! I plumb fergot ter check fer irks."

"Here, bend lower while I check for more . . . Nope, you seem to be clear now. Remember to stay alert for the symptoms: irritation, criticizing others, wanting your own way, taking offense."

"Yeah, I guesses I manifested all o' thet back in Tren's tent, didn't I?"

"Well, if I was your captain, I'd have you horse-whipped and the welts rubbed with salt."

"C'mon, Bonu, yer wouldn't really, would yer?"

"No, of course not—our salt supplies are too limited."

The two laughed.

Then Bonu said, "Whatever the generals mete out will be fair and redemptive, you can be sure of that."

"Bonu? Is that you?" A shadowy form approached from behind.

Bonu and Scung turned. "Jeda? Why are you away from your campsite?"

"I can't explain it. I just got this feeling I ought to find you."

"Well, I'm afraid this isn't a good time. I'm summoned to a meeting in the generals' tent; officers only. I'll join you later at your campsite. We'll talk then."

"Is Scung accompanying you? He's not an officer."

"Yes, well, that's a little hard to explain."

"I been disrespectful an' gotta go git me whacks," Scung said in a singsong tone that evoked a laugh from Bonu and Jeda.

"He was irk-bit and acted—well, he was downright rude to the generals and Captain Varter, if you can believe it. They told him to come back after they deliberated his discipline. In fact, we've just contacted all the brigade leaders we encountered in the jungle back when we were on our way to Pitland to rescue you, sending them to the same meeting. This is probably going to be the last big meeting before we set out on the campaign in earnest."

"I sensed something like that, too, which is why I felt the Advisor prompting me to seek you out."

"The Advisor prompted you?

"Spoena and I were in camp tolling our swords when a sudden urgency to find you came over me. Bonu, something very significant is about to happen tonight. I must be at your side. If the generals don't want me in attendance, well, they can tell me themselves; but I'm coming with you. I need to be right there alongside you."

"Bonu?" a youthful voice spoke out of the darkness.

"Now who's that?" Bonu challenged.

"It's me, Artil. I've been summoned to accompany you."

"Artil? What's going on? Who summoned you?"

Artil stepped into the combined sword-glow from Scung, Bonu, and Jeda. "The Advisor," she said matter-of-factly. There was no debate about it.

"Ho there, wait up," came another feminine voice from out of the forest. "I'll accompany you, too."

"Now, this is getting out of hand," Bonu muttered. "Vawella? Is that you?"

"It is. And Kyleah is with me. We have business in the officer's meeting."

"Who told you there was an officer's meeting? I was instructed to invite only leadership of the various brigades that Scung and I sent into camp. Now, Jeda, Artil, Vawella, and Kyleah, you're all crashing this invitation-only meeting."

"And I," said a masculine voice from behind the women. "Dr. Kraga, at your service. I should be there, too."

"Oooh, Bonu, yer be's in big trouble fer bringin' too many people ter the meetin'," Scung taunted.

"But I didn't—I give up. Come on along, we might as well have a picnic while we're at it." Bonu, with Jeda at his side, tramped off toward the command tent, leading the others.

As they approached Tren's tent, they heard a disconcerting jumble in the hollow, many voices chattering where, for security reasons, silence was to be maintained. Bonu also noted a larger-than-usual contingent of sentries surrounding the tent. The tent walls had been rolled up, and a crowd overflowed around the outside. Bonu glanced behind at the entourage he'd inadvertently gathered, took a deep breath, and pushed his way under the tent roof with Jeda beside him and Scung and the others close behind. He found a narrow aisle open down the middle of the gathering that went directly to the seated officers who presided from behind a table along the rear of the tent. Jeda followed Bonu as he approached the table.

"Silence, everyone," Tren ordered, rising to his feet, banging the pommel of his sword on the table. "Bonu, Jeda, and you, too, Scung, come down here. Sentry, tie all the flaps open, so those arriving can participate. Bonu, I see you've brought some extra people with you."

"Sorry, sir, begging your forgiveness, some of them just sort of tagged along. I tried to dissuade them."

"Never mind, Bonu. You've accomplished your task admirably, Captain."

Jeda stole a quick look at Scung.

It took a moment for Bonu to catch Tren's misspeak. "Uh, excuse me, Tren, but I think you—"

Tren laughed. "No, Bonu, I didn't misspeak." He turned to the generals and raised both palms up. The generals and Captain Varter, taking the cue, stood, wide smiles on their faces. "Tonight," Tren resumed, "I have an announcement, then three duties to perform. First the announcement: I don't quite know how to explain this. But although we've begun planning our attack, Logon would have us return to the cliffs for just a little while."

Murmurs buzzed inside and outside the officer's tent. Consternation showed on the faces of many; others just stood dumbfounded, staring at Tren.

"Yes, we are to pack up and head back to the cliffs. Do not think for one moment that we've ended up here aimlessly like Somem leading the king's battalions so long ago. King Elyon did so to prepare his people for warfare, using their prolonged, circuitous march to strengthen and equip his forces to take the land from their mortal enemies."

Tren paused to ascertain the mood of the throng. Seeing they weren't indignant, he continued, "In the same way, Logon confirmed to us senior officers that we were brought here to plot our advance toward Cosmopolis in stages. While here, much unifying in camp was accomplished, things needed to be agreed upon to avoid confusion. It took some doing, but each one of you is now aware of his or her place in Logon's service. Upon our return, it will be the time for the all-out assault on Lurcan's forces."

Tren noted relief on some faces, while others exhibited trepidation. "Prince Logon knows what he's about; don't give in to doubt or fear. Perhaps it remains for the other trumpets of the runes to sound and be fulfilled before the final attack is launched. At any rate, returning to the cliffs gives us more time to toll our blades and practice mock combat, honing our skills in rescuing lives to the king.

"Now, as to the duties that I must now perform—deeds of a joyful nature—I regret only that we do not have time to render the full traditional ceremony bestowing commission of authority as would be done under better circumstances. Because these proceedings are, of necessity, truncated, they are nonetheless valid and binding. With the express leading of Logon and the Advisor"—Tren held his sword aloft, so its light was visible to all inside as well as outside the tent—"and the four generals here, along with Captain Varter, all bearing witness, we hereby commission you, Bonu, as captain in good standing of the Ecclessite realm and, in particular, commanding officer of the newly amalgamated brigade comprised of the wandering brigades and company fragments you sent to the cliff encampment. They are merged into one unit under your command. Your immediate task is to organize these various factions into one unified fighting unit by resolving disagreements over tolling the Children of the Stars.

"It's necessary that all our units be of one mind—that there be no division, which would allow the enemy opportunity to drive a wedge between our forces and weaken our strength. Over the years, varying traditions and interpretations inconsistent with the pure rendering of the runes have gradually been inserted by the king's enemies into this or that brigade, causing mistrust and even hostility between soldiers who are supposed to be on the same side. Now we are on the eve of a great battle, contending for the very souls of those who hate us. Unless we become united by adhering only to the runes and all the runes Logon had engraved on our blades, great losses on both sides will mount, leaving devastation so tremendous . . . " Tren's eyes moistened, and his voice became choked.

Then he turned to the officers gathered around. "I hereby urge you to lay aside any and all differences; heed the instruction of Captain Bonu. He's dispatched a dread singlehandedly and was instrumental in the destruction of Pitland and its sorceress. He has experienced battles with creatures that not many captains or generals have encountered. Trust him; he's a worthy leader, and so is his adjutant, Lieutenant Scung"—Tren glanced at the nonplussed Eroton—"who stuck faithfully by his friend's side and proved invaluable to the mission that these two undertook at great risk to themselves."

"Hear, hear!" echoed Ollo, Leton, Marn, and Captain Varter. All five officers at the table, now standing, withdrew their swords and, in turn, tapped Bonu and then Scung on both shoulders.

A rousing cheer reverberated into the benighted forest glen, rolling over swamp, hill, and vale of the kingsman encampment. Kingsmen posted on every surrounding campsite heard the shout and felt a surge of joy course through them. Something glorious was taking place, and not a few of them burst into runesongs of victory. Many left their campfires and headed for the source of that shout to investigate and join in the celebration.

Bonu turned to Scung, tears in his eyes. "I guess that's your discipline, Scung; you are sentenced to serve as my adjutant." Scung's brawny arms encircled his newly appointed captain and lifted him off his feet. Scarcely able to draw a breath from the pressure on his ribcage, Bonu squeaked, "Put me down before you crush me."

"Oops! Sorry, *Captain*." Scung unceremoniously lowered him and did an awkward salute, a wide, toothy grin shining through his gnarly beard.

"Don't look so happy, Lieutenant Scung; your life is about to become a nightmare," Bonu teased.

"Yer means worser than getting' et by a man-eatin' plant or dueling harlequins in the Scrarth an' Avangar, fleein' from Hod-ya an' her henchmen? I cain't hardly wait."

"That concludes two of the three tasks before us," Tren resumed. "Ahh, I see our commotion has drawn an even larger crowd." Tren peered out through the open tent walls as kingsmen came running from every quarter. He held his hands aloft to quell the hubbub.

The assembly shushed each other, as well as those just joining outside. The new arrivals slowed to a trickle.

Tren called out, "Please, please, find a place to sit if you can; there's one more solemn duty Logon would have me perform before we adjourn."

Bonu, Jeda, and Scung settled to the ground beneath Tren's upraised arms. Jeda slipped her hand in Bonu's and looked questioningly into his eyes.

Bonu's lips formed a thin line as he slowly shook his head and shrugged.

Tren reached down and, with his right hand, lifted Bonu, then with his left, pulled Jeda to her feet. They both stood before him, bewildered, curiously looking around, no longer holding hands.

"We"—Tren sounded very officious—"are gathered here in the sight of Logon and this august company to join . . . "

Bonu and Jeda jerked their heads straight ahead, staring at Tren, then at each other.

"This man and this woman . . . "

Jeda's and Bonu's jaws dropped, their eyebrows raised.

"In the sacred union of wedlock." Tren took their hands, joined them, and held them aloft before the assembly.

Much of what transpired after that, including what Tren said, was lost due to the state of shock the couple were in, until he proclaimed, "Upon statement of your troth and fidelity to each other, I ask, Jeda of the house of Kway, do you receive this man, Captain Bonu, to be your sole husband, provider and protector, father of your children, yielding allegiance to him as his helpmeet in all things?"

Jeda stared into Bonu's tear-rimmed eyes and heard herself say, "I come under your covering, Bonu, accepting your name as my own, your life and fate as my own, your pursuits as my own, as long as we both shall live." Tears flowed freely down her cheeks.

"And do you, Captain Bonu, captain of the 'Wandering Brigades Regiment,' receive this woman, Jeda, formerly of the house of Kway, to be your sole spouse, providing for her in all things; protecting her from all harm; siring her children and raising them in love, obedience, and awe-filled respect of Logon Xychirion and obedience to his runes?"

Jeda's face blurred before Bonu's eyes as he declared, "Jeda, I accept the responsibility of always covering you with my love, providing for you in accordance with Logon's will for mated pairs, protecting you from all harmful elements of this world with my own life and limb, and do undertake to raise our children under the Advisor's tutelage in service to Logon Xychirion."

Tren presented a beautifully braided rope, which Vawella had clandestinely placed in his hand during Jeda's and Bonu's exchange of vows. He held it aloft for all to see, and said, "Let this band of espousal unity be a symbol of your binding oaths to each other." He extended his arms around both Jeda and Bonu, draping the braid over their heads and down to their waists. Then he drew it tight, forcing the couple toward each other in an embrace as he tied a knot. "You are hereby known no longer as you were but as you now and henceforth are—man and wife." Then in a whisper, he said, "Go on, lad, kiss the girl."

Before Bonu's and Jeda's lips parted, brawny arms encircled and raised them off the ground. Scung's raucous laughter vibrated right through them as joyous pandemonium broke out in and outside the tent.

"Did you know?" Jeda shouted above the din when their feet touched down.

"Not a clue; did you?"

Before either could say another word, blindfolds were put over their eyes and, still bound at the waist, were guided by many hands through the throng and outside the tent.

"Where are you taking us?" Bonu challenged.

"You'll see," teased Spoena. "There's a special lean-to set up in an isolated vale just for your wedding night—"

A sudden hush overcame the festive atmosphere.

The procession leading the newlyweds stopped abruptly. Bonu reached up and removed his blindfold, as did Jeda.

Scung surged to the fore, drawing his sword, yelling, "A life for the king!"

A wavering voice responded to Scung's challenge. "Put away your sword, kingsman. You already stabbed me with one of those things, remember?"

Tren forced his way around Jeda and Bonu and came face to face with a bedraggled stranger. "Who are you, interloping on our ceremonies like this? Put your sword away, Scung. He's no threat." Stepping closer, Tren took the stranger's chin in his hand and turned it to the light.

"I remembers thet scar, but it cain't be," Scung muttered lowly, also drawing closer. "Yer got kilt! I seen yer a lyin' dead as a squished bug on the floor, stomped by one o' the dreads." A look of utter amazement covered his face.

Jeda gasped and reached out to touch the scarred face. "Gragnold?"

THE END OF BOOK FIVE

More of J.M. MacLeod's short stories and articles can be found at
Lordswordwords.blogspot.com
Email—swordrunes@gmail.com

For more information about
J.M. MacLeod
&
Turit's Rise
please visit:

www.facebook.com/john.macleod.188
Lordswordwords.blogspot.com

For more information about
AMBASSADOR INTERNATIONAL
please visit:

www.ambassador-international.com
@AmbassadorIntl
www.facebook.com/AmbassadorIntl

If you enjoyed this book, please consider leaving us a review on
Amazon, Goodreads, or our website.

More from Ambassador International

Humanity has spread and colonized regions of the galaxies. As their reach expanded, countries, colonies, and planets joined to form the Federated Nations, providing a centralized government among the stars. In this dystopian anthology, follow along as humanity discovers new beings, wondrous worlds, old temptations, and strength in horrendous trials.

Rune has lived her whole life in the mountains of Kansanai. When everything is turned upside down, will she be able to let go of the life she thought she deserved for something far greater than what she could have ever imagined? Rolf goes through the motions of everyday life yet, his routine is disrupted when a voice claiming to be the one true God speaks to him. While listening to his heart, he is thrown temptation after temptation on his journey. Will he be able to resist the temptations?

How far would you go to protect the ones you love? During the apocalyptic final days of Noloro, three orphaned teens have nothing left in the world but each other. A sardonic sorcerer offers them a way off their dying world, but at what cost? Family, courage, and faith are at the heart of this end-of-the-world adventure.